Also by WILLIAM BERNHARDT

CAPITOL THREAT

CAPITOL THREAT

A NOVEL

WILLIAM BERNHARDT

BALLANTINE BOOKS • NEW YORK

Published in the United States by Ballantine Books, an imprint of The Random House Publishing Group, a division of Random House, Inc., New York.

BALLANTINE and colophon are registered trademarks of Random House, Inc.

ISBN 978-0-345-47017-1

Library of Congress Cataloging-in-Publication Data

Bernhardt, William.
Capitol threat : a novel / by William Bernhardt.
p. cm.
ISBN 978-0-345-47017-1 (acid-free paper)
1. Kincaid, Ben (Fictitious character)—Fiction. 2. Legislators—United States—Fiction. 3. United States. Supreme Court—Officials and employees—Selection and appointment—Fiction. 4. Libel and slander—Fiction. 5. Washington (D.C.)—Fiction. 6. Political fiction. I. Title.

PS3552.E73147C39 2007
813'.54—dc22   2006048503

Printed in the United States of America on acid-free paper

www.ballantinebooks.com

246897531

First Edition

Text design by Meryl Sussman Levavi

For Michel

My sister, my friend

Lad of Athens, faithful be
To Thyself,
And Mystery—
All the rest is Perjury—
—EMILY DICKINSON

Prologue
Ten Years Earlier

I wish it didn't have to be this way.

That's what I kept saying to myself, throughout the entire ordeal, and long after it was over. But there was never any choice, not really. I did what I had to do. I knew someone would probably end up dead. I just assumed it would be me.

As we embarked on this misbegotten adventure, I checked to make sure my weapon was primed and loaded and simultaneously reminded myself that Schopenhauer postulated the existence of an indifferent universe. An Immanent Will shaping our destiny. Not that the cosmos is actively opposed to us, as some of the nihilists might have you believe, but simply disinterested. There is no such thing as luck, because the concept of luck presupposes a sentient being dealing out favors. So in Schopenhauer's view, the ease with which the whole job went down, at least initially, was due not to providence but merely to the chance occurrence of inconceivable and uncontrollable forces.

As it turned out, Schopenhauer was wrong. I had a huge load of luck coming my way. I just forgot to duck before the inevitable reckoning.

I couldn't believe how simple the break-in was. We bought the costumes at a party shop, for heaven's sake, right next to the pointed hats and the noisemakers. I suppose the dubious authenticity didn't matter—we looked, at least at first sight, like two members of the local police. Flipped the fake IDs Jack had bought and we were inside. I was stunned at the effortlessness of it all. Granted, we weren't breaking into a bank. I didn't expect security at that level. But I expected something, given the value of the merchandise. The lack of security was why Jerry accepted the gig when Renny came calling. This is the second most profitable criminal enterprise in the world, he told me, but the security is no better than what you'd expect at a comic-book convention. Jack didn't care about the merchandise; he certainly had no appreciation for it. It was a job, one he couldn't do alone, so he dragged me along. Into the fire. We are tested by fire; that's what Nietzsche taught. What does not kill us makes us stronger. So I accepted. So I would be stronger. At least I told myself that was the reason. Maybe I just wanted to make enough money that I didn't have to take every petty job that came my way. Maybe I wanted enough money so that the next time I had to make a decision—like the one that took Catherine away from me—I wouldn't make the wrong one.

Must've been the way I carried myself, or the look in my eye, or perhaps the fact that I was way too underweight to be a police officer. Maybe it was my long blond hair, or excessive makeup, or the party-shop shoes that didn't quite fit. I'll never know for certain, but one of the museum guards began scrutinizing me intently almost immediately after we arrived. I knew he was suspicious. And I knew that the more time passed, the more opportunity he would have to do something about it. So I cold-cocked him in the face. Elbow to the nose, sudden flash of searing pain, blood everywhere. His partner reacted, but not fast enough. Jerry flattened him before he could unsnap his holster. A few more blows to the head and they were both laid out on the cold marble floor, their faces looking as if they'd been scraped with sandpaper. That was the problem with these security guys—they didn't really expect trouble. They didn't have the wariness of true beat cops, the subliminal awareness of possible death lurking behind every door. Maybe we were teaching them a lesson, I thought, just as Locke argued that all life, all experience, was instructional. In the future, they would be more careful.

"Have a reason for that," Jerry asked, "or just didn't like the way he looked at you?"

"He made me," I answered.

"He didn't have time. Suspicious, maybe."

"We were going to have to do it eventually."

"Yes, but you didn't have to do it so quickly and with such gusto. Better hope that basement is where we think it is." He grinned in a way that made me disgusted with myself just for being with him. "You really do hate men, don't you?"

I didn't bother trying to deny it. "I have my reasons," I said quietly.

We made our way down to the basement, where the goods we wanted were stored—the ones that didn't appear on the official inventory. It was a dark, dank, and dingy place, obviously not meant to be viewed by the public. But what was stored there! Beauty and banality, all commingled in one subterranean package.

We went to work. Jerry had a list. We were very selective. I used my X-Acto knife to cut a lovely oil of a wooden ship loaded with men being tossed about by a wicked storm. It looked old, but I wouldn't know; philosophy was my gig, not art history. We were almost finished when I heard Jerry say the single simple sentence that changed everything:

"I'm keeping Isabella."

"You can't do that."

"What—you come this far only to balk at a little kidnapping?"

"We have a list, Jerry. If we go off-plan we risk getting caught."

"We took that risk the second we put on these cop suits."

"They won't pay a ransom. This is supposed to be a snatch and run, pure and simple."

"Then I'll keep her. She can be mine. All mine." He hugged the statuary as if it were an actual naked woman. A wild, dangerously crazy look flickered in his eyes. "I'll be good to her. I'll be so good she'll never want to leave me."

I'll just bet he would. I stopped cutting and drew myself up to my full height, which not incidentally was three inches taller than his. "I won't let you screw this up, Jerry. It's too important. I need this." And I did need it. I felt that in my inner core, for reasons I couldn't even begin to explain. It was like a Kantian imperative.

"So that's it?" he growled. "End of discussion?"

"Pretty much, yeah." I returned to my work. The sooner we were out of there, the better.

Naturally, he wouldn't let it go. "Did you forget that this is my job? That you're working for me?"

"Yeah, and you're working for Renny, and this is not what he told you to do."

"You've always been a pain in the butt, you know that? Too damn smart to have anything to do with the rest of us morons. Except the way I see it, for all your supposed brains, you're here in the same cellar with me, doing the same grunt work, living hand-to-mouth, hoping today isn't the day the feds finally show up at your doorstep. Hell, you couldn't even keep your own kid—"

"*Jerry*! End this!" I didn't mean to point the knife at him. I mean, how much damage could I really do with an X-Acto? It was just a gesture, an unintended one. But Jerry took it as a threat. He kicked the knife out of my hand, then threw himself on top of me. I might have been taller, but he was a lot heavier. He pinned me down, his hot, sweaty, disgusting body much too close to mine.

A moment later, his fingers wrapped around my neck.

"I don't need you anymore," he whispered. "You've already done everything I needed you to do. You're expendable." He clutched my throat even tighter. His fingernails pierced my flesh, drawing blood. I felt light-headed, unfocused, like my consciousness was slowly slipping away. "News flash, Vickie. You're not the only one who knows how to hate."

I wanted to fight. I tried. But trapped in that position, pinned beneath him, I was helpless. Struggling was useless; there was simply nothing I could do. He crushed my windpipe in his iron grip. As I felt blackness sweeping over me, knowing with sudden and fearful certainty that I would never wake up again, a million thoughts raced through my brain. Bertrand Russell thought that death was a doorway, simply the next part of the journey. But what the hell did that atheist know about it? One thing was certain—higher learning could not help me now. I was going to the one place where philosophy was of no avail.

No one could have been more surprised than I was to find myself awake and alive. Bound and gagged, bleeding from a dozen places, in tremendous pain, but alive. A blessing, or a curse? Coin toss.

Jerry had hogtied me and thrown me in the back of the van with the goodies. Including Isabella, the stupid fool. We'd brought a lot of rope, anticipating that we might run into trouble. I should've known the primary source of trouble would be Jerry. I was tied so tightly the ropes burned my flesh through my clothing whenever I wiggled. Blood mingled with hemp to create a nauseating, frightening smell that permeated the truck. I don't know why he didn't finish me off—probably just didn't want to leave a telltale body at the scene of the crime. He'd get around to murdering me soon enough. He'd make me so much roadkill on the side of the Boston Turnpike.

I was lying on my side, unable to move my hands or legs. With extreme effort, and despite the protest of every muscle in my body, I managed to push myself upright. But how did that help? I couldn't possibly get free. There was no slack in the ropes at all.

Unless . . . I created some.

It was a class I'd taken in American history—under protest. Required reading included a series of short biographies. One of them was about Erich Weiss, better known as Harry Houdini. An American icon. Scholars still didn't know how he managed to accomplish many of his escapes. But they knew the secret to one of them: they knew how he managed to escape from all those straitjackets. Seemed he was able to dislocate his shoulder. Hurt like hell, but the suddenly limp and lowered limb created enough slack to allow him to wriggle out of the jacket.

Hell, I was a philosophy major, not a damned magician. No way I could do anything like that. Right?

Then I thought of Jerry, his hot fetid breath in my face, his hand clutched around my throat, using me and then disposing of me, like so many men before him. So many.

Catherine . . .

I clenched my eyes tightly closed. I could taste blood on my lips. I didn't know where it had come from. Didn't matter—there was likely a lot more forthcoming. I concentrated on my left shoulder—it was the more flexible. I remembered the diagrams of the ball-and-socket joint we had studied in Zoology 101. And then I strained, twisted, feeling as if I were pulling my muscles against themselves, forcing the shoulder bone out of its natural home . . .

It hurt—dear God in heaven it hurt so much—as lightning flashes of pain raced down my entire body. I'd never felt anything like that before. Before I started, I thought I couldn't possibly hurt more than I already did, but I was wrong, so pathetically wrong. I was sure I would lose consciousness again, for the second time in an hour . . .

It took three attempts and I don't know how long—too long—till I heard the snapping noise, followed by a momentary sensation of release, followed by a wave of agony so intense I threw up all over the floor of the truck. I hoped I didn't damage any of the goods, but at the moment, that wasn't my primary concern. I fell forward, my head hitting the floor, vomit followed by drool and blood, over-whelmed by the mind-numbing aching in my left shoulder. I babbled and spit and breathed in short, quick gulps, as if spastic respiration might somehow fix my shattered body. The pain was so intense—if I had been cut open with a knife, it couldn't possibly hurt any more . . .

Know thyself, Socrates said. Well, I knew myself well enough now.

If I could do that, I could do anything.

Maybe twenty minutes later, Jerry exited the turnpike and pulled the truck over to the side of the road. I was ready. He was grinning when he opened the back doors—probably planning to play with me awhile, violate me a few more ways before he killed me. But he never got the chance. My left arm was useless, even after I'd popped it back into the socket, and my right wasn't much better, so I made do with my feet. My foot clipped him under the chin the moment he pulled the rear doors open and sent him reeling back-ward. I jumped out of the truck and kicked him in the face ten more times, sending blood and flesh flying. I followed with several clenched fists to the solar plexus. I never gave him a chance to fight back, never even gave him a moment to figure out what was happening. I just punished him, over and over again, making him hurt like he'd hurt me, only a thousand unbearably intense times worse. I dragged his face back and forth over the gravel till he was totally disfigured, then I kicked him some more until at last I heard several ribs break. Then I kept on going, kept on going, long past the point where he had any chance of recovering. I wasn't just killing him. I was killing him, and my father, and everyone else who ever hurt me or used me or pretended to love me. They all deserved to die.

When it was over, I pushed Jerry's body down a hill into the bramble and rolled the truck onto a side road. I knew he would be found. So what? By that time, Renny would have recovered the loot and I'd be gone. He couldn't care less who got paid, just so he got the goods. I didn't know what he would do about Isabella. Not my problem. I had no problems, not anymore.

At least that was what I kept telling myself. There was one difficulty I tried to pretend wasn't there: the inevitable conflict arising from Rousseau's postulation of the noble savage theory—that is, the idea that to have civilization, we give up freedom, because civilization must have rules. And I had broken damn near every one of them.

I wasn't stupid enough to pretend I could get away with all this without suffering a few repercussions. I'd had the temerity to short-circuit that indifferent universe and win a big one for the home team. But the other shoe would drop. I knew it would. I had quite literally escaped death. I had gone too far, taken too much. There would be a reckoning.

Damn karma, anyway. Even as I stuck out my thumb to hitch a ride, I felt a hollowness, an inability to feel pleasure, a certainty that it would all come to an end before I had a chance to enjoy it. Funny how sometimes you just know these things. I was as certain about this as I was that when I licked my lips I was tasting my own blood. And not for the last time.

Three Weeks Before

Judge Rupert Haskins folded his wife's hand into his own and squeezed. "Heck of a way to be spending our twenty-seventh anniversary, isn't it, Angel?"

His wife, Margaret, smiled, causing crow's feet to form around her eyes. "I don't mind."

"Damned bother, all this Inns of Court rigmarole. But it would be awkward if I didn't attend, since I founded the chapter."

"I understand."

"It's important work, mentoring the next generation of lawyers. Trying to instill in them the ethics and values lawyers had—hell, everyone had—when we were young."

This time it was her turn to give his hand a squeeze. "Rupert . . . we're still young."

"I'm sixty-two, Angel."

"And you've never looked better."

"I've lost the hair on my head and gained it in my ears."

She laughed. "You've never looked better."

The Inns of Court was a fraternal organization within the Denver Bar Association. A select number of the local, state, and federal judiciary with the city's most prominent lawyers met once a month for dinner and discussion of legal issues, mostly relating to maintaining the high standards of the bar. Every year a new class of young lawyers was chosen for one-on-one guidance from the permanent members of the Inn. It was a highly sought position, not only for the educational experience, but for the chance to become acquainted with judges the lawyers might well be appearing before one day. There were three different Inns in Denver, but the one Judge Haskins had founded was the first and was generally considered the most prestigious, since he was the senior judge on the Tenth Circuit. And this year, to his dismay, the premiere session for the new class of acolytes at the downtown Hilton ballroom had fallen on his and Margaret's wedding anniversary.

Haskins was about to reply and rebut when he was cut off by the sound of a baby crying at the next table. "Can you believe that lawyer brought his wife and their newborn? To a professional banquet? What kind of lawyer would bring a wife who just gave birth and the child? You never would've seen that in our day."

Margaret patted his hand gently. "Darling . . . the wife *is* the lawyer. And I don't think she has a husband."

"But—that's not right."

His wife shrugged. "Times have changed."

"She should've hired a babysitter."

"Babysitters are expensive. And we don't say 'babysitters' anymore. We say 'caregivers.'"

"Right. Very important that we don't demean the teen workforce." He leaned closer. "I'm going to have to give some damn speech in a minute. I'm sorry. But tomorrow night, Angel—I'm taking you out to dinner. To compensate for this scheduling snag."

"That's not necessary."

"It's our twenty-seventh anniversary!"

"Yes, it is. We've been together twenty-seven years. So you can skip the dinner, and the champagne, and whatever bauble it is making a bulge in your jacket." She leaned in closer. "All I want is you."

He came close enough that they brushed noses. "Do you know why I call you 'Angel'?"

"I've assumed it's because you're beginning to have difficulty recalling my name."

"It's because someone like you could only have come from heaven. Beautiful, pure, and untouched by the wicked world. I'd be nothing without you."

She laughed again and her face flushed slightly. "You *are* in a sentimental mood tonight, aren't you? Rupert, you would've been a success no matter who you—"

"No. Not without you. And what's more—I wouldn't want it, without you." He planted a kiss on the tip of her nose.

She pushed him away. "Oh, honestly. I think you get more foolish every day," she protested, but without much vigor. "Now start putting your thoughts together for your speech. And please don't tell that musty old story about when you were in the freshman moot court competition and the judge criticized your argyle socks. They've heard it more times than they've heard the Pledge of Allegiance."

Judge Haskins had almost reached the point in the story where he notices the judge is staring at his ankles when he was rocked by an explosion from behind the podium. The first wave knocked him and the podium to the floor. He fell on top of it and immediately felt blood coursing from his nose. The second wave was even stronger— and hotter. He tumbled off the edge of the dais, falling sideways onto his left leg. It felt as if it might be fractured. But neither that nor the dozen other injuries he had suffered registered for more than a moment. His primary concern was the heat that continued to emanate from the kitchen behind him.

The ballroom was on fire.

Haskins slowly pushed himself to his feet, but he was sent reeling by someone rushing in the opposite direction. The sudden burst of flames had thrown everyone in the room into a panic. Husbands and wives were rushing across the ballroom toward the main entrance. The screams and shouts were deafening; some were calling the names of loved ones, others just screaming in abject panic. The heat was already unbearable. Haskins felt as if he'd been dropped into a deep-fat fryer. The lights exploded, plunging the room into darkness. Everyone was coughing, struggling to breathe. People were rubbing their eyes, or extending their arms to feel their way through the dense smoky gloom. There seemed to be a problem getting the doors open. The smoke was billowing up in the enclosed ballroom, making it almost impossible to get air.

"Margaret!" Haskins cried, as he pushed himself to his feet once more, ignoring the blood streaming down his face, the aching in his left leg. "Margaret!"

He felt her more than heard her, given the enormous confusion and tumult in the room. That was the advantage of being married to someone for twenty-seven years—he could literally sense her presence. Haskins fought his way across the crowded room, brushing shoulders and kneecaps with the hundreds of people rushing in every direction. His leg hurt so much that his knee buckled with his first step. A woman in a flaming ball gown flew past, knocking him back onto the floor.

This will never work, he told himself. I need to stay on my feet. My Angel is depending on me.

He pushed himself up again. The pain in his leg was excruciating, but he kept his knee rigid and continued walking. There would be time enough for pain later.

He found Margaret lying on the floor, half-hidden under one of the banquet tables. She was unconscious, maybe from the explosion, maybe from all the people who had kicked and trampled her after she tumbled to the floor.

There was only one thing to do; whether he felt able to do it or not. He bent over, his back screaming—it had never been the same since the disk replacement two years before—and cradled her in his arms. She felt three times heavier than she really was, but he put that out of his mind and headed toward the door. A crowd was gathering. A few of the men were making panicked, disorganized efforts to get the doors open, but nothing worked. Haskins guessed that the explosion had created a vacuum. Even though people on the other side must be trying to open the doors, they weren't budging.

"Just a moment, Angel," Haskins murmured, as he placed his wife gently into a nearby chair. He stood on a table and bellowed, hoping he might be heard over the tumult.

"Listen to me!" he shouted, not attracting much attention. It was hard to stand on such a rickety table, especially with a rickety leg. He drew in his breath, inhaled smoke, and went into a coughing spasm. Water streamed from his eyes, but he forced himself to try again.

"Listen! Can you feel that fire? Do you know how quickly fire spreads? We've got to get organized—or we're all dead."

"What can we do?" one of the young men shouted back.

Damn good question. What could they do? Waiting for help was not an option—the fire would consume them in minutes, maybe sooner.

"Let's grab the podium," he said. "You and you and you."

Haskins and the three men he had chosen at random ran back to where the podium lay on the floor. It was mostly intact, although its proximity to the fire had made it extremely hot. Haskins touched one end, then jerked his hand back.

"We have to do this," he muttered. "Use your clothes to protect your hands!"

Together the men tore off their jackets and shirts and used them to insulate their hands. It was not a complete fix—Haskins still could feel his flesh searing—but it at least made it bearable in the short term. On his cue, they lifted the podium and carried it toward the nearest door.

"We have to work together," he shouted, coughing and choking with every word. "On three!"

Haskins delivered the countdown, and together they used the podium as a battering ram against the door. It buckled but did not break.

"Again!"

They rammed the door one more time. The plastic molding splintered, creating a narrow opening. People streamed forward, desperately trying to escape the unbearably intense heat. Haskins hoisted his wife back into his arms and carried her through the threshold, barely a few steps ahead of the flickering flames.

"Is everyone out?" he shouted, once he had his wife to safety and made sure she was breathing. "Is everyone safe? Buddy up. Make sure you can account for everyone you came with. Look for the people at your table who were—"

The next sound he heard, barely discernible over the buzz of the crowd and the power of his own voice, shook him even more than the explosion, even more than the sight of flames slowly consuming the room.

A baby was crying.

"No," he whispered, under his breath.

He raced back toward the doors, but one of his fellow federal judges stopped him. "Don't be a fool, Rupert. You can't survive in there. The firefighters should be here any moment. Let them—"

Haskins didn't wait for the end of the sentence. He returned to the center of the inferno.

He had one advantage the firefighters would not have—he knew where the baby was, or at least where it had been. The problem was, visibility was now almost zero. He felt his way forward, using the walls and the tables to thread his way back to his former seat, even though everything he touched was red hot.

Haskins heard the baby cry again. That helped. Even with flames crackling all around him, he could zero in on that heart-wrenching sound.

The baby was still in her carrier, but her face was completely covered in black. The plastic molding of the carrier had begun to melt.

Haskins lifted the baby into his arms, wiped the smoke and soot from her face, and held her close. "Breathe, child. Breathe."

Now he had a bigger problem—how to get back. A trail of flames cut across the center of the room, separating him from the main entrance. He knew he didn't have the strength to get another door open. Already he was feeling faint. Must be the thinness of the air, he thought. Most of the oxygen had been burned out of the room. His knees wobbled. This couldn't be the end. Surely he hadn't gone through all this just to have the poor child die in his arms.

Like a ray of light piercing the darkness, Haskins saw a white arc stream through the flames. It hit him in the face—and it was wet.

Water. Someone was putting out the fire. Praise God—someone was putting out the fire!

A moment later he saw uniformed firefighters crossing the room. One of them took the baby and immediately put an oxygen mask over its tiny nose and mouth. Someone threw a blanket over

Haskins and escorted him to the outside corridor. Just in time. His brain was as smoky as the room; it was getting very hard to think clearly.

"If you ever get tired of judging," he heard one of the men say, "we'd be honored to have you join the Firefighters Brigade. You're a hero, Judge. A real-life hero."

He didn't want to appear rude, but he felt sick and tired and had no stomach for compliments. "Angel," he whispered.

"Your wife is over here," another voice said. "She's fine."

Haskins allowed himself to be led to her side. Her eyes were open, though streaked with soot and tears. Even though his clothes were hot and filthy, he threw his arms around her and hugged her tightly.

"Looks like we'll be around for our twenty-eighth, Angel," he said. He heard nothing back from his wife. But he could feel tears of joy cascading down his cheek, renewing him, making him feel young all over again.

Haskins and escorted him to the outside corridor. Just in time. His brain was as smoky as the room; it was getting very hard to think clearly.

"If you ever get tired of judging," he heard one of the men say, "we'd be honored to have you join the Firefighters Brigade. You're a hero, Judge. A real-life hero."

He didn't want to appear rude, but he felt sick and tired and had no stomach for compliments. "Angel," he whispered.

"Your wife is over here," another voice said. "She's fine."

Haskins allowed himself to be led to her side. Her eyes were open, though streaked with soot and tears. Even though his clothes were hot and filthy, he threw his arms around her and hugged her tightly.

"Looks like we'll be around for our twenty-eighth, Angel," he said. He heard nothing back from his wife. But he could feel tears of joy cascading down his cheek, renewing him, making him feel young all over again.

Book One

The Politics of Motion

1

Ben Kincaid rushed into the magnetic train in a blind panic. He knew he shouldn't have taken a meeting with that woman from the foreign-policy think tank, but she'd told him that it was urgent, that American civil rights might crumble into dust if he didn't meet her at Jimmy T.'s, a favorite hangout for senators and lobbyists not far from his office in the Russell Building.

"You can see why this is so urgent," the thin, earnest woman said, brushing a shock of brunette hair from her face. She was even younger than Ben, which undoubtedly accounted for a good deal of the earnestness. "This country has endured the torture of prisoners at Abu Ghraib. We've endured Gitmo Bay and the Salt Pit and all the other places where the Constitution has been violated."

"Technically," Ben said, "the Constitution only applies to U.S. citizens. Not foreign nationals."

"So you're saying you're okay with torturing prisoners?"

"Nooo," Ben countered. "I'm down on torture. But I'm down on terrorists, too."

"If we allow this to continue, then we become the terrorists."

Ben could see he would get nowhere with this woman using only logic. "You do understand that I'm not Todd Glancy, right? Senator Glancy resigned. I was appointed by the governor to fill out the remainder of his term."

She flipped her hair back again. "Like I don't know that already."

And in that instant, Ben realized that she not only knew that already—that was the reason she had singled him out. She would get nowhere with any experienced member of the Senate, so she was going after the new kid on the block. "Look, if you have a report or something, I'll be happy to forward it to the Foreign Relations Committee. Of which I am not a member."

"You seriously think we haven't done that already? I don't think you understand how dire this situation is . . ."

And it probably was dire, too, as was the predicament of every lobbyist, politician, and private citizen who had contacted Ben in the few short months since he became a senator. If he'd had the time, he would have been happy to listen to what she had to say. Maybe. But in this particular instance, the time did not exist. He still had the memo Christina had given him in his suit pocket: the Democrats were planning a filibuster and he was late.

As soon as he'd managed to extract himself from the earnest young woman, which was none too soon, he'd raced down the sidewalk, run into the Russell Building, and taken the elevator down to the small private subway train that shuttled back and forth between the Senate office buildings and the Capitol. Ben liked the train—it was quiet and clean, unblemished by graffiti and advertisements. A series of state flags, arranged in order of admission to the Union, ornamented the track. Ben knew that by the time he reached the baby blue flag of Oklahoma, the forty-sixth state in the Union, he had almost arrived at the Capitol building. But he couldn't enjoy the ride today. He was late. For his first filibuster! His party was hosting a party and he wasn't there!

He ran into the building only to be stopped for an interminable period of time at the security checkpoint. How long before they would just wave him past? Probably forever. Finally he smiled at the Capitol Police and raced down the corridor. He sped past the pillared Capitol crypt, past the vice-presidential marble busts in the spectator gallery, past the historic Ohio clock in the hall outside the chamber. He had heard some of his new colleagues talking about the politics of motion—the need to appease the public by creating the appearance of movement, even when none is actually taking place. At the moment, Ben's feet were giving the phrase a whole new meaning.

Moving as quickly as decorum would allow, Ben made his way inside the Senate chamber. He emerged on the carpeted center aisle but veered left toward the curving rows of nineteenth-century mahogany desks (exactly one hundred of them) arranged in concentric semicircles. Ben found his assigned desk on the Democrat side: Desk 101 on the far rear left of the chamber, the desk reserved for the most junior freshman senator in the assemblage. He slid behind it, sat up straight, and tried to act as if he had been there all along and knew exactly what was going on.

Ben had been in such a rush it took him a moment before he noticed that no one else was there. The other desks were all empty.

What was going on? Had he gotten the dates confused? He checked the memo Christina had given him. No, she had told him to be here thirty-five minutes ago, and Christina did not make mistakes. Where was the rest of the Senate?

There was one other person present, but he wasn't at a desk. The junior senator from Alaska, Byron Perkins, was on his feet, milling aimlessly about the Senate floor in the general vicinity of the rostrum. He was a tall, prematurely gray senator in his second term, but Ben knew he had already managed to get appointed to some of the most prestigious committees. He appeared to be reading from the newspaper—something about grape imports in Pago Pago.

Perkins spotted Ben and made his way toward Desk 101. He eventually stood directly in front of Ben, winked, and continued reading.

". . . while the commerce secretary assured the crowd that a steady stream of fruit would continue throughout the spring season.

The representatives from the agricultural community were pleased by the announcement. In other news . . ."

Ben listened to the scintillating prose from the *Washington Post* read aloud for the better part of an hour. Could this really be what he was supposed to be doing? And if so, why was he the only person here? He wanted to ask someone, but he was afraid to get out of his chair. Could one false move end the filibuster? Perkins never took a breath long enough for Ben to ask him anything. What should he do? Eventually, a potent combination of confusion, fear, and boredom gave him the courage to raise a hand.

"No, sir," Perkins rambled on, "I will not yield to the young senator from Oklahoma, because if I did, my filibuster would come to an end and the Republican majority could seize control of the chamber. However, the weather forecast for this week in D.C. looks exceptionally rosy . . ."

Ben lowered his hand.

". . . but despite the fine weather outside, I might do well to offer the eager but rather inexperienced senator from Oklahoma the knowledge that during a filibuster, although the senators have to remain on the premises in case a quorum call is made by the opposition, only the most inexperienced rube would actually go to the Senate chamber and listen to the continuous drivelous spiel that makes up the actual filibuster."

Ben shrank down into his seat.

"Interested parties might find the members of the Senate in the large conference room across the hall. If such interested party will be going there now, I wonder if he might consider fetching me some coffee. I don't want to presume, but when one is the most junior senator in this august legislative body, and one has been foolish enough to actually attend a filibuster in progress, a certain degree of errand-running might not be utterly inappropriate . . ."

Across the hall in the large conference room, Ben found a vast expanse of cots stretched as far as the eye could see. The other ninety-eight members of the Senate, with few exceptions, were resting on the cots, for the most part sound asleep. Ben gazed at the field of legislators, some of whom he had admired his entire life—Senate

Minority Leader Hammond, Senator Keyes from Texas, and numerous others, all arrayed before him, many of them stripped down to T-shirts and boxers, and also—

Snoring.

Ah, the glamorous life of a United States senator.

2

It still didn't seem like his office.

Ben, aided by Christina's eternal resourcefulness and dubious decorating taste, had tried to remake the place in his own image. Almost everything that had belonged to Senator Glancy had been removed—including that creaky copying machine that printed only in blue ink. Ben had ordered the walls painted, the carpet replaced, and new furniture imported. Christina had contributed plants, a mostly dying breed from her nearby apartment on "C" Street. The walls were loaded with family photographs and press clippings pertaining to some of Ben's more high-profile cases. He'd noticed that most of the other senators decorated the walls with campaign memorabilia, but since he'd never campaigned for anything in his life, he'd have to make do with mementos of trials gone by.

He'd made his private retreat in the right rear of Senate office S-212-D in the Russell Building a near replica of the one he had back at Two Warren Place in Tulsa: a cozy nook in which he could

deal with the endless stream of memos, e-mail, phone calls, lobbyists, and constituents. He needed a place for personal privacy or private meetings. He still hadn't been assigned one of the basement
hideaways—just as well, given the unpleasant memories of Glancy's
hideaway he still retained, not to mention his inability to navigate
the basement without becoming hopelessly lost. And no one seemed
to use the Senate library anymore. It was dusty, musty, poorly lit—
and worst of all, they didn't carry either of the two books Ben had
written. There was a rumor circulating that Christina was mounting
a boycott.

Speaking of whom . . .

Ben stared up into the vivid blue eyes of his law partner,
Christina McCall, currently serving as his chief of staff, who was
seated on his desk, hovering over him. Her strawberry blond hair
encircled her head like the flaming halo of the Angel of Retribution;
her arms were akimbo, her brow was creased, and she had called
him "Benjamin J. Kincaid," a certain sign that she meant business.

"You have to make a decision. Now."

"I—I don't see the urgency."

"That's why you have a chief of staff. So what's it going to be?
Decide!"

"Look, I'm a United States senator—"

"Which is precisely why you can't dither about the way you
usually do. Decide!"

Ben tried to push his chair back, but the wall blocked his escape.
"It's only been a few months since the governor appointed me to fill
out the remainder of Senator Glancy's term. I don't even know if I
like it, much less whether I want to run for reelection. Well, I don't
know if it's really reelection when you weren't elected the first time,
but I still—"

"Stop." Her eyebrows knitted together. "You thought I was
talking about deciding whether to run for a full term?"

"Everyone has been hounding me for a statement. The press, the
governor, Senator Hammond—"

"I don't give a damn about that."

Ben blinked. "You don't?"

"Well, I mean, I do—but I already know what your decision
will be."

"Is that so. Perhaps you'd like to enlighten me."

"Nope. Violates the Prime Directive."

"Excuse me?"

"Forbids interference with the natural development of a dithering personality."

"Then what are we talking about?"

She thrust the back of her left hand into his face. "This!"

The sizeable diamond glittered in his eyes. "Oh, that. Well, gosh, we've only been engaged for, um . . ."

"Thirteen weeks, two days, and roughly four-and-a-half hours."

"Yes. Exactly." He pressed his hand against his brow. "I thought it was understood that we'd get married after this term ended and we were back in Tulsa."

"And that was acceptable when I thought we were talking about one abbreviated term. But I'm not waiting around another six years! I've been waiting for you half my life as it is!"

They both heard the chuckles emanating from the back of Ben's office. "Could you be kinda less subtle, Chrissy? I'm not sure Ben gets your drift."

Loving. Ben's barrel-chested investigator, currently serving as Senator Kincaid's research aide, though most of his research didn't involve library books. "Something I can do for you?" Ben asked.

"Just remindin' you it's time to take off for the Rose Garden. Don't want to miss a chance to visit the White House."

"I was thinking I might skip it."

"*Skip the White House?*" Christina and Loving both erupted at once.

Ben shrugged. "There's so much security. I can just stay here and watch it on C-SPAN."

Christina gripped him by the shoulders. "Benjamin J. Kincaid. When the leader of the free world invites the junior senator from the State of Oklahoma to the Rose Garden to hear firsthand who he's nominating to the Supreme Court of the United States, the junior senator doesn't go couch potato on him."

"He invited everyone in the Senate."

"Doesn't matter. You have to go." She paused. "Especially if you're thinking about running for another term."

Ben sighed. "Oh, all right. But I won't enjoy it."

"You're breaking my heart."

"I'm s'prised it's taken the President so long to make the nomination," Loving offered. "This whole thing's been orchestrated from the start."

Ben wasn't sure what was stranger: the statement itself, or the fact that Loving had used the word "orchestrated." "Huh?"

A low, subguttural snigger. "You don't really think the late Justice Cornwall died of a heart attack, do you?"

"Spare me your conspiracy theories."

"When a man in a position of power in his early sixties dies of a 'heart attack' "—Loving made little snicker quotes in the air as he said the words—"you can be certain the Powers-That-Be are making a play."

"The Powers-That-Be? And who is that? The Trilateral Commission? The Freemasons? The Thirteen Old Men Who Rule the World?"

Loving stepped closer and spoke in hushed tones. "Microsoft."

Ben rolled his eyes. "Give me a—"

"Think before you scoff, Skipper. Everyone knows Microsoft is in bed with the Chinese."

Christina stared at him. "We do?"

"Who else uses icons to convey meaning, huh? Do you know how widespread the Windows operating system is? In twenty years, the English alphabet will be extinct."

Ben frowned. "And this relates to the late Justice Cornwall because . . ."

"He was well known to be a staunch anticommunist."

"I would like to think everyone in our government—"

"In the new era, Americans will all be illiterate computer jockeys. Easily conquered by the Marxist-Maoist-Microsoft consortium."

"And this is all being engineered by that pinko fink Bill Gates?"

Loving guffawed. "You know, Skipper, for a senator, you're not very well informed. There is no Bill Gates."

"There isn't?"

"Bill Gates is a virtual character created by Microsoft technicians and played by a succession of actors. Honestly, do you think he looks like a real person? I don't even know where you'd go to buy a pair of glasses like that."

Ben pushed past him. "On second thought, I *will* go to the Rose Garden. I'm desperate to go to the Rose Garden. Anywhere I might find a small morsel of sanity. Come—"

He collided with Jones, his administrative assistant, currently serving as his administrative assistant. "Boss! Are you taking appointments yet?"

"Do I ever stop?"

"Christina told me not to let anyone in your office till she came out."

Ben gave Christina a long look. "Indeed. Well, it'll have to wait. We're going to see the Presid—"

"Senator Kincaid!" Ben was all but flattened by a large woman in a sundress who pushed past Jones and slammed Ben back into the doorway. She slapped her hands against his chest. "I have to talk to you."

"This is the U.S Senate! Don't we have . . . guards or something?"

The woman ignored him. "I'm Geraldine Pommeroy."

Ben ran the name through his mental Filofax. "I talked to the chairman of the Foreign Relations Committee about that furlough for your son—"

"I don't have a son. I have four daughters."

"Four . . . daughters. Oh—there's a Senate page position opening up in—"

"They're not old enough to be pages. The oldest is twelve."

"Okay, I give up. What do you want?"

"They told me you could get us tickets for the White House tour. My eldest is doing a report on what she did over the vacation break, and she needs pictures of the White House to bring up her 'C' average."

Ben rolled his eyes. Good thing U.S. senators deal with only the most urgent and important crises. "Jones?"

He stepped forward. "Sorry, Boss. We're all out of tourist passes."

Ben shrugged. "My apologies, ma'am. I couldn't get anyone into the White House if my life depended on it. If you'll excuse me—"

"Where are you going?"

"Me? I'm going—" He stopped short. "I'm . . . um . . . I'm going on an important . . . senator . . . thing." He ducked under her arm and slid past. "Be seeing you!"

The woman whirled on him. "I'm not voting for you next time!"

"I'm pretty sure you didn't vote for me before," Ben said under his breath. "Jones—is the car ready? Get me out of here!"

3

Sometimes Ben had to shake himself just to remember that it was real—he was an actual U.S. senator. And he had been invited to the White House. As his car whizzed down the stretch between Lafayette Park and 1600 Pennsylvania Avenue, he marveled once again at his great good fortune. The elm trees and retractable bollards were lovely, and they kept you from noticing the camouflaged guard booths. Couldn't have the White House looking like a penitentiary—even though at times Ben thought that was exactly what it was.

Ben had seen the Rose Garden a million times on television, but it looked like an entirely different place when you visited in person. For one thing, you noticed that there actually were roses, long rows of tall flowering red and pink rosebushes. The air was sweet and the endless green expanse of perfectly trimmed lawn was an amateur golfer's dream. All in all a wonderfully tranquil location—or it would be, if it hadn't been infested with a thousand or so reporters, politicians, and sundry other dignitaries, not to mention a tangled weave of minicams, boom mikes, and miscellaneous technical equipment, all centered around the currently unoccupied podium bearing the seal of the POTUS—President of the United States.

"A rather impressive display, isn't it? Even when no one's up there."

Ben turned and found himself face-to-face with the top dog in his party, the Senate Minority Leader, Robert Hammond. Ben glanced at his watch. "President Blake is late."

Hammond chuckled. "President Blake is always late. Haven't you noticed? He likes to build anticipation, put on a show. It's because he's from Missouri." The wind whistled through Hammond's thinning silver mane. "But I suppose when you've gone to all the trouble of running for the highest office in the land, you're entitled to a few idiosyncrasies."

Ben smiled. During his short time in Washington, he had repeatedly been impressed by Hammond's warmth and good humor. He couldn't help but be pleased that this senior legislator had taken so much interest in him, a puny appointed fill-in senator from Oklahoma. Ben almost felt as if the man were grooming him for a future in politics, as if Hammond saw a potential in him that no one else was seeing, including himself. Hammond was also the author of the federal Environmental Protection Wilderness Bill, a sweeping piece of reform legislation designed to undo the damage of previous administrations and declare an unprecedented amount of untouched wilderness and national parkland free from development. It was the legislation closest to Christina's heart. She had spent hundreds of hours trying to make the bill a law. Hammond was also assembling a coalition to pass the largest aid bill in history for the millions of Americans living below the poverty level.

"Have we got the votes yet, Senator?"

"For the Wilderness bill? Still three short. Don't worry. I'll find them."

"You're the only man who could."

Hammond grinned. "Might be right about that, Ben. Might be right. I'll let you know when we've got a plurality."

"Great. I'm hoping to give Christina a signed copy of that bill for a wedding present."

"Can't think of anything that would please her more. Or me."
He turned his attention to the empty podium.

"You already know who it is, don't you?" Ben asked.

"Well . . . a small group of the senior legislators did have a private heart-to-heart with the President this morning."

"It's Judge Haskins, isn't it?"

"That would be telling."

"Can you at least say whether you're pleased about the selection?"

"Yes. I can tell you that, under the circumstances, I'm very pleased. It could've been a lot worse, given the deeply Republican President who's doing the picking. I can only assume the President wants to end his administration on a high note with a popular, quickly confirmed addition to the Court."

"Well, that's a relief." Ben knew that the Supreme Court, in the wake of the death of Justice Cornwall, was evenly divided among conservatives, liberals, and centrists. The next person appointed to the Court might well cast deciding votes on the death penalty, gun control, abortion, right-to-die, and a host of other critical constitutional issues.

"They've been planning this dog and pony show for days," Hammond said. "No coincidence this is happening on a Friday afternoon, either. Most of the press won't be on the story until Monday. In the meantime, the President's staff will blanket the Sunday news shows with flunkies selling the candidate, rattling on about how he's God's gift to jurisprudence. They'll get endorsements from the Christian Congregation and law enforcement organizations and anyone else who needs a favor from the White House. They'll distribute puff pieces and video clips, stuff the media can regurgitate until they have a chance to do a little digging on their own. By Monday you'll be reading stories about people whose lives were changed for the better by this judge's courtroom brilliance. The press will look for something negative. But the truth is, they won't find much, because if there were anything to find, the President's men would've found it first—and he would never have been nominated. By the end of the week, most Americans will have heard something that gives them a favorable first impression of the man. And the President's battle will be four-fifths won."

"The President's investigators have missed things before," said Ben. "Remember, they don't do a full-fledged FBI investigation until the President makes his nomination. That's the one wild card in every nomination—the President can never know what the Feebs might find. I was still at OU when my contracts professor Anita Hill went to Washington to testify about Clarence Thomas."

"That was eons ago. Today, these boys take no chances. Sad result is, the only people who can get nominated are nebbishes with no lives." He winked. "But at least this time we're getting a fairly reasonable nebbish."

"Good to know."

The applause began before anyone was even in view. Advance men, Ben reminded himself. Even the President depended upon them. A few moments later, as the applause reached its crescendo, the Commander-in-Chief appeared, shaking hands as he walked, smiling, slapping people on the back, until he reached his podium. He was not a tall man, but his bearing was so straight and self-confident that he seemed taller than he truly was. He had a smile so perfect, so carefully calculated for the television cameras, that in person, Ben thought it seemed almost external to his body, something he could put on or take off like a necktie.

"Some have said that the power to appoint justices to the Supreme Court is the greatest of all executive powers," he began, reading off an almost invisible translucent teleprompter, flashing the telegenic good looks that had gotten him elected. "Even greater than the power of war. While this administration opposes judicial activism, and judges who think they're legislators, we nonetheless recognize that the appointment of a new member to the Supreme Court is a matter of grave import."

A wind whistled through the Rose Garden, bathing Ben in the aroma of rose petals. The President was doing a good job, he thought, getting straight to the point yet simultaneously letting the suspense build, so the ultimate announcement would seem all the more dramatic—even if no one had heard of the man before.

"Ideally, Supreme Court justices should be many things—wise, impartial, insightful, full of idealism yet imbued with a keen eye on the wicked ways of the world," President Blake continued. Ben thought his slow Missouri drawl—not that different from a western

Oklahoma accent—effectively conveyed a sense of "regular guy-ness" without mitigating the importance of the occasion. "They must interpret the letter of the law, yet at the same time they must see beyond the letter to the people: the people who wrote the law, and the people it was designed to protect and defend. They must be intellectual, but never so much as to elevate the head over the heart, because every time they hear a case, every time they sign an opinion, lives are changed. This is not a mere exercise in logic, but a sacred trust with the power to alter and affect millions of Americans. Most important, Supreme Court appointees must make sure that justice—equal justice—rings out in this hallowed land of ours, now and forevermore."

"Is he announcing a judicial nomination," Ben whispered, "or canonizing a saint?" Hammond motioned him to shush.

The President smiled. "Fortunately, today I am proud to announce that after an extensive search, we have found someone worthy of and equal to this daunting responsibility. It is my very great privilege to announce this day my nominee for the office of the Supreme Court of the United States—the Honorable Thaddeus T. Roush."

Another round of applause broke out as a tall, thin man emerged from the restricted area behind the podium. He waved to the crowd, then approached the President, who gripped him by the shoulder and shook his hand.

"Am I supposed to know who he is?" Ben whispered.

"No," Hammond answered. "But you will."

Roush was wearing a blue suit with a red tie—standard politico television wardrobe since Ronald Reagan. He was obviously unaccustomed to the attention, not to mention the crowd, the lights, and the microphones, but he held himself together and approached the podium, readjusting the microphone to account for his greater height.

"Thank you, Mr. President. And let me say that it is my very great honor to even be considered, much less chosen, to be your Supreme Court nominee." His slow, precise voice did not contain much inflection, highlighting his almost ascetic, intellectual appearance. "While I have enjoyed my work for the Court of Appeals, I am humbled by the possibility of playing an even greater role in the judicial affairs of this great nation. Again, I thank the President for this opportunity and assure you all that I will do the best I can to earn this honor and to respect and dignify the great tradition of the Supreme Court."

A spattering of applause. Roush hesitated. Ben wondered if he were done. He'd said enough—no rule required a Supreme Court justice to be a great orator, after all. Not part of the job description.

"There is one thing, however," Roush continued, "that I feel I must say, and Mr. President, I hope you will pardon me if I go off script here, because as important as the rest of it is, this must come first."

Ben saw President Blake smile, but there was an awkwardness about it that convinced Ben that Roush's extemporaneous remarks weren't just for dramatic effect.

"I hadn't planned this," Roush said, much more quietly than before, "but as I gaze out into this sea of faces I am reminded once again that this is a good nation, a great nation, filled with large hearts and great souls, people who would always rather know the truth than be placated with a lie." His face seemed to change. He was more nervous now. His slow voice became almost stuttering. "Throughout our history we have experienced prejudice and inequality, but time after time and year after year we have fought the good fight, and watched as the old ways and the unfair ways were extinguished. We were once a nation plagued by the stench of slavery, but we fought that battle, both for freedom and, later, for equal rights. We were once riddled with gender inequality, but slowly and surely we have made this country a better, fairer place for people of both sexes. People of differing races, creeds, and colors are equal in the eyes of the law, as the Fourteenth Amendment says they must be. Today there is only one group of Americans that remains constrained by inequality with the full sanction of the law, and just as with the other terrible inequalities of the past, this blight on our collective conscience must fall, must pass away, and those who work to that end will be remembered as freedom fighters, tireless soldiers in the battle for truth and justice."

Ben searched the faces of all those who surrounded him in the garden. Everyone else seemed just as puzzled by this strange and sudden turn of oratory as he was.

"This has nothing to do with my service as a judge or justice," Roush continued. "This is a matter of conscience. I would rather you hear it from me than read about it Monday morning in some supermarket tabloid. I thought the truth might emerge during the prenomination screening process, but since it did not, I will make the announcement myself. I will not be a part of a lie, because lies are what hold us down, keep us from attaining our greatest potentiality as a nation. Ladies and gentlemen, the man you see sitting behind this podium is not my brother, not my uncle, not my cousin, not—as the Secret Service believes—merely my best friend. He is my partner, my life partner, and he has been for almost seven years."

Roush paused, then looked directly into the camera. "Ladies and gentlemen, I am a gay American. And I will not live in the closet any longer."

4

The phones were ringing so incessantly that Jones was certain he had developed tinnitis. In the wake of the previous day's dramatic development in the Rose Garden, everyone, it seemed, wanted to talk to the junior senator from the state of Oklahoma. If Ben was getting this volume of calls, Jones could only wonder what senators of the slightest importance had to handle. The administrative assistants in the other senators' offices, however, would at least have the pleasure of seeing the pile of messages from other politicians, lobbyists, constituents, press, and various and sundry cranks occasionally diminish. Ben's stack wasn't shrinking at all. Because Ben wasn't anywhere to be found.

Jones saw Christina burst through the door and tried to take advantage of the three seconds or so before she disappeared into her office. "Any sign of the Boss?"

"None." She stopped just outside her door. "And I can't waste any more time looking. Someone has to start returning calls before the villagers revolt."

"They're going to want to know what Ben's position is on the gay Supreme Court nominee."

"Which will be challenging, since I have no idea."

"What, you two don't go in for pillow talk?"

She looked at Jones sharply. "Not about politics. In fact, I expressly forbid it."

"So what are you going to do?"

She threw up her hands and disappeared into her office. "What politicos do best. Equivocate."

Jones didn't blame her for feeling overwhelmed. There was always a wave of publicity following the announcement of a new Supreme Court nominee, but no one had been prepared for the tsunami that followed the revelation of the nation's first openly gay nominee—nominated by a very conservative Republican President, no less. The White House had been marshaling their forces and ducking all the important questions, such as: Did you know he was gay? Will you still support him? Don't you risk losing the fundamentalist Christian support that got you elected in the first place? Similarly, everyone had expected to see presidential flak pieces saturating the airwaves over the long weekend. Instead, literally from the second Roush made his surprise announcement, the pundits' attention had been focused not on the candidate himself but on the cause he might represent. His nomination had stopped being about his qualifications as a judge and had metamorphosed into a referendum on gay rights.

Loving wandered in from the outside corridor, his head hung low.

"Any luck?" Jones asked.

"Not a trace."

"You're supposed to be a private investigator. Surely you can locate one U.S. senator."

"Not if he doesn't wanna be found."

"You think he's hiding? Why?"

" 'Cause that's what I'd do, if I represented the very conservative state of Oklahoma and somebody put up a gay Supreme Court justice. What do the people callin' say?"

"They're opposed, by a six-to-one margin. Most of the calls are from rural towns in the western part of the state." A quick phone call to Paula, Jones's librarian wife back in Tulsa, had told him that the consensus of opinion was no different in the second-largest city in the state.

"That doesn't mean much. The outraged always speak the loudest. We need some real intel."

"There are about half a hundred pollsters working on that as we speak."

"I could fly home, visit a few bars, and give Ben a more accurate picture of the public opinion. Be a lot cheaper, too."

"He might want you to do that. It's hard to tell. Since we don't know where he is!"

Even though it was Saturday and the Senate was not in session, Ben had come to the Senate chamber early in the morning and sat at the little desk in the corner bearing his nameplate. Actually, he liked it better when the Senate was not in session and he could enjoy the historic setting without having to listen to people bickering with one another. He gazed across at the expanse of brown antique desks, row after row, curving toward the center. He was reminded of Arlington National Cemetery; it had essentially the same effect, except with desks instead of graves. Symbolic? He hoped not. The inkwells, snuff boxes, and spittoons reminded him that this was a very old room, with a hallowed and distinguished heritage. All the Presidents since John Adams had walked down that center aisle and taken their place behind the elevated rostrum to deliver their State of the Union addresses, flanked on either side by a long succession of outstanding party leaders. All the Vice Presidents had sat in that chair at the rear center, serving as President of the Senate, nine of them future Presidents themselves. Behind that raised dais, the electoral votes were counted every four years so the President of the Senate could announce the identity of the next President. This was a room that had been a bastion of excellence, a home to brilliant minds and daring idealism. In truth, Ben had never been particularly political, but sitting here always reminded him that despite the distastefulness of much of modern politics, the U.S. Senate was part of a long-standing and important tradition, one that had shaped a nation, and as a result, shaped the world.

"Place kinda gives you the willies, doesn't it?"

Ben turned to see Senator Hammond sitting beside him. He started to rise, but Hammond waved him back down. "This is my second private audience with you in as many days," Ben said. "If you don't watch out, someone's going to mistake me for a person of importance."

The corners of the Minority Leader's lips turned upward. "Modesty. I like that. And I don't get to see it much in this town. Made up your mind yet?"

"You and Christina. To which of my many undecided decisions do you refer?"

"Thaddeus Roush."

"Oh. Well . . . I'm torn."

Hammond leaned back and rested his head against his hands. "Between what and what?"

"Between a gut instinct that the time for a gay Supreme Court justice has come and might do the country a lot of good, and my realization that gay or not, if he was nominated by this oh-so-Republican President, he must be evil."

Hammond grinned. "I told you yesterday, Ben—he's a lot more to the center than you might expect. We could do a lot worse."

"We could do a lot better."

"Not with this President."

Ben frowned. Good point. "Did you know he was gay? Yesterday, I mean."

"I did not."

"Did the President?"

"No way. Oh, they might've had some intimation. The man is in his late forties, never married, has a male roommate, that sort of thing. But it wouldn't have been a problem, even for the Republicans, as long as he stayed in the closet. There are a lot of gay people in this town, Ben. We've known that ever since Gerry Studds became the first openly gay congressman back in 1983. No one cared about Mark Foley—till his suggestive electronic messages to congressional pages started surfacing. You've seen The List—the unofficial roster of gay congressional staff members. Even the Republicans have them. We call them the Pink Elephants. As long as they keep their private lives to themselves, no one much cares. Try to make a fuss about it and you get labeled homophobic. Hell, people were speculating that Justice Souter was gay when he was nominated to the Supreme Court—the man lived with his mother, for Pete's sake. But that didn't stop Bush the First from nominating him. Long as it's not in the public eye, it's not a problem."

"But now it *is* in the public eye. And there's no taking it back. Will President Blake stand behind him?"

"Well, he can't exactly withdraw the nomination, can he? That would be too blatantly anti-gay even for that rascal. Especially after that swell speech he gave yesterday saying what a brilliant legal mind Roush has, and how he'll be a crusader for truth, justice, and the American Way. But the inside skinny is that Blake feels hoodwinked, and frankly, I can see the man's point. Word is he wants the nomination to fail so he can appoint someone else quickly, before his second term expires, but he doesn't want to be the hatchet man. He's counting on the Judiciary Committee to do that for him. The Constitution gives them the right to advise and consent. So the Republicans are most likely hard at work searching for some nongay reason to withhold their consent. And given that there's more of them than us on the committee, they probably will succeed.

"And," Hammond added, "whether we like the man or not, if his nomination fails, it'll be a major-league slap in the face to gay rights. What Roush said yesterday is accurate—we've corrected a lot of the prejudices and problems that have haunted the nation, or at least put laws into place that make it clear we don't tolerate disparate treatment. But the law still doesn't protect gay and lesbian people. We actively discriminate against them, prohibiting gay couples from sharing medical benefits and passing legislation with code names like the Defense of Marriage Act. Defense against what? Gay people, obviously."

"Change takes time," Ben said. "It's a mistake to force it before the populace is ready. Could create a backlash. I know a lot of good people who nonetheless have sincere religious objections to homosexuality."

"You always think the best of people—even when they're at their worst, don't you, Ben? You remind me of my boy."

Ben blinked. "I didn't know you had a son."

"Not many people do. He died . . . well, quite some time ago.

But he was a great kid. So full of optimism. Such a good spirit." He paused reflectively. "Losing him was about the toughest thing that ever happened to me."

"I can only imagine."

"Hieronymous Carroll, we called him."

"Hieronymous?"

Hammond grinned. "I know—it's awful. What can I say? I was a Latin major."

"Ah," Ben said, nodding. "I studied Latin in college myself."

"But your point is correct, Ben. There is still a lot of homophobia in this country."

"Nonetheless, I believe we will eventually have gays on the Supreme Court. Even in the White House. Eventually."

Hammond slapped the back of his chair. "You know what? So do I. I'm just not sure I'll be alive to see it." He ran his fingers through his graying hair. "But if someone's going to go down in the history books as the senators who took a stand against the last bastion of prejudice—why not us?"

"Tempting, I must admit. But I keep coming back to the same stumbling block: he's a Republican."

"Like it or not, Ben, the next justice appointed to the Court is going to be a Republican, this one or some other." He gripped Ben firmly by the shoulder. "Will you do something for me? Come out to the man's house with me tomorrow. He's setting up a press conference—to make an announcement as to whether he'll comply with the President's unspoken request, or whether he's going to tough it out. There'll be people swarming all over the place. Everyone wants to talk to him, but he's promised me a solid hour when he'll talk to anyone I bring him."

"An hour's not long. Especially if you've invited a lot of people. Perhaps another day would be better."

"An hour will be long enough. And tomorrow he'll be expecting visitors. It's not far from here, Ben. What better have you got to do? Meet him. Talk with him. See if he doesn't impress you as much as he impresses me. Then make your decision."

Hard to turn down such a reasonable request. "May I ask another question? Why me?"

"Modesty rearing its ugly head again?"

"No. I just know that there are more influential senators around than yours truly."

"Who says you're the only person I've invited? I've been shaking the bushes all morning. Getting a regular junket going. But I know many of our brethren will never support a Republican candidate. They may not oppose him too hard, especially now that such a position could be perceived as anti-gay. But they won't support him. They've got constituents. Careers."

"And I don't?"

"You weren't elected. You didn't raise campaign funds. You're not beholden to anyone. Last I heard, you hadn't even decided whether you'll seek another term. For a U.S. senator, you have a rare degree of independence. And let me also say that I think I'm a pretty good judge of character. I've read your résumé, Ben. I remember that big case you had in Chicago, the gay-bashing hate crime."

"But I represented—"

"I know. Nonetheless, everyone recognized where you stood on the fundamental issue of equal rights, and I don't imagine that's changed much since then, has it? Bottom line—you'll do what your heart tells you to do, and damn the consequences." He leaned forward eagerly. "This boy Roush—he needs someone like that. He needs a friend."

Ben walked to a window and gazed across Constitution Avenue to the Supreme Court building, the home of the most momentous legal decisions in the history of the nation. Could anything possibly be more important than helping determine who would write the next nation-shaking opinion? "I don't know . . ."

"So come meet the man. That's all I'm asking. Bring that pretty little fiancée of yours. You know," he added, looking Ben directly in the eye, "a lot of our colleagues serve in this chamber for twenty, thirty years, and never do a damn thing of any consequence. You've been here a few months and you've been given a chance to make history. To change the face of the world. Can you really afford to pass that up?"

5

They trampled the petunias.

Thaddeus Roush had known his actions would attract a certain degree of attention. No, he had known he would set off a firestorm. But it hadn't really sunk in—it hadn't seemed real—until he found a platoon of reporters buzzing around his house like ants in an ant farm, shouting for him to smile or toss them a quote, as if he were a trained seal performing for their damned minicams. Yesterday he was an unknown; today, they all wanted a piece of him.

The grass was ruined, positively ruined. And the petunias were destroyed.

Ray's petunias.

Roush sat in his library, one hand pressed against his forehead, the other clutching a Scotch-and-soda that he had not even sipped. Never in forty-seven years had he experienced a day like this one. Up before dawn for a meeting with the President, who behind the closed doors of the White House asked all the questions he was not supposed to ask. Abortion. Gun control. Even gay rights. And Roush hadn't lied, either. He didn't for a minute believe the framers of the Constitution intended to provide any rights to homosexuals, penumbral or otherwise. Such a thing would have been unheard of at that time. Any rights of that nature had to come from the legislature, not from the Constitution—and certainly not from the Supreme Court. And so President Blake, confident that the forty-seven-year-old bachelor posed no overt risks, had led him to the Rose Garden and publicly bestowed ringing praise about his judicial acumen, even though Roush was quite certain the President had never read any of his opinions and never would.

Then Roush sandbagged him. He dropped his little surprise in full view of the nation, the tiny revelation that changed everything.

Even as he had approached the podium, he wasn't sure he would be able to do it. He'd known he should; it was a matter of conscience. As he'd said, he would not live a lie, not once he became a public figure. Furthermore, by coming out as he did, he could make a stand for tolerance in the political arena that could benefit thousands, perhaps even millions, of Americans.

But only at a cost. Yes, he'd known he should do it. Yet in the final seconds leading to the utterance of the speech, he was not certain that he would. Did he have the courage, not only to look the unblinking camera in the eye and tell it who he really is, but also to face the subsequent consequences? The painful price of honesty?

The questioning following his announcement had been extremely awkward and was soon curtailed by the POTUS staff, who treated him as if he had sold nuclear secrets to a hostile nation. The President himself disappeared, probably never to be seen by Thaddeus Roush again. Blake's chief of staff harangued him for the better part of an hour, saying Roush had abused their trust to forward his personal agenda. And perhaps she was right. Who could say? Roush never felt as if he were advancing an agenda; he was a judge, not an advocate. But he did have a core instinct for the difference between right and wrong. Hiding would have been wrong.

Although he had used the phrase in his speech, he never saw what he had done as "coming out of the closet." He'd never considered himself in the closet. His sexual preference wasn't a secret; it was simply something he never talked about. Heterosexual judges never talked about their sex lives; why should he? He knew many of his friends suspected the truth; for that matter, he knew that the President's investigators who had been burrowing into his life for the past two weeks suspected it. So long as it wasn't out in the open, it wasn't an issue, not even for the farthest of the far right. But he had brought it into the open. He had changed everything.

When the White House had finally released him and he came home, Ray was waiting for him. They stared at each other for the longest, most excruciating time. But neither spoke.

Should he have told Ray what he planned to do? Of course he should have. It seemed so obvious now. By outing himself, he had outed his lover as well. Ray should have had some say in that. Chalk it up to Roush's muddled state of mind. He was running on instinct, blind instinct, more impulsive than compulsive, more feeling than planning. Ray had always been adamant about remaining apart from Roush's political and judicial work—in part because he wasn't really interested, and in part because he was a fiercely left-wing liberal.

Roush wondered what the press would do with that, allowing himself a tiny smile. Strike Two for the President's investigators— they hadn't discovered that, either.

And Strike Three was the Big Secret. The major-league blot that the investigators had missed altogether. The hidden piece of his past that made his homosexuality utterly unimportant by comparison.

Surely that was too long ago, too far in the past.

Who was he kidding? If he had learned anything from his brief foray into politics, it was this: There's no such thing as too long ago.

He should have told the President about that secret. Or at the least, declined the nomination for unspecified reasons. But how could he pass up such a momentous opportunity? The crowning achievement of his career—an intellectual feast! It would take a stronger man than he to say no to the Supreme Court, even though he knew that if the truth were ever revealed . . .

But he was worrying himself unnecessarily. Why should it ever be revealed? No one had discovered the truth in the past. None of the investigators associated with any of his previous appointments had so much as sniffed the scent of the truth. There was no reason to believe anyone ever would. It was long ago and far away, water under the bridge. It had been a mistake, but we all make mistakes, and Roush was entitled to move on. No one could stop him . . .

Or so he had believed. So he had tried to tell himself until he saw the phone message, the single pink slip in a massive pile of pink slips that actually mattered. It seemed there was another downside to being the subject of the latest media blitz.

The past can find you. Ghosts can return to their old haunts.

Enough. He would need rest if he were going to face the onslaught of the new day. Senator Hammond was bringing over a junket of potential friends. Sadly enough, having been virtually abandoned by his own party, he was forced to look across the aisle to the Democrats for support. That would give Ray a good deal of pleasure.

He needed to be in top form. Since his previous press conference had been abruptly curtailed, he would have to answer more questions from the press. He would be expected to tell them whether he would bow to the call from dozens of right-wing organizations to step down.

And he would have to try to find some way to reconcile with Ray, some way to atone for what he'd done.

He would have to deal with the consequences of revealing his secret, while simultaneously praying that the Big Secret never came to light. He could survive being labeled a traitor, a liar, even a faggot. But no one was likely to lend their support to a murderer.

6

*B*en had never before visited Montgomery County, Maryland, a well-heeled suburb outside D.C. He didn't much care for it; it didn't seem so much like a real town as it did an overgrown, over-priced housing development—or several housing developments ab-sorbing one another like a multicelled bacterium to create the semblance of a community. Prefab cottages and sprawling McMan-sions stretched as far as the eye could see, huge spreads located far enough away from the urban centers that they remained affordable to the upper middle class in a way that anything older or closer would never be. There were neighborhoods like this back in Tulsa, Ben knew, especially as you moved south of midtown, where more square footage could be obtained for less. The distance from the no-toriously high crime districts of D.C. probably worked in the neigh-borhood's favor, too. Still, he didn't like it. There was something creepy and artificial about it. Like a Stepford town. An overgrown theme park. Not a real city.

But of course, that was the opinion of a guy who lived in the up-stairs apartment of a semi-seedy boardinghouse, so what did he know? Christina's eyes lit up like a pinball machine as they pulled into the driveway. She had been urging Ben to look at houses. They would need something larger, she said. She understood Ben's attach-ment to the boardinghouse, to the legacy Mrs. Marmelstein had left him, but they would need more space after they were married.

After they were married. He still couldn't say it, or even think about it, without picturing a fleecy word balloon above his head reading *"Gulp!"*

Judge Roush's front lawn was so encrusted with reporters that Ben couldn't tell whether he liked the exterior of the house or not. But the interior was definitely to his taste. Lots of wide open spaces, not much clutter. Ben hated houses that were filled to the brim with tchotchkes, a never-ending array of doodads. He didn't do that with his place. Of course, he didn't really own any doodads.

If Christina moved in, she would bring all of hers. The ceramic pig collection. The knickknack tribute to all things French.

Was it a bad sign that shivers ran up his spine?

This house appeared to have been decorated sparely by choice, and that said a lot about its occupants. It had a modern feel: straight lines, white paint, lots of light flooding in from the wide windows, flat ceiling—almost Frank Lloyd Wright flat—and modern art on the walls.

"Is that a Chagall?" Ben asked, pointing to a predominantly pink and blue watercolor above the sofa in the living room.

"Indeed," Senator Hammond answered. "You have a good eye, Ben."

Well, a good eye for the signature at the bottom. "I'm going to assume it's a print."

"Actually, it's a page removed from an art book. But the signa-ture is genuinely Chagall's. One of the last things he did before he passed away. It's quite valuable."

"And this," Ben said, pointing to the spot-illuminated painting on the opposite wall, "is a Dalí?"

"Right again. From the *Paradise Lost* series."

"Wasn't there a problem with forgeries after Dalí's death?"

"It wasn't forgeries, exactly. It was the difficulty of distinguishing actual Dalís from the work of his students, which he sometimes signed, particularly late in life. But this is the real thing. Thaddeus knows his art. He's been collecting for many years."

"It's my passion." Ben turned and saw the new Supreme Court nominee standing behind him. "One of them, anyway."

Ben shook his hand. "And what are your other passions?"

"Truth. Justice." He motioned Ben toward the nearest sofa. "And unicorns. I love anything with a unicorn on it." He smiled. "That last part was a joke."

"Thank goodness." Ben eyed the man sitting opposite him. He looked different up close than he did on television, or even on a somewhat distant brightly lit dais. He supposed anyone would. He was tall and trim, dark-haired—just a hint of gray—with prominent brows and a crescent nose. Roush was dressed casually in a polo shirt and khaki chinos, but he had clearly paid close attention to what he was wearing. Probably obsessed over exactly what image he wished to convey, Ben suspected. He knew *he* would. And now Roush had the added problem of having to dress in a manner that was attractive but not . . . fussy. Dandified. Or any of the other euphemisms his opponents would be using to remind everyone that he was gay. "You must be exhausted. Bob tells me you've been talking to senators all morning."

"I'd rather be grilled by senators than by that horde amassed on my front lawn." Ben didn't doubt it. "I haven't had so many people around my home since we hosted the block party. The press conference isn't until four in the afternoon. They started setting up their equipment at four in the morning. Can you believe it? I'm the scourge of the block. I'll be lucky if they don't drum me out of the neighborhood association."

Ben doubted that was much of a threat. "Looks like you have quite a spread here."

"Oh, two acres. Honestly, I only bought the surrounding lots to prevent them from being developed. This town was in danger of becoming a little too cookie-cutter, if you know what I mean."

Ben raised an eyebrow.

"Then Ray got into gardening and, well, you can see for yourself."

"Where is Ray, anyway?" Hammond asked. He turned to Ben. "Did you know this man's partner used to be my law clerk? About a million years ago."

"Small world, huh?"

"So it seems," Roush said. "Anyway, after Ray put his green thumb to work, this little house became the tail that wags the dog. Can I show you around?"

Roush took Ben through the rear sliding doors and gave him a guided tour of the grounds. The backyard reminded Ben of the Philbrook mansion in Tulsa—which had the most magnificent garden he had ever seen in his life, until now. What Roush had called the "backyard" was actually a rectangular expanse that stretched almost to the low horizon, all of it planted, all in excellent shape. The lawn was virtually manicured. The flowering plants were clipped, the bedded flowers were in bloom. Roush identified each for Ben as they passed, usually offering the Latinate name as well as the common. As they strolled down the cobbled path, Ben marveled that a garden could seem so rich and wild, yet simultaneously seem perfectly planned and ordered. Even if Roush wasn't the primary gardener, it was clear he took great pride in it. Ben wondered if all the senators who were visiting today had gotten the backyard tour, and what effect Roush imagined that might have on them. He couldn't help thinking of *Pride and Prejudice:* Elizabeth Bennett initially rejects the presumptuous Darcy, but her feelings change when she sees the artistry and majesty of his estate, Pemberley. Perhaps Roush was hoping for a similar transformative effect.

After the tour, Roush took Ben into his private library; the walls were lined with beautiful Folio Society editions of the classics. The man Ben recognized from the press conference as Roush's partner, Raymond Eastwick, was sitting on the sofa reading a magazine.

"Ben," Roush asked, "have you had a chance to meet Ray?"

"Haven't had the pleasure," Ben said, extending his hand. As he did, he couldn't help but notice the contrast between the two. Eastwick was larger, a little heavy, stronger-looking. He was dressed in jeans, and one of the knees was soiled. Early morning weeding, perhaps.

"Pleasure's mine," Eastwick said, "and I mean that. Been with Taddy for seven years, and I think this is the first day in all that time there's been another Democrat in the house."

"You're on the side of the forces of goodness and light?"

Eastwick laughed. "Yeah. It's a mixed marriage. But somehow, we make it work." He gave Roush an odd look. "I'll leave you two alone."

Roush poured Ben a glass of lemonade, then took a seat across the coffee table from him. Senator Hammond came in from the other room and joined them. "What can I tell you about myself?" Roush asked.

"As far as your public life goes," Ben said, "that's all over the airwaves. Not to mention the Internet. Your personal life is a little sketchier. Any problems?"

Roush tugged at his collar. "No. The President thoroughly vetted me. How could I possibly have any secret bigger than the one I revealed yesterday? And that wasn't a secret. That was just none of anyone's business."

"Well . . . are there any other tidbits of information that are none of anyone's business but might nonetheless derail your confirmation?"

"Absolutely not."

"I'll go out on a limb and assume you tilt to the right."

"I am a Republican. I've voted for the Republican presidential candidate all my life." He paused. "But I'm a reasonable man."

"I read your Fifth Circuit opinion in *Chalders v. Boring*. You struck down the parental notification requirement in the state abortion law. Even though the Supreme Court upheld the one in Oklahoma."

"They were very different statutes. The one in *Chalders* clearly violated the right to privacy—even allowed the state to put women's names on the Internet. I wasn't ruling on the constitutionality of abortion. I was ruling on the appropriateness of a specific statute."

"I got that," Ben said, eyeing him carefully. He saw no hint of dissembling, no sense that the man was putting on a show. "But it's a distinction a lot of die-hard Republicans I know wouldn't have perceived."

Roush held out his hands. "Like I told you, I'm a reasonable man."

Ben kept watching the eyes. "At the same time, you buried the Connecticut gun control bill. The one the state legislature spent five years getting passed."

Roush remained unruffled. He maintained eye contact the entire time he spoke. He was firm, but not insistent. "The statute violated the Second Amendment. Plain and simple. I know you probably don't agree, but there was a sound Fifth Circuit precedent that provided persuasive authority. And just for the record, I didn't 'bury' the bill single-handedly. It was a unanimous opinion. Even my distinguished Clinton-appointee colleague agreed."

Solid reasoning, even if Ben didn't much care for the result.

Hammond arched an eyebrow. "What did I tell you, Ben? He's the real deal."

"The real what? An honest man?"

"A thinking Republican."

Ben decided to steer the conversation away from politics and judicial opinions. Christina had prepared an extensive brief on the man's public life, and as far as Ben could tell, he was a dutiful and honest judge who did his work in a prompt and efficient manner. But there should be something more than a good work ethic in a man who wanted to be considered for a position on the highest court of the land.

"I know you probably don't want to address specific issues like the death penalty—"

"Reprehensible," Roush said, without blinking. "I don't know if any government has the right to take lives. But we certainly don't, given our gigantic error rate. How many people have been released from death row because DNA evidence proved they didn't commit the crime of which they were convicted?"

"Over a hundred," Ben said, more than a little stunned.

"Besides, we all know executions have been applied disparately on racial grounds. If they can target racial minorities, who's next? I'm familiar with the Jay Wesley Neill case from your home state, Ben. The prosecutor repeatedly referred to the defendant's homosexuality during his closing plea for the death penalty. He ended up executed by lethal injection—while his partner and co-conspirator got life. Appalling."

Ben felt his eyes widening of their own accord. That case was a notorious blight on the history of Oklahoma jurisprudence. Although the appeals court criticized the prosecutor's remarks, the decision was not reversed and the defendant was executed.

"The whole death penalty situation is an international embarrassment," Roush added. "We run around the world preaching to others about human rights, while simultaneously carrying out a practice considered unjust and inhumane by virtually every other civilized nation." He drew in a breath. "So, you see, I part ways with my party on this issue."

And how often did that happen in this day and age? Ben wondered. He glanced at Hammond, who was beaming from ear to ear.

"You're probably familiar with Senator Hammond's Environmental Protection Wilderness Bill," Ben ventured. "My fiancée has been working for months to get that bill to the floor."

"She must be glad Senator Hammond is in the Senate," Roush replied. "He's the only man on earth who could get that bill passed, especially in the current political climate. Ditto for the Poverty bill, and that stands to benefit—what—around three million poor and indigent people?"

"Yes. But the bill hasn't passed yet."

"And you're concerned that even if it does, the Supreme Court will kill it. Not without reason. It does raise some constitutional issues regarding congressional power and the interstate commerce clause that are not frivolous."

Ben waited. He didn't want to ask the question.

"Of course," Roush said, "it would be inappropriate for me to comment on a specific pending law." He leaned forward and smiled. "But just between you and me, if I killed a piece of environmental legislation, that handsome young man you met a few minutes ago would never forgive me. And if I killed an antipoverty bill, I would never forgive myself."

Ben tried to be skeptical. "Even if there were constitutional issues involved? The rules say you have to enforce the letter of the law—and damn the result."

"The rules." Roush turned his eyes skyward. "Even the most

conservative, I'm-opposed-to-judicial-activism jurists in the country apply the rules when and where they see fit, and we all know it. Are you telling me *Bush v. Gore* was decided based on judicial precedent, or the letter of the Constitution—both of which require judges to stay out of the election process? Nonsense. The Republican members of the Supreme Court saw an opportunity to pick the next President and they took it." He leaned forward. "I hope you don't mind, Ben, but I've taken the liberty of asking my clerk to do a little checking up on you. It appears to me your whole career has been about applying the rules when it served a righteous cause—and looking the other way when it didn't."

"I don't know about—"

Roush held up his hands. "Don't get me wrong. I'm not accusing you of anything—except maybe being a lawyer who actually cares about his clients. But it seems to me you always keep your eyes on the prize. You do what it takes to see that justice is served. You understand that the rules exist to help people—not the other way around. People come first." He settled back into his chair. "That's the kind of Supreme Court justice I'd like to be. You got a problem with that?"

7

Half an hour later, Ben conferred with Minority Leader Hammond in the foyer. Roush had moved on to another senator, Eastwick was at work in his garden, and a few select reporters and photographers had been admitted inside. The place was buzzing like a beehive, swarming with people, disturbing much of the charm and all of the ambience. Nonetheless, Hammond found a semiprivate corner and pulled Ben aside. "So?"

Ben shrugged. "What do you want to know? He's a charmer. He opposes the death penalty. He's on what I believe is the morally correct side of many critical social issues, and he's at least reasonable about the others." He paused. "Roush is either an incredibly slick con man or the best nominee we could hope for from the current administration."

"And which do you think it is?"

Ben pursed his lips. "I think he's the best nominee we could hope for from the current administration."

"What did I tell you?"

"But I've been wrong before. I'm really not that good at judging people."

"Stop waffling. Can I assume you're on board?"

"On board what? It's not like I'm going to convert the Senate Judiciary Committee. I'll be lucky to get a seat in the gallery."

Hammond looked at him levelly. "Once the far right is mobilized, and the Christian Congregation begin their inevitable attack ads, he's going to need all the friends he can get. A voice of support—especially one with a high approval rating from the buckle on the Bible Belt—will be very welcome. I'd like to be able to tell Thaddeus you've got his back. What do you say?"

Ben considered for a long time. This would not be a prudent move, especially for someone who was contemplating an imminent Senate race. But when did he ever do the smart thing, anyway? "Tell the man I've got his back. Now how can I get a seat for this press conference?"

"Seat?" Hammond took Ben by the arm and smiled. "You're going to be standing just to the left of the podium, Ben. Let's get your nose powdered."

Roush locked the bathroom door behind him, sat on the toilet, put his head in his hands, and breathed deeply. He was beginning to feel claustrophobic out there. He'd never been in the eye of the hurricane before and he didn't like it. Normally judges don't attract that much attention. All these people swarming over the grounds, thinly veiled enemies looking for any scrap of information that might be used against him—it was overwhelming. Nightmarish. His asthma was acting up, and he couldn't have that. By the time the cameras were rolling, he had to be calm and utterly in control.

He hated this business of trying to win over the Senate, one senator at a time. It was as if he were auditioning for the job. Totally inappropriate. But essential, if he was going to survive the tidal wave he had started. The toughest conversation had been with the new guy, Kincaid. He was smart, and so utterly without any political agenda or ambition that he remained free to act according to his conscience—the kind of person Washington feared most. The look that man had given him when he asked if Roush had any secrets! It sent chills down his spine. Or maybe it wasn't the look. Maybe it was the fact that Roush knew how disastrous it would be if the truth ever emerged.

He and Ray still hadn't talked, exchanging nothing more than a few casual pleasantries. First, the man is publicly outed on national television; then, the next day, his home is invaded. His private nest. No wonder he was hiding in the garden. Roush would have to think of some way, of any way possible, to make it up to him. He could just imagine the rage that must be boiling behind that gardening apron. When Ray lost his temper—

"Judge Roush?"

"Yes?" Camilla was on the other side of the door. She was the housekeeper three times a week, but on this day her job description had mutated into gatekeeper and bouncer.

"There's a woman outside the gate who wants to speak with you. She buzzed me on the intercom."

"Reporter? Politician?"

"Neither. She says she called you yesterday."

"Just tell her—"

"She insists that you will want to see her—before it's too late."

"Did she give a name?"

"No. But she said to tell you—it's about Savannah."

Every muscle in Roush's body stiffened. Every nerve tingled. He stopped breathing.

"If you want, Judge, I'll just tell her—"

"I'll take care of it."

"Are you sure? You've got so much—"

"I'm sure. It's nothing serious, Camilla. Just a reporter trying to play on your good nature to trick her way in. I'll take care of it. You go help Ruth in the kitchen, would you?"

"If—if you're sure."

Roush waited until she was gone before he did anything, before he even moved.

Victoria had waited this long to try to contact him. She could surely wait a little longer.

So it had finally happened. What he dreaded most. The one thing that could ruin his plans, his entire future. That was the problem with having your face splashed all over the airwaves. People remembered. People knew where you were.

The front yard was still cluttered with media. He would have to send her through the garden gate. Even that was hardly secluded—a crew was setting up for the press conference. And Ray was back there gardening.

He would have to get this over with as soon as possible. No one could know. Not the press. Not Ray. Not anyone.

His future depended on it. His *life* depended on it.

8

Ben listened to the pitiful deliberation between Hammond and Roush's advance crews as they tried to decide where to stage the press conference. They walked all over the grounds, looking for the perfect visual backdrop. Ben favored the small rear herb garden surrounded by stately hedges, but the rest thought the enclosure was too small to accommodate everyone who would want to attend. In addition to that problem, a Ford SUV illegally parked on a dirt road at the far end of the property was visible at that angle. Hammond favored the central garden with the flowering plants, since it was beautiful and would create a positive impression. Roush's people worried that being photographed surrounded by brightly colored flowers would seem too "gay," whatever that meant. Perhaps it was an indicator of Roush's eagerness for the job; Hammond's crew won. The podium, the nominee, the supporters, and the press were artfully arranged at the south end of the garden among the tulips, pansies, and hanging lilies, just in front of a round-top wooden door covered with green climbing ivy—like something out of *Alice's Adventures in Wonderland.*

"Once we're married, I want a garden like this," Christina said, tugging gently at Ben's sleeve. She had left her work on the Wilderness bill administrative committee midday to attend the conference.

"Christina, please don't start . . ."

"I'm not starting anything. I'm just telling you that whether we end up in your boardinghouse or someplace nice, I expect to have a garden. A good one."

"Then you'd better see if Ray Eastwick can fly out to Tulsa. Because I don't know from gardening."

Christina squeezed his arm and smiled. "You don't know from women, either. But you're going to learn."

A few discreet coughs from the President's representative—a junior staffer from the fund-raising department, about as low-level a rep as the President could possibly send without admitting he no longer supported the candidate—told Ben it was time to begin the conference. At Hammond's request, and against his better judgment, Ben had agreed to introduce the nominee after a few humorous introductory remarks from the Minority Leader. He couldn't help but dwell on the irony of it—a Republican nominee reduced to being introduced by two Democrats.

Ben waited for the laughter at Hammond's jokes to subside before he began speaking. He had never been very good at getting people's attention. He had read that some politicians seemed to grow larger than life when they stepped behind a podium. Ben was pretty sure he shrank. Here in Alice's garden, he might as well sip from the bottle labeled DRINK ME.

"You may be asking why I—the most junior of the junior senators—am delivering this introduction," Ben began. "The answer is simple. This is a time in our nation's history when we must reach across party lines and remember that we are one nation. The nomination of someone who is actually qualified for the job—eminently so, in this case—is a cause for rejoicing, not mud-wrestling in partisan politics. So I am here, like many of my Democratic brethren, to show that we not only believe that this nomination is appropriate—it is important."

Enough speechifying. He wasn't very good at it, anyway. "Judge

Roush has a few preliminary remarks, and then he'll entertain any questions—any reasonable and appropriate questions—you may care to ask."

Ben stepped back and Roush squared himself behind the podium. Ben noted that he was carrying only one sheet of paper, which suggested that he either intended to devote most of the time to questions or did not as yet understand what would be required of him. These people weren't going to let him by with a paragraph of platitudes.

"I suppose it may seem a little unusual," Roush began, "to hold another press conference so soon after the last. But to my great surprise, there seems to be a significant interest in . . . well, me."

A few chuckles. Good, Ben thought. Put them off guard with a little humor. Harder to be tough on someone they like.

"At least the media seems to have a consuming interest. The rank-and-file Americans—I'm not so sure. I don't expect to be invited on *Total Request Live* anytime soon." More chuckles. Very nice. Pity he would eventually have to say something serious. "So I invited you to my home to ask me whatever questions might be appropriate. I must warn you, though, when I made my full disclosure in the Rose Garden, I did so in the spirit of honesty and forthrightness—and frankly, to avoid having it revealed in some tawdry way that would inevitably give the impression that I was hiding something. I was not, however, attempting to make my nomination a referendum on gay rights, which would be grossly inappropriate. Nor was I throwing the door open on my private life. My private life is just that, and I see no reason why that should change. There is no precedent for invading the personal privacy of a Supreme Court nominee, and I do not see any reason to start one. Nor will I be willing to answer any hypothetical questions regarding how I might rule on particular judicial or political issues."

Okay, this part, not so good, Ben thought quietly. The press never like to be told what they cannot do. It almost guaranteed that they would try to do it.

Roush smiled. "I will be more than happy, however, to entertain questions that relate to my qualifications for the job for which I have been nominated."

He didn't get any. "Judge Roush," said an attractive brunette in the front row. Ben thought he recognized her from a CBS news show. "Did you inform the President of your homosexuality during your prenomination interviews?"

Roush sighed, obviously disappointed. "I don't recall that he ever asked me about my sexual preference. Nor, for that matter, did I ask him about his." Another light round of guffaws. "Why would it come up? It has nothing to do with my qualifications to sit on the Supreme Court."

"There are millions of Americans who might disagree with you."

"Not if they were the nominee, they wouldn't."

All things considered, he was handling this rather well, Ben thought. Admirably. Particularly for a political novice.

"Throughout the most recent decades," Roush added, "we've seen a continual erosion of standards in our political discourse. Topics that would've been taboo before are now openly explored. Invasions into the sex lives of public figures are rationalized as reflecting on 'character' or 'trustworthiness,' when in fact they are just excuses to engage in the most scurrilous tabloid forms of reportage. The only way that I can see to stop this trend is to refuse to participate. So I will. And I urge each of you to do the same."

In the dead center of the throng, a man with more hair spray than hair spoke. "Can you confirm or deny rumors that the President will withdraw his support from your nomination?"

Roush shook his head. "I'm not going to talk about rumors at all. Rumors are not news. I can tell you that no one—including the President—has indicated to me that he will withdraw his support." He paused, a small smile playing on his lips. "And I personally find it difficult to imagine that he would."

Roush was right of course, Ben thought. Much as the President might like to pull out of this mess, he couldn't. It was one thing to oppose gay marriage or gay health benefits; it was quite another to cancel the nomination of a man he had said was eminently qualified for the job simply because he emerged from the closet. Even if it wasn't illegal, it smacked of bigotry and prejudice. The press would eat him alive.

"Do you think," another brunette, this time an NBC anchor, asked, "that the Senate will confirm your nomination?"

"I think it would be foolish to make predictions in advance of facts." He paused, then grinned. "But they should."

"The Judiciary Committee is mostly Republican—"

"So am I," Roush replied.

A voice from the back shouted, "Could we meet your partner?"

"No, I don't think that would be appropriate. The President did not nominate—"

"The President always introduces the First Lady!" a voice in the rear called. "Where's yours?"

Ben could feel the burning in Roush's cheeks, but Roush managed to maintain control. "How many Supreme Court nominations have you covered, sir?"

There was a long pause, then: "Four."

"And how many times have you asked to interview the nominee's spouse?"

Silence.

"I'll take that to mean none. So I see no reason to break with precedent. Ray has nothing to do with my legal work."

"Did he have anything to do with this garden?"

More laughter. "Well, yes. That he did. I suppose there's no reason for him not to take credit for his extraordinary horticultural efforts."

Mild cheering and a spattering of applause followed. Ben knew this would be awkward, but the mob could be ignored only so long. "Perhaps a brief introduction would be in order. I think he's out back, puttering in the peat moss or something."

Roush turned and grabbed the iron circle that opened the rounded-top door directly behind him, the door that, Ben remembered from his tour, separated the main garden from the enclosed area with the herbs and the fountain.

Roush tugged at the door but couldn't seem to get it open. "I would assume it was locked," Roush muttered, "but there's no lock." He tugged a little harder, but it didn't give. Ben got the impression something was jamming it on the other side.

"This is ridiculous," Roush said, still tugging, trying to save face. "Serves me right for going off-script." He got another nice laugh, but it didn't mask his apparent frustration. Ben could see beads of sweat forming on his brow. Finally, he pressed his foot against the adjoining wall and pulled the door handle with all his strength.

The door flew open. Roush lost his balance and tumbled backward, almost knocking over the podium. A second later, another figure fell through the doorway.

The crowd screamed. Ben craned his neck to see who it was, what had happened, but the body fell too fast. All he could tell for sure was that it was a woman—and that she was covered with blood. Once she hit the ground, she did not move, and it was readily apparent why.

Her throat had been cut, deeply. A pair of garden shears protruded from her back.

The press moved six different ways at once. Some panicked and ran, some raced forward for a closer look. Talking, screaming, running. Minicams readjusted their focus from the podium to the fallen figure in the grass. Commentators all talked at once. The network reps shouted into their cell phones, urging their bosses to interrupt the regularly scheduled programming.

And standing in the doorway, just beyond the opening, Ben spotted Ray Eastwick.

9

Ben felt Christina appear at his side. "Do something," she urged. "These reporters will destroy the crime scene."

Ben moved forward to block their way, but he could see already that he would be inadequate to stanch the flow of the hundred or so press reps bearing down on him. Fortunately, two Secret Service agents emerged from the wings and stopped the traffic. Ben had to admire their quick-witted professionalism. They were here strictly on a ceremonial security detail, never dreaming they would have to take charge of a murder.

"Who is she?" Christina asked.

"Don't know," Ben answered, trying unsuccessfully to sneak another glance at what was now clearly a corpse. "I only saw her face for a fleeting instant. But she didn't look familiar."

Ben moved toward Roush, who was in turn moving toward Eastwick, who seemed stunned, dazed. Roush started to embrace him, then stopped. Whether it was because he was undoubtedly being filmed, or because Ray had been found in such a compromising location, Ben wasn't sure.

Just beyond them, through the door, Ben noticed that the illegally parked red Ford SUV he had noticed earlier was gone.

"What happened?" Roush asked.

Eastwick just stared at him, eyes wide. "I . . . I don't know."

Hammond emerged from the doorway and made a beeline toward Ben. "You've got to take charge of him."

"What are you talking about?"

Hammond pointed toward the house. On the street, red flashing sirens created an eerie strobe-light effect.

"The local police will be here any minute. I expect the feds will show shortly after that."

"Good," Ben said. "They need to take charge—"

"No, you need to take charge. Of them." He pointed toward Roush, who was holding his partner by his arms. His eyes were wide and moist.

"Me? Why me?"

"That's what you do, isn't it? In real life? Represent the accused."

"They haven't been accused of anything."

"And I expect that condition will last about another five seconds. Go."

Ben sidled toward the couple, who were still staring at each other speechlessly. "Look," Ben said quietly, "the police will be here any minute. The press are still watching. Do not, under any circumstances, say anything."

Roush frowned, obviously confused. "What?"

"The press will be asking you questions. Exercise your Fifth Amendment rights. Say nothing."

Slowly, Eastwick seemed to come around. "They'll arrest me."

"They can't arrest you just because you were standing in the doorway at the wrong time." Unless, Ben thought, you were there because you just murdered the woman.

Roush's voice cracked. "But—all that blood—"

"Stop!" Ben said. "Don't you see those huge boom mikes?" He

jabbed a thumb behind himself. "They can pick up a baby's gurgle from three hundred feet. When I said say *nothing,* I meant say *nothing.*"

Roush drew himself up. "You want me to take the Fifth. Like some sort of . . . pimp or something. I won't."

"Do you know what could happen to Ray? Even if they don't arrest him, they could make his life a misery for—"

"Excuse me. Lieutenant Fink, Montgomery County PD." He was a small man, but muscular and tidy, every hair on his receding hairline exactly where it should be. "Which one of you is the judge?"

An hour later, the local police had the crime scene more or less under control—just in time to thwart the efforts of the FBI to take over. The FBI claimed that the presence of so many congresspersons and executive branch staffers mandated federal involvement, while the police argued that it was a state crime that wasn't committed on federal property and didn't involve any element that would trigger a federal crime statute.

The crime scene investigators scrutinized the doorway and the surrounding garden while detectives quizzed everyone present. The garden teemed with hair and fiber experts, soil samplers, blood spatter consultants, coroner's office interns, and videographers—not that there was any lack of videotape of the crime scene before the officials arrived. Both Eastwick and Roush claimed they did not know the victim. For that matter, neither did anyone else. A housekeeper recalled letting the victim on the premises, but said she didn't follow the woman around, didn't get her name, and didn't tell anyone she was there. A gardening apron was found stashed behind some hedges—covered with blood. Eastwick maintained that he had seen the woman from a distance, her body pinned to the back side of the door by the garden shears. He had approached rapidly but, before he arrived, Roush opened the door.

All around him, Ben could hear various reporters doing live remotes from the scene of the crime, talking about "yet the latest bizarre turn of events" regarding the Roush nomination. Some reported that unidentified senators were already calling for Roush to step down. Roush had no apparent connection to the crime. But his partner was another matter.

Ben was desperate to talk with Roush, or Eastwick, or both, but the police were keeping them incommunicado—and since he had not been asked to represent either of them, he had no basis for interference.

Not that he'd ever let that stop him in the past . . .

"I guess she'd probably been stuck to that door for some time, huh?" Ben said casually, as he watched Lieutenant Fink examine the body with an infrared scanner.

"Don't think so. Blood was still fresh."

"Looked to me like she was killed somewhere else, right? Probably planted on that door by someone hoping to disrupt the press conference."

Fink pushed up on one knee. "Senator Kincaid . . . how can I put this? Do I look like a stupid man?"

"No, of course not."

"Then don't treat me like one." He returned to his work. "I'm positive she was D.R.T.—Dead Right There. The killer slashed her throat, then pinned her to that door. What's your interest in this, anyway?"

"I'm just a friend of Thaddeus Roush. Hope this doesn't interfere with his nomination."

Fink gazed up at Ben with a seriously arched eyebrow. "We've got no reason to suspect Roush was involved. Anything's possible, but I'd like to think he wouldn't have opened the door on national television if he'd known there was a corpse there. Now his little snuggle bunny—that's another story. Far as we can tell, he was the only one in the rear garden."

"You can't know that. There are several ways back there."

"Eastwick himself said he saw no one."

"That doesn't prove anything."

"Not saying it does. I'm just saying . . . it's a good thing Eastwick hasn't been nominated for anything."

"Can I talk to him?"

"Which one? Roush? Sure—we've got nothing on him. Eastwick is going to be spending a lot of time downtown."

Ben found Roush sitting on the periphery of the action, out of the way, but not so far the police couldn't question him whenever they liked. "You realize," Ben said quietly, "this changes everything."

"I won't give up," Roush said. His chin trembled a bit, but his expression was resolute.

"I'm not suggesting you should. But you have to realize—this was an uphill battle from the start. Maybe an impossible one. And it just got about a thousand times worse."

"Do you—do you think that's what this murder is about? My nomination?"

Ben shrugged. He was tired, and he hated pretending he had answers when he didn't. "I don't know. Hell of a coincidence if it isn't." He paused. "I got a friend back home in Tulsa, a cop. Mike Morelli. He doesn't believe in coincidences. Says that's the word we use when we don't know enough to discern the connections. I tend to agree."

"But—why?"

"Again, I don't know. But that's what we have to find out. Because it looks to me as if someone wants your nomination to fail bad enough to kill for it."

Book Two

Dead Nominee Walking

10

If it hadn't been for the reflection in the silver lenses of the hooker's sunglasses, Loving never would have seen the barrel of the machine gun emerge from the rear window of the black sedan in time. As it was, he barely had a second to react, but that second was the difference between staying alive and becoming as porous as an SOS pad.

"Duck!" Loving shouted, but the poor hooker, her reflexes undoubtedly slowed by whatever she was taking this week, didn't obey. The machine gun fired, a sweeping rat-a-tat-tat that cascaded across the sidewalk and ricocheted against the brick buildings behind them. Two bullets hit her in the back and she fell.

Loving caught her in his arms. She was already dead. Blood poured out of her wounds, spilling onto his arms and face. Damn! She was a junkie and a hooker and it was entirely possible she was HIV-positive. Before he had a chance to worry about that, however, he noticed that the sedan was still within firing range. Another shower of gunfire burst out of the rear window. He held the woman's body up to shield himself until the sedan was out of range. An awful thing to do, but it wasn't as if the bullets could hurt her anymore.

Two men emerged from opposite sides of the backseat of the sedan, both of them wearing dark pants, dark T-shirts, and long dark dusters. One of them, like the woman he held in his arms, was wearing sunglasses, even though the sun had set and the Georgetown street lamps barely emitted enough light to see ten feet in front of your face. He was tall, purposefully nondescript, and carried what appeared to be a Sig Sauer with a silencer. He was a professional, an enforcer. Loving could tell just by looking at him; he was the spitting image of Leon in that movie. The other man was shorter, fair-haired, pretty, hair combed back and every lock in place. He wasn't an enforcer; no professional would use an automatic weapon on the streets of Georgetown. Probably a personal representative of the client, tagging along to make sure the job got done.

They were moving toward him.

Loving dropped the corpse and ran. Hated to be unceremonious about it, but under the circumstances, he figured God would understand. As soon as he moved, a hail of lead cascaded down all around him.

He dove, flinging himself flat on the pavement. That wouldn't get him anywhere fast, but it would get him out of the line of fire. For a little while. He hugged the concrete, hoping the darkness would give him a few seconds before they adjusted their aim.

It worked. The gunfire stopped, and the instant it did, Loving dove into the alleyway to his left. Out the corner of his eye, he saw the two men moving toward him, Leon on the left, Pretty Boy on the right. They were maybe fifty feet away—more than close enough to connect with either of their weapons.

Loving raced down the alley, kicking empty soda cans and upended trash cans all the way. For a man as large as he was, he could still move fast when he needed to, which was a good thing, because his pursuers were not far behind. Loving had used this passageway to meet the hooker, who supposedly had a lead on a friend of the woman who was murdered at the Roush press conference. He knew it would lead to the NorthPoint shopping mall, where Loving had left his car. If he could only get there in time, there was some slim chance he might survive. On foot, he was a dead man. It was only a matter of time before one of those slugs connected, and then—game over.

Another round of gunfire sent splinters of brick and mortar flying past his head. Guess they'd figured out where he went, not that he was surprised. He'd thought he was running at top speed, but somehow he managed to triple it as soon as he heard the bullets dancing about. Funny how that worked.

It was a long, dark, narrow stretch. The dark part worked to Loving's advantage; the narrow part did not. Even if his two assailants couldn't see exactly where he was, all they needed to do was spray the width of the alley and wait to get lucky. He had to get out of there.

Ahead of him, Loving saw, both literally and metaphorically, the light at the end of the tunnel. He focused his eyes and ran hard—so hard he didn't see the trash can lying across his path. He hit it full speed and went flying, landing in a pile of refuse and human waste. His head banged against the brick side wall. He could tell he was getting woozy. Consciousness was fading . . .

The clanging sound of bullets riddling the trash can brought him back around. The damn thing might have practically crippled him, but it had undoubtedly saved his life. Loving supposed that made it a draw. He pushed himself to his feet and resumed running.

He bolted across the street and made a beeline for the side entrance to the mall. Surely his pursuers wouldn't be insane enough to fire when there were so many innocent bystanders. Maybe he could even lose them. All he needed was enough time to get to the parking garage . . .

He burst through the glass-paned doors and headed toward the escalator. There were still people in the mall, but it was far from crowded, damn it. Too close to closing time. He pushed past several people, muttering his regrets, and jumped onto the fancy acrylic-sided escalator.

Leon and Pretty Boy opened fire. All at once, the mall was blanketed with screams. Shoppers dove one way or the other to get out of danger. Panic seized everyone in the vicinity. The people on the escalator—those who weren't wounded—began stampeding to the top amid the frenzied cries. Loving ducked, but there was only so much he could do, stuck on the escalator with two assassins at the bottom. He was swept along by the rising tide of humanity, unable to do anything to help or escape. In effect, they were creating a barrier around him—but a barrier that might well cost someone their life.

At the top of the escalator, he almost crashed into a blond woman in her early thirties pushing a stroller. The baby girl inside couldn't have been older than six weeks. The mother was in shock, frozen in place.

"Get outta here!" Loving shouted, checking over his shoulder to see if Leon and Pretty Boy had made it to the top.

The woman did not move.

Loving slapped her. A bit brutish, even for him, but it always seemed to work in the movies, right?

She didn't budge.

Like he had time for this. Loving grabbed the handlebar of the stroller. That seemed to snap her out of it a bit.

"Are you gonna push this thing, or am I?" Loving shouted.

"I—I—"

Loving pointed the stroller toward a nearby shoe store and gave the mother a push. "If you stay in there, you should be safe. They're following me."

The mother moved rapidly toward the shoe store. Loving bolted in the opposite direction. Leon and Pretty Boy announced their arrival on the second floor with another round of gunfire. Loving dove into a nearby department store occupying a corner slot. The display window smashed into pieces and Loving was almost buried beneath a shower of safety glass. He kicked a mannequin out of his way and kept running. The store had another entrance on the opposite end of the mall. From there, it was a short sprint to the parking garage. His only hope.

He raced down an aisle of perfumes he didn't have time to sniff. Bottles and display items crashed and exploded all around him. He'd been lucky so far, but he knew that couldn't last forever. The two men were stalking him, and at least one of them knew what he was doing. Loving would never make it to the parking garage at this rate. He had to take them down or get the hell away from them. The trouble with taking them down was—there were two of them, and they had guns. The trouble with getting away from them was—

A bullet creased Loving's thigh. Searing pain radiated through his body. He cried out, stumbled, then rolled to the floor. He clutched his leg and took another roll, dodging behind a makeup counter. The wound didn't feel serious, but it would make it seriously difficult for him to outrun two thugs determined to kill him, regardless of who got hurt along the way.

In one of the overhead security mirrors, Loving saw the two men round the corner. They were barely twenty-five feet away. A panicked shopgirl came too close and Pretty Boy whipped the butt of his gun across her jaw. She screamed and fell to the floor.

Loving clung low to the carpet, gritting his teeth. That was unnecessary. She was no threat to them. Pretty Boy was not only unprofessional—he was cruel.

That made Loving mad.

No more running. Not that he could anyway, with his leg screwed up. He tore a strip off his T-shirt, wrapped it around his hand, found the largest shard of shattered glass on the floor, and waited.

He was still somewhat hidden by the makeup counter, and Leon and Pretty Boy had their attention focused upward, still looking for an upright runner. They'd figure it out soon enough, but with a little luck, not until . . .

When they came parallel to the opening between the wall and the makeup counter, Loving lunged. He jabbed the jagged glass into Leon's stomach. He knew Leon was the pro, the tougher of the two; he had to take him out first. Pretty Boy whirled and fired, but in his haste his aim was far off the mark. While Leon reeled from the blow, Loving grabbed his gun and pounded the butt against Pretty Boy's hands, making him drop his own gun. Loving followed with another blow to his face, shattering his nose. Blood spurted in all directions. Loving raised his wounded leg and kicked the man in the solar plexus, sending him crashing to the floor, unconscious.

Leon grabbed Loving by the throat, knocking the Sig Sauer out of his hands. Loving had known glass in the gut wouldn't stop a pro, but he had hoped it would buy him more time than this. The man had him in a perfect elbow lock that Loving couldn't break. He tried to jab backward with his elbow, without avail. He tried to shake loose—no dice. Leon pinched harder, cutting off Loving's air. He was beginning to feel light-headed.

It was now or never again.

Loving reeled forward, flipping Leon over his head. Leon crashed into a display counter, sending more glass flying. Loving recovered the gun, but it wouldn't fire. Probably damaged when he used it as a battering ram against Pretty Boy. He could leap on top of Leon while he was down, but in his heart he knew that, tough though he was, he was unlikely to win a fistfight against a man who killed for a living.

And that left him with his original option. Run.

Running was a lot harder now. His leg was aching even more than it had before; all the fighting had inflicted wear and tear on the wound. He forced himself to ignore the pain and keep running. He made it out of the department store and into the parking garage. For once, he actually remembered where he had parked. He found his van and started it.

The engine coughed, and for a brief moment he panicked, thinking he was going to be stuck, just waiting for Leon to show his ugly face. *Come on, damn you!* The second time he tried, the engine turned. He backed out and straightened the van.

Leon was standing in the middle of the lane, not fifteen feet away. And he was holding Pretty Boy's automatic weapon.

Loving didn't have time to think. He lay flat across the seat and floored it. The van shot forward. A spray of gunfire riddled the windshield. Loving kept driving, trying to keep the steering wheel steady.

A second later he felt the thump. He sat up in time to see Leon's body fly over the hood and roll off the roof. A second later, the van smashed into a stone pillar, bringing it to a dead halt.

Hard to steer when you're lying down across the front seat.

Still weak, Loving crawled out of the wreckage and hobbled to the side until he could find a wall to support him. He was breathing like an asthmatic, his heart pounding out of his chest. As the adrenaline rush faded, he began to realize just how badly hurt he really was.

After resting another moment, he flipped open his cell and called the police. Then he hobbled over to the approximate area where he thought Leon's body must have landed.

He found the bloody wet spot that indicated the point of impact, but Leon was gone.

Loving shook his fists at the ceiling. *What had Ben gotten him into this time?*

11

Senator Robert Hammond's office had the largest and most well-appointed conference room of any save that of the Majority Leader himself, so that was where they all met, even though the number of people who had been chosen to attend was small and select. Thaddeus Roush was the center of attention, and the amalgamation of talent was gathered to make sure his nomination was not derailed by partisan politics, anti-gay fervor, or murder.

An image consultant named Gina Carraway held color swatches next to Roush's face. "No, red," she said finally. "Definitely a red tie."

Roush squirmed. "A bit flamboyant, isn't it?"

"You wore red in the Rose Garden."

"The President's staff insisted. They even gave me the tie. I typically favor earth tones, myself."

Carraway wrinkled her nose. "Won't play on television. Recedes into the background. You need something bright, something bold, something that emanates confidence."

"Maybe a pair of Bermuda shorts," Ben said—then immediately regretted it. No one was laughing.

All in all, the mood was somber. In the wake of the disastrous press conference, the general consensus in the political world was that Roush was a dead nominee walking. Many people in both parties had called for him to resign to prevent any further embarrassment to the President, or for that matter, to himself. No one gave his nomination any chance of success. What had initially been seen as a breakthrough advance for gay rights was now looking like a tremendous setback for them. Almost every lobbying group in town had taken a position, and almost all of them were opposed. Even some of the gay rights organizations had removed their support after the murder—support that was fairly tepid in the first place. After all, Roush might be gay, but he was still a Republican.

"I think we've fussed about the man's tie long enough." This came from Bertram Sexton, a high-powered D.C. attorney Hammond had recruited to act as Roush's "advisor" during the confirmation hearings. Sexton had represented various nominees and appointees at congressional hearings almost a dozen times in the past. "We need to craft a good opening statement, then strategize how to control the questioning."

"I'm not finished," Carraway protested. "I have to match skin tones. He'll need to wear a good foundation during the hearings."

Roush twisted his shoulders. "I am not wearing makeup."

"If you don't, you'll look hideous under the bright lights. You've got circles under your eyes and tend toward a five o'clock shadow. Plus, you're likely to sweat."

Roush folded his arms across his chest. "I repeat: I am not wearing makeup."

Carraway pinched the bridge of her nose with her long red fingernails. "Bob, I can't work with this."

Senator Hammond smiled, but it was not a happy smile. "Let's leave it for now. We'll revisit the issue later."

"We will not," Roush said emphatically. "Are you insane? I am the first openly gay Supreme Court nominee. No way in hell I'm going to be seen wearing makeup. It's just too . . . obvious."

"Antonin Scalia wore makeup," Carraway replied.

"I'm sure Ruth Bader Ginsberg did, too," Roush grumbled. "But I won't."

"His concerns about makeup raise all kinds of public opinion issues we have to address." This was Kevin Beauregard, a professional pollster. "Our research indicates the opposition to his nomination is almost evenly divided between those who oppose him because he's gay and those who are concerned about his possible connection to a violent crime. He's right to avoid anything that might be perceived as stereotypically gay."

Roush raised an eyebrow. "Such as?"

"Oh, you know as well as I do. Probably better. No pastels. Pink shirts are out. We want you to look sharp, distinguished. But not 'pretty.' No fussy hair styles. No Dippity-Do."

"Am I allowed to shampoo?"

"Yes, but under no circumstances can you exfoliate." He sighed. "If I had my way, I'd give you a buzz cut."

"Not going to happen."

"Then you wouldn't need shampoo."

A line creased Roush's forehead. "I repeat, sir: Not going to happen."

"And that thing you do with your wrist—don't do it."

"What thing?"

"That thing. You just did it. That has to go."

"I don't know what you're talking about."

"It's that thing you do, especially when you get worked up. It's not exactly a limp wrist, but . . . uncomfortably close. You have to avoid anything that might seem effeminate."

Roush's face was reddening. "Will there be anything else?"

"Yes. Can we do something about all the refusals to reply?"

"I don't know what—"

"You won't talk about your personal life. You won't talk about your sexual preference, other than to identify it. You won't talk about Ray. You won't talk about the murder. You won't express an opinion on issues that might come before the Court." He shook his head. "The American public does not like to be told no. Makes you come off very negative. People will suspect you're hiding something."

"My personal life is none of their damn business."

"And when do people normally say something is 'none of your business'? When they're hiding something. I'm telling you, Thaddeus—every time you refuse to answer, you lose three percentage points."

"I don't care what you or anyone else thinks. I will not express opinions on political issues or hypothetical cases. It is grossly inappropriate."

"Another thing: don't say 'grossly.' It sounds, well, gross. Turns people off."

"Are you planning to police my vocabulary now?"

"Absolutely. Try to avoid the big multisyllabic words. People don't like it—makes them feel stupid. And it seems kind of pompous. Maybe even a little gay."

"My vocabulary is gay?" Under the table, Ben could see Roush's fists balling up. "Have you people forgotten that I am not running for office? All I need is the votes of nine senators in committee and fifty-one in the full assembly. The opinion of the American public doesn't matter."

"I'm afraid it does. This is already a hot-potato nomination. People are up in arms. Calling their senators."

"I can testify to the truth of that statement," Ben offered. "My phone has been ringing off the hook since the announcement in the Rose Garden."

"And it's going to get a lot worse before it gets any better," Sexton added. "Thaddeus, you should prepare yourself for the worst."

"Moreover," Beauregard said, "I can guarantee that the distinguished members of the Senate will be taking the temperature back home before they decide how to vote. You'll have to win over Middle America if you want this position."

"Swell." Roush swiveled his chair to face Ben. "You're from Oklahoma. Could you please deliver the Heartland for me?"

"If possible," Ben said somberly. "But the sad truth is, most of my phone calls are running against your appointment."

"That's to be expected," Hammond said hastily. "People don't know you or anything about you, other than your sexual orientation. We can change that at the hearing."

"Look," Roush said, "I'm not planning to put on any dog and pony show. I'm a D.C. Circuit judge, not a damn circus performer."

"Another thing that has to go," Beauregard said, making a *tsk*-ing noise. "That attitude. Temper, temper."

"What, is my temper too gay for you?"

Ben scooted his chair between them. "Gentlemen, please. We're on the same team here, remember?"

"Could've fooled me," Roush grumbled.

"If you don't mind," Ben continued, "I have a few questions of my own."

"Like what?" Senator Hammond asked.

"Like what the heck am I doing here?"

"Well, I was planning to spring this in private, but—I want you to be Tad's lead counsel at the hearings, Ben. I want you sitting beside him from start to finish."

"What? *Me?* Why me?"

Hammond's eyebrows bounced up and down. "Why not you? You're a member of Congress and an experienced lawyer."

"You've already got a lawyer."

Hammond shook his head. "Bertram is brilliant when it comes to strategizing the Senate hearing, but he has no experience in criminal defense."

"This isn't a criminal trial."

"Damn close. You know as well as I do that they will try to drag the murder of that poor woman into it."

"Probably right. But there are other senators—"

"Actually, there are few senators with genuine criminal defense experience, and none with as much as you."

"But at best, the criminal defense aspect will be a small part of the confirmation hearings. You need someone with political savvy. Experience with hearings of this sort."

"Bertram will be sitting right behind you."

"I should be sitting right behind *him*."

"No, I don't think so. You're an Oklahoman and everyone knows it. You're young, earnest, popular, and as Mom-and-apple-pie as they come. That's what I want America to see. Bertram won't be far away. But when people turn on their sets to look at Tad, I want them to see the fresh-faced kid from Oklahoma at the same time. I want them to think, 'Well, if Kincaid likes him, a member of the opposition party for heaven's sake, maybe he's okay.' "

"I think you're overrating my influence."

"Got nothing to do with influence," Hammond said. "It's about image. You've got exactly the image Tad needs. Am I right, Gina?"

She nodded. "He is right. Why are you paying me so much money, Bob? I think you've got the image concept down cold."

"Thirty years in the Senate will do that for you. But I still like to get a second opinion." He leaned forward and grabbed Ben by the shoulders. "So whaddaya say, slugger? Your country needs you. Thaddeus Roush needs you. Will you do it?"

"Have you made a decision?"

Ben stood in the doorway, a briefcase and coat under his arm. He had just returned from the big powwow in Hammond's conference room and Christina nailed him before he even had a chance to sit down. "Could I at least hang up my coat first?"

Christina considered. "I'm not sure there's time."

"Make time. Do you have any idea how hard it was to get through the swarm of press vultures outside?"

"Yes, because I walked the same path, except two hours earlier."

"Show-off." Ben tossed his coat and case into a chair, then grabbed the loaded message spindle. "This many calls? Since I left for the meeting?"

"And it's going to get worse."

"Politicians or constituents?"

"Mostly the latter."

"And the general tenor—?"

"Either they're mad at you because you backed a gay nominee or they're mad at you because you backed a Republican nominee."

"Swell. Anything else?"

"Got a call from a friend at the governor's office. He's looking into the possibility of withdrawing your appointment."

"Is that possible?"

"Probably not. But the fact that he's considering it doesn't exactly fill my heart with a rosy glow."

"That's just . . . lovely." Ben riffled rapidly through the stack of messages. "Any calls supporting me?"

"Just one. But you know your mother never likes to stay on the phone very long."

Ben stuffed the messages into his pocket. "Any other news?"

"No, Ben. There is no other news. Every information outlet in the country is obsessing about this story and this story alone. If someone dropped an A-bomb on Boulder, Colorado, they would still only be covering the Gay Supreme Court Justice story. And re-running that clip of you introducing him to the world, just minutes before he introduces a dead body to the world."

"Any opinions on whodunit?"

"Oh, Ben, you know perfectly well what everyone thinks. East-wick was seen standing behind the body. On national television."

"Has he been arrested?"

"Not yet. They're still questioning him."

"How's he holding up?"

"Pretty darn well, all things considered. Still hasn't seen fit to hire an attorney."

"Any idea what he's been saying?"

"No. But since he hasn't been charged, he must not have said anything tremendously useful."

"Any word from the White House on the nomination?"

"President Blake's official position is that since Roush himself isn't accused of anything, there's no reason to delay the confirmation hearings. The inside skivvy is that the President wants to move things along so that Roush's nomination can die in time for him to nominate someone else. Heaven forbid his term should end before he has a chance to appoint the ideologue of his choice."

Christina crossed her arms, always a sign that she wasn't going to brook any shilly-shallying. "Now, as to the tiny matter of your decision."

"Which one?"

"I know, there are so many from which to choose. I was refer-ring to whether you're going to represent Roush at the hearings."

"You know about that?"

"I get around."

"Hammond just asked me a few minutes ago."

"As I said, I get around."

Ben drew in his breath, then slowly released it. "I think I'm going to do it."

"You think that's wise?"

"Not particularly."

"Right. Stupid question. As if there were any doubt. Gina Carraway is already choosing your tie." Christina stepped closer and, with an extended finger touched his lips. "I just wish you could make your other pending decisions with the same alacrity."

12

Lieutenant Albertson of the DCPD pounded on his desk. "What the hell did you think you were doing?"

"Trying to stay alive," Loving grunted. "You got a problem with that?"

"I got a problem with three innocent spectators getting shot and a hooker getting killed. Miracle it wasn't worse."

"The miracle's that I wasn't perforated in a hundred places."

"That's your story."

"That's the truth."

Albertson took a banana out of a desk drawer and began peeling it. "I really don't need this right now. I'm in the middle of a very high-profile investigation."

"Yeah, so am I."

"Probably the same one. Lieutenant Fink has asked me to help him figure out what happened at the Roush press conference." The police detective inhaled half the banana in a single bite. "Loving—walk with me."

"Your wish is my command." Loving limped beside him.

They left Albertson's office and emerged on the busy streets of D.C. Loving knew Albertson from the work they had done on the Glancy case, and he liked to think the man trusted him, at least a little, but at some level the professionals were always suspicious of the amateurs. And when two thugs are so desperate to kill you that they open fire in a shopping mall, he was probably right to be suspicious. Loving still felt wobbly from the car crash, not to mention the bullet wound, but he managed to hold himself together long enough to walk. Outside, he breathed deeply of the fresh air—which was actually not all that fresh, given the heavy traffic whizzing down "E" Street. It was hot, too. All in all, Loving wondered why Albertson didn't prefer the nice air-conditioned environment of his semiprivate office.

Albertson pointed and they strolled north. The aroma arising from a hot-dog cart on the corner was supremely tempting, but Loving supposed this wasn't the time for chow.

"You're trying to figure out who the girl is, right? The one who was killed at the Roush press conference," Albertson said.

"As a starting point."

"To what? Figuring out who killed her? Had to be Roush or his little boyfriend."

"Killin' her at their own home? When about a million people were visiting?"

"I'll admit, that part is troublesome. Still, I think we could make it stick if we came up with a little proof."

"Hard to prove who did the killin' when you don't know who the victim was. How can you prove motive?"

"Yeah. That's also a sticking point." Albertson finished his banana and, to Loving's surprise, ordered a hot dog. Well, when in Rome. Loving got his loaded with onions and sauerkraut. "So—had any luck?"

"I'll tell if you'll tell."

Albertson inhaled half his dog. "What do you want to know?"

"Why's it so hard to figure out who the woman is? Doesn't she have fingerprints?"

"Yeah, but they don't match any prints on record. Something weird about them. My forensics boys think they may have been tampered with."

"What about the face? Gotta be someone who recognizes her."

"No one has come forward, discounting the cranks." He devoured the rest of the dog in a single bite. Loving was no shrink, but this guy had to have a major oral fixation. "I'm surprised. The whole thing is weird, though."

"How d'ya mean?"

"What was she doing at that press conference? Why doesn't anyone know her? Why would anyone kill her there when, as you say, there were about a million people roaming about?"

"Maybe it wasn't planned."

"That would be my guess, too. Crime of passion, fit of anger, whatever. Were you there?"

Loving shook his head. Private investigators didn't get invited to important political functions.

"Well, the million or so people in attendance present another problem. Too many suspects. Even the possibility that it was someone who wasn't actually invited to the press conference. After all, the victim wasn't invited. But there she was."

Loving frowned. He had hoped this conversation would be useful. If anything, it was only making the case more complicated.

"But enough about me," Albertson said, wiping his mouth. "I gave, now you follow suit. Who the hell was trying to kill you?"

"I wish I knew."

"But you said they were professionals?"

Loving nodded. "At least one of them was. I think the other guy was some sort of keeper. He wasn't as good; in fact, if anythin', I think he was crampin' the pro's style. I probably wouldn't have gotten away if he hadn't had that clown weighin' him down. I mean, come on. A machine gun in a shoppin' mall? That's like somethin' out of one of them *Terminator* movies. No pro would ever do that."

"Agreed. Where did they go after you crashed your buggy?"

"Don't know. I mean, the pro probably knew how to roll with the car and land on his feet. That wasn't so much of a shock. But the mall security men said the other guy was gone before they could even get to the scene, and I left him hurtin' pretty bad. I think they must've had backup."

"Cleaners?"

"Somethin' like that."

"Okay. Give me more."

"I don't have more to give."

"Try. I got people breathing down my throat, expecting me to explain three wounded people and over a million dollars in property damage. What were they after?"

"Well, judgin' from appearances, me."

"Why?"

"Don't know."

"You were meeting someone?"

"Right. I've been trollin' all the low-life hangouts in the vicinity, crook bars and pool halls and stuff. Finally found a guy who said he knew a guy who knew a girl . . . that sort of thing." Loving made a strategic decision to delete the one identifying feature that helped him close in on the person he wanted—the red Ford SUV Ben had seen parked at the rear of Thaddeus Roush's garden. "She was a workin' girl who supposedly knew a woman who knew the woman who was murdered. Got the impression the victim has some kind of criminal past, so I'm surprised you didn't get a match on her prints. Anyway, before this lady of the evening could tell me anythin', those coldhearted assassins riddled her with bullets. Just because she was in the way." Loving swallowed. "Looked like she wasn't more than eighteen. Maybe younger."

Albertson was silent for a moment. "Well, I have to assume you were getting too close to something someone didn't want you to know."

"Like the person who's really behind the murder?"

"Maybe. Or someone who sent the victim to the press conference to be killed. Or someone who doesn't want you to know who she is for some other reason. Point is—it's big. Whoever was behind this has some serious money and serious crime connections. Sufficient to bring in a very serious hit man. And a keeper."

"Yeah. That's a problem."

Albertson raised a eyebrow. "Getting scared?"

"Nah," Loving bluffed. "Gettin' curious. And a little depressed. If there's major crime figures in this—maybe even the mob—it's gonna be a tough nut to crack. Those boys are very good at keepin' their secrets." He stopped walking. "So what are we doin' here, Lieutenant?"

"I don't follow you."

"Why are we out here soakin' up the sunshine instead of inhalin' the asbestos fumes in your office?"

Albertson smiled slightly. "Don't you like to get out on occasion? Feel the rays of the sun warming your face?"

"Cut the crap. There was somethin' you wanted to tell me in private. So spill already."

Albertson rummaged through his pockets, presumably looking for something to put in his mouth. "I propose a deal."

"And that would be?"

"We share information. We're both working the same case, more or less. You learn something, you tell me about it. I learn something, I do likewise. Sound like a good deal?"

"Well," Loving said cheerfully, "it sounds like a good deal for you. Since I appear to be on the trail of somethin' big. And you got nada."

"Look, Loving, I've cut you breaks in the past—"

"Never said otherwise."

"And I got you that provisional P.I. license so you could work while your boss is playing senator."

"Most kind of ya."

Albertson's eyes lowered. "But I could revoke it just as easily as I got it."

"I qualified for that license. I'm over twenty-one, got no felony convictions. I passed the psych evaluation and I completed my twenty-one hours of trainin' to get certified by the Oklahoma Council on Law Enforcement Education."

"All of which might get you somewhere back home. But Dorothy—you're not in Kansas anymore."

"Oklahoma."

"Same difference."

Loving turned to face him squarely. His shoulders were about twice as broad as Albertson's, so he made a particularly effective roadblock. "Now you're playin' dirty pool. I don't take kindly to bein' pushed around."

Albertson stood his ground. "I don't much care what you like. I got people breathin' down my neck for a breakthrough in this case. So if you get one, I expect to hear about it. Understood?"

"And what do I get in return?"

"You get to keep your license."

"Not good enough."

Albertson frowned. "We're bound to figure out who the victim was eventually. If we do, you'll be the first one I tell. And if you get a name first, I'll let you run it through the FBI databases. You'll get more info in ten minutes online than you could get from a month of pounding the pavement."

Loving considered. That was at least marginally tempting.

"And I won't press charges."

"Huh? For what?"

"Destruction of private and public property. Assault with a deadly weapon. Apparently you attacked two men and ran over one of them with your automobile."

"They were tryin' to kill me!"

"That's your story. A lot of the witnesses thought you were the bad guy. Thought you were on the lam from the police."

"That's crazy."

"Crazy enough to keep you in jail for a very long time awaiting trial. The D.C. courts are so overcrowded these days."

"I don't believe you'd do that."

"But can you be sure?"

"You've always seemed like a kinda sorta honest person. So far."

"I'm taking that as a compliment."

"Suit yourself."

"But the threat still stands."

"All right, already. We'll share." Loving poked him with a finger. "But don't forget. This is supposed to be a two-way street."

"I won't," Albertson said.

"Good. You've got my cell number."

They returned to the police station, having circled the entire block.

"Enjoyed our little chat," Loving said.

"Likewise, I'm sure. Stay in touch."

Loving watched as Albertson trotted up the stairs. Albertson was desperate, plain and simple. Didn't know what was going on, didn't have a clue how to proceed, so he was grasping at straws. Even the particularly desperate straw of aligning himself with a private investigator. The problem was, Loving really didn't know what to do next. His only lead was lying in the morgue. The pond scum who had put him on to her had disappeared. He had nothing, except a queasy feeling formed by the knowledge that someone had wanted him dead—and probably still did.

Well, he'd figure something out, right? Back to pounding the streets. He turned and—

The man was standing so close behind Loving that he'd bumped into him before he could stop himself. He took a step back to gain a clearer view.

The man in front of him raised his sunglasses slightly as a sort of salute. His right hand was in the pocket of his overcoat. There was a bulge in the pocket that resembled the barrel of a gun. "Hello again."

It was Leon.

13

Common Beltway wisdom dictated that in reality, it was not senators, congressmen, or Presidents that controlled Washington—it was lobbyists. Richard Trevor was thinking about having that etched into a paperweight.

"Mr. Trevor," said his young-and-gorgeous-but-much-too-eager-to-please new assistant, Melody McClain. "Do you want to see my report?"

"Behind me, Melody. At least three steps behind me."

Trevor didn't mean to be rude—well, in truth, he supposed he did—but he had to get his point across. He had an image to protect. People saw him as a maverick, a Washington outsider, even when he was very much inside the city limits, jogging his third lap around the Reflecting Pool at the foot of the Washington Monument in the Main Mall. It was a beautiful day; he could smell the cherry blossoms. In truth, he hated jogging, thought it was as boring as anything on earth, except possibly golf. But he liked to maintain a vigorous, youthful image. It was important for the leader of the Christian Congregation, one of the most powerful lobbies in the country, one that helped put the last three Presidents in office, to maintain the proper image. So he jogged. His staff could accompany him, but they had to maintain a respectful distance—which was exactly far enough to ensure that they wouldn't appear in any photos the stalkerazzi might be snapping.

Melody continued huffing several steps behind him. She was unaccustomed to jogging. Especially with a clipboard in both hands. "Sir, I think the report will tell you everything you need to know about Thaddeus Roush."

"I already know everything I need to know about Thaddeus Roush," he replied. "The man is a homosexual." He pronounced the word with two long "o's" and a strong accent on the first three syllables. "He is not a suitable candidate for the highest court in the land."

"He does have a good record. Sound decisions, persuasive reasoning. And consistently conservative."

"Doesn't matter. We cannot place our trust in a man who would lie down with another man." Of course, he quietly reminded himself, many Old Testament figures who for sometimes difficult-to-comprehend reasons were the chosen children of God did it. But never mind that. "Sodomy is a plague upon our great country. It must be eradicated."

"Sir, homosexuality has existed since the dawn of time. I don't think it can be eradicated. Only persecuted."

"Melody," he said, without breaking his stride, "are you disagreeing with me?"

"Of course not, sir. Just . . . playing devil's advocate. Previewing what your opponents will say."

"I already know what my opponents will say, the heathen and the communists and the godless lesbian feminists and their ilk. Please do not talk to me in that manner again."

"Yes, sir. Sorry, sir. I just—"

"That is exactly the kind of soft liberal thinking that has brought our nation to the low place where it is today. Immorality destroyed the Roman Empire, you know."

"Yes, sir. I'm so sorry, sir."

Was he perhaps a trifle oversensitive on this subject? Yes, he would be willing to admit that he was. Particularly since he had so often been accused of being homosexual when he was growing up. There was no truth to it—none whatsoever! But the accusation kept rearing its ugly head, time after time. It was because of the way he looked, his eternal baby face. Maybe the somewhat high pitch of his voice. He had tried growing a beard—didn't help. It came in wispy and unpersuasive. He tried lowering his voice, but it never sounded natural. Like Jim Nabors when he sang. Fake. Better to be himself and let the world judge him by his actions, not his God-given appearance.

He rounded the corner of the pool and started toward the Lincoln Memorial. There was a time when he would have been flattered by the attention of a lovely woman such as Melody, someone who had shown up at his office professing her devotion to the cause of Christian politics, someone who had made it all too clear that she would do anything—and she did mean *anything*—for him. Not bad for a kid who used to be a supply youth minister in one of the poorest churches in Miami. But this was a temptation he could resist, that he must resist. It was important that he remain free of entanglements. That was why he had never married. His work—the holy task of reforming the nation and returning it to its fundamentalist Christian roots—took precedence over everything else.

"Will we be seeing Judge Haskins today, Melody?"

"No, sir. He had a conflict."

"Did he, now?"

"Ever since that fire at the Hilton, he's been red hot. No joke intended, sir."

"So he's too busy to see me? Is that what you're telling me, Melody?"

She hesitated. "He says he never intended to draw attention to himself. He thought it would be unwise to be seen in public."

"You mean—seen with me in public."

"Well, yes. I'm sure it's nothing personal, sir. He probably just felt that being seen with the leader of one of the top lobbies in the country could make it appear as if he were campaigning. As if he had a political agenda."

As if there was someone in this town who did not. "Don't be

naïve. He's balancing the damage that could result from being seen with a lobbyist against the damage that could result from offending a lobbyist. And he has evaluated the problem incorrectly. Lobbyists—"

"—run this town. Yes sir, I know."

Was she being sharp, or just stupid? "There are over fifteen thousand lobbyists in this city, Melody. Think of it. More than all the senators and representatives and their staffs combined. Our influence is enormous."

"That's the Golden Rule, sir. He who has the gold makes the rule."

He decided to ignore the blasphemy of her lame little joke. This time. "Money is important. Especially with the new campaign reform laws, they're all sucking at whatever special-interest teat they can find, issues be damned. No Republican appointment in the last ten years has been made without my approval, and that includes congressional committee appointments. I buried Harriet Miers and I can bury this Roush chump even easier. The Senate has rejected twelve nominees over the years and sixteen have withdrawn under pressure—and someone like me has been behind every one of those outcomes. Politicians who want to go somewhere play ball with me. Those that don't find every door slammed in their faces."

"Money certainly will buy influence, sir."

"It's not money, at least not predominantly. What gives lobbyists our real power is information. We constantly gather information. I know more about Senator Keyes's constituency, what they believe and what they like, than he does. Small wonder we've managed to maintain such a positive relationship. There are simply too many bills, too many issues. No politician can keep up with it all, be the expert on everything. So when some new issue arises and they suddenly need to do ten minutes on *Larry King* on a subject they know nothing about, they call the lobbyists. They can't admit to ignorance—that's simply not done. If they get caught with their pants down, they look like fools. More than one political career has been ended by a single bad interview or press conference. So we help them out. That's how Washington works, Melody. We inflate their egos. And they give us everything we want."

Trevor reached the end of his run. Another assistant was wait-

ing with a towel and a chilled bottle of Gatorade. "Tell Judge Haskins I will see him in my office this afternoon at two."

"He told me he has a—"

"Tell him to cancel it." Trevor smiled. The blood slowly faded
from his cheeks as he wiped the sweat from his brow. "Regardless of
whether he wants to be on the Supreme Court, I'll bet he won't turn
it down if it's offered." He laughed and tossed her the dripping
towel. "If he's the right man for the job, I'll get him marching in
step."

"Whether he likes it or not?"

"I will not accept—will not tolerate—a gay Supreme Court justice. Especially not this one."

"Do—do you know Judge Roush?"

"I was at the press conference when that poor Christian soul
was murdered. So were you, Melody, remember?"

"But you sound as if you really know him."

"Oh yes. I know him. All too well. Him and all of his kind." His
eyes narrowed. "I will not allow this nomination to be confirmed.
And if I have to crush Roush in the process—" He shrugged, then
started back toward his office. "The will of God be done."

14

"Could we get a picture of you with the baby?"

Judge Haskins looked down at the ground modestly and shuffled his feet. "Well . . . if it's all right with her mother."

"Is it all right?" Lynda Paul, the statuesque redhead standing beside the judge, beamed. "I can't think of anyone with whom Nikki would be safer than her own guardian angel." The crowd of reporters smiled appreciatively. She passed the baby into Judge Haskins's arms and the flash bulbs went off like small rapid-fire explosions. "Next week, Nikki is going to be baptized. I've asked Judge Haskins to stand in as her godfather." Her comment was greeted by a warm and enthusiastic response, even before she added, "If the man weren't hitched, I'd ask him to marry me."

Everyone laughed, and once again the minicams went into action. Margaret Haskins, her face still showing signs of the bruising she suffered in the fire, stepped beside them. "I might have a few words to say about that, young lady."

Lynda wrapped an arm around Margaret and hugged her tight. "Why is it the good ones are always already taken?"

Judge Haskins looked seriously flushed. "This is too much fuss over too little. I only did what any other—"

"That's obviously not true," Lynda interjected, not even allowing him to finish. "There were over a hundred people trapped in that ballroom. But you were the only one who had the perspicacity to organize a team to get a door open. You saved your wife and my little Nikki." She addressed the reporters. "I'd passed out. Someone got me outside, but they didn't know about the baby, and I was far too out of it to tell them." She looked at Haskins solemnly. "We wouldn't be here if it weren't for you, sir."

"Oh, stuff and nonsense."

"It's true. You're a hero. A bona fide American hero."

The enthusiastic response from the press suggested that they concurred. They were gathered outside the Denver Children's Hospital. The occasion was Nikki's release and first day home after the explosion. Nikki's mother had asked that the man who saved her baby's life be present. He'd agreed; since the accident, he and his wife had become quite close to Lynda and her infant.

"Any plans for the future, Judge?"

He shrugged. "I'm just hoping all you people will go home and let me proceed with my work on the Tenth Circuit."

"What do you think about the President's nomination for the Supreme Court?"

Haskins's neck stiffened. He turned slowly, his face emotionless. "I . . . don't think it would be appropriate for me to comment."

"A lot of pundits predicted that you would be the most likely nominee, given the enormous positive publicity following your heroic actions during the Hilton fire."

"That—hardly proves anyone's qualifications for the highest court in the land."

"Maybe not," another reporter rejoined, "but it suggests that you'd get confirmed in a heartbeat." Pause. "Unlike the current nominee."

Haskins shook his head, appearing extremely uncomfortable with the new topic. "I doubt if I'm even on the President's radar. I'm just a humble federal appeals court justice—"

"So was John Roberts. Before he became the Chief Justice."

Haskins started to speak again, but Lynda beat him to it. "Speaking for myself, I think he'd make a heck of a good Supreme Court justice. The Court could use someone with his courage. His inherent decency." She looked at the judge lovingly. "And after you were appointed, you could hire me to be your clerk."

Another round of laughter followed. Margaret tugged at her husband's sleeve, as if to indicate that the conference was over. The reporters, however, were not willing to give up so easily.

"Judge Haskins, is it true you've been contacted by representatives of the Christian Congregation?"

"Oh, my phone rings off the hook every time you people do another story about me. Really, you need to move on to someone else."

"The Christian Congregation is one of the largest and most influential lobbies in Washington. Some say they put President Blake in office. Surely if they back you, the President would have to consider nominating you."

"I have no idea what the President might be thinking. I've never even met the man. And I really don't think it's appropriate for us to speculate—"

"At least tell us this, Judge, since everyone seems to agree that Thaddeus Roush's nomination is doomed. If the President wanted to nominate you to the Supreme Court, would you accept?"

Margaret was still tugging at his sleeve, and his reluctance to answer was evident, but he finally managed. "A nomination to the U.S. Supreme Court is the highest honor any judge can receive. Obviously, I would have to give any such compliment serious consideration. But I want to emphasize that I do not seek—"

It was too late. The reporters had their story at the end of the second sentence. The rest was drowned out by footsteps and the background chatter of live remotes.

"Good heavens," Haskins muttered under his breath as he and his wife headed for their car. "What have I done?"

His wife looked up at him, her eyes beaming with affection. "I'm no lawyer," she said quietly. "But I think that very soon, you might be getting a call from the White House."

15

"A little more, Senator Keyes?"

Keyes held up his hand as if to refuse, then wavered. "Well, just a smidgen, Johnny. Helps me think."

He smiled as his top aide poured the smoky liquid into his snifter. Keyes was pretty sure that whiskey did not in fact help anyone think, but it did help him get through the night.

Senator Josiah Keyes, chairman of the Senate Judiciary Committee, leaned back, propped his feet on the edge of his long mahogany desk, and addressed his guests: Senator Matera of Wyoming, vice-chairman of the Senate Judiciary Committee, and Senator Potter, the fresh-faced kid from Oregon who was the newest member of the committee. For entirely different reasons, Keyes knew these were the two committee members he could count on most for unqualified support.

"This whiskey sipping is all right," Matera said, a thin smile on her face, "but shouldn't at least one of us be smoking?"

Keyes chuckled. Potter appeared puzzled.

"Ten years ago," Keyes said, "I'd have filled the bill with a big Havana stogie. But not anymore." He patted his ample stomach and swigged some more booze. "Gotta be careful about my health."

"I don't understand," Potter said, working up enough nerve to admit his ignorance. "Why would we want to smoke?"

Keyes tried to prevent himself from appearing too patronizing. "So this would be a smoke-filled room." He winked at Matera. "Didn't you learn anything in civics class, son? That's where all the real deals are made in Washington."

"Ah." Potter scratched his chin. "So, are we about to make a deal?"

"Would that we were in a position to make a deal. Probably be more accurate to say . . . we're laying plans. Preparing for the future. Like any good generals might do."

"I imagine we're not the only ones in this town making a few plans tonight," Matera ventured.

"That much is certain. Did you see the latest televised Haskins appearance?"

"At the hospital? Sure. Such a modest man! So unambitious."

"That's his story. But I'm willing to bet he read every one of those op-ed pieces recommending him for the nomination after Justice Cornwall died. I bet he was just as mad as I would be when he was passed over." Keyes chuckled, which sent his considerable girth jiggling, girdled though it was by the vest of a three-piece suit. "Rule One of Washington politics: Never count your nominations until they're hatched."

"Whether he wanted the job before or not," Matera replied, "now he's got a second shot. If Roush fails, the President will want a sure thing so he can appoint a justice before his term expires. Everyone said before that Haskins was the most likely candidate."

"Which is exactly why that dog won't hunt." The Texas aphorisms didn't come to Keyes as easily as they once did, just as his Texas twang had faded after decades of spending the better part of the year in Washington. Except when he needed it. "How do the President's boys explain why he wasn't chosen before?"

"The President was punishing Haskins for his decision in *Bar-*

nett v. Adams. He had a chance to narrowly conscribe *Roe v. Wade.* He didn't take it."

"And the Christian Congregation wanted him punished. But now that he's had his hand slapped a little, they're willing to reconsider. Assuming he's willing to give them the assurances they require on certain hot-button issues."

"You think he will?"

"You saw that media event at the hospital, right?" Keyes paused. "Hell, yeah, I think he'll give them what they want. I think he'll give it to them wrapped in gold leaf. The President will get everything he wants."

"You're missing the point," Matera said. "It isn't about what the President wants. It's about what he can sell to the people who put him in office. If Haskins was unacceptable once, he's still unacceptable."

"Unless he does something to make himself more acceptable," Keyes said sagely. "Which is, I would imagine, the whole point of his visit to our fair capital city. He needs to show he can be of invaluable service. Win back the good graces of the President via intermediaries." He took another sip from his snifter. "If either of you hears about Haskins visiting with Richard Trevor or anyone else at the Christian Congregation, I want to know about it immediately."

"Yes, sir," Potter piped in.

"Meanwhile, we must focus on giving the President what he wants from us. Thaddeus Roush dead." He polished off his drink and motioned for a refill. "Dead in the water. Dead as a Supreme Court nominee." He held his refilled beveled glass snifter up to the light, watching it refract into a rainbow of colors. "This is probably the biggest embarrassment of Blake's career. Gives a rousing speech about what a great jurist this guy is, then the guy outs himself. Hell of a note, isn't it? The Democrats are rallying support around a Republican nominee, and the Republicans no longer want anything to do with him." He chuckled. "Suddenly President Blake, the staunch supporter of the Defense of Marriage Act, has nominated the first openly gay Supreme Court justice. If something doesn't happen fast, he'll lose his base of support. His approval ratings are already plunging. This mess could have negative ramifications for us all." He stared at the prismatic glass a little longer. Maybe this stuff did help him think. "Has the Congregation taken any official position yet?"

"They're stuck in the same conundrum as the President," Matera explained. "Can't afford to publicly denounce a Republican candidate. My people think they may be creating or funding a third-party lobbying group, something not officially tied to them, an organization with the freedom to speak out about this nomination. Sort of a Swift Boat Veterans for torpedoing a homosexual judge."

"Wonderful." Keyes drew in his breath slowly, his eyes becoming reflective. "Jessie, do you believe these people choose to be gay?"

Matera coughed. "Well, I . . . I . . . don't really know much about it."

"Did you choose your sexual preference?"

"I don't recall ever having to give it much thought."

"Exactly." Keyes stretched, his hands behind his neck. "I don't think people choose to be gay. Why would they? All the scientific studies indicate that it's not chosen, not learned. Nature rather than nurture. And yet like it or not, this inclination written into the genetic code is enough to keep this man off the court. Damn shame, really. Fine man like Roush. Fine mind. Head in the right place on most of the issues. Little soft on the death penalty, but no one's perfect. In Texas, we have to insist upon the efficacy of the death penalty—otherwise we've killed a lot of folks for no good reason. Elsewhere, a man can afford to have reasonable doubts. Fact remains—Roush could be a fine justice. A lot better than some of the idiots on the court now, men and women who only got there because their lives have been so damned boring they could survive the confirmation process. But we've got to kill this nomination. Whatever it takes, we've got to work together and do it."

"Actually," Potter offered, "I don't think we have to do anything. According to my unofficial straw poll, Roush doesn't have a chance of clearing the full Senate."

Keyes smiled again. There was nothing quite so refreshing—if a bit exasperating—as youthful naïveté. "Roush can never get to the full Senate. He can't survive our committee vote."

"But—why?"

"Because if he does, every senator in our party will be forced to take a public stand on what by then will be, if indeed it is not already, a referendum on gay rights."

"But our party has always opposed—"

"And the people do not need to be reminded of that point. Polls show it's a major bone of contention. Possibly second only to our stance on abortion. The plurality of the people do not share our view. That's why we must protect our brethren by preventing them from being forced to vote."

"But—the only way they could *not* vote—?"

"You've got it exactly. They don't vote if we kill the nomination in committee. But we have to come up with a reason for it. Something that isn't about him being a homosexual. Even if it really is all about him being a homosexual."

"And that would be . . . ?"

"Don't know yet." Keyes polished off the last of his drink. "But I will. Soon. That's my job. To protect the President from his own stupidity."

"But—with what?"

"Don't know yet." Keyes's eyes narrowed. He stared directly at his two companions, one, then the other. "But I have men looking for it. And I want you two to join the search."

Matera leaned forward. "What it is we're searching for?"

"If I knew that, I wouldn't need your help." Keyes steepled his fingers before his face. "But I do. Make no mistake about it. This is important. Quite possibly the most important thing you have ever done or ever will do in your entire life. The Supreme Court is evenly divided ideologically. The new justice could well cast the deciding vote on every issue of importance for years to come. What's more, if we don't act swiftly and decisively, the fundamentalist support that has been the cornerstone of this party for at least twenty years could be lost. And that, my friends, could eviscerate the entire party and put us all out of work."

Keyes paused, then sat up. "Equally important, we cannot give the Democrats a victory. Is it a coincidence that they picked up Roush the instant our party let him go? Of course not. We must stop the encroachment of rampant amoral permissive liberalism, the plague that is tearing this country apart, eating away at our moral fiber. Make no mistake about it—this is an ideological war. A battle for the soul of this once great nation. And as in every war, there will likely be casualties." He hunched over his desk, staring straight ahead. "So—find me that smoking gun. The one that puts a bullet in the center of the forehead of Thaddeus Roush." Keyes lowered himself slowly back into his chair. "And anyone else who gets in our way."

16

Loving's first instinct was to run, but he managed to suppress it. Surely Leon wouldn't try to plug him here, on "E" Street, in front of dozens of witnesses—would he?

What was he thinking? This was the man who had tried to kill him in the middle of a shopping mall. He turned to run—

Leon laid a hand on Loving's shoulder. "You have nothing to fear from me."

Somehow, the reassurances of a trained killer did nothing to stop his stomach from churning. He tried again to turn. Leon held him in place. Even though Loving outweighed the man by at least fifty pounds, he couldn't break his grip.

"I just want to talk. Please. It would be in your best interest."

He had a thick accent. Loving thought it sounded Germanic, but he wasn't exactly Henry Higgins when it came to dialect. " 'Cause you plan to get it over with quick and easy?" he jeered, feigning a confidence he did not feel.

Leon smiled. He had a gold replacement tooth on the top right row. "Because I'm off-duty."

"Hit men get coffee breaks?"

"I was retained to accomplish a single task. Regrettably, I failed, so I forfeited my payment. My employer informed me that my services were no longer needed."

"Sorry to put a black mark on your résumé, Paladin."

"It's not your fault. My . . . associate did not care for the experience of working with me. He gave a rather negative report to our employer."

For some reason, Loving believed the man did not intend to harm him. At least not at the moment. "Gosh, that's a tough shake. So who is this employer?"

Leon released Loving's shoulder and held up a finger. "That would be telling."

"Uh-huh. And what exactly was your job?"

"To prevent the young lady of the evening from conveying her information to you. Regrettably, we arrived late. When I saw that you had already spoken to her, it became necessary to eliminate you as well."

"You're wrong. We barely said hello. She told me nothin'."

"I hope for your sake that is true." Loving noticed that his right hand remained firmly clasped on whatever was in his pocket. This man could kill him in less than a second if he wished. "But I fear it will make little difference. You will have a hard time convincing my former employer."

"So the hit is still on?"

Leon shrugged slightly. "As I said, I have been told that my services are no longer required."

"So you really didn't come here to kill me?"

"My dear fellow, why should I? I hardly know you. My contract has been terminated."

"I guess I should feel proud," Loving replied. "I'm thinkin' you don't have too many blots on your record."

"You would be correct. Unfortunately, I was hampered by my . . . associate. My employer's son. A difficult partner, at best."

"Because he's trigger-happy and stupid?"

"I tried to tell my employer that his . . . assistance was not needed. But he insisted."

"He sent the idiot offspring to keep an eye on you."

"They sent him to observe, to perhaps learn skills that would enable him to be of use at some time in the future. Unfortunately, I fear that is impossible. Many things can be cured with experience and training. Stupidity is not one of them."

Loving's gut instinct told him it would still be smartest to turn tail and run from this man who was, after all, a killer. But his curiosity got the better of him. "Why are you here?"

"I thought . . . I thought I might be of some assistance to you."

"You want to help me?"

"You find that so difficult to believe?"

"Usually I don't get to be best buddies with guys I run over with a car."

"I'm not one to hold grudges. Would you care for a latte?"

Loving raised an eyebrow. "You're joking, right?"

"Well, we are standing directly in front of police headquarters. And as dim-witted as they are, it is probably not prudent for me to remain here forever."

Leon gestured toward a coffee bar across the street. Oookay, Loving thought. In for a penny.

Inside, they found a booth in the rear, away from the windows, and sat on opposite sides. Loving ordered black coffee and told the waitress he didn't give a damn what blend it was. Leon ordered a white chocolate mocha, Genvalia ground, with whipped cream and chocolate sprinkles.

"You seem surprised."

"Well . . ." Loving searched for words. "I guessed I had you pegged as more the bourbon-straight kind of guy."

Leon gave a little shudder. "Stereotypes are so banal." He took a sip of his gourmet coffee, which left a white foamy cream mustache on his upper lip. "As I was saying, I did admire the way you handled yourself last night."

"Even the part where I stabbed you in the gut?"

"In fact, I was wearing Kevlar. The wound was not nearly so serious as you probably imagined."

"And when I hit you with the car?"

"That stung a bit. It would never have happened if I hadn't already been off my game. Decentered, if you will, by the handicap of an accomplice. But I must admit it's not my first time rolling over a speeding car. One learns to deal."

Loving rubbed the side of his face. Last night the man had tried to kill him; today they were sitting in a booth sipping overpriced yuppie coffee. It was surreal.

"So I guess as a reward for my fabulous performance, you're plannin' to give me the name of the woman who was killed at the press conference?"

"Would that I could. I don't know that poor unfortunate's name. But I do know someone who might be able to give it to you."

"And you're gonna tell me?" Loving asked incredulously. A moment later, he snapped his fingers. "You're pissed."

"I've had nothing to drink."

"I mean you're angry. Because they fired you. You're tryin' to screw the pooch."

"I assure you that never in my life—"

"You're ticked off 'cause you got canned."

"It was . . . unjust. The fault was all with my partner. And at least at some level, deep down, I believe my employer realizes that. But what can he do? The man is his son." He paused. "That said, I assure you my motives are not entirely petty."

"Don't worry about it," Loving said, sipping his cup of coffee. "I don't care what your motives are. Who is this person? Give me a name."

"Trudy."

"And she can give me an ID on the murder victim?"

"Yes, I believe that Trudy—" He coughed into his hand. "—uh, might be able to help you along."

"Got an address?"

"As a matter of fact, I do." He passed Loving a folded sheet of paper. "Don't be fooled by the office space at the front of the building. The den of iniquity you seek is in the basement."

"Aren't they always." Loving shoved the paper into his pocket. "Got any other leads?"

"I'm afraid not."

"Well then, I should probably push off. It's been . . . um . . . in-terestin'."

"Indeed it has."

Loving hesitated. "So . . . I don't need to worry about you sneakin' up behind me and tryin' to kill me? 'Cause we're friends now."

Leon tilted his head to one side. "Mmm . . ."

"I see. You're still hopin' they'll hire you back."

"A man's got to eat."

"And if they do, you'll be back on my ass."

"I think that very unlikely." He smiled. "But if it does occur—I won't enjoy it."

Loving knew he shouldn't be smiling, but he was.

"Let me warn you, Mr. Loving—even if it isn't me who comes for you next, if you do not discontinue your investigation, there will be someone."

"Why?"

"Because there are people who do not want the identity of the lady in question to be revealed. They will stop at nothing to prevent it. And they are swimming in resources. Money. Power. Armies to command." He paused. "I can't assure you that all of these minions will adhere to the same code of conduct that I do. Be very careful—danger may lurk in the most unexpected places."

That sent a shiver down Loving's spine. "Gotcha. Thanks for the tip."

"It was my pleasure." He extended a hand. "Best of luck to you."

Loving couldn't believe it, but he was actually shaking the hand of the man who had tried to kill him only hours before. "Very kind of you."

"Not at all." Leon looked up over the brim of his frothy mug. "You're going to need it."

17

I should've started down here, Ben thought, mentally beating himself up for having wasted so much time trying to find Senator Keyes in his office, or in one of the meeting rooms for his many committees—or heaven forbid, on the Senate floor. When a senator of his stature wanted time alone, away from the prying eyes of reporters or the outstretched hand of whatever constituent happened to be touring Washington that week, he retreated to his hideaway. Nestled in the subterranean basements of the three Senate office buildings, the hideaways did not appear on any of the tourist maps—or even on the official blueprints—but they were there, just the same. You had to know how to wind your way down the stairs and through the narrow corridors crowded with disused furniture and outdated equipment. You had to brave the suction and noise of an air-conditioning system more ancient than Methuselah. But the difficulty of the approach was part of the appeal; senators came here when they did not want to be found, sometimes for work, more often for pleasure. Given the tumult currently under way upstairs, Ben should have known to check the hideaways first; a senator of Keyes's stature probably had three of them.

He caught the senator just as he was leaving, locking the door behind him. Inside the room, he could hear high-pitched, rather feminine giggling, but he decided not to ask. Keyes saw him, but he still turned away and started down the corridor.

"Senator Keyes! Could I have a few words?"

"Can you talk while you walk?" he replied, buttoning the vest of his three-piece suit around his ample girth.

"Ever since I was nine months old," Ben muttered under his breath. Then, audibly: "I wanted to talk to you about the Roush confirmation hearings."

Keyes checked his watch. "Main committee room. Ten minutes."

"Yes, I know that. I wanted to talk about how you plan to conduct the hearing."

"With my usual enthusiasm and bonhomie, I'd like to think," Keyes said, smiling slightly.

They turned a corner, and the racket from the antiquated air-conditioning system became so loud Ben could barely hear. "I wondered if we could come to a few agreements in advance. About how the hearing will be conducted. How we'll conduct ourselves."

"Why? You're not on the Judiciary Committee."

"I've been asked to represent Judge Roush during the hearings. To act as his representative."

"Isn't that a conflict of interest? One of the people who will vote on his confirmation acting as his legal representative?" Keyes acted surprised, even though Ben was quite certain he wasn't.

"But I won't be acting as a lawyer. Not really. I'll just be acting as his advisor. Since he's unfamiliar with the ways and procedures of the Senate."

"Ah. Clever work-around." He winked. "I thought your fearless leader was going to run interference for him."

Ben assumed that was a reference to Minority Leader Hammond. "We're both working with Thaddeus. He's going to be helping me with—"

"Even so, this seems quite a high-profile position for a first-term not-really-a-senator."

They reached the foot of the stairs. There would be reporters waiting at the top in the gallery, and once Keyes felt the embrace of a klieg light Ben knew he would have no chance of talking to him. He took hold of the man's arm and held him back. "I wanted to see if we could come to an agreement about these hearings. Before we're forced to start performing for the cameras."

Keyes looked down at him, one eyebrow cocked high. "All right. What did you have in mind?"

"I assume we both want a dignified and expeditious confirmation process."

"You assume a lot."

"I hope we will both remember the constitutional role of the Senate in this process. To advise and consent."

"The Constitution and I are well acquainted, Senator Kincaid."

"It's not an excuse to engage in personal attacks."

"Heaven forfend."

"No McCarthyite tactics."

"Perish the thought."

"No prying into the nominee's private life."

"Well . . . there are times when a nominee's private life becomes relevant. Certainly your party found it very relevant when Clarence Thomas was nominated."

"No one's going to be bringing sexual harassment charges against Thaddeus Roush and we both know it."

"Mr. Kincaid, you seem to be assuming I will be hostile to Judge Roush. May I remind you that he is a member of my party, and was nominated by a President who is a member of my party?"

"Don't waste your breath. I know perfectly well the President wants this nomination killed."

"I didn't get that memo."

"So your staff hasn't been taking my fellow senators' temperature regarding a possible Haskins nomination?"

Keyes turned slowly, his eyes widening.

"When the media-darling wife-and-baby-saving judge from Colorado flies to Washington and visits the President," Ben added, "it suggests that someone is lining up a successor."

"Nonsense. The President just wanted to formally acknowledge Judge Haskins's achievements. The man is a national hero."

"And the President could use a national hero. Just as soon as Roush's nomination goes down in flames."

"It's hardly a crime to consider alternatives, Ben. Especially when the current nominee's 'partner' is being interrogated in connection with a murder."

"That sounds to me like a good reason to delay the hearing. Not to rush it forward."

"Delay is not an option." Keyes was quiet for a moment, then shrugged, apparently deciding that denials were not worth the effort. "You could hardly blame the President for forging ahead. Most pundits expect this nomination to fail, and his days in office are limited. If we don't move forward quickly, he might not have a chance to select the next nominee."

"This nomination doesn't have to fail. It shouldn't fail."

"Some things are outside our control."

"I'm not sure I think anything's outside your control. At least as it relates to the Senate Judiciary Committee. You could stop the character attacks and the tabloid testimony cold if you wanted."

"We still have many questions—"

"You already have Roush's written answers to your interrogatories."

"Pitiful. Haven't seen a more evasive, less informative bunch of hogwash since Harriet Miers. And you know what happened to her."

"Mister Chairman, I am well aware that you run this committee, at least with regard to the Republican members."

"I'm only the chairman, Kincaid. Not the gatekeeper. I can't prevent other senators on the committee from raising issues—"

"You can, and we both know it. That's how it's done. You get other party loyalists to do your dirty work so you can retain the appearance of impartiality."

Keyes pressed a hand against his chest. "Senator Kincaid. Your accusations offend me. Surely you don't suggest that I would use this hearing to engage in partisan skulduggery."

"With all due respect, Senator—save it for the cameras."

To Ben's surprise, the senior senator chuckled with merriment. He placed a hand on Ben's shoulder. "I like you, Kincaid. I really do. You're so . . . well, unlike everyone else in this town. I wish the Senate had ninety-nine more like you. Except Republican." He laughed again, then looked Ben straight in the eyes. "What is it you really want?"

"I want you to promise there will be no discussion of Roush's sexual preference."

"I can't do that. It may not seem relevant to you, but to my constituency, it is the most important issue relating to Roush's confirmation."

"Then I want you to agree to proceed with fundamental fairness. No character assassination. No slimy slurs or insinuations. No gay stereotyping. We keep it all aboveboard and conduct ourselves as befits members of the United States Senate."

Keyes looked at him levelly. "That I can agree to."

Ben paused. Something about this conversation was extremely unsatisfying, but how could you go on arguing when the man agreed to your terms? "Fine." Ben extended his hand. "Here's to a fair fight."

"Indeed," Keyes said. "A fair fight."

Ben was relieved to finally get Roush inside the Old Senate Caucus Room, where the confirmation hearings would be conducted. It was a beautiful room, one of the most ornate and elegant in the entire Senate complex, and virtually unchanged since its construction at the dawn of the nation's history. The high ceiling gave the room a sense of being larger than it was; the gold crown molding imparted a sense of dignity and history that Ben could only hope imprinted itself on the participants. Most important, there would be no mob of reporters. In here, the select few allowed inside were assigned seats and were expected to remain in them. There was one camera strategically placed on the left side of the room, and its feed would be shared by all the television networks.

Ben took advantage of the fact that the rest of the assembly had not yet been admitted. He and Roush walked the room, getting a feel for it, getting comfortable, if such a thing were possible.

After they had explored the room, Ben and Roush made their way to the front-and-center table. There were two chairs, a pitcher of water, two glasses, and a microphone.

It was terrifying.

Maybe it wasn't the table. Maybe it was the raised semicircular bench upon which eighteen senators would sit, ten Republicans, eight Democrats, each of whom in turn would question Roush about his fitness for the job of Supreme Court justice. No, Ben couldn't blame Roush for seeming nervous. Just the thought of it made Ben's stomach churn, and he wasn't the one who was going to be grilled.

The rest of the assembly would be admitted soon. Best to get into position.

"Ready to go?" Ben asked, as he motioned toward the center chair.

"Ready as I'll ever be." Roush sat, and Ben took his strategic place beside him. "Is it too late to decline the nomination?"

Ben almost smiled. "If you were going to withdraw, I think you'd have done it by now."

"Yeah." Roush paused again. "Do you think I did the right thing?"

Ben didn't have to ask what he was talking about. "As a matter of fact, I do. With the enormous amount of scrutiny and investigation given a Supreme Court nominee, it might've come out anyway."

"The President's people didn't get it."

"They didn't get Anita Hill at first, either, but she still testified, putting Clarence Thomas on the defensive for the rest of the hearings. No, you were right, Tad. Better to do it yourself. That way, everything is on the table. You don't have to worry about being discovered. All the secrets are out."

"Yes," Roush murmured quietly. "All the secrets are out."

The rear doors were flung open and in an instant, the subdued edginess was transformed into brash panic. Eighteen senators took their seats on the bench, Senator Keyes in the center. Members of the press, of the Senate, and of the Washington establishment all took their positions in the gallery. Senator Hammond, their legal advisor, Bertram Sexton, and Christina took the seats directly behind. Gina Carraway, the media expert, stood on the left, where she could see the image in the television monitor—in effect, she could see the hearings as America saw them. Once Ray Eastwick was released from the police interrogations, he also would sit behind Roush, but they had decided not to leave an empty seat for him now—that would only remind America why he wasn't present today. The cameraman adjusted the boom mikes and turned on the bright white spots. An anticipatory buzz swept through the Caucus Room, making the already unbearable suspense about a thousand times more intense. Ben could feel the heat bearing down on them, and that wasn't just from the overhead lights. He knew he wasn't the only one feeling it. Roush was already sweating.

Christina strode up to the table and placed a hand on Ben's shoulder.

"Ready to go?"

Ben smiled nervously. "No."

"Good."

"Good?"

"Good. You always do better when you're on edge. Comes with being mildly neurotic."

"How sweet."

She leaned forward and gave him a kiss on the cheek. "I know you'll be great," she whispered. "You always are."

"I think you're seeing me through rose-colored glasses."

"Perhaps. There's a word for that."

"Which is?"

She patted his shoulder one last time. "Well, if you don't know already, you'll hear it during the wedding ceremony. Whenever that happens."

Ouch. Ben winced. He glanced at the other end of the table and saw Roush grinning broadly. "What?"

Roush shook his head, still greatly amused. "And I thought I had problems."

Keyes tapped his microphone, as if to make sure it was working.

"This hearing is called to order," Keyes said, with what Ben estimated to be approximately three times his usual Texas accent. "Would the nominee please do us the favor of rising?"

Ben leaned sideways and whispered into Roush's ear: "Showtime."

18

Thanks to the concerted efforts of Senator Hammond and Bertram Sexton, Ben felt as if they were well-prepared for what would soon take place—or at least had the illusion of being prepared, perhaps the best that could be hoped for under the circumstances. Senator Keyes, he knew, was taking his marching orders from the White House. They wanted the nomination killed, but Keyes, as chairman, had to remain impartial and nonpartisan. His main go-to girl would be Senator Matera of Wyoming, a staunch ultra-Republican woman in her fifties who didn't mind playing the attack dog, and had a fiercely independent constituency that remained loyal to her—and possibly even liked her more—when she was at her worst. Her opposite number was Senator Dawkins from Minnesota, a Democrat who did not plan to run for reelection and thus was free to challenge the Republican majority whenever they acted inappropriately—for whatever good it might do. Each of the eight Democratic senators had prepared or been given prepared questions that would elicit favorable testimony: discussions of some of Roush's best opinions, his charitable work, his sterling judicial record. Ben had remarked at how much the whole proceeding resembled a trial; an enormous amount of work went into the preparation, yet everything remained uncertain.

The sergeant-at-arms held the Bible while Roush raised his right hand. "Do you swear to tell the truth, the whole truth, and nothing but the truth, so help you God?"

"I do," Roush replied.

"Point of order," Senator Matera said, raising a finger in the air. "Does the nominee attend a church?"

Senator Keyes appeared surprised, although Ben thought that very unlikely. "Well, I . . . I don't have a record—"

"Neither do I. How do we know an oath to God means anything to him?"

"Well," Keyes sputtered, "I think we can assume—"

"I don't think we can assume anything. The man has acknowledged that he participates in a—an atypical lifestyle, contrary to the laws of God."

Ben and Keyes both spoke simultaneously, but Keyes had the advantage of the raised platform. "Perhaps we could just ask a simple question regarding the man's religious beliefs."

"Excuse me?" Ben said, grabbing the microphone in front of Roush. His voice echoed throughout the chamber, reminding him that he was being watched not only by the hundreds in the room, but the thousands, perhaps millions, viewing the hearing on television. A cold chill shot down his spine. "I—I—" He took a deep breath and started again. "I've been told that you have a passing acquaintance with the Constitution, Senator. Have you read the First Amendment?"

Keyes smiled avuncularly. "I'm allowing you to speak freely, aren't I?" A small titter of laughter arose in the gallery.

"I was referring to the separation between church and state." In fact, Ben knew that Roush did not attend church regularly and he rather suspected the man was an agnostic. Pegging silence on the Constitution, however, seemed wiser than absolute honesty. "This line of questioning is entirely inappropriate."

"Well, we have a right to know if this oath he took that called for him to swear to God means anything to him."

The oath was probably unconstitutional itself, but since they'd been using it for two hundred–plus years, Ben doubted they would change it now just to make him happy.

"He took the oath," Ben said, "so he's governed by the penalties of perjury and contempt of Congress. That's all you need to know."

"It's not enough for me," Matera interjected. "The oath a new Supreme Court justice takes also invokes the name of the deity. I believe the American people have a right to know if that name holds any importance to him."

"I'll second that," Senator Potter, the youngest member of the committee, said.

"I object," Ben said. "This is grossly—"

"You are not in a courtroom, Senator Kincaid," Keyes said. "You may call for a point of order, but objections are not a part of our procedure."

Thank you so much for the hand-slapping on national television. "You can call it anything you want, but this inquiry into religion is improper and you know it. This has been stage-managed to create an unfavorable impression of the nominee—"

"Now let's not get paranoid, son."

"I object to that remark, too."

"And I will remind you again that this is not a courtroom."

"Tell me about it," Ben muttered. "No judge on earth would allow a stunt like this in the courtroom."

Keyes pounded his gavel. "Senator Kincaid. I find your lack of respect for this assemblage appalling. I think you owe us all an apology."

"I'll second that, too," Potter echoed.

"I didn't raise this issue," Ben said firmly. Despite his tendency toward nervousness, the fact that he was being observed by millions, and the fact that Senator Hammond was wincing and Christina was motioning for him to shut up, the words were flowing easily. Maybe hearings weren't that different from courtrooms after all. "Don't blame me for a stunt you prearranged with the distinguished flunky from Wyoming."

A loud murmur from the gallery followed. Keyes pounded his gavel. Matera grabbed her mike. "I will have the distinguished . . . whatever you are in your current capacity, Mr. Kincaid, know that I've been in the Senate almost twenty years, and I am no one's flunky."

"I only hope," Ben rejoined, "that will prove to be true."

Keyes was still pounding. "Could we please proceed with the matter at hand? The witness has sworn the oath and understands that he is subject to the criminal penalty of contempt of Congress. Let's move on. Does the nominee have a preliminary statement?"

Ben settled back into his chair and passed the microphone to Roush. He only hoped Tad did better with it than he had. "I do, Mister Chairman."

Roush spoke in a cool, clear voice, rarely looking at his notes, speaking with a calm earnestness and apparent spontaneity—just as he had done during the hundred or so times they had rehearsed the speech. Even though he was sitting right beside the man, Ben watched him in the video monitor to gauge his performance, a trick he had learned from Gina. Roush looked good; his strong cheekbones photographed well and his smooth facial lines gave him a pleasant on-camera expression. Most important, at least from Gina's perspective, he did not look effeminate.

Despite the constant emphasis on image, it was the content of Roush's statement that concerned Ben. As the pollster had told Roush earlier, it was laced with too many taboos, too many things he would not do: He would not comment on specific issues or potential cases. He would not discuss his political or—he added this extemporaneously—religious beliefs. He would not provide details about his personal life. This not only potentially created a negative impression, it was like dropping bait in a fish pond. Ben knew with certainty that one of the Republican senators would attempt to quiz him on each of the supposedly forbidden subjects, if only to put him in the position of having to refuse to answer on national television. Taking the Fifth, however justified the cause, rarely endeared anyone to the audience.

"It is paramount that the judiciary retain its independence from the political spheres, both the legislative and the executive branches of our government, as contemplated by the doctrine of separation of powers enshrined in the U.S. Constitution. Similarly, the public and the private realms are distinct, and always must remain so. The political and the legal worlds are distinct, and it was the framers of the Constitution's fervent and express desire that they always remain so. It is its independence that gives the judiciary its true power, the ability to perceive issues clearly and without interference, without prior judgment or bias, to apply the law as it is and not as one might wish it to be. Since the days of *Marbury v. Madison,* the Supreme Court has—"

Senator Matera interrupted. "You're talking about accountability, aren't you?"

Roush hesitated, obviously unsure whether to continue with his prepared statement or to respond to the question.

Matera filled the gap. "When you talk about the importance of maintaining independence, you're talking about activist judges doing whatever they want without accountability to the American people."

Roush stuttered. "I—I assure you—"

"I mean, that's how we ended up in the mess we're in today, with thirteen-year-old girls having abortions and the Ten Commandments being removed from courtrooms. It's all about activist judges who aren't accountable to anyone."

Ben leaned into the mike. "Ma'am, this is supposed to be an opening statement. The questions come later."

Senator Matera was not chastised. "I can't let a statement like that one pass without comment. The American people know that I am firmly opposed to any godless judges who support the homosexual lifestyle and the homosexual agenda. I am certainly not going to sit still while any such person is enshrined in a position of great power where he will not be accountable to the American people."

"I must protest—"

"Immorality breeds immorality. Do you think it's a coincidence that just after the man announced his decadent lifestyle choice, a woman turned up dead?"

"This is absurd," Ben said, but it didn't prevent him from experiencing the sinking sensation that the hearing was already getting away from him. What could he do to stop this? He felt powerless, desperate. The buzz from the gallery was almost as loud as he was. Matera was ignoring him, steamrolling him. "At this time, Senator, it is inappropriate—"

"Where do you get off lecturing me on procedure, young man? You don't even know the difference between an objection and a point of order." A little awkward laughter from the gallery. "You don't set the agenda in this chamber."

"It is traditional to allow the nominee to make a statement."

"That doesn't make it an entitlement. That's all we need—a homosexual activist judge creating another entitlement."

"I second that," Potter interjected.

Ben clenched the mike tightly. "This is outrageously inappropriate."

"I wasn't put on this dais to improve the décor," Matera continued. "I'm here to represent the people, and I will not be silenced or otherwise prevented from doing so. The American people are angry about what this man has done and they do not want to see it proceed any further."

It was clear he would have no success appealing to her reason, so Ben turned his attention to Keyes. "Mister Chairman. *Point of order.*" He gave each word its own emphasis. "Are you planning to allow the nominee's opening statement to be interrupted with questions?"

"Well . . . perhaps it would be best to let the man make his little speech," Keyes conceded, now that the damage was done.

"Thank you."

"Senator Matera, I would take it as a personal favor if you would reserve your remarks until it is your turn to question the nominee."

Matera folded her arms across her chest. "If you wish, Mister Chairman. But I refuse to sit still and listen to this self-serving godless diatribe." She stood and walked out of the Caucus Room, leaving almost everyone present gaping in her wake.

Keyes appeared surprised and shaken, even though Ben suspected the whole drama-queen scene had been planned and scripted, possibly even rehearsed. They had been one step ahead of him from the outset—well, more than one, actually.

Keyes waited until Matera was outside, then added, "Regret-table. But I suppose some members of the committee feel that certain remarks are of such egregiousness that they demand explanation. Judge Roush, please continue."

He did, but Ben knew no one was listening. Matera's scene-stealing stunt had totally upstaged him. The remainder of Roush's opening speech would be only empty words, soon forgotten. All anyone would remember, all that would be discussed and replayed on the news shows, would be Matera's outrage and walkout. She had effectively guaranteed that Roush would have no "honeymoon" period—he would be perceived as stumbling from the outset, which would only hasten the failure of his nomination.

And Ben, his astute legal advisor, had done nothing to stop it. Hadn't even slowed it down.

19

Loving hated driving in Washington, D.C. It seemed there was no good time, just one endless rush hour. Traffic was never like this in the small Oklahoma town where he grew up. Even in Tulsa it was never like this, not even on the Friday afternoon before Christmas vacation. He was almost creamed by a semi as he tried to merge onto Interstate 66. He took the Key Bridge exit and traveled straight across the Potomac, then veered right onto "M" Street. Eventually he fought his way to Thirty-first, a main drag through one of the most upscale parts of Georgetown. Personally, he preferred the bars and honky-tonks of rural Oklahoma to the endless shopping emporia surrounding "M" and Wisconsin. Did everyone in this town own a cell phone? Were they permanently attached to their ears? Might as well dangle them from the end of a pierced earring.

When he was in the vicinity of his destination, Loving parked his minivan and crawled into the back. Since Ben had decided they were relocating to D.C., at least until his senatorial term expired, Loving had taken the time to drive his official P.I. van up from Oklahoma so he could use it when needed. The tinted windows were completely opaque; he could see out, but didn't want anyone seeing in. A dark sheet hung between the front seats and where the rear seats used to be; he'd removed them to create a nest and to make more room for his surveillance equipment.

He opened the cabinet bolted to the side wall of the van. This was his private stash: digital camera, pencil-thin flashlight, twenty-power binoculars, bottled water, peanut butter sandwiches, and a lifetime supply of beef jerky. He also had a fan he used to keep cool during stakeouts. He wasn't sure he needed any of this equipment at the moment, but he ate a sandwich, just so the trip wouldn't be wasted. Then he slid outside the van and disappeared into a nearby alley.

He had become all too familiar with the network of alleys that seemed to unite most of commercial Georgetown; they were useful, but never ceased to send a chill or two up his spine when he entered. They were dark and oppressive, even in the daytime, and it would be all too easy to get trapped in them—as he had learned a few days before when he was fleeing from Leon and Pretty Boy.

He walked through the alley until he emerged at the opposite end and his ultimate destination, the address Leon had given him.

Loving pressed himself against the stone wall of the alleyway, carefully inching forward in tiny increments toward the street. Perhaps he was being excessively cautious. On the other hand, after two killers have tried their darnedest to blow you away, then one of them sits in a coffee bar and suggests there's probably still someone gunning for you, maybe there's no such thing as excessively cautious. The stinging sensation in his leg where the bullet creased it reminded him that wariness might be prudent.

He'd feel better about this if it were nighttime. Skulking about in the shadows was his specialty; he'd had a lot of practice. But Leon had made it clear that if Loving wanted to bump into this "Trudy," four in the afternoon would be the optimum time. Broad daylight. Heavy Georgetown traffic. A line of high rises that provided a never-ending succession of potential snipers' nests.

The street was smoggy to the point of choking with a sheet of cars whizzing by, not to mention the buses announcing their passage with hydraulic brake squeals and noxious fumes. How many different bus lines did this town have, anyway? Judging from the traffic, he put the number at somewhere around a hundred billion. A wonder there was anyone left to drive a car.

Loving plunged across the street, weaving a serpentine pattern through traffic, dodging cars and, at least in his mind, imaginary Leons who might be gunning for him. He made it to the opposite side and raced to the front door of the office building.

Except when he arrived, he realized it wasn't an office building. Big enough to be one, but it wasn't. *Trinity Baptist Church of Georgetown,* read the lettering on the door.

Loving did a double-take. This place looked nothing like a church, at least not from the outside. It was a five-story brownstone with barely any windows, much less any made of stained glass. He supposed space downtown was at a premium, and even churchgoers had to make do with what they could find. Inside, he saw more signs of churchliness, even though it wasn't Sunday. Religious posters— HAVE YOU BEEN WASHED IN THE BLOOD?—and tract displays hung over the functional, if unexciting, airport-beige carpeting. He spotted two large double doors and peeked inside. He found a cavernous room larger than most auditoriums, with an immensely high ceiling; he speculated that it probably reached to the top of the building. The altar at the front was decorated with flowers and a podium and flanked on either side with huge movie display screens. High-tech preaching, from the looks of things. A lot bigger than anything they'd had back in Loving's hometown.

Loving would have loved to stop and gawk, but he recalled that Leon told him that Trudy wouldn't be found in the business operation proper—she'd be in the basement. That was starting to make a lot of sense to him. What better front for a criminal operation than a church? Or maybe the church was legitimate, but rented its basement to raise extra cash. Either way, it was likely to escape the scrutiny of law enforcement eyes. Very clever, in a satanic sort of way.

Keeping careful watch to make sure no one spotted him, Loving began searching for the way to the basement. He moved sideways down the main corridor, keeping his face to the wall as if he were intensely scrutinizing something, while searching for a stairway that led downward. He spotted a heavy reinforced door with a black nameplate that looked as if it might fit the bill. Just before he reached it, however, two women emerged from opposite ends of the adjoining hallway.

Loving rapidly turned away from them.

"Well, hello, girlfriend!" one of the women said.

"Back at ya, sweetheart!"

Loving stood in front of a glass window—the display case for an immense library, as it turned out—and he could see the two women reflected in the glass. They were hugging. Both appeared thirtyish. One was blond and petite, while the other was a larger, but still very attractive, brunette. The brunette was wearing a tight-fitting dress and had a pink boa wrapped around her neck—not exactly standard church garb.

"You understand what's going down today?" the brunette said in hushed tones.

"Sure do. I think Michael has really been sweating," the blond replied.

"I know I would be. Who would've ever imagined—"

"I know, I know. It's unbelievable."

Loving strained to pick up their words. Were they talking about the murder of the mystery woman at the Roush press conference?

"I'm still not sure about . . . you know," the brunette said.

"Oh, I do, I do. But at some point . . . maybe change is good."

"Maybe. Maybe it's time to take . . . a new position."

"Just so Michael stays calm. Just so everyone stays calm. That's the main thing."

"Agreed. Got to keep our heads together."

"Absolutely, honey. I better get downstairs."

"Understood. But I'm going to see you tonight, right?"

"Count on it, Trudy."

Loving's neck stiffened. It was her!

Should he confront her now, or wait until she was alone? Loving wasn't sure which approach would be best, and while he was deliberating, the two women slipped down the stairs.

He waited a respectful few seconds so it wouldn't be obvious he was trailing them. Maybe his caution wasn't necessary—the women didn't exactly look like contract killers—but at this point, Loving didn't feel it was possible to be too careful. The door squeaked as if it hadn't been oiled since the Rock of Ages was formed, and the steps weren't much better. Loving did his best to enter stealth mode, but the environment made it challenging. By the time he reached the foot of the stairs and turned left, the women had disappeared.

No matter. There were only four doors off the passageway. Two of them were dark, not that that necessarily ruled out the possibility of a clandestine meeting. He crept close to the first and cupped his ear to the window.

Nothing. Silly to think there would be anything. He started toward the next door, relaxing a bit—and then he remembered what Leon had told him. Danger may lurk in the most unexpected places.

He took a deep breath, steadied his nerves, and moved on. Still nothing.

The third door was slightly ajar. Though the room was dark, Loving was able to ascertain that there was no one inside. And that left the last door on the left . . .

As he crept closer, he could hear talking. No, as he continued to approach, he realized it was only one voice, one voice speaking in a steady tone, almost a monotone. No, several voices, but all speaking in unison—that was it. He couldn't make out the words, but something about the voices gave him the creeps.

He moved in even closer, then crouched beneath the window in the door so he couldn't be seen. There was movement inside, and some music playing softly in the background. Someone's boom box? Maybe playing to drown out the voices? Something to prevent electronic eavesdropping?

Slowly, gently, he tried the doorknob. Locked.

Still crouched, he examined the lock. Just a simple push-button number in a flimsy wooden frame. He knew he could break it. But not without being noticed.

He heard more movement inside, followed by the sound of a door opening. Was there another entrance? Was it possible Trudy was escaping through a rear exit?

There was no more time to waste. He took off his T-shirt, wrapped it around his hand, then thrust it through the glass.

The window shattered, sending glass flying. Moving as quickly as possible, he turned the knob to release the lock, then rushed through the door.

Inside, he found three rows of people sitting on the floor. Little people. Children. Five and younger. All of them sitting with their thumbs and forefingers touching, palms turned upward, in the lotus position, staring at the man who just broke into the room.

"*Ommm . . .*"

"What the hell was that?" Senator Hammond asked, pounding on his own conference table. "They walked all over us!"

Ben stared at the floor. "I wasn't expecting them to go attack dog so soon."

"You should've been!"

"I thought they would at least let him get through his opening statement!"

"You were dead wrong. Anyone with any political sense—"

"Which would exclude me, something I've been trying to tell you since you started roping me into this! This was your idea, not mine, remember?"

Roush came between them. "Boys, calm down. You're misdirecting your anger."

Christina concurred. "He's right, you know. You should be

ticked off at Keyes and Matera, who couldn't wait ten minutes before they started with the dirty tricks and sabotage."

Hammond passed a hand across his wrinkled brow. "They've made it clear with their opening salvo that there will be no pretense of fairness in this confirmation struggle. It's going to be partisan politics right down the line."

"Then we're already dead in the water," said Roush. "There are more of them, I mean, more of me, I mean—" Roush took a deep breath. "More Republicans than Democrats. If they all follow the leader, I lose."

"But will they?" Sexton, the D.C. lawyer asked. "Some of the Republicans on the East Coast are in a bit of a bind with this one. Roush was selected by their President, after all. If they reject someone who is still technically the President's nominee, it might look as if they're voting against him just because he's gay. The backlash in New England, or perhaps California, could be considerable. Safer to just pass the party's nominee."

"Not if President Blake doesn't want them to."

Sexton shrugged. "The President is a nice man. But he can't get them reelected."

"Unfortunately, the poll data indicates that most of the American voting public is not on our side," Beauregard said, passing around the latest figures from a late-night phone poll. "A plurality of Americans oppose Roush's confirmation."

"Why?"

"Variety of reasons. Mostly because he's gay, but there are also Democrats who think he's too conservative, Republicans who think he's too liberal, or will emerge as a closet liberal now that he's emerged from another closet. A few people are actually knowledgeable about real issues, and have concerns about his position on the death penalty, abortion, and other topics in perpetual political limbo. There's a wide spectrum of concerns. Problem is, when you add all those things together, you get a lot of people who don't want to see Thaddeus on the Supreme Court."

Roush's head fell into his hands. "And if the people are against me, I can't count on anyone's support. Maybe I should withdraw."

Hammond's jaw stiffened. "Is that what you want?"

Roush shook his head. "No, it's not what I want, but—"

"I don't think a man with your background gets where you are today by quitting."

"But if it's all futile—"

"That's what they said about desegregation, fifty years ago. Most Americans initially opposed that, too. Like it or not, Tad, you've become a symbol. And let's be honest—in some respects, you've asked for it. The only question is what you're going to symbolize. The futility of fighting? Or the dawn of a new era."

Roush sighed. "Right at the moment, I'd be content to symbolize 'hardworking judge most people have never heard of.'"

Christina laid a hand on his shoulder. "That ship has sailed, Tad. Are we going to throw in the towel, or are we going to go back out there and give as good as we got? Or better."

Roush smiled a little. The expression in his eyes made a verbal response unnecessary. "Wish I knew where they'd hit next."

"I may be able to help you there," Carraway interjected. "PR 101. Your biggest audience for any televised hearing will be on the first day of questioning."

Beauregard passed around another file. "Remember, even Justice Roberts was grilled about advice he gave gay rights advocates a decade before he was nominated, and that man had a wife and children. They're sure to hit you on the issue that troubles Americans the most. Play on their greatest fear. Xenophobia. The fear of the different."

"The 'gay lifestyle?'" Ben asked.

Beauregard nodded. "Count on it."

21

Richard Trevor waited about a fourth of a mile down the main trail on Theodore Roosevelt Island, near a huge statue of the famed Rough Rider. The clearing was ornamented with two stone bridges crossing small canals and a pair of large decorative fountains. Despite being permanently lodged in the center of the Potomac River, it was not a common stop for tourists. Easy to get to but not heavily populated, it constituted an ideal meeting place for the city's top lobbyist and a somewhat timid judge who still wasn't sure he wanted to campaign for an opening that didn't quite exist yet.

"Judge Haskins?" Trevor said as the older man approached.

Haskins was gazing at the statue, which showed the former President standing with his right hand raised.

Trevor shared the view. "Looks like he's being sworn in right before your eyes, doesn't he?"

Haskins was slow to respond. "I was thinking he looks like he's in one of those great girl groups from the fifties." He noted the lack of response from Trevor. "Never mind, son. You're too young."

"You know, there's a swearing-in ceremony just like the one that big bronze man is experiencing—for new Supreme Court justices."

Haskins raised a finger to his lips. He was wearing a coat with the lapels up and his reading glasses. Not exactly anything that could be called a disguise, should he be spotted, but enough to minimize the chances of being recognized, just the same. "Are you Trevor?"

"I am, sir. And let me say that it is an honor—"

"Yes, yes, I know. Your assistant . . . what was her name?"

"Melody."

"Yes, that was it. Very persuasive young woman." He glanced at the gentle downward slope of the trail. "Shall we walk?"

"Sure." No problem for an experienced lobbyist like Trevor. He did half his business this way. Keep moving. Less likely to attract attention. Politicians acting like spies. "I want to thank you for meeting with me. It's quite an honor, chatting with a hero such as yourself."

"Oh, please don't—"

"Especially when I've been trying for so long. Without success. Mind if I ask what changed your mind?"

"Well . . . your assistant suggested the possibility that the President was considering another Supreme Court nominee. I mean, if the current one fails."

"Not much of an 'if.' More like a certainty."

"Yes, that's what my friends in high places tell me."

"But that's been true since the day Roush was nominated. Why are we meeting now?"

Haskins walked a good hundred yards without speaking, kicking the leaves and staring at the horizon. "Did you watch the hearing this morning?"

"Of course."

"I don't mean to be unkind, but . . . that was a pretty pathetic spectacle. Appalling."

"I couldn't agree more."

"Whatever you may think of his personal life, Roush clearly is not ready for the public spectrum. National attention. And who is that idiot they've got acting as his advisor? It's almost as if someone on his support staff wants him to fail. Or his handlers are sabotaging him from within."

"Sad, but true. So what are you thinking?"

"I'm thinking there's going to be another nomination made soon."

"And you're wondering if it could be you."

Haskins pursed his lips. "I've never sought a higher position. I am very content with my job on the Tenth Circuit. I don't—"

"It's nothing to be embarrassed about, sir. Most of the people I know think you should have been chosen in the first place."

"Well, I don't know . . ."

"Your heroism at the Hilton brought you into the national eye for a reason, sir. God has a plan; he doesn't play dice with the universe. If I may be so bold, I believe the President made a mistake ignoring that in the first place. I'm told he regrets it."

"Really?"

"Of course. I'm also told that when the Roush nomination is crushed, or more likely he withdraws, President Blake wants to be ready to make an immediate replacement nomination, one that everyone will support."

Haskins stopped, leaning against a tree and brushing mud off the soles of his shoes. "I can understand that. His time is ticking. But what's all this got to do with me?"

Trevor smiled. "Modesty aside, sir, I think you know. I represent a number of lobbying interests, all of which share some common . . . philosophical beliefs. And we all believe that you would be the perfect next choice for the Supreme Court."

"And these interests would be . . ."

"People who do not accept the nomination of a man who flagrantly violates the tenets of the Old Testament in his daily life."

"Ah." Haskins continued to walk silently down the grassy pathway. "The Christian Congregation."

"So, what do you think? Are you interested?"

"Am I interested? What judge wouldn't be interested in a promotion to the Supreme Court of the United States? The question isn't whether I'm interested."

"I can assure you I can deliver the support of the people I represent."

"That's just it. It isn't a matter of what I want. It's who I want to get into bed with."

Frown lines crossed Trevor's face. "What are you—?"

"It's just an expression, son." He looked back and gazed at the statue behind them, sighing quietly. "Would you prefer a military metaphor? The question is which hills I want to capture."

"I don't quite—"

"I only get one ride, son. One chance and then it's over. I didn't ask for all this attention. I have no experience in these matters. I don't know anything about Washington politics. If I take this step, plunge myself even further into the limelight, I have to make sure I've got the strongest backers possible."

"With respect, sir, you'll never have a better opportunity. The need for a nominee coming so soon after your feats of heroism—"

"You think I don't know that? Nonetheless, the President passed me over the first time. He could do it again. For that matter, how can I be certain the Roush nomination will fail?"

"Well." Trevor stopped walking. "I think I can promise you that."

"Nothing personal, but you can't guarantee anything. Not even if you own every politician on the Judiciary Committee. I've always been an honest man and I've conducted an honest life. I can't risk anything that might undermine my integrity. If you can't offer assurances—"

"I think I can." He popped open his briefcase and produced an envelope.

"What's this?"

"See for yourself. It's the reason the Roush nomination is certain to fail."

"If this is about him being gay—"

"It's ever so much more than that."

Haskins held the envelope as if it were a dirty diaper. "I can't open this here. Out in the open."

"Then don't. Take it home. Show it to Margaret. Then reach your decision."

Haskins stared across the horizon. The sun was beginning to descend, and the orange of the sky melted into the orange of the falling leaves. Times like this, Washington, D.C. seemed like the most beautiful city in the world. So long as you didn't travel too far from the center.

"This has to be on the up-and-up. I have a good life. Wonderful wife, three lovely daughters. I can go back to Denver and be perfectly happy."

"I know you can, sir. God has blessed you many times over. So take a look at the information in the envelope. Please."

"I suppose there's no harm in just looking."

Trevor took Haskins by the shoulder and steered him toward the end of the trail. "Of course not. There's only divine providence. God wants you on the Supreme Court, Judge. I'm certain of that. He wants you in there pitching for him. Fixing so much of what's wrong with this country today." He patted the judge on the back. "Just read the file. And know this." He peered deeply into the judge's eyes. "If we can bring down one nominee, we can guarantee the next."

22

*L*oving stood stupidly at the front of the room while twenty-four pairs of underage eyes stared at him from the floor. To their credit, none of the children broke out of position and only a few stopped chanting. Loving wasn't sure what to do. So he just stood there staring, shirtless, in a pool of broken glass, wondering what den of evil he had stumbled into this time.

A middle-aged woman wearing warm-up shorts and a tank top walked agitatedly from the side of the room. "I thought I made it clear. The class is full!"

Loving cleared his throat. "I need—"

"Yes, I know it's hard to find a placement in Georgetown this time of year. But these grandstand dramatics won't help you. I assume you'll pay for the door."

"Well . . . yes . . ."

"Please put your shirt back on. As you may have noticed, there are children present."

Loving meekly shook the glass out of his shirt and put it back on.

"If you'd like to place your child on the waiting list, please do so. But at present, there are no—"

"I'm lookin' for a girl—"

The woman gave him a long look. "You must like them young."

"No, I'm lookin' for a *woman*. A woman named—"

"Excuse me." She turned back toward the class, which appeared to be foundering somewhat without leadership. The chanted mantra had been replaced by private whispering. "Class, listen to me. I want you to use your imagination and go to a happy place."

Loving rolled his eyes.

"I want you to envision somewhere that always makes you happy. An amusement park. The zoo. McDonald's. The ocean. Imagine that place, then let your mind take you on a vacation there while I talk to the nice man who broke the window." She bent down and turned up the volume of the boom box slightly.

"That somethin' classical?" Loving asked.

"The Tao of Healing." She put one hand on her hip. "Now kindly tell me why you've burst into my yogababy session."

Loving knew he should stay on topic, but he couldn't resist. "Yogababy?"

"What, you haven't heard of it?"

"I've heard of Yogi Berra."

"Very amusing. For your information, the yogababies movement is nationwide. Our DVD has sold over a hundred thousand copies."

Loving's eyes wandered to the happy faces and sunflowers painted on the walls and ceiling. "Aren't these toddlers a little young for yoga?"

"Absolutely not. Balanced lives begin with balanced children."

"Well, yeah, but—"

"It's very good exercise."

"So is T-ball."

The woman cringed. "And the meditational tools they learn here can benefit them throughout their lives. Why, I have students who started with me when they were two who are in their teens now, still practicing the same asanas I taught them."

"The same . . ."

"Asanas. Yoga positions."

"There's more than one?"

Her eyes traveled skyward. "This is beside the point. Could you please explain what you are doing here?"

"I'm looking for a woman named—"

She whirled around and clapped her hands. "Students. Unflap your butterfly wings."

In unison, the small children wiggled their arms and legs.

"Now I want you to adopt the shavasana."

The children lowered themselves to the floor mats, lying on their backs, and closed their eyes.

"Shavasana?" Loving asked.

"It means 'corpse pose.'"

"Lovely. Look, while the kids are nappin'—"

"They are not napping," she said indignantly. "They are meditating."

"Whatever. Listen, I'm lookin' for a woman named Trudy."

"I don't know anyone named Trudy."

"Well, that's odd, 'cause I just followed her down here."

"Maybe she's Nadya's friend. She was late bringing Chandler."

"Is Nadya a blonde wearing a bright orange pullover?"

"I'm sure I didn't notice what she was wearing. All the parents drop their children off and then they disappear, usually to the Starbucks across the street. I don't allow the parents to observe. It destroys the children's ability to focus, to ascend to a higher plane."

"How much higher can they get when they're . . ." He glanced at the room and calculated an average age. ". . . three?"

"You might be surprised. It's actually much simpler for these children. Their minds are still pure and unsullied by the cynicism and stress of the modern world. They reach spiritual equilibrium much more readily than you or I."

"Well, when will this Nadya—" As if in answer to his question, in the rear of the room, through a windowpane, Loving spotted the blonde he had seen upstairs. "Excuse me."

The woman grabbed his wrist. "What about the window!"

Loving reached into his pocket and threw back one of Ben's cards. "Send the bill to this address."

He raced to the back of the room, trying not to step on any of the tiny yogis trying to get in touch with their inner adults—although actually, he noticed that several of them were sound asleep—and pushed through the rear exit.

Nadya had walked up the steps to street level and was about to cross the street. "Stop!" he yelled.

To his surprise, she did.

Loving ran to her, huffing breathlessly and wondering, once again, if it was safe for him to be seen in the open. "Where's Trudy?"

Nadya looked at him strangely, or rather, as if he were very strange. "I don't know. Who are you?"

"My name . . ." He pondered for a moment. Was it really safe to give the woman his name? Or advisable? Sure, kiddie yoga seemed innocuous enough. But Leon had warned him that danger lurked in unexpected places. He had suggested that Trudy could give him the information that he needed. But that didn't mean she—or her friends—were safe. Maybe he shouldn't give her any details that would help any other trigger-happy friends she might have track him down.

He wasn't quite sure what won out—his sense of honesty or his lack of imagination. "My name's Loving. I work for Senator Kincaid."

"I don't believe I know—"

"Don't sweat it. No one does. I'm lookin' for Trudy."

"Really?" Her nose wrinkled. "Do tell." She gave him the once-over. "Who would've guessed? You seem so—well, I shouldn't stereotype. Takes all kinds, right?"

Loving stared at her dully. "Huh?"

"It's none of my business—"

"Look, lady, I'm a private investigator. I'm tryin' to get a lead on the woman who was killed at Judge Roush's press conference."

All at once, Nadya's face became serious. "I'm sure Trudy had nothing to do with that."

"How can you be sure?"

"I just—I just know it's not something Trudy would go in for."

Loving grunted. "I appreciate your vote of support, but I'd still like to talk to her. Could you please tell me where I might meet her?"

Nadya backed away from him. "No . . . No, I don't think I can do that. I don't think I want anything to do with you. And I don't think Trudy will, either."

"Please," Loving said, grabbing her hand. "Help me find her."

"No." She shook her hand loose. "And if you touch me again, I'll scream."

Well, I'm handling this masterfully, aren't I? Loving thought. He released her hand. "Just tell me where Trudy is."

Nadya continued retreating. "No."

"I know you're going to meet her later tonight."

"How do you know?"

"I just do. Where are you meeting?"

The woman bumped backward into a small Toyota hatchback. "I'm warning you. Leave me alone."

Loving noticed that the stack of books she carried contained a small Filofax calendar. He considered making a grab for it, but doubted he would be successful. "Please tell me where you're going to meet."

"I'll scream! If you don't stay back, I'll scream!" She jammed a key into the car door, threw all her belongings in the backseat, then locked the car again. "I'm going to get my coffee now. I have a cell phone. If you don't leave me alone, I'll call the police."

"Are you meeting Trudy at Starbucks?"

"No! I've got maybe an hour to myself, for once in my life, until I have to pick up my boy. I do not expect to be disturbed."

"But all I want to know is—"

"See?" she said, holding up her cell phone. "All I have to do is punch one button and the police are on their way."

"But all I want—"

"Leave me alone! Me and Trudy both!" Nadya turned and ran down the sidewalk, then disappeared into the coffee shop.

Loving stood on the sidewalk berating himself for his stupidity. He'd handled that like a prize chump. If only they'd been sitting around a bar or something—that was more his natural milieu. He understood those people. Neurotic moms who take their tots to yoga class he didn't know.

He stared at the Filofax calendar in the backseat, probably containing the vital information about the rendezvous he wanted. He could break the window, but it was a crowded street and that would undoubtedly attract attention, possibly even set off a car alarm. He could wait until Nadya emerged from the coffee shop and try her again, maybe follow her, but that was risky, especially given her excitability. He'd do it if he must, but there had to be a better way.

All he had to do was figure out what that better way was.

23

Ben was not surprised to hear that the first person to question Roush would be Senator Matera, who had decided to grace the committee with her presence once more. The opposition knew what Gina Carraway knew: the biggest audience, and thus the opportunity to make the biggest impression or do the greatest damage, would come on the first day of questioning, before most of the home audience switched their attention back to *The View* or *General Hospital*. During the break, Ben visited Senator Keyes's chambers to try to persuade him to select a more neutral initial interrogator, in the name of "dignity and justice," but Keyes's AA told Ben he was "unavailable."

The second Ben and Roush passed through the gabled double doors, the bright lights came on and Ben's sweat glands kicked into overdrive. He still couldn't believe he had been chosen for this high-profile role—he, the least experienced senator in Congress. Even Beauregard seemed to support Ben's involvement as Roush's advisor, despite the information he was getting from his polls. Did that make any sense?

Christina, just a step behind him, whispered into his ear. "The big red is on. Don't look."

Meaning the big red light, the one that informed the gallery that their image was being broadcast from coast to coast, and for that matter, throughout a sizeable chunk of the rest of the world. They had been coached to never look directly into the camera. As with actors in a sitcom, a direct stare broke the fourth-wall illusion that was the fundamental assumption of television programming, even purportedly nonfiction programming like this. Viewers wanted to believe they were flies on the wall, watching while their subjects were unaware—when in reality no one could forget for a moment that they were being televised.

After the committee had retaken their seats, Ben pulled the microphone closer. "Before we begin," he announced, "I want to remind the committee that Judge Roush will not entertain any questions—"

"You have not been recognized, sir," Keyes said. "If you wish to speak, you must be recognized by the chairman of the committee." He paused. "That would be me." A tittering of laughter from the gallery ensued.

Ben took a deep breath. "Very well. May I be recognized to speak, Mr. Chairman?"

"No. You are not a member of the committee, and you are not the nominee. Your function here is simply to advise the nominee."

"Nonetheless," Ben said, undeterred, "in the interests of saving time, I would remind the committee that any questions posing hypothetical cases or probing into his personal life—"

His voice went dead. Or more accurately, his microphone went dead. Ben's voice became a whisper of what it had been before.

Senator Keyes smiled. "I control the microphones, sir. I will turn that one back on when you are recognized to speak. I must remind you again that this is not a courtroom, and you are not here to perform as an advocate. We have rules designed to help us get at the truth with a minimum of fuss, and I will enforce them."

Ben sat in his chair and glowered. Two options presented themselves to him, neither of them good. He could continue to insist on making a statement, perhaps instructing Roush not to speak until he had, but that would only make them appear obstreperous and suspect to the television audience. Or he could cave and let Keyes bulldoze by, at the risk of looking a total wimp to the television audience and setting a precedent that would make him worse than useless for the remainder of the proceeding.

While Ben pondered what to do, Senator Keyes recognized the distinguished senator from Wyoming to lead the questioning of the nominee. Looks like the die is cast, Ben thought. I'm a wimp on national television.

"Judge Roush," Senator Matera said, pulling the microphone closer, "I've reviewed the cases you've handled on the Tenth Circuit and I have a few questions."

"I expect you do," Roush said, smiling. The power returned to the microphone just after he began speaking. "But first I believe my advisor Mr. Kincaid wanted to remind the committee of a few of the ground rules. And," he said, looking directly at Keyes, "this is my time, so I would appreciate it if the wind didn't suddenly go out of the microphone's sails."

Bless you, Ben thought, as he took the mike. "As I was saying before: no hypothetical cases, no questions about political positions or issues, no prying into personal matters."

"Why, Mr. Kincaid," Senator Matera said, flashing a smile that could have belonged to a woman thirty years younger, "you're taking away all the fun stuff." Laughter filled the gallery, easing much of the tension. She was good, Ben realized as he gazed across the dais at her twinkling eyes. Be afraid. Be very afraid.

"Judge Roush, let me ask you a question I think won't bother even Mr. Kincaid. As I said, I've been reviewing your record," which of course meant her staff had been reviewing his record and had provided her a summarized coverage, "and it appears to me you fancy yourself something of a judicial activist. Why do you—"

"Excuse me," Roush said, interrupting, "but I'd like to correct that."

"Judge," Matera said, still smiling, "I haven't asked you a question yet."

Roush spoke over the laughter. "Maybe not, but you've made a statement that is patently incorrect. I am not a judicial activist. To the contrary, I am a judicial conservative. If I had to label myself with a single judicial philosophy, it would probably be fundamentalist positivism."

"Well . . . you're using words too big for a simple country girl like myself. Perhaps you could explain the difference."

"The theory of judicial activism—and here I use that phrase as it is used in legal and academic circles, not as it is bandied about by politicians—is that a judge can interpret the law so as to advance political beliefs that are not currently enshrined in established law. A fundamental positivist recognizes that society does change over time and that occasionally the law requires modification, but nonetheless considers it a judge's foremost duty when interpreting the law to ensure continuity. To follow precedent. To recognize that the law must be a knowable, predictable entity."

"So you don't think judges should usurp the role of legislators?"

"Certainly not. I don't know anyone who does. That's a charge leveled by critics who don't like a decision. Rather than simply acknowledging that intelligent people can still have different opinions, they blame 'activist judges' and imply that they have done something illicit or improper, something judges aren't supposed to do."

"And what exactly are judges supposed to do?"

"Enforce the Constitution, and the lesser laws to the extent that they do not conflict with the Constitution."

"And nothing more."

"Nothing more." Roush smiled. "Believe me, that's plenty enough to keep a man busy."

Ben eyed Senator Matera carefully. She had a way of looking out the corner of her eyes that reminded him of Brer Rabbit in the Disney cartoon—the look of the trickster. He kept waiting for the other shoe to drop.

"Well, then," Matera continued, "how do you feel about these so-called penumbral constitutional rights?"

"For starters," Roush said, "I think it was a terribly poor choice of language. When Justice Brennan wrote that a woman's right to choose was a constitutional freedom that could be found in the penumbra of the Constitution, he implied to some readers that it wasn't really there."

"That is what the word 'penumbra' means, isn't it? Something on the outside, like an aura. But not contained within the entity itself. One of my clerks was kind enough to bring a dictionary."

"Exactly my point. I don't think that's what Justice Brennan meant. I think he meant to say that there are rights squarely embedded in the Constitution that are not expressly delineated."

Matera wagged her head. "I must tell you, Judge, this is sounding very activist to me." More laughter. She may not say much, Ben thought, but she does know how to entertain.

"With respect, ma'am, I disagree. A firm tenet of the fundamental positivist's judicial outlook is the fact that the world changes. We all know that. *Tempus mutantor.* The founding fathers could not have anticipated developments like the automobile, television, the Internet. The increased ability of the government to oversee, and potentially control, our lives. The widespread technological innovations that have made invasion of privacy so easy. That being the case, we have two choices. We either admit with resignation that the Constitution is no longer relevant—or we look to the core values that underlie the Constitution and apply them to new issues as they arise. The individual's right to privacy was clearly one of the fundamental concerns of the Constitution. You can see it in the First Amendment, the Second, the Fourth—almost everywhere, especially in the Bill of Rights. The founding fathers never contemplated that a government would attempt to ban abortion; women had quietly been obtaining abortions since the first European settlers came to this country. All Justice Brennan did in *Roe v. Wade* was apply the fundamental principle of privacy to a new issue."

Matera peered down through her glasses. "I take it then that you support *Roe v. Wade?*"

Ben grabbed the mike. "No specific cases, remember?"

Roush smiled. "It's all right, Ben. I can answer that. The truth is, as a judge, I neither support nor fail to support any individual decision. I review the facts of an individual case and apply the law. So long as there are no other intervening considerations, I apply precedent."

"And *Roe v. Wade* is one such precedent?"

"Yes, ma'am. Has been for more than thirty years."

"But it could be reconsidered?"

"Any decision can be revisited in a subsequent case, if there are grounds. New issues. But that can't be based on anyone's—any judge's—personal beliefs. It must be based upon new consideration presented by the case at bar."

"So you wouldn't strike down *Roe v. Wade.*"

"Ma'am—"

"Right, right. No specific cases." She paused, then turned a page in her notes. Ben mentally commanded his fingers to stop drumming on the tabletop. This little exploration into legal philosophy had been fine, possibly dry enough to persuade a large portion of the audience to switch channels, but Ben knew that Matera had other more malevolent goals for the first day of the hearing, and waiting for her to show her true colors was giving him an ulcer.

As it happened, he didn't have to wait much longer.

"Judge," Matera continued, "if you won't talk about *Roe v. Wade,* perhaps the single case of greatest interest to everyone in America, would you consent to discussing *Powers v. Georgia?*"

Ben felt his heart drop. They had known this was a possibility, of course. But somehow, he had thought that even Senator Matera wouldn't have the effrontery to try this tactic.

"What about *Powers,* sir? Would you have any interest in repealing it?"

Roush licked his lips, pulled the microphone a little closer, all the while doing what Ben thought was a magnificent job of keeping his emotions in check. "I can't address any ruling in the abstract. I have to know the circumstances of the case at bar."

"Oh, come now, Judge. You must have some personal feelings about this."

Ben winced; it was the least emotive facial expression he could manage. *Powers v. Georgia* was the infamous 1988 Supreme Court case which, in a decision written by Justice Rehnquist, upheld a Georgia sodomy law, declaring that it did not offend the Constitution to criminalize consensual relations between male homosexuals. What the *Dred Scott* case was to African Americans, *Powers v. Georgia* was to the gay and lesbian community.

Roush's face reddened only a bit, but on the television screen he looked as if he were wearing rouge. "Whether I do or do not have any personal feelings would not be relevant to my work on the Supreme Court. My work as a justice would simply be to determine whether the state statute offends the U.S. Constitution."

"Oh, please, sir. With all due respect, I'm nobody's fool."

"I never said—"

"The first moment in your life you were in the public spotlight, you were compelled to declare to the world your participation in the homosexual lifestyle. Do you seriously expect me to believe that you wouldn't jump at the chance to overturn *Powers?*"

Roush spoke in careful, measured tones. "I seriously expect you to believe that I wouldn't overturn anything unless there was a constitutional basis."

"Then you'll find one. That's what you activist judges do, isn't it? I bet you'd love to bury that opinion."

"As a matter of fact," Roush said, "I have a lot of respect for that opinion." Red blotches were creeping up his neck, but Ben hoped he was the only one close enough to notice. "Just as I have a great deal of respect for the late Chief Justice Rehnquist. I don't believe for a minute that Justice Rehnquist or those who voted with him made their decision based on any personal prejudices, homophobia or anything else. As Rehnquist explained, antisodomy statutes are as old as this nation. It simply isn't credible to suggest that the framers of the Constitution would've been offended by such laws." He took a deep breath. "That of course doesn't mean that enlightened senators such as yourself couldn't pass a law prohibiting statutes they deem discriminatory. It just means they aren't unconstitutional."

Ben released his breath. Damn—this man was good. He could almost stop worrying about him—or he might have if the good senator from Wyoming had left it at that.

"Judge Roush, let's cut through all this judicial rigmarole and talk turkey, shall we? You are a self-professed homosexual."

"Objection," Ben said. "Or—point of order. Whatever you want to call it, Mr. Chairman. This question is obviously veering into private matters."

"There's nothing private about it!" Matera said, slapping the table. "The man came out of the closet at a press conference!"

"I'd have to agree with her on that one," Chairman Keyes said, as if his opinion were a surprise to anyone.

"I don't care," Ben replied. "If you allow questions in this direction, it will only set a precedent for subsequent committees to find excuses to pry into people's private sex lives. We already do that to our political candidates. Must we do it to judicial nominees as well?"

"It's all right, Ben," Roush said, placing his hand on the mike, making his voice echo through the chamber. "The senator does have a point. What I haven't heard yet is a question. Is there one?"

"Well then," Matera said, leaning forward, "here it is. How can we know that your sexual preference won't influence your judicial reasoning?"

"How can you know anyone's private life won't affect their judicial reasoning?" Ben shot back. "This is a frivolous question being asked for the sole purpose of generating opposition based upon intolerance."

"It's an important question, Mr. Kincaid. We've never had a gay Supreme Court justice."

"That you know of."

"Who was openly gay." She paused. "Is it all right to call you gay, Judge Roush? What term do you prefer?"

Roush gave her a long look. "You may use any term you feel appropriate, ma'am."

"Thank you. I appreciate your generosity. But my point is, when a man's thinking is so dominated by one issue and cause, how can we know it won't control his work on the bench?"

"It never has before," Roush replied. "I've been on the bench a long time, but no one outside my immediate friends and family even knew I was gay until I announced it in the Rose Garden."

"Why did you keep it secret?"

"It wasn't a secret. I just didn't talk about it."

"You're splitting hairs."

"Do you go around talking about your sexual preference a lot?"

"Well . . ."

"Neither do I. But let's get real—if I had come out of the closet beforehand, I wouldn't be here now."

"So why come out at all?"

"As I said when I accepted the nomination, I felt it would be dishonest not to do so."

"Still, my concern is that your highest controlling authority might be . . . well, something or someone other than the Constitution."

"Your concerns are misplaced."

"My understanding is that you are in a long-term relationship—"

"Which is absolutely none of your business."

"What if you contract AIDS?"

"What if you contract syphilis? Nobody ever got disqualified from a job because of something they might get someday."

"This is totally different. If confirmed, you would be a representative of a . . . a lifestyle . . ."

Roush shook his head. "This is so sad. These are the same arguments people used against Kennedy—vote for him and the country will be controlled by the Pope. The same arguments they used to keep women from voting, to keep them off the Supreme Court till the 1980s, when Ronald Reagan—a Republican—appointed Justice O'Connor. Sometimes it seems as if we haven't made any progress at all."

"You can compare yourself to Kennedy and women if you like, but they were both in the mainstream in a way that you simply are not. You represent a minority lifestyle, one that many people oppose and most people do not share. How can you possibly claim that you can represent the thoughts and interests of the American people when you are so different from them? When you are nothing like them?"

"Nothing like who?" Roush exploded. "You?"

Ben pulled the microphone away. "These questions have in fact become quite offensive. We will not be answering any more of them."

"Mr. Kincaid—"

"You heard me. I'm not going to change—"

Chairman Keyes leaned forward. "Mr. Kincaid, I guess I need to remind you again that you are not in a courtroom. You can't plead the Fifth. Refuse to answer and the nominee could be held in contempt of Congress."

"You can huff and you can puff," Ben said firmly, "but I'm instructing the judge not to answer any more offensive questions."

"Just a minute, Ben," Roush said, laying a hand on his arm. Damn it, why wouldn't the man let him do his job? "I do want to say something before we leave this subject, once and for all, I hope. In the first place, I haven't been nominated to the Senate. I'm not a representative of the people. That's your job, Senator. The judiciary is specifically designed to be independent of the legislature, a check on the legislature. It is not a judge's job to represent the thoughts and interests of the American people—it's a judge's job to enforce the law, pure and simple."

"Without any regard to the wishes of the people?" Matera looked as if he had just suggested torching the Washington Monument.

"Frankly, yes. And let me make a second point. You talk about representing America—there are many Americas. And they don't all look like you. From the outset, America has been a melting pot. Our diversity has been our strength. It still is, even if some misguided folks want to re-create the whole country in their own image. We do not have a national religion, or a national race or color. We do not all have the same sexual preference and we never have. America has many faces. And we are better and stronger for it."

24

Loving stood on the sidewalk and idled about, pretending to read a discarded newspaper, admiring the display windows of overpriced Georgetown boutiques, and otherwise purposelessly killing time until he was certain Nadya had disappeared into the coffee shop and wouldn't be watching or returning—at least not until her son's journey to his inner self was over for the day. Sweet Jeepers, why couldn't she just hire a babysitter? Given what she'd said, he had a little under an hour, so he couldn't afford to waste time. Didn't like standing around in plain view, anyway. He tried to convince himself there was no danger, despite what Leon had told him. There was no logical reason to think assassins were watching his every move, right? That was just paranoia, and with the Senate committee hearings already under way and Ben left with no way of explaining the murder at the press conference, he couldn't afford to give in to paranoia. That was just craziness.

Yeah. And if he kept saying it to himself long enough, maybe the pain in his leg where the bullet creased him would stop suggesting he was in total denial.

He tore a scrap of paper from a newspaper in a trash bin, bummed a pencil, then casually strolled up to Nadya's Toyota. He crouched beside the driver's door, peered through the windshield, and copied down the VIN from the embossed metal label on the dash. He almost felt bad about doing this. Well, he rationalized, it was her own fault for not covering up the number. It was illegal to remove the VIN plate, but nothing prevented you from putting a strip of electrician's tape over it. For that matter, an index card wedged into the bottom of the dash would work—anything to prevent criminals from doing . . . exactly what he was doing.

He flipped open his cell phone and activated the scrambler. The scrambler would not affect his call; he and the person on the other end of the line would be able to speak naturally. But to anyone trying to intercept the signal, it would sound like gibberish. He was still fighting the urge toward paranoia, but he knew that it was pathetically easy to eavesdrop on cell phone calls. Anyone with a receiver purchased at Radio Shack could do it. Amateurs could simply roam the frequencies, listening for interesting chatter, but professionals knew how to triangulate onto a cell phone's signal or hack into a database to get its serial number and thus determine the perfect frequency for eavesdropping. He'd never used a scrambler before Ben and his crew had come to Washington, but then, he'd never been able to afford one before, either.

He stepped away from the car, then called Information to locate the nearest Toyota dealer.

"Georgetown Imports."

"Hey, this is Al Loving. Sorry to bother you, but I've locked the keys in that car I bought from you guys a while back and I have to be at an important meeting in thirty minutes. Is there any way you can cut me a duplicate key?"

The voice on the other end of the line sounded bored to tears, as if she had heard this story a thousand times. "Have you got the VIN number?"

"Sure." Loving read it off.

The woman took it down. "Can you get a ride down here?"

"Not a problem."

"We'll start cutting the new key now. It'll be ready for you when you arrive. You can also get a keyless lock controller, if you wish. Sounds as if you might need one."

"Thanks, just the key will be great."

"We'll get right on it."

Loving disconnected, then stuffed the phone into his pocket. He'd pulled this scam at least a half dozen times. It was ridiculously easy. Someday, he supposed, someone was going to get wise to it, put it in a book or something, and then car dealers would start being more careful. But in the meantime, why should this only be available to car thieves who used the VIN to hijack a car in broad daylight and drive it to the chop shop? Seemed only right that the trick should occasionally be used by the forces of good and righteousness.

And he *was* working on the side of good and righteousness. Right?

Less than thirty minutes later, Loving was back at the side of Nadya's Toyota with a brand-new sparkling door and ignition key. He slid the key into the lock, trying not to attract any attention, although there was no reason for anyone to believe that he wasn't the owner of the car. After all, he had a key, didn't he? Unless Nadya happened by. That would be bad.

Loving didn't waste any time. He opened the Filofax calendar to the present month, then removed his handy-dandy DocuPen R700. The gizmo was no bigger than your average writing pen, and that's what it looked like, but in reality, it was a miniature scanning device. He rolled the pen over the pages for the entire month; the DocuPen would record everything—text and graphics—and it took only four seconds. Later, he'd take it back to the office and Jones would upload it to his computer via a USB port. So easy even Loving could understand it, despite his acute computophobia.

He closed the Filofax, crawled back out of the car, shut the door, relocked it, and had started moving away when he saw Nadya approaching from the opposite direction. She saw him, too. This left two options: he could try to make some excuse for his presence, or he could run. The latter would probably be more prudent, but the former would be more fun. And what was life without a little fun?

Nadya marched right up to him, her expression angry. "Why are you hanging around my car?"

"I was waitin' for you to return."

"Why?"

"I told you already—I need to find Trudy."

"And I told you already—I'm not telling you anything. Remember?"

"Yeah, but I thought you might be more agreeable after you got your caffeine fix."

She glared at him. "You thought wrong."

"Well, can't fault a man for tryin'."

"I think I could."

"Say—do you do this yoga stuff, too?"

"Of course. You think I'd indoctrinate my son in a discipline I don't practice myself?"

If it bought you an hour's peace in a coffee shop, probably so, he thought. For that matter, if you drank less caffeine, you might need less yoga. But he opted not to voice either observation. "I was just wonderin', you think maybe I could do that, you know, that yoga stuff?"

She eyed him dubiously. "Are you seriously interested in leading a balanced life? Trying to find inner tranquillity?"

"Absolutely. If you'd be my spiritual guide."

She took a step closer. "You'd . . . you'd want that?"

He stepped even closer. "Absolutely." He stared deeply into her eyes. Their noses were inches apart.

Her lips pursed. "You're playing me, aren't you?"

"Totally." He grinned. "Kind of fun, though, wasn't it?"

"It might be, if I didn't think you were trying to get my friend in trouble."

"I won't get her in trouble." He paused. "But I can't promise she isn't already in trouble. Somebody out there has a secret they want kept secret. And they're playing for keeps."

25

"Now that was more like it," Senator Hammond said, slapping Roush on the back. "You really came to life. That little speech was just what we needed. Don't you agree, Ben?"

Ben nodded. He was enjoying this little post-game rehash a lot more than he had the last. "I thought it was perfect. I was worthless, but happily, Tad was able to save his own bacon."

"More than that," Hammond continued. "You showed Keyes and his cronies this mudwrestle isn't over yet. If you can speechify like that, son, you could have a career in Congress."

"Thanks," Roush said, shrugging, "but I think I'll stick to the bench. If the bench will still have me."

"I concur with the senator," Beauregard said. "Tracking polls suggest that many people have a higher opinion of you now than they did before."

"But none of those people will be voting on my nomination."

"In effect, they will. The Republicans will back off if the public starts to perceive this as an anti-gay witch hunt. Not even the staunchest Republicans want anything to do with that."

"We're not out of the woods yet," Sexton interjected. As the senior strategist on the team, Ben assumed it fell to him to be the perpetual wet blanket. "They didn't get the coup they wanted on their first day before the cameras. But since it's still a horse race, the second-day audience will be above average. They'll redouble their efforts to trash Judge Roush."

"How?" Ben asked. "Keyes has to call a Democratic senator next. He indicated he was going to move to Senator Dawkins, since he's the senior Democrat on the committee. And we know he's friendly."

"And a friendly witness is a good thing. But it's still Keyes's playground. He'll come up with something." He leaned closer to Ben. "You're going to have to be ready. And be tough. Tougher than you've been so far, if you don't mind my saying so."

Ben liked to think he was thick-skinned and above taking offense at constructive criticism, but he wasn't sure this was all that constructive. "I'm doing my best out there."

"Don't give me that 'doing my best' crap. That's what children say. It's a way of making excuses for failure."

"Excuse me? Where do you get—"

"You're playing in the big leagues now, Kincaid, so you're going to have to act like it."

"If you'll recall, I didn't want this job in the first place!"

Sexton tugged at his three-piece suit. "I don't care if you did or you didn't. You're there now and it's too late to make changes. It would be perceived as a sign of weakness. And you're already fighting a wimp image."

Ben bristled. "Look, here in Washington, you may think it's always best to come on like a two-ton pile of bricks, but in my experience, most people respond better to a calm and reasoned approach."

"That's our problem." He paused. "Your experience doesn't mean crap here."

Ben clenched his teeth. "No one is persuaded by somebody who acts like an asshole."

"You're not trying to persuade anyone. Tad is!" Sexton shook his head. "Damn it, Ben, you've got to stop thinking like a trial at-torney. This is a whole new arena. Tad is the one who has to be calm and reasonable. You *should* act like an asshole. You're there to be his asshole. An attack dog in heat. You fight the fight so he doesn't have to. You protect him."

"I *have* protected him."

"Bull. You left him hanging out to dry, morning and afternoon. He saved himself."

Christina stepped forward. "That's more than a little harsh. I to-tally disagree."

Sexton acted as if she weren't there. "Did you think that was bad out there today, Kincaid? Let me tell you something—that was nothing. Kid-glove stuff. They were going easy on you because they thought the nomination was dead in the water. Now that they know we have a little fight left in us, they'll likely bring up the murder."

"We can deal with that."

"How? Your investigator has nothing. Listen to me, Ben—I was at the press conference when that woman's corpse was uncovered. So were Gina and Charles. We saw the expressions on people's faces. It doesn't matter whether the police have linked Ray to the crime. It's a blot on his record. A serious problem."

"I don't think they'll play that card."

"Then you are living in a dream world. Now that Tad has had a good day, made a good impression, they'll be pulling out all the stops. Firing with all chambers. Shooting with—"

"I don't mean to interrupt the stream of manly metaphors," Ben said, "but I don't need you to tell me that we face some tough oppo-sition. I've known that from the start."

"I have, too," Roush said, stepping between them. "So cool it, both of you, okay? I'm the one whose butt is on the line. We need to be fighting our opponents, not each other."

"And on that note," Christina said, deftly joining the effort to change the subject as soon as possible, "am I the only one who heard that the lovely Senator Matera of Wyoming was seen with the leader of the Christian Congregation yesterday?"

Hammond sat up. "Richard Trevor? I hadn't heard that. Who's your source?"

Christina fluttered her eyelashes. "Oh, I get around."

"Been here a few months and she's got better intel than my senior staff." He gave Ben a direct look. "Hang on to that lady."

"I will. I mean, I want to. I mean—" Ben pressed two fingers against his forehead. "You know what I mean."

"I for one wouldn't object to a little clarification," Christina said, lips pursed.

Ben slouched lower into his seat.

"So Trevor and Matera are talking. Probably wooing a replacement Supreme Court nominee. And I have a pretty good idea who that will be." Hammond batted his finger against his lips. "I have to tell you, Tad. This isn't good news."

"What's the problem?" Roush asked. "I'm the one with the nomination."

"For the moment," Sexton said. "But the Christian Congregation represents a huge voting bloc, and they're not all nutcases who think God sends hurricanes to Florida to punish gays and career women, either. If both the President and the President's biggest pocketbook are backing the same nominee, and the powers that be know it, they're going to be fighting even harder to kill this nominee. They're going to aim for the head. Fire with both barrels. Charge like—"

"Yes, yes, we know," Ben said, cutting him off. "They'll go nuclear." He turned to Christina. "Any idea whether Judge Haskins is interested?"

"In an appointment to the Supreme Court? I think we have to assume he is."

"I saw him give a press conference with his wife and the mother of that baby he saved, and he indicated otherwise."

"No one wants to be overt about it," Gina Carraway said. "These are judges, not politicians. Presidents usually avoid anyone who appears to be campaigning for the job. On the other hand, if the President needs a candidate who is sure to be confirmed quickly and without objection, he could hardly do better than the man who saved a baby from a burning building. Never mind arguing about judicial qualifications and deliberative theories; most Americans don't really understand what appeal judges do anyway. As soon as the President starts calling him a 'bona fide American hero,' he'll be unstoppable."

"So we have to make sure he never gets a chance to be nominated," Ben said quietly.

"Yes," Sexton concurred. "That's what you have to do."

Thanks, Ben thought, drumming his fingers on the table. I always work best under pressure. *Not.*

26

Senator Dawkins spent the first few minutes of the day's session hurling some of the softest softballs ever lobbed in the marbled walls of Capitol Hill. He began by asking Roush questions about his background: growing up in a poor—that is, economically challenged—family of coal miners in West Virginia, putting himself through college and law school, and eventually rising to the D.C. Circuit Court of Appeals. Then he took Roush through a guided tour of his judicial record, sparing him the immodesty of bragging about himself by doing all that dirty work for him.

"I was particularly moved by the language you used in the *Smoot* case when you upheld the states' rights of eminent domain." He quoted the opinion, reading from his notes. " 'We must always remember one paramount lesson from our constitutional studies: the Bill of Rights was not created to bestow powers to the federal government, nor even to individuals. It was conceived, drafted, and executed to ensure the continuance of the most sacred principle of federal law—that all rights not expressly given to the federal government are reserved to the states.' "

"Thank you, sir," Roush said, bowing his head slightly. "I thought that was a pretty good line myself." A spattering of laughter followed.

Of course, Dawkins had not chosen to talk about states' rights by accident, as Ben well knew. He was reminding all those present that despite the opposition of his party, this nominee was a Republican, sufficiently conservative to attract the President's attention in the first place. States' rights was a good way to do it, since it was a catch phrase Republicans had used for decades to promote political agendas that could not be identified by their true name.

"Now if we may," Dawkins continued, "I wanted to discuss your somewhat controversial dissent in *State v. Victor.*"

"I only dissented in part," Roush clarified. "To some of the language in the majority opinion. I concurred in the result."

"Just so. But your dissenting opinion does appear to leave open the possibility that, despite Supreme Court precedent to the contrary, you believe there are at the very least some instances in which the death penalty might be unconstitutional. Could you please explain what you meant?"

This discussion, too, had been prearranged. Ben and Sexton both agreed that his position on the death penalty was likely to be targeted by the Republican opposition. It would be the next item on the agenda, now that they had done about all they could with his professed homosexuality without appearing totally bigoted. So Sexton made the strategic decision to have the issue first raised by a friendly source. It wouldn't prevent other committee interrogators from treading the same ground, but it might make them appear redundant.

"I can explain what I said in the context of that particular case," Roush replied, "but as I indicated earlier, I can't prejudge future cases or consider hypothetical applications of the opinion. My point was simply that the Constitution forbids cruel and unusual punishment."

"Point of order," Senator Matera said, interrupting. "Isn't there direct Supreme Court precedent stating that the death penalty does not offend that passage of the Constitution?"

Ben grabbed the mike. "I believe this is Senator Dawkins's turn to ask questions."

Matera smiled. "I was merely interposing a point of order, Mr. Kincaid. You need to study your procedure if you're going to continue to appear at this hearing."

Well, Sexton wanted him to be an attack dog, Ben thought. Here goes nothing. "A point of order is a request for a procedural clarification addressed to the chairman of the committee. What you just asked was a substantive question addressed toward the nominee. By no stretch of the imagination could that be a point of order. What you did was what my mother used to call by its technical term: butting in."

The laughter in the gallery only made it sting the worse. Matera's back stiffened. "Did your mother teach you to be disrespectful to United States senators, Mr. Kincaid?"

"No, ma'am. Did your mother teach you how to take turns?"

Matera slid back into her chair, a thin smile on her face. Ben wanted to think he had perhaps earned a small measure of the woman's admiration—but he doubted it.

Roush recovered his microphone. "Regardless of who asks the question, I think we all know that the Court has flip-flopped on this issue. First the Supreme Court abolished the death penalty, citing the cruel and unusual punishment clause. A few years later, a newly re-constituted court reversed that opinion."

"And would you have the Court flip again?" Dawkins asked.

"Absolutely not. Again, I can't prejudge a case that isn't before me. But I have spoken earlier of the great importance of stability and continuity in the law. Sudden reversals such as the one I just described undermine the law and diminish people's confidence in the judiciary."

"Getting back to the original question, sir: what was the point you were trying to make in the *Victor* dissent?"

"It's simple, really. The majority opinion took the position that the death penalty is always constitutional and within the power of the state. I simply made the point that, while there was no reason to believe it was unconstitutional in the case at bar, it was possible that the death penalty might be applied so inconsistently, or might be obtained so fraudulently, that it would constitute cruel and unusual punishment—the position taken by virtually every other highly industrialized nation on the planet. We've all heard about the capital convictions obtained in Oklahoma based upon evidence that was falsified by a forensic scientist who sacrificed her conscience in pursuit of her boss's quest for a high execution rate. We know more than a hundred people have been released from death row because DNA evidence proved they did not commit the crime of which they were convicted. We've seen the studies that show that minorities are given the death sentence at a vastly higher rate than white defendants. We saw the governor of Illinois commute the sentence of every single prisoner on death row due to irregularities in the system. At some point, the Supreme Court might have to consider whether the state is required to establish some degree of certainty before it executes. We know a conviction is no guarantee of guilt. Maybe each state should establish an ombudsman or watchdog committee to oversee the process. Maybe the forensic evidence in capital cases should be double-checked by independent agencies. Those are matters for state legislatures to consider. My point was simply that, absent guarantees of fairness and accuracy, it was possible that a particular execution might be deemed cruel—because guilt was obtained by fraud—or unusual—because the sentence was applied disproportionately due to reasons of race or sexual preference."

"Sounds to me like judicial activism of the worst kind," Matera interjected.

Ben reached for the mike, but Roush responded before he had a chance to object. "That is exactly what this is not, ma'am. I specifically said that these are matters for the legislature to consider. The role of the appeals judge would simply be to consider whether the guarantees that lie at the heart of the Constitution are being observed."

"Would those be the guarantees at the heart of the Constitution," Matera asked, "or somewhere in the penumbra?"

"If I may be so bold as to interrupt the distinguished senator from Wyoming," Dawkins said, "I was under the impression that this was my time with the nominee."

"Well, when I hear activist balderdash like that," Matera ranted, "I just can't contain myself."

"You'll have to," Dawkins said. "Because I'm not done."

"Tell us the truth, Judge Roush," Matera said, charging ahead. "You're planning to repeal the death penalty first chance you get, aren't you? That's your secret agenda. One of them, anyway."

Attack dog, Ben reminded himself. Attack dog. "I'm instructing the nominee not to answer."

"Because you're afraid of what he might say?" Matera asked.

"Because you do not have the floor, ma'am."

Matera turned toward Senator Dawkins. "Will the senator from Minnesota yield the floor?"

"I will not," Dawkins replied succinctly.

"Are you planning to filibuster?"

"I am planning to finish taking my turn."

"Well, I've had about all of these touchy-feely-friendly questions I can stand."

"I didn't care much for the questions you asked yesterday, either, madam. But I still managed to keep my mouth shut while you asked them."

"Mr. Chairman," Matera said, "may I pose an interlocutory voir dire examination to clarify this point before Senator Dawkins proceeds with his questioning?"

May she pose a *what*? Ben thought. That wasn't in the copy of Robert's Rules of Order that he read.

"I'll allow it," Senator Keyes replied.

Dawkins appeared outraged, but Matera plowed ahead before he had a chance to say anything.

"Mr. Roush, I—and all of America, I think—would like a straight answer. Are you planning to repeal the death penalty?"

"I'm not planning to do anything," Roush answered, "except consider the cases that come before the Court and rule on them to the best of my ability."

"Can you promise that you will not attempt to repeal the death penalty—a penalty which, I might add, sixty-eight percent of all Americans favor?"

"It would be gross—" He glanced across the room at media-savvy Gina. "—er, wildly inappropriate for me to answer that question."

"I'll take that as a 'no.' "

"You will take it the way it was given," Roush shot back, his voice rising. His eyebrows knitted together. "You are asking me to predict how I would rule on a hypothetical case that is not before me, not before anyone—because it doesn't exist."

"All I'm asking for is a straight answer."

"Mr. Chairman," Ben said, jumping in, "this is not any kind of voir dire examination. This is harassment."

"Oh, the nominee looks like he's doing just fine to me," Keyes said calmly. "But I think it might be time to return the questioning to Senator Dawkins."

"Point of clarification," Matera said, not giving Dawkins a moment to inhale.

"Very well," Chairman Keyes said, with a touch of feigned weariness.

"Judge Roush, is your fanatical opposition to the death penalty based upon your fear that your boyfriend will be the next person who gets it?"

The Caucus Room erupted. Not just the press, but almost everyone in attendance gasped, whispered, cheered, booed, or raced for the door. On a side monitor, Ben could see that the camera was moving in for a close-up of Roush. He was trying to remain calm, but for perhaps the first time in the entire proceeding, he was losing the battle. Sparks of anger seemed to leap from his eye sockets.

"I have been instructed by counsel not to discuss the tragic death that occurred at my home—"

"I don't care what your lawyers said," Matera snapped back. "A woman was found dead in your garden, and it looks like your longtime homosexual lover killed her."

"He did not," Roush replied, clipping off each word.

"How do you know? Were you with him in the garden?"

"I know."

"If he didn't," Matera said, "the only other person who could've done it was you."

"That's not true, there were hundreds of—"

"Listen to me, both of you," Ben said, snatching the microphone away. "You are not supposed to be discussing this. We have been told not only by counsel but by the police—"

"I think the American people have a right to know!" Matera said, pounding the bench. "They have a right to know who we're putting on the Supreme Court. A murderer's accomplice? Or the murderer himself!"

Roush leaped to his feet. Ben tried to pull him back, but it was no use. He had totally lost it. "I have known Ray Eastwick for seven years," Roush shouted. "He is not a murderer."

Matera scoffed. "Love is blind."

"He did not kill that woman!"

Pandemonium ensued. The chairman pounded on his bench, but the uproar was not quelled. Ben tried to object in his most fiery attack-dog manner, but no one was listening. Despite their best precautions, the murder had been dragged into the hearings, dragged into the living room of every American watching. Matera would be criticized tomorrow in the press, but what did she care? She was retiring at the end of this term, and now she would retire the hero of her party and her President. Roush would go down in flames. Haskins would be nominated, and a week later, no one would remember who Roush was. A hard-liner would replace a man with a conscience.

And it was all Ben's fault.

27

Once again, Loving fought traffic on the elevated Whitehurst Freeway, wondering how a nice Oklahoma boy like him had ended up in D.C. Sure, Ben had helped him when he needed it most, and he would do anything for the guy—within reason. This East Coast relocation was really pushing it, though. At least the Potomac was quiet tonight. He'd come from the south, near the Woodrow Wilson Bridge, and the engine noise of the police patrol boats was happily absent. He took the usual crisscross of highways and by-ways to Georgetown, then parked near a rather dilapidated neighborhood. Loving could tell it had once been a thriving commercial center, but apparently the rise of the nearby Georgetown Waterfront Complex had stolen the tourists and the shoppers. He didn't know who might be having a meeting in a neighborhood like this. No one he wanted to meet.

Except for Trudy, of course.

He walked parallel to the waterfront, then took a shortcut

through Francis Scott Key Park. Nice place, especially for a guy whose main accomplishment was writing the lyrics to a song no normal human could sing. Loving tried to pretend the neighborhood wasn't giving him the creeps, but it was, and no degree of self-disciplined self-denial was going to make him forget it. As the environment grew worse and worse, it became harder and harder to believe he was still in the nation's capital. Granted, you only had to travel half a mile from Capitol Hill to be in the slums, but even the slums weren't as bad as this sleazy, dirty, depopulated neighborhood. The street itself seemed to reek; the stink rose from the waterfront, the abandoned buildings, even the pavement. The only people he saw were pimps and prostitutes. He couldn't even retreat to the alleyways, as was his usual wont, because every time he tried he bumped into a drug deal in progress. He couldn't wait to get out of there.

Loving had taken the DocuPen back to the office, and Jones—when Loving could pry him away from the C-SPAN coverage of the hearing long enough—plugged it into a USB port and brought up the calendar pages he had scanned. The listing for that night didn't give any indication of what Nadya was planning to do, but it did give an address, which in the long run was far more valuable. He'd find out what Nadya and her friend Trudy were up to when he got there.

He rounded a corner and saw three white punks huddled around a fire set in a metal trash can. It was not a cold night; he supposed this had been done just for dramatic effect. Didn't take a genius to figure out they were gang members. He kept his eyes focused front and center and hoped he could pass without incident.

"Whatchoo doin' on mah street, bee-otch?" one of the punks sang out.

Loving had to suppress a grin. He loved it when white boys tried to talk black. It was so pathetic.

"Just passin' through," Loving said, with a nod of the head. He didn't stop walking.

"Betchoo I know whatchoo want," another offered. "I'll give ya some," he added, wiggling his ass.

Loving sighed. It would be so pleasurable to stop and beat the living crap out of these kids. But he supposed he'd best stay on task.

Halfway down the street, a bullet whizzed by, just above his head. *Damn!*

Loving ducked and ran. Crouched but still in motion, he made tracks toward the street corner. None of the shops were open; there was no place to duck into for safety. Another gunshot, and even the street punks scrambled. Loving saw a bullet hit the brick wall just beside his head. Judging from the angle of deflection, it was coming from somewhere above him.

Sniper. And him with no place to hide.

This could be a problem.

Loving raced across the street and dove toward a small grocery on the corner, hoping it would be open. It wasn't. He considered breaking in, but he knew that by the time he managed that, even the clumsiest of snipers would have nailed him. He kept running, dodging in one direction, then another, hoping that if he stayed sufficiently serpentine and unpredictable he might last a little bit longer. He had almost made it to the end of the street when he saw a black sedan pull up on the opposite side.

A rear door opened. Pretty Boy appeared.

He was carrying his machine gun.

Someone else was getting out of the back of the car, too, but Loving didn't stop to take notes. He backtracked a few steps and then turned left, hoping to get as far as possible as quickly as possible. As soon as he saw an alleyway, he raced into it. He didn't care who was in there; he needed cover, fast. He flung himself between two sleazy-looking old men who were taking something down, knocking away everything they held in their mutual hands. Might be a trillion dollars of heroin hitting the pavement for all Loving knew, and for all he cared. He had to stay safe. He searched for a trash Dumpster, anything that might shield him. There was nothing. Probably just as well. If he stopped anywhere, Pretty Boy and his new playmate would close in quickly.

He stopped for a moment to catch his breath, wondering if he were still within the sniper's range. Another gunshot rang out, ricocheting off the walls and burning into the pavement not a yard from his foot. Well, that answered that question.

He resumed running, wondering how close the killer really was.

It was entirely possible he was not pinned down to a sniper's nest but mobile, moving from rooftop to rooftop, able to follow Loving almost anywhere. If that were the case, he was a thousand times more dangerous.

Loving wasn't safe in the alley, obviously, so he plunged out the opposite opening and kept running. He started right, but another bullet burned a trail before him. He whipped around and started in the other direction. He'd been lucky so far, given that the sniper had an obvious advantage on him. In fact, he'd been far too lucky. There was only one possible conclusion.

The sniper wasn't trying to kill him. He was trying to herd him. Probably toward Pretty Boy.

Sure enough, at the end of the street, well before he arrived, Loving saw Pretty Boy and his new companion whip around the corner, arms at the ready. The new guy was probably a professional, but Loving could tell he wasn't in Leon's league. They'd fired Leon to punish him for his previous failure, which was mostly Pretty Boy's fault, and now they were suffering for it. This man was older, more haggard, tall and too relaxed for modern-day murder, especially when the target not only knew someone was after him but had some experience at avoiding trouble. Definitely not a Leon; more like Max von Sydow in *Three Days of the Condor*. Who, Loving recalled, never did manage to plug Robert Redford. But Loving supposed he couldn't expect this story to have the same happy ending. This wasn't a movie, and besides, he was much better-looking than Robert Redford.

He had about a third of a second to make a decision. The two hit men were in front of him, the sniper was behind, and the only other thing on the street was a flight of stairs leading to the subway.

Loving hated to do it. He knew that once again going into a crowded place would endanger innocents, especially given Pretty Boy's proven penchant for firing his weapon in public. But there was no alternative.

He hit every other step on his way down the metal stairs, then plunged into the throng. He pushed his way through the crowd and leaped over the turnstile. He didn't have time to pay the fare. He realized that it might get him arrested, but at the moment, that would be a good thing. If he could attract some law enforcement attention, it was just possible the killers might back off. He tore down another flight of steps and moved toward the trains.

A bullet whizzed just in front of his face, this time so close there could be no question in his mind: these people were trying to kill him, no matter who else got hurt. Some of the people around Loving realized what had happened and ducked or screamed, but the station was so crowded and so noisy most people didn't notice at all.

Where were they?

When he looked up, Loving got his answer—one he didn't like at all. Pretty Boy and Max were perched on the upper level. They'd found an overlook, a balcony of sorts, and it gave them a perfect view of everything below. There was no way he could escape them, especially if Pretty Boy opened up his automatic weapon on the crowd. It wasn't nearly packed enough for Loving to get lost in the melee. And there was no telling how many people might die if serious gunplay ensued.

He didn't have time to deliberate at length. He just went for what seemed like the smart thing at the time. Loving cupped his hands to his lips and bellowed: "Look out! Sniper!"

As if in answer, another shot rang out, and the crowd went crazy. Everyone was screaming at once, moving a dozen different directions, colliding and fighting with one another. Despite all the movement, no one was getting anywhere. It was a frenzied crowd. Men, women, and children panicked. Loving felt bad about creating terror in these terror-filled times, but his actions had the desired effect. Now there was far too much activity for the assassins to get a clear shot. Pretty Boy might not care if he hit a stray bystander or two, but apparently he drew the line at wholesale slaughter.

Good. Keeping a crowd packed tightly around him, Loving managed to slide down the passageway until he was out of sight of the balcony. He ran up another flight of stairs, but instead of crossing to the trains moving in the opposite direction, he kept going to the street level.

Loving emerged gasping, desperate for air. He looked both ways down the street, then above to the rooftops. As far as he could tell, he'd lost the assassins. But how could he be sure? And what if he was still within the snipers' range?

He leaned against the wall, trying to slow his heart, trying to get a grip on himself, wiping the sweat from his brow. Twice now he'd managed to escape what looked like certain death. How long could he realistically expect to keep this up? He had to find out what was going on, and not just for Thaddeus Roush's sake—for his own sake as well.

Loving limped to the corner until he could read the street sign by the poor illumination provided by a nearby lamp.

He had to laugh. Maybe it was just the emotional release that follows periods of great anxiety, or a final kick of adrenaline, but he found himself laughing and crying all at once, so hard his sides shook.

He'd ended up exactly where he'd been planning to go in the first place. Even the right city block.

He'd have to remember to send Pretty Boy and Max a thank-you note for helping him find his destination. He was usually so poor with directions.

And then a thought hit him, one that sent shivers right up his spine.

Was it possible the killers already knew where he was going? Is that why they were able to have a sniper in place before he got there?

Loving raced down the remainder of the street, even though his side and his sore leg ached, until he found the number he wanted. He ran up the short porch steps and down the hall to a door and peered through the window at what appeared to be the backstage of a small auditorium. What kind of criminal operation took place here? he wondered. Drugs? Is that what this case was about? Is that why someone was so determined to kill him—to protect his stash? Maybe the place had been converted into a bordello. Maybe some kind of gambling ring. A gangland hideout.

There was no way for Loving to know. The only thing of which he was certain was that he was better off inside than out, so he stepped into the dark auditorium.

He took a cautious step forward, trying to make as little noise as possible. He could hear someone on the stage talking. As he approached, he realized that there was not only someone on the stage, but several rows of people sitting in the audience.

What was this? An underworld crime boss meeting? A perverted sex show? What kind of den of iniquity had he stumbled onto this time?

He took a tiny step closer—and that was when the man on the stage spotted him.

"Ah—here he is!" he said, gesturing offstage toward Loving. The audience burst into applause. "And what kind of poem will you be reading, sir?"

28

Thaddeus Roush waited until he heard the click that told him the door had opened.

"Ray?"

No answer. He set down his gin and tonic and made his way toward the front door.

"Ray." He held out his arms, but his partner did not accept the embrace. The only thing he gave Roush was a long look. Then he turned away and directed his attention to the winding staircase.

"Ray, how long is this going to continue? You can't sulk forever."

Roush could almost see the short hairs on the back of his lover's neck stand at attention. "Sulking? *Sulking*? Do you know what I've been doing all day while you've been the center of attention on national television, playing mind games with senators? I've been in a crappy little hellhole of an interrogation room surrounded by six detectives accusing me of all manner of crimes, while my lawyer sits there instructing me not to answer, and the chief of police threatens to have me thrown in jail. I'm lucky I got to come home tonight! Eventually they're going to get sick of this tap dance and lock me up. Probably would have done it already if it weren't for those hearings of yours. So excuse me for *sulking*."

Roush stood at the foot of the stairs clinging to the newel post. "You can't blame me for this, Ray. I had nothing to do with that woman's death."

"I wish to God you did. Until the police figure something out, I'm their best suspect."

"That's absurd. You wouldn't hurt a flea."

"I know," Eastwick said, eyes like daggers. "You're the one with the dangerous past. Maybe I should tell them that."

"Ray . . ."

"You'd think they might dig it up on their own, but I guess not. If the FBI didn't get it, what are the chances that these clods will?"

"Ray, please." Roush held out his arms, his eyes welling. "Come here."

"No. I don't want anything to do with you."

"I need you."

"Do you? Do you really? Apparently you don't need me enough to consult with me before you throw our lives out in the open."

"You knew I was talking to the President."

"I didn't know you were planning to out me! On national television! One day you say you're going to meet the President. The next day I'm on the cover of *People*!"

Roush looked at him helplessly. "Ray . . . I didn't know myself. I didn't plan it. I just— When I got up there, behind the podium with the big bright presidential seal, and I saw the cameras, I thought— my face is going to be all over America. I don't want that to be the face of a liar."

"So you just did it. Without so much as a thought to how it might affect other people. Like me!"

"I'm sorry. I was as surprised as anyone."

"Really? Were you as surprised as . . . say, my mother? Who had invited her whole Baptist book club over to see me at the White House? How do you think she felt when all of a sudden her friends realized I wasn't standing behind you because I was your research aide? How do you think that made my seventy-six-year-old mother feel?"

"Ray . . . I can only say I'm sorry so many times."

Eastwick marched down the stairs, then stopped and turned back, as if he were torn between wanting to give Roush another piece of his mind and not wanting to come anywhere near him. "Next thing I know, I have people calling me wanting to know all the intimate details of my lurid homosexual relationship with the great almighty judge. I'm tabloid fodder."

"We always knew we might be exposed one day."

"Yeah, but I didn't think my lover would be the one to do it! I didn't think he'd do it without telling me!"

"Ray—"

"I'm still reeling from that, from the calls, the snickers, the gasps, my mother, and the next day, you're entertaining guests! In my house! My garden!"

"I had no choice."

"Don't you dare try to tell me that! That's a cop-out and we both know it. You had a choice and you chose. You chose to hang me out to dry!"

"I would never do that, Ray. I love you. You know—"

"Don't start! Don't start with that!" His fists clenched till they were white. "You don't have the right. Not after what you've done. Not after what you've subjected me to."

"Ray—I would never intentionally hurt you."

"You already have!" His voice cracked. He took a deep breath, got himself back under control. "And you know what hurts the most, the very most? All this time I've had to deal with police officers and detectives and everything else—where were you? Nowhere near me, that's for damn sure. You were off playing big-time Supreme Court nominee."

"We tried to get the hearing delayed. The Republicans refused."

"You could've withdrawn."

"I—I—"

Eastwick folded his arms across his chest defiantly. "Am I wrong? Was there some cosmic force that prevented you from walking out?"

A long silence ensued. Finally, Roush said, "I didn't want to."

"Now at last you're being honest. You didn't want to. You didn't want to give up anything for me. Being on the Supreme Court was more important to you than me!"

Roush held up his hands helplessly. "I . . . wanted both."

"Well, you screwed that up, didn't you, buddy? 'Cause you've lost me. You've lost me forever. And the odds of you getting on the Supreme Court aren't looking great, either."

"I understand that you're mad now. But you'll get over it. You'll—"

"I will never get over this." He paused, catching his breath. "You haven't even left a seat open for me at the hearings."

Roush's head slowly fell. "My advisors didn't think it would be a good idea. They thought it would be a negative reminder."

"Reminder of what? That you like to sleep with men? Would that not play so well with Middle America?"

"It would be a reminder that my lover is a murder suspect." Roush looked at him sadly. "That's all it ever was. The opposition has already tried to use the murder controversy against me. And they will again. But maybe after you're cleared—"

"Yeah, maybe after I'm cleared. Maybe after I'm cleared and after I've had a sex change operation!"

"Ray, you're not being fair."

"Why should I be fair? Who says I have to be fair? I have to be angry! I have a right to be angry!"

"Ray . . . please." This time, Roush didn't wait for permission. He moved swiftly up the stairs, his arms outstretched, but Eastwick turned away long before he got there. A moment later, he heard the bedroom door slam closed.

Roush collapsed on a sofa, his head in his hands. He was destroying his life, the love of his life, seven years together. And for what? A seat on the Supreme Court he didn't have a ghost of a chance of getting. Nobody wanted him anymore, not even the President who'd nominated him.

But he couldn't give up now—could he? With so much at stake, both personally and beyond. He was the first-ever openly gay American nominated to the Supreme Court. He stood for something. If he went down, he had to go down fighting. He couldn't afford to appear the "pansy." That would be giving them what they wanted, playing to the stereotype. Besides, there was a lot of good he could do on that court. He was still young. He might be on the bench for thirty, forty years. He could change the course of the nation.

He would lose Ray.

And there was still a chance that his other secret would be revealed.

Was there a chance that Ray would tell, if they questioned him hard enough? That he might crack under the strain? Or worse—do it for vengeance? He seemed mad enough, just now, on the stairs. He seemed mad enough to do anything.

No. Roush refused to believe it possible. Ray was angry, sure. Maybe their relationship had come to an end. But he couldn't believe Ray would betray him. Not like that. If word got out, it would have to come from someone else. And if it did . . .

He would deal with that when the time came. If he had to. Right now, it looked as if they wouldn't need that to bury him anyway.

What did it say in the Gospel of Matthew? *For what is a man profited, if he shall gain the whole world, and lose his own soul?* Worse yet to lose the world, and also lose the man who had been his soul mate for the best years of his life.

What should he do?

That night, before he attempted unsuccessfully to sleep, he prayed for guidance. But in the morning, as he prepared for another grueling day before the Inquisition, no guidance had come.

29

*L*oving swallowed hard. "P-p-poem?"

"Yes, of course," the moderator said. He was wearing a collarless cambric shirt, a beltless pair of khakis, and loafers without socks. "You're next, aren't you? Why else would you be backstage?"

In the rear, on the other side of the stage, Loving saw two burly men in tank tops take a tentative step forward. He made them for bouncers—poetry bouncers?—just from the way they swaggered while they stood still. He knew he could take them, but that wouldn't get him any closer to Trudy. After he'd practically gotten himself killed getting here, he wasn't going to give up so easily.

"So . . . the cover charge to get in is . . . I gotta recite a poem?"

The moderator looked only mildly puzzled; his brow line soon gave way to a smile. "This is part of your persona, isn't it? The Accidental Poet. I get it. Not bad. I think you can make it work. You don't really look much like a poet."

Loving considered: he was wearing jeans with a hole in each

knee, a sweat-soaked white T-shirt, and a buzz cut. Didn't look like a poet? The moderator was a master of understatement.

"You're in the Independent division, right?" the moderator continued.

"I . . . suppose?"

"Thought so. I would've recognized you if you'd come from one of the 'burb teams. And you definitely don't seem like the Georgetown type." Out in the auditorium, they both heard the roar of the crowd intensifying. "Look, I've got to get this show rolling again. What's your name?"

"Uhh . . . Loving."

The moderator grinned broadly. "Loving. Oh, that's just so . . . so . . . perfect. How did you ever come up with it?" He placed his cheek against Loving's and whispered, "I think the judges are going to go for you in a big way."

Loving watched as the slight man walked back onstage to thunderous applause and foot stomping.

Judges?

"Ladies and gentlemen," the moderator said. The microphone squeaked with reverb at the sudden increase in volume. Everyone squealed and covered their ears until the pain subsided. "I'm pleased to introduce the next entry in the D.C. division qualifier for the National Poetry Slam. In the division for independent nonoriginal poetry interp, I give you—Loving!"

He extended his arm, cuing Loving to enter.

Here goes nothing.

Loving shambled onto the stage. The lights were so bright he could barely see faces past the second row. After that, it was all shadows—but so many shadows! It was a large auditorium, packed to the brim. He wasn't sure there'd been this many people in the audience the last time he saw John Prine in concert. And all these people came to hear poetry?

The moderator stepped away from the microphone and Loving took his place. His mouth went dry. All those eyes were staring at him, expecting him to say something. What? He didn't know anything about poetry—he'd never even finished high school. Ben's friend Mike was always spouting off little bits of poetry, which Loving found keenly annoying. He never understood a word of it.

Another amplified voice emerged from the gallery. "You must begin within thirty seconds or you will be disqualified."

And booted out the back door? Far away from Trudy? He tried to speak, but no words came. Earlier he'd been facing two thugs and a sniper, but he'd managed to keep his head together. Now he was being taken apart by a bunch of poetry freaks.

"Ten seconds remaining."

His jaw worked like rusty hinges on a graveyard gate. "I—I—I—"

"Please speak up!" the same voice commanded. "Five seconds remaining."

Loving cleared his throat. "I—I never saw . . . a purple cow . . ."

He paused, catching his breath. He could see the heads in the audience turning, looking blankly from one to another.

"And . . . And I never hope to see one."

In the front row, on the faces of the three people with pencils and clipboards who he now realized must be judges, he saw eyes narrowing. One of them smiled a little. From the rear of the theater, someone laughed out loud.

"But I can tell you anyhow . . ."

More laughter. The judges leaned back, one pondering, one scrutinizing, one drumming the eraser of her pencil.

Loving took a deep breath and finished. "I'd rather see than be one!"

The laughter intensified till it filled the auditorium. Loving wasn't sure what they were laughing at—the poem wasn't that funny—but the merriment only intensified. The female judge grinned, as if resigning to it against her will, then finally broke out in full-fledged laughter. The other two judges followed. Thunderous applause burst out. Loving bowed solemnly, and the room was filled with cheers.

Oookay, he thought—what do I do now? He started back the way he came, but the moderator raced onstage and took his arm, restraining him.

"Just a minute, Loving. This is a poetry slam, not a reading. Now we have to hear what the judges think of your performance. Terrence?"

The man sitting at the far left of the judges' table, the youngest of the three, removed his reading glasses and laid them on the table. "Well, I must admit—he had me going at first. I mean the whole package—the trailer trash outfit, the redneck haircut, the feigned awkwardness. I knew he was shamming, but he did it so well, I just couldn't be sure. And then he added the stuttered delivery of quite possibly the most trite bit of doggerel ever written—well, it was perfect. It exceeded the parameters of a poetry slam. It was more like performance art."

The female judge on the other end concurred. "I thought it was brilliant, too, Terrence. But did you hear the way he recited the poem? The way he manipulated the presentation of the syllables? It reminded me of nothing so much as Borges—do you know the story 'Pierre Menard, Author of the *Quixote*?' The fictional critic and autodiagenetic narrator considers an author who has copied Cervantes's work, and because it comes from a new source, it takes on new meaning, new irony. I believe that's what Loving was doing with Burgess's 'Purple Cow.' "

The man in the middle, an older gentleman in a herringbone jacket, jumped in. "Speaking as the only academic on the panel, I also wish to add my appreciation of Loving's deceptively simple performance. What he has done is take an undistinguished bit of verse and give it a parodic deconstructionist modernist interpretation. It is exactly what the French theorist Barthes did in *S/Z*—taking a simple sentimental story by Balzac and by applying a reductionist reading showed that literary depth can be plumbed from all forms of literature. He has made 'The Purple Cow' not a readerly, but a writerly text."

Another round of applause spread through the auditorium, and soon thereafter, Loving heard a throng of people screaming wildly and chanting, "Ten! Ten! Ten!" He had no idea what they were talking about, but then, he hadn't really understood anything that had been said for the last several minutes. The moderator returned, took him by the arm, and escorted him offstage.

"Fantastic job, Loving. Just fantastic. I love your creative spirit. How long have you been in the arts?"

"Umm . . . prob'ly not as long as you might think."

"Well, it doesn't matter. I just have to ask." He turned and laid his hand on Loving's chest. "Would you be willing to play on my team?"

Loving picked up his hand with two fingers and removed it from his chest. "Look, pal, I—I don't play for . . . for the other team. Or both teams. Or . . . anythin' like that."

"Are you sure? Middleton needs a fourth, now that Rufus has dropped out. Nationals is only a month away."

"Nationals." Loving's head was beginning to throb. "Look—can I think about it awhile?"

"Sure. I'll escort you to the waiting area. There are a few more contestants reciting before the judges make their decisions."

"Uh—could you by any chance seat me next to . . . Trudy?"

"Trudy?" A huge smile spread across the moderator's face. "So that's what you meant when you said you didn't play for my team?"

The most intelligent thing Loving could think of to say was, "Huh?"

"Please don't think I'm criticizing. Different strokes, right? Live and let live."

They stepped down a side staircase into the audience gallery. Up on the stage, a plump woman with spiky hedgehog hair was reciting: "Man did not give me language. Man cannot take it away from me. I have a voice and I will not be silenced . . ."

Loving took a vacant seat on the end of a row and wondered what to do next. While he contemplated his options, a woman in her midforties wearing a bridal gown scooted down two seats and sat beside him.

He nodded. "Evenin', ma'am."

She returned the nod. "Back to you. Everyone treating you right?"

"Well . . ."

"Thought not. These people are so obsessed about the Nationals, they've lost all perspective."

There was that word again. "Nationals?"

"The National Poetry Slam. In D.C. next month. Biggest one ever. Teams from thirty-two states will be participating. Huge crowds are expected. Big prize money."

"Big prize money?"

"Well, two thousand dollars. But in the poetry world, that's Bill Gates money."

"Bill Gates? He's really—" Loving decided not to digress. "What exactly is a . . . poetry slam?"

Her eyes narrowed. "Still playing with me, or are you really that naïve?" She adjusted the bodice of her gown. "Think of it as the Olympics of poetry. The Vatican of Verse."

"It's a competition?"

"Correct. A panel of judges—sometimes pros, sometimes selected from the audience—pick the winners."

"How can you decide whether one poem is better than another?"

"I know, it's so subjective, but they do it every week. It's crazy, but it's a last-ditch effort to keep poetry from dying out altogether. The whole thing was invented by this guy in Chicago, Marc Smith— a former construction worker, of all things. Then it took off—all across the nation, people trying to revitalize the poetry world, bring it to new audiences, rescue it from the pit of obscurity where academia left it, all so remote and inelegant that no one wanted to read it anymore. Poetry slams are about poetry from the people, not the eggheads. Sure, we bring in an egghead every now and again, just to give the thing some legitimacy, but this is a populist movement. It's not about professors. It's about people like you."

Loving glanced at her intricate white lace gown. "I like your outfit."

"This is a costume. It's meant to bring home what I'm going to say about the tyranny of the patriarchal system, the whole antiquated notion of marriage, which they call a sacrament but is really more like an extended date rape. It's about women taking control of their own bodies. You know what I mean? I don't care about being someone's possession. His sex slave. Hausfrau. I want to find my social consciousness."

"Where did you lose it?" Loving asked, blank-faced.

She stared at him for a second, then smiled. "You're really good, you know it? For a moment, I almost took you seriously. Would you be interested in joining my team?"

Loving hadn't been this popular since grade-school dodgeball. "Are you with Middleton?"

"God, no. Like Michael? I hate those queer banana Emily Dickinson knockoffs. I'm with Waverly. We're more in the Walt Whitman school. We go head-to-head with Middleton next week. It'll be an American poet smackdown. And then the week after that—Head-to-Head Haiku."

"Haiku?"

"I got a surefire winner. Wanna hear it?" She closed her eyes before he made his apparently irrelevant response, then began: "But just because you/Put your tongue inside my ear/Don't mean we're betrothed." She opened her eyes. "Pretty good, huh? Smacks you right in the groin."

"It does. It really does."

"Last time we competed with Middleton, we tied after the first round. Then I served up a little inner wisdom and Middleton's leader, Michael, the moderator tonight, did his usual loss-of-childhood-innocence riff. So trite. After round two and my piece on my sister's death—very spiritual—we pulled ahead by .03 points. But then Malcolm—their token black member—did this racism thing that sounded as if it were written in the beatnik era. They ended up winning by a paltry .01 points. I was so disgusted. I'm dying for a rematch. And I think you might be just what we need."

"Well . . . let me give it some thought. By the way, I've been looking for someone who I think was planning to come here tonight—name of Trudy. You know her?"

The bride's eyes widened. "You're with Trudy?"

"Well, I'm not exactly—"

"I never would've guessed. I guess that tough-guy exterior really is a costume, isn't it?"

"What is it about this woman? Every time I tell someone I'm lookin' for her, they practically bust a gut. Do you dislike her?"

"No, I adore Trudy. Tried to get her on my team once, years back. I just didn't think you were . . . you know. The type." She giggled. "I'm sorry. That's rude."

Loving was long past trying to understand. "If you could just help me find her—"

"I'm afraid I have no idea."

"If you could give me a detailed description, maybe? I saw her once, but not for long."

"She's gorgeous. Big wide eyes, blue as the ocean surrounding a Caribbean island. Strong. And long hair—you can't miss that. Brunette hair almost to the waist."

That filled out his earlier glance of her reflection nicely. Shouldn't be too hard to spot. At least it gave him a chance. " 'Preciate that."

"Give some thought to my offer."

"I will."

"And good luck. You're sure to qualify for the finals. What piece are you going to recite then?"

"You mean I have to know another poem?"

"Of course. You can't milk the same performance piece all night long. You must've prepared something else, right? I don't think you can get by with the 'burly-redneck-who doesn't understand-poetry' thing again. I mean, it had a nice, sort of Andy Kaufman quality the first time around—like a nail-hard comic not afraid to take a joke too far. But to try it a second time—that really would be taking the joke too far."

"Thanks for the tip. And if you see Trudy, please let me know."

Loving glanced up at the stage, eyes wide, hands already beginning to tremble. There must be hundreds of people in this auditorium. And if he didn't find Trudy fast, he was going to have to come up with a parodic deconstructionist modernist interpretation for "Twinkle, Twinkle, Little Star."

Loving searched the entire auditorium, gallery, backstage, balcony, even behind the concession stand; but he never managed to locate anyone who remotely matched Trudy's description, or anyone who knew where Trudy was. He systematically inspected the entire building, all while trying not to disturb the shouting, crying, wailing, pontificating, and various other modes of performance emanating from the stage. Stealth was for other private eyes; Loving much preferred the in-your-face, tell-me-what-I-want-to-know approach. Perhaps it lacked subtlety, but it worked for him. At least, normally it did.

After about an hour of searching, he decided to call it quits. She just wasn't there. He hated to abandon the search—he had no other leads—but this was getting him nowhere. He was wasting his time, and worse, if he hung around much longer, he would be forced to take the stage again. That was to be avoided at all costs.

He decided to leave the same way he had come, by the backstage exit. No one seemed to mind him being there; they probably thought he was preparing for another performance. He slipped out and soon found himself back on the street. He wasn't greeted by another round of gunfire, either from behind or above, and that was a considerable relief. Apparently the bad guys had gone home, at least for now. He cut through a nearby alleyway and headed for his van.

The blow came so swiftly he barely saw it, had no time to duck. Something hard and metal smashed into the back of his skull. Loving fell to his knees, fighting unconsciousness. He held up his hands, trying to block the next blow. Damned if it wasn't a brick.

He wrestled with the strong arm holding it, fighting to get free. In the dark shadows, he couldn't make out the face of his assailant. Max? Pretty Boy? He didn't think it was either, judging by the silhouette. Maybe the sniper had climbed down from his nest. No telling. At the moment, he had to focus on making sure that brick didn't make contact again with his head.

A sudden swift kick to the groin took the fight out of him but fast. Where had that come from? he wondered, as he felt the strength ooze from his arms. The shoe felt . . . pointed. As his attacker moved in for the next blow, he spotted the shadowy trace of hair, very long hair, so long the bearer could almost sit on it. Loving tried to grab a handful of it, but he wasn't nearly fast enough. The brick came down again, this time making contact with the base of his skull.

He fell to the wet, slimy concrete pavement, his head swimming. The pain was immense. He tried to summon some strength somewhere in his body, preferably his feet, but it did not come. Before he could do anything to defend himself, the brick came barreling downward once again, the blackness enveloped him, and he was gone.

30

Ben entered the Senate Caucus Room with an almost unreasonable sense of optimism about what was yet to come. Despite the unmitigated disaster of the last session, he hoped this one would be a pleasant change of pace. The gauntlet of interrogations was over, all eighteen of them; now they called witnesses who had testimony that might be of use to the Senate Committee in the course of its deliberations. The friendly witnesses would be first—co-workers, friends, character witnesses, anyone Ben or Sexton could drum up to say a few nice words in support of Thaddeus Roush. Of course, each would be interrogated not only by the senator who called them but also by any other senator who wished to do so, with no set time limit other than those that might be imposed at the whim of the chairman. In effect, it would be cross-examination, though they didn't call it that. But there was no reason to believe that would lead to any trouble. No one was being called who was remotely controversial.

After all the friendly witnesses testified, the opposition had the right to call anyone whose testimony might be of use, but so far they had given no indication that they would. Despite the widespread opposition to Roush's nomination, no one seemed to have unearthed anything negative about him. They couldn't hang him on his sexual preference. The police had been unable to link the murder to Roush or Eastwick. Besides, the whole procedure—calling witnesses, examining them, cross-examining them—was much closer to what Ben was accustomed to dealing with in the courtroom, and as a result, he hoped he might be somewhat more helpful than he had been so far.

The first witness sworn was a woman named Amelia Haspiel, a judge from the D.C. Circuit who had served on the bench with Roush for the previous eight years. She spoke in glowing terms about his dedication to his work, his fidelity to the law, his relentless work ethic. She called him a driven professional, but also made the point that he was genial and agreeable to work with, not obsessive or insulting, despite his obvious great intelligence.

"I don't know that I've ever had a co-worker whose company I've enjoyed more. Or in whom I had greater confidence."

"But you're a peer. A co-equal Circuit Court justice," Senator Dawkins said. "Do you think the same would be true of those who work under him?"

"I know it would," Haspiel said without hesitation. "I've heard Tad's secretary comment more than once that he was the best boss she ever had. And I know that whenever a clerkship in his chambers came available, there were always more applicants than Tad could begin to fill. He was popular with everyone."

"Did you ever hear anyone say anything negative about Judge Roush?"

"Never. Not once in eight years. That includes remarks from lawyers who appeared before him, some of whom, of course, lost. Didn't matter. Even when lawyers or fellow jurists disagreed with him, they always respected his opinion. He's a man of integrity. I wish our courts had more judges like him."

Can't get much better than that, Ben thought, watching from the sidelines. And the best part of it was, neither he nor Tad had to do a thing. They could just sit back and watch.

Senator Potter, R-Ore., took the mike for what Ben knew amounted to cross-examination. He was a potential threat, someone whose devotion to Keyes would never waver. Didn't matter. As long as it wasn't Matera, Ben wouldn't worry about it.

After about ten minutes of hemming and hawing, Potter finally got to what he had obviously wanted to talk about all along. "Judge Haspiel, did you think at any time that Judge Roush's . . . sexual preference interfered with the performance of his judicial duties?"

Ben frowned. What could the purpose of this question be? Surely Potter didn't expect a positive response. Was it just a bit of thinly disguised mudslinging, a chance to remind Middle America that Roush was gay?

"No, sir, there was not. But of course, none of us knew he was gay."

"Ah. He kept that secret even from the other members of his court."

Haspiel barely blinked. "Senator, he did not keep it secret. He just didn't talk about it."

"And none of you ever had the slightest suspicion?"

She paused. "How do you define suspicion?"

"Did you know or did you not know?"

"Sir, anytime you have an attractive man of Tad's age who is not married and has never been married, there are always going to be people who suspect he is gay. So what? I don't listen to that kind of gossip. And I'm sure you don't, either."

"Do you think there was perhaps . . . a tendency to go easier on him because he was believed to be a member of a minority group?"

Haspiel stared at him incomprehensibly. "Like someone might cut him slack because he's gay? Not in this world."

"I just wondered if it was ever a disruptive factor."

"Sir, it wasn't any kind of factor. We didn't know. We didn't care!"

"So you think it doesn't make any difference?"

Her head tilted. "I don't see—"

"Judge . . . do you consider yourself a Christian woman?"

"Wait a minute," Ben said, rising from his chair, careful not to use the word "objection." "This is inappropriate."

Senator Potter appeared taken aback. "I am not embarrassed to say that I am a man of faith."

Ben stared at Chairman Keyes. "Don't let the hearing degenerate into this, Mister Chairman. Show some spine."

Keyes drew himself up. "I do tend to think that questions about religion are not necessary to this hearing, although I'm sure the senator from Oregon, being a devout man of faith who observes all the Biblical injunctions, New Testament and Old, is genuine in his concern—as are many of us—regarding a nominee who stands in flagrant disavowal of the articles of faith."

"And that goes for my constituents as well," Potter added. "They've read the Book of Leviticus."

"Have they read the First Amendment?" Ben asked. "Specifically, the part about freedom of worship? The separation between church and state?"

Ben managed to shut down the questioning, at least for the present, but Potter had made his point for whatever it was worth. A long succession of friendly witnesses ensued, running late into the day. Ben wasn't sure any of them were doing Roush much good—certainly they weren't going to change the minds of the diehards on the committee—but at least they did serve the fundamental purpose of making the proceedings far more boring than they had been before. In his mind's eye, Ben could see hands all across America reaching for their remotes. By the end of the day he imagined more adults were watching *Teletubbies* than this confirmation hearing. There wasn't enough of interest happening to fill a sound bite.

Until Jennifer Tierney took the stand.

She was a perfect character witness, or so they thought, because she had known Roush for decades. They had met in law school and remained friends. She had vacationed with him, worked with him, been with him through fun times and hard times. And she had nothing but the most complimentary praise for him. He remained calm in the face of adversity, but he was strong when strength was required. He loved children, played with her two daughters for hours at a time. He was generous but frugal. Ben was waiting for trustworthy, brave, and reverent, but before they got to that point, the chairman yielded the floor to the senator from Idaho.

Senator Northrop was technically a Democrat, but she was so

conservative and had such a right-wing constituency that she usually voted with the Republicans and was expected to do so at the conclusion of this committee hearing. This not only reduced the number of votes upon which Roush could count—already in the minority—but also raised the even more difficult issue of who Hammond and the others backing Roush could trust.

"You've been out with Judge Roush on a number of social occasions?"

"Yes, of course. We live barely a block from each other in Montgomery County."

"And you work in similar arenas?"

"Well, I'm on the state court of criminal appeals, but . . . yes. We get invited to the same parties."

"And were you invited to the gathering at Judge Roush's house the day after his nomination? When he gave the tragedy-tinged press conference?"

Meaning: when the corpse was discovered in his garden. Ben started to rise, then stopped himself. He didn't have quite enough yet.

"Yes, I was."

"Did you see what happened?"

"I saw what everyone else saw."

"Were you surprised?"

"When a woman was discovered dead in the garden? Who wasn't surprised?"

"Of course." Senator Northrop pressed her long fingernails against the base of her microphone. "I don't want to ask you about the murder, ma'am. I know some feel that would be irrelevant to the present proceeding, and I'm sure Mr. Kincaid would protest and none of us would get out of here before the Beltway was packed bumper to bumper." Like any professional comedian, she paused for the ensuing laughter. "But I wonder if you noticed where Judge Roush was before the press conference began."

Tierney paused, obviously surprised by the question. "No. I don't really recall."

"You didn't see him?"

"I saw him when I entered the home."

"And that was . . . ?"

"Perhaps forty-five minutes before the press conference. He was very busy taking meetings with people."

"You know that for a fact?"

"Well, I know that's what I was told."

"That seems to be what everyone was told. But I've yet to find anyone who actually saw Judge Roush in the minutes immediately prior to the press conference. And the police are having the same problem." Ben remained silent but rose to his feet, something he knew Northrop would see out of the corner of her eye. "But let me change the subject. You've told us you didn't see Judge Roush. Did you see his . . ." She coughed slightly. ". . . lover, Mr. Eastwick? Do you know where he was or what he was doing?"

"No. I never saw him at all. Not until the press conference, when he was discovered with—"

"Just a minute," Ben said. "This is improper questioning. It has nothing to do with the nominee's qualifications for the Supreme Court position."

Chairman Keyes looked at Ben with a blank expression. "Are you interposing a point of order?"

"You can call it a point of anything you like. This is wrong."

"And what exactly is it you find so wrong?"

Ben knew how this game was played; he'd seen it done a million times in the courtroom. Keyes wanted him to make a great fuss about discussing the murder—with the unavoidable result that the jury would be left with the impression that Roush was hiding something. Here, the jury was an American viewing audience of several million people. And the tens of millions more who would read about it tomorrow morning or see the clips on the evening news.

"I object to turning this hearing into a murder trial. The police are investigating the murder. We're here to appoint the next Supreme Court justice."

"Well, to consider an appointment, at any rate."

"So leave police matters alone."

"Mr. Kincaid," Senator Keyes said slowly, his Texas drawl coming to the forefront, "are you not aware that the Constitution expressly grants Congress certain police powers to investigate matters of national interest?"

"This isn't the payola scandal, Senator. This is a slimy back-door attempt to impugn the reputation of a distinguished jurist by making constant references to an unexplained death."

The senator smiled benignly. "If you would allow us to ask our questions without interruption, perhaps the death would cease to be unexplained."

Ben resisted the temptation to roll his eyes. "I will not permit any more questions relating to that young woman's death."

Senator Potter grabbed his mike, showing a rare bit of spine. "What is it you're afraid of, Mr. Kincaid?"

"I'm afraid of seeing the highest governing body of the nation demeaned by partisan mudslinging. We're all aware that there are people both pro and con to this nomination, as there are with every nomination. That doesn't mean we have to sink to this level."

"We can't ignore reality, son," Keyes said.

"Evidently you can. We expressly asked for a continuance of this matter pending the police investigation and you refused."

"Well . . ."

"So we have no choice but to ignore the crime for now and let the police investigate. If they come up with something that relates to Judge Roush, we'll deal with it at that time. Until then, this is just cheap, petty character assassination—worse, implying guilt by association. And frankly, sir, I'd like to think you're better than that. I'd like to think we all are."

Ben resumed his seat. If he had hoped for a round of applause, he was disappointed.

"Well," Keyes said, "perhaps these matters are best left alone for now. I feel certain there are many other topics we could be discussing. I'll call the next witness."

O frabjous day! As impotent as Ben had felt throughout this entire proceeding, apparently his little fuss had been sufficient that Keyes, weighing the benefits of continued trash talk against the detriment of appearing to be engaging in trash talk, decided to let it go. Sexton would be pleased—Ben had been tough, sort of, and it appeared to have accomplished their goal. At least in the short term.

Two things about the exchange still bothered Ben, though. First, he knew that Keyes would never have given up, not under any circumstance, unless he thought he had something better waiting in the wings.

And the second concern was: Throughout the ordeal, Senator Matera had remained silent. Their top attack dog had played no role whatsoever. That made no sense.

Unless they were saving her for the something better that was waiting in the wings.

31

oving awoke to mixed sensations: his head felt like a rock—
but a rock resting on a pillow. Not that the pillow made it
throb any less. But it suggested an unusual degree of TLC from a
mysterious back-alley brick attacker.

"Is Sleeping Beauty awake at last?" a soft, high-pitched voice
asked.

Loving turned his head in the direction from which it came, but
the movement hurt so much he decided it wasn't worth the effort.
By this time he had realized that his feet were cuffed to the posts of
the bed on which he lay. The knowledge that he wasn't going anywhere, combined with the knowledge that his head ached every time
he moved it, left him with seriously diminished curiosity.

"Long as you've been out, you'd think I hit you with my baseball bat."

Loving wondered if it really could have made much difference.
The feminine voice was very appealing, friendly, with a trace of a

Southern lilt. He would probably find it sexy if the possessor hadn't recently beaten him into unconsciousness.

"Where am I?"

"In my room." And a pretty shabby room, from what little Loving could see of it. Flimsy furniture, tacky wallpaper. Some kind of flophouse. Not even Motel 6 quality. "It's not far from the poetry slam."

"Why did you—"

He felt a fist suddenly grab the collar of his T-shirt and twist it around his throat. "Why were you looking for me?"

This time, he didn't have to crane his neck. Trudy was hovering over him, just as she had been described. Long brunette hair, muscular figure, strong arms, which combined with the element of surprise had very much worked against him in the alleyway.

"You heard me, stalker boy. I want to know why you were looking for me."

"I—" His first attempt to speak was not successful. His throat was filled with some filmy residue of unconsciousness, and his tongue was thick and unresponsive. "I was followin' a lead."

"Well now, isn't that what they all say." She had a way of looking at him that was positively . . . alluring. Loving didn't usually go in for the bondage scene, and he didn't think he'd been captive long enough to fall victim to the Stockholm syndrome, but there was something about this Trudy that was working for him in a big way.

Which only made it all the more difficult to talk. "I—I'm working for a man who's working with Thaddeus Roush, that guy who's up for the Supreme Court."

"I know who Roush is. Don't treat me as if I'm stupid just because I'm pretty."

"Wouldn't dream of it."

"So what's Roush got to do with me?"

"I think you know somethin' about the woman who was killed at his press conference."

"Do tell. And what makes you think that?"

"Got a tip from a man who tried to kill me."

"And you considered that reliable?"

He shrugged. "Frankly, it was all I had to go on. Do you own a red Ford SUV?"

Her neck stiffened. "What if I do?"

He nodded. "Figured you did. Your car was spotted in the rear of the Roush garden that day. Ford SUV, '01 or '02. Didn't appear on the list of cars owned by people known to be present. They went in more for expensive foreign cars and bulky camera vans."

"Must be a million people who own SUVs like mine."

"It was yours."

"Uh-huh. So you figured I loaned my car to this poor murder victim?"

"I figured you gave her a lift. Since the car disappeared shortly thereafter and she was in no condition to drive. This other guy in our office—name of Jones—is very good with computers. He managed to hack into the database for the Maryland Turnpike Authority."

"How'd you know I took the turnpike?"

"I didn't for sure," he smiled slightly—even that hurt—"until now. The police all assumed you headed back to the capital. But that wasn't gettin' 'em anywhere, so I decided to take a different approach. 'Sides, the turnpike has surveillance cameras."

"It does?"

"It does. Several points down the stretch. You can't get on or off without being spotted. Jones tapped into their video records—they're all stored on hard drives for months—gauging the approximate time someone leavin' the press conference might hit the turnpike. Only spotted one cute little gas guzzler like yours at what we estimated to be the time you made your getaway."

Trudy tossed her hair back with a whip of her head. Loving felt his heart skip a beat. Totally a turn-on. "And those little cameras let you follow me all the way home to Georgetown?"

"Nah. Jones tried to enlarge the video image and get your license plate number, but it was too muddy. I figure you did something to the plate. I wasn't able to connect the name Trudy to that car for certain. Until now."

She tapped a long fingernail against her lips. The nail was painted bright red. "You been at this private-eye game long?"

"A fair piece. Why?"

"Well, I don't mean to criticize, but you don't seem very good at it." She leaned in closer. "I think every friend I've got in the world—

including some I haven't seen since high school—has called in the past few days to tell me some big, beefy hunk of a guy was looking for me. If I had anything to hide, I would've disappeared a long time ago."

"But you didn't."

"No, I didn't."

"Is that supposed to prove you have nothing to hide?"

She leaned in even closer. "Or maybe I just wanted to see this big, beefy hunk of a guy for myself. And at the moment—I'm glad I did."

It would take a stronger man than Loving for a statement like that to pass without making an impression. He knew it was unprofessional—the woman was not only a suspect, she had clubbed him over the head. But damn, she was hot.

"You're . . . not . . . totally unappealing yourself," Loving mumbled.

She ran a hand across his stubbled head. "I like you, Mr. Loving."

"Just Loving."

"Whatever. I like you. Even though I shouldn't. But that's the story of my life. I always fall for the bad boys."

Loving tried to pull his head back into the case. "Would one of those boys by any chance use a .35-gauge sniper-scope rifle?"

"What on earth are you talking about?"

"I'm talkin' about some guys—professional guys, wiseguys—who have been tryin' to take me out ever since I started lookin' for you. They've come within a whisper of killin' me twice now."

"Oh, please. Paranoid much?"

"It's true. You read the papers? Hear about the whack job who shot up the NorthPoint shopping mall a few days ago?"

"Yeah . . ."

"Well, it wasn't a whack job. That was the cover story the cops put out. It was really two heavily armed, highly dangerous professionals. Tryin' to kill me. Came damn close to succeedin', too. And later, one of them told me they weren't gonna stop. Not as long as I was lookin' for you. Said to watch for danger in unexpected places."

"What, you had a nice little chat with a man who was tryin' to kill you?"

"Long story. Point is—evidently you know somethin' someone else is willin' to kill to make sure doesn't get out."

Trudy's breathing became faster and deeper. "But that . . . doesn't make any sense."

"It does to someone. So what is it you know, Trudy?"

She was visibly shaken. "I don't know anything."

"Evidently you do."

"I don't!"

"You know who got killed at the Roush conference."

"But I don't—not really."

"You must know her name."

"She went by Victoria."

"Victoria what?"

"She never told me."

Loving propped himself on his elbows. This is the part of the interrogation when he would normally try to intimidate her with grim, threatening expressions, but that was hard to pull off when you were chained to a bed. "What are you tellin' me? You just picked up a stranger and gave her a ride to her death?"

"Yes! I mean, no! I mean—"

"What do you mean?"

She took a deep breath. "I was doing a favor."

"For a woman you'd never met."

"No. For Renny."

Finally they were getting somewhere. "And who is this Renny?"

Trudy sat on the edge of the bed, barely inches from Loving. He could feel his internal temperature rise at her nearness. Even as she was spilling her guts, and probably lying about half of it, he found himself liking everything about her—the way she moved, the way she talked. The worried expression on her face made him want to reach out and cradle her in his arms. For starters.

"Renny owns this club. Bar, I guess. Called Action. Kind of a hick place, but not really."

"A faux hick place?"

"Exactly. Well, you don't see so many of these joints on the East

Coast. Renny is a very high-class guy, but he disguises it by catering to dislocated rednecks, kind of like—" She didn't finish the sentence. She didn't have to. "But it's all a front. The peanut shells on the floor, the arm wrestling, all that. All for show. Renny is very . . . cultured."

" 'Zat a fact."

"It's true. He's all refined. Civilized. Knows about philosophy and poets and stuff."

"And I guess you'd go for that in a big way. Bein' the yoga and poetry buff."

"Hey, I do the best I can, okay? I didn't get a fancy Ivy League education. Couldn't afford it. I'm an autodidact."

Loving's eyes fairly bulged. "And you admit it to people? I mean, sure, everyone does it, but—"

She glared at him. "It means I'm self-educated. Taught myself. Broadened my horizons."

"Oh." He swallowed. "So you're attracted to this Renny clown because he's so educated?"

"Kind of, yeah. He's a good business contact, you know? Kind of guy who can hook you up with whatever you need." Loving wondered what exactly it was she needed. "So when he asked me to do a little favor for his gal Victoria . . ."

"You did it. Played chauffeur." Loving sighed. He wished he could convince himself that Trudy was lying, but he didn't think she was, and that wasn't just because she was turning him on ninety miles a minute, either. He could see it in her eyes.

Trudy placed a finger on Loving's expansive chest and slowly walked it toward his neck. "Am I in a lot of trouble?"

"Hard to say," he replied, trying to ignore what she was doing to him, "since I don't know what the heck is goin' on. But offhand, I'd say yes. What's this Renny into?"

"I don't know what you mean." Trudy's hand crossed his neck and began gently massaging his ear.

"There has to be more to this than some redneck bar. No way Thaddeus Roush would be involved in a place like that." Loving cleared his throat and tried to ignore the stroking of his temples. "There's something going on, some major crime in here, somewhere. Is Renny using this bar as a front for drug smuggling?"

"I don't think so. I know druggies, but I've never seen any at Renny's."

"Prostitution, maybe?"

"No way. Renny's too classy. I mean, he's got girls all over the place, but I don't think they're working girls. More like . . . sex slaves."

Loving was curious what the difference was, but thought it might be dangerous just at the moment to engage Trudy in a discussion of anything relating to sex.

"There must be somethin'." She was so close now he could feel her breath on his face. "Can you get me in to meet this Renny?"

"I can take you to the bar. But I can't guarantee you'll see him. He stays in the back rooms, and they're pretty exclusive."

"I'll get in."

"He has lots of security."

"Crooks always do. I'll get in if I have to flatten a platoon."

"Is that your solution to everything? Rush in and bust some heads?"

"As I recall, you're pretty good in the head-busting department yourself."

She leaned in closer, inches from his face. "You probably liked it."

"I'm pretty sure I didn't."

She grabbed his ear and twisted it, pulling his head toward hers. "I bet you like a woman who takes control."

"Unlock those cuffs on my ankles and I'll show you what I like, lady."

"No, I think I prefer you like this. Completely under my control."

"In your dreams."

"You think you're tough, don't you?"

"Tough enough for you."

She swung herself around, straddled him. "Are you as turned on as I am?"

"More."

When they kissed, it was more like two torpedoes flinging themselves at each other. He pressed hard against her and she pressed hard back, sliding her body across his. He kissed her as if he were trying to penetrate her skull; she bit his lower lip till it bled.

"Oh my," one of them groaned, and then the kissing resumed. Loving leaned up as best he could and wrapped his arms around her, pulling her tight. She took his T-shirt by the collar and tore it right down the center, ripping it off him, revealing his massive muscular chest. She shoved her face between his pecs and licked him, working her tongue up to his neck, then to the side of his face, and then they were kissing again, just as hard and powerfully as before.

"You're incredible," he said, pushing himself against her as hard and firm as was humanly possible. They kissed again, and this time he placed his hand on the back of her head. He grabbed her hair tightly, tight enough for it to hurt, and he pulled and—

And it came off. All those endless brunette locks.

It was a wig. And without the wig, Trudy's appearance changed dramatically. The peekaboo hair no longer softened the hard ridges of her face. The full breadth of Trudy's shoulders became apparent.

Loving wiped a finger across her moist upper lip. Makeup. Disguising just the faintest hint of whisker.

Trudy was a he.

32

Christina had tried chocolate milk. She had tried word games. She had even resorted to playing Bobby Darin songs on her harmonica. Nothing worked. Ben was in a blue funk and showed no signs of emerging.

"That was disgraceful," he muttered, over and over again. "I let Keyes and his cronies walk all over me."

"You did not," Christina assured him, stroking the side of his face. "You fought like a tiger."

"Please."

"Keyes backed off."

"Keyes backed off after he had accomplished everything he wanted. He couldn't push it any further without betraying whatever semblance of impartiality he thinks he still maintains." Ben's eyes darkened. "And worst of all—he isn't done yet. Of that I'm certain. He has something big planned. And we don't have a clue what it is."

Kevin Beauregard entered the conference room, a clipboard in one hand and a cell phone pinched between his ear and his shoulder. "Have you seen this?" He punched a button on the television set and it flickered to life. CNN was replaying key moments from the previous session.

"Ugh," Ben said, wincing, then turning away. "The only thing worse than being there being trounced is watching myself being there being trounced." Now and ever, he hated seeing himself on television. All he noticed were the flaws—every stutter, every slouch. His bottom teeth were crooked and the camera appeared to be intentionally positioned to highlight his bald spot.

"Actually, the overnight polls aren't bad," Beauregard said.

Ben looked at him incredulously. "You must be joking."

"I'm not. A lot of people think Keyes went too far. I think you'll see him pulling back next session. Acting with a greater facade of impartiality."

"He'll get someone else to do the dirty work. Potter, or Matera, or some other toady."

"Very likely. But every little bit helps, right?"

Ben was forced to agree, which went against his almost pathological instinct to oppose anything said by any person who made decisions based upon polling results.

"If only there was some way to stop the murder investigation," Beauregard added.

"What? Why?"

"In most Americans' minds, the murder is a big unresolved question mark. The fact that the police are still investigating—and apparently not getting anywhere—only makes it harder for us to make a case for Roush. Even if we can't solve the murder, it would be better if we could get the investigation stopped."

"And how exactly do we do that?" Ben asked.

"Make it political. Call it persecution. Act like it's all something that's been trumped up by Roush's opponents. Polls show that Americans love conspiracy theories. The more complex and unlikely the better."

"Kevin . . ." Ben said, not sure just how to put this. "A woman is dead! She was murdered. In Tad's garden."

"I'm aware of that. But the police don't know who did it. They probably never will. Can't you get them to close the investigation? Maybe call one of your friends in law enforcement?"

"No, I can't. And I won't. If the police decide to give up, they're going to have to do it on their own."

Beauregard frowned, then changed the subject. "Here's another thing we learned from the polls. You struck a chord with many viewers when you told them you tried to have the hearings delayed until after the police had completed their investigation of the murder. A lot of people didn't know that, and it raised some questions in their minds. Gave the whole proceeding a political taint."

"Swell. But how does that help us?"

"Should make Keyes back down even more," Christina suggested.

"I agree," Beauregard said. "And it will make it harder for the President to rush in with a replacement nominee. If he can't do that, there's no point in trying to terminate the hearings prematurely."

"There are still more votes on that committee against us than for us."

"We'll have to change their minds," Christina said.

"We're not going to change anyone's mind. Who knows what really lurks in people's minds? The votes are being controlled by power brokers like Keyes. That lock isn't going to be changed by anything they learn during the hearing."

"You can change the committee votes," Beauregard said firmly.

"Excuse me? How?"

"By turning the tide of public opinion. If popular sympathy swings in favor of Roush—admittedly a long shot at this point, but if it does—you'll see Keyes and his cronies back down. They'd have no choice, really. They're elected officials. And most of them would like to be elected again at some time in the future."

Ben shook his head. "I don't see how Roush is going to accomplish that."

"I don't, either." Beauregard snapped his cell phone shut and passed the clipboard to Ben. "I think it has to be done by you."

33

Roush repeatedly assured Ben that they had nothing to worry about from Harvey Gottlieb, but it didn't make him feel any more at ease. Yes, Gottlieb and Roush knew each other, once upon a time, before he met Ray, but that was long ago and they had parted amicably. Moreover, it was entirely personal, and Ben could pitch a fit if Keyes went after Roush's personal life, so what was there to worry about?

Answer: Ben didn't know, but he did know that the opposition forces wouldn't be calling him unless they thought the man could do their cause some good—and do Roush some damage. When Ben learned that Senator Matera would be handling the questioning, goose pimples coursed across his body. That settled it—this was the one.

"How did you happen to meet Judge Roush?" Matera asked.

Gottlieb was wearing a tailored Brioni blue suit, sitting up straight, looking quite distinguished, even with the reading glasses. "I was working in the D.C. Circuit Court as a clerk."

"Were you working under Judge Roush?"

"No." Darn. No sexual harassment action this time.

"But you met Judge Roush in the course of your duties?"

"Yes. I took some documents into his chambers for signature the first week I was there." Gottlieb was a tall man, dark-eyed, about a decade younger than Roush. He was dressed to the nines, but Ben supposed that wasn't unusual for someone who was about to appear on national television. He seemed elegant and—well, it had to be acknowledged—a bit effeminate. Playing into stereotype. "I don't remember now what they were. Doesn't matter, I suppose. I thought it would take thirty seconds. Imagine my surprise when Judge Roush asked me to sit down and started chatting with me."

"What did he want to talk about?" Ben braced himself. Matera wouldn't be asking these questions if she didn't already know the answer. And like it.

"Well, at first it was just idle pleasantries. You know. Ball game scores. Gossip about the Chief Justice's wife. But soon, he was asking me if I liked to party."

Ben felt his gut clenching.

"And within ten minutes," Gottlieb continued, "he had asked me out on a date."

A small stir from the gallery. Ben weighed whether to interfere—the conversation wasn't particularly damaging yet—or to let it proceed. He opted for the middle road: a gentle reminder.

"Mister Chairman," Ben said. "Point of order. I thought it was understood that we would not be prying into the nominee's private life."

"I recall hearing the nominee say he wouldn't answer any questions about his private life," Keyes said. "I don't recall any understanding regarding the sworn testimony of others. And I don't believe you have the right to decide what other witnesses you do not represent say or don't say."

Well, that was effective, wasn't it? Ben retook his seat, deciding to reserve his moral outrage for a later time when it would be of greater service.

"Getting back to the witness," Matera said with a harrumphing noise, "did you say that the judge asked you out on a date?"

"Yes. He was trying to pick me up."

"And were you receptive to this proposition?"

"If you're asking if I'm gay, yes, I am."

"And he knew this."

"I guess his 'gaydar' was up and running that day." Gottlieb smiled slightly. "Mine doesn't work quite so flawlessly. But I suppose he's had more experience."

Matera squirmed, coughed, fingered her collar. Ben recognized these all as visual cues she was sending her constituency to express how supremely uncomfortable she was talking with all these gay people about gay things. Despite her personal misery, like a dutiful warrior she soldiered on.

"So you and the judge . . . went out?"

"For about six months."

Matera arched an eyebrow. "Six months. Indeed. Where did you go?"

Gottlieb breathed in deeply, then released it. "Tad was very fond of . . . gay bars."

Ben wasn't sure how to characterize the low threshold sound that blanketed the gallery, but there definitely was one. And it wasn't a good thing.

"Uh . . . gay bars?"

"Yes, places where men—well, most of them were just for men—went to meet other men. You know what I mean?"

Matera cleared her throat. "No, I am quite sure I do not."

"Well, judging from the interior, they're perfectly ordinary places. Bars. Music. Dancing. Tables. Mediocre food. What's different is the clientele. Men. Black leather outfits. Chains. Much more chatter about furniture and hair gel."

"And these were the kinds of places the two of you frequented?"

"Hey, he did the choosing. I'm more of a homebody myself. Tad liked to party."

"And precisely what did this 'partying' entail?"

The time had come. Ben rose. "Mister Chairman, I must object."

"Mr. Kincaid, this is not—"

"You can call it a point of order, or a point of clarification, or a point of I'm-mad-as-heck-and-I'm-not-going-to-take-it-anymore. This is an unwarranted intrusion into the nominee's personal life."

"I disagree. I think we're uncovering points that relate to the character of the nominee and—"

"What's worse," Ben continued, raising himself to full dander, "is that the committee is permitting what is nothing more than blatant prejudice based on sexual preference."

"You're out of line, Mr. Kincaid."

"I don't think so. If Judge Roush had attended a straight bar, no one would care. If he had dates with a woman who worked for another judge in his office, no one would care. This whole line of inquiry is only of interest because he's gay. This is a prurient line of questioning designed to exploit anti-gay prejudices and it is beneath the dignity of the Senate!"

"I'm always interested to hear opinions regarding what is appropriate for the Senate from members who have been with us for several weeks," Keyes said, with a quiet cough, "but based on my thirty-three years of experience here, I believe this question is of value. If your nominee wishes to remain silent with regard to the matters being discussed that is his prerogative, but you do not have the right to silence a witness properly called and sworn by this assemblage."

Ben knew what that remark was about. Keyes was baiting Roush, hoping he could get him to talk, a move that would likely make him seem defensive and would only open the door to more inquiries into his personal life.

"We will not discuss personal matters," Ben said firmly. Out of the corner of his eye, he could see Roush peering up at him. He was not happy. "There will be no exceptions."

"Then please take your seat so that we may continue our discussion with someone who is willing to talk," Keyes said. "Someone who has no secrets to hide."

What could he do? Keyes had him in a corner and he knew it. Ben reluctantly took his seat.

"At first all we did was dance," Gottlieb explained. "Sometimes normal pop tunes, sometimes campy stuff, old disco, Gloria Gaynor, Village People. Those guys love to boogie. Don't be fooled by his age—Judge Roush is a zippy little dancer."

"An important qualification for a Supreme Court justice," Matera murmured.

"But he wasn't content with mere dancing. Soon he was asking me if I was willing to experiment."

"Experiment . . . how?"

"Well, I'm not going to talk about everything he wanted to do. I feel that would be inappropriate."

Ben was relieved to hear that the witness had such high standards. He assumed that nothing ever happened that the committee would find particularly titillating. The undescribed horror left to the listener's imagination played much better than boring revelations.

"But anything that happened in a bar, in a public place—well, that can't be private, can it?" Matera asked. "I don't believe anyone can have a reasonable expectation of privacy regarding conduct in a public place. So I ask you again: what kind of experiments took place?"

"Well, some of these bars were . . . specialty houses. Catered to gay men with particular interests."

"Such as?"

"Primarily S and M. Bondage."

Ben didn't have any problem identifying the murmur that traveled through the courtroom this time. They weren't happy thoughts.

"And did the judge like these sorts of activities?"

"I don't think he'd ever engaged in them before. I don't think he had acknowledged he was gay for very long. But he was curious. So we gave it a try."

Matera looked up at the sky as if she couldn't believe what she was hearing, what she was in fact begging the witness to reveal. "And how did this experiment go?"

"Not so well. I wasn't comfortable with it. Eventually he got the message and gave it up. We moved on."

"Moved on to what?"

Gottlieb drew in his breath. "Threesomes. And after that—gay orgies."

The Caucus Room descended into chaos. Ben didn't think cameras were even allowed in here, but nonetheless, a flurry of flashes went off throughout the room. Cell phones flipped. The usual whispering became a tumult. Chairman Keyes tried to bring the hearing back to order—although not as hard as he might, Ben thought.

"This is an outrage," Ben heard Roush mutter under his breath. "A moral outrage. A crime against decency."

"Did the nominee have a comment?" Keyes asked, above the noise.

"No, he did not!" Ben answered for him. "I renew my objection to this disgraceful, irrelevant line of questioning."

"I think at this point, Mr. Kincaid, you must be the only person in the room who thinks this is irrelevant. The country has a right to know who—what kind of person—they're putting on the Supreme Court. His character. His moral fiber."

"That's just an excuse."

"No, Mr. Kincaid. That's why we're here."

Once the room had been restored to some reasonable semblance of its previous calm, Matera continued the questioning.

"Mr. Gottlieb, when you say that Judge Roush engaged in . . . threesomes," her lips actually curled as she said the word, "are you talking about . . . sexual intercourse involving three people, er, three *men* at once?"

"Yes, ma'am."

"And did you in fact engage in any of these . . . threesomes?"

Gottlieb's head lowered. "Yes, ma'am. I did. We did."

"And, well, I won't ask you for the details, obviously. But did these . . . sodomistic encounters with other men—"

Ben clenched his teeth. Thanks for not going into the details.

"—appear to be something that Judge Roush enjoyed?"

"Yes, ma'am. Very much. I think he was actively pursuing some . . . journey of self-discovery. Which is what led him to move forward to an even greater number of partners. Orgies."

"Unacceptable," Roush muttered under his breath. "How much did they have to give this assassin to get him to talk?"

Senator Matera continued. "And when you say orgies, you mean—"

"Many men. Sometimes as many as twenty. All having sex in the same room."

"And where would these encounters occur?"

"There were certain bars. Private clubs. Bathhouses. They didn't advertise it, but word got around."

"And these men would all be . . . ?"

"Gay, obviously. Mostly exhibitionists. Some in costumes, some in drag. Some using . . . utensils for intercourse."

"This is inexcusable!" Ben bellowed. He rose to his feet, feeling just as enraged as he sounded. Sexton might criticize him later for being ineffectual, but he wouldn't criticize him for not being sufficiently angry.

"Are you calling for a point of order?" Keyes asked.

"I'm asking for a moment of decency! You can keep all your parliamentary niceties. This is just wrong and you know it! This is tawdry wallowing in the sex life of a private individual for no purpose other than to indict him for his sexual preference."

"Mr. Kincaid, your hyperbole does not impress us. Take your seat."

"No, sir. I will not. This line of inquiry will end now. Or I will withdraw from the room and take the nominee with me."

"Sir, that would constitute contempt of Congress. I could have you both jailed."

"At the end of a protracted quasi-criminal trial, yes. But that could take months." Ben looked at Keyes levelly. "And that would really screw up your timetable, wouldn't it?"

For the first time since he had met the man, Ben thought he had finally caused him to stop and think for a moment. Maybe it was the polls that showed Americans were suspicious of the Republican insistence on pressing ahead with the confirmation process. Or maybe it was just possible that even Keyes realized they had crossed the line with this witness.

After an eternity—which Ben realized when he watched it later on CNN was actually about ten seconds—Keyes spoke. "As it happens, Mr. Kincaid, I tend to agree that this questioning has gone long enough. I think we all have the general idea. While I do think this is of relevance to the character issue, we have been given sufficient detail on the . . . sexual issues to reach our own conclusions. Do you have anything else you wish to ask this witness, Senator Matera?"

"Only this. Mr. Gottlieb—how did your relationship with Judge Roush come to an end?"

"I broke it off, eventually. I didn't like all the constant sexual aberrations. I wanted a loving, committed partner, but I always got the feeling that I was just his young stud. Not someone he loved. More like someone he might pick up on a street corner for a night of fun and revelry."

"Thank you, sir. That's—"

"*I would like to be heard!*"

To Ben's shock—and horror—he saw that Roush had risen to his feet.

"Judge Roush," Chairman Keyes said, "you do not have the floor."

"I don't care." His rage was palpable. His shoulders shook as he spoke. "I will not have these things said about me without responding."

"All in good time."

"No, sir. I will be heard!"

"I'm sure you will, but only when you are recognized by the chair."

"Now."

Keyes adjusted his granny glasses. "I must say, you share your counsel's difficulty with procedure. Which I for one think would be a problematic quality for a judge."

Ben tugged on Roush's sleeve, but was ignored. "You cannot trash a man's reputation without giving him a chance to defend himself!"

"I assure you I will allow you to speak, sir, at the appropriate time, but as you can see, it is five o'clock, our traditional closing time."

"I tell you—I will—"

Keyes slapped his gavel on the bench. "This session is adjourned."

Roush tried again to speak, but he was drowned out by the sounds of reporters flocking to his side. Many rushed to Gottlieb as well, no doubt seeking more of the details that Ben had squelched. Roush stood there, twisting in the wind, looking impotent and useless.

"Should I try to talk to these reporters?" Roush asked Ben.

"Under no circumstances."

"But—"

"No buts. No exceptions. No talking."

"I have to deny—"

"They've heard your denial. We need to get all our heads together and prepare a response. And it has to be good. Smart and carefully calculated. Speaking prematurely can only limit our future options."

Ben could tell it pained him, but Roush obediently offered the gathering press a "No comment at this time" and turned away. Christina and Ben gathered their materials and retreated to the back door.

Ben knew they would all be waiting for him in the conference-room headquarters: Carraway, Sexton, Beauregard, and worst of all, Senator Hammond. They would be furious, both at Keyes and Matera. And at Ben.

Before this latest revelation, Roush's nomination had seemed a long shot at best.

Now, it seemed utterly impossible.

34

"What in the name of—Trudy!"

Loving tried to push away, but since she—*he*—was straddling him, and Loving's feet were still cuffed to the bed, there wasn't far for him to go.

Trudy appeared distraught. "What's the matter?"

Loving wiped the back of his hand against his mouth, as if desperately trying to remove all traces of the earlier saliva swap. "What's the *matter*? You're—you're a guy!"

"Well, duh. I thought you knew."

"Knew? If I knew, do you think I'd be—be—"

"Yes?"

"Aarghh!" Loving twisted back and forth, trying unsuccessfully to get out from under Trudy. "Get off of me!"

"Are you sure?" Trudy traced a line down the side of his face. "You didn't seem to mind being near me a minute ago."

Loving slapped the hand away. "A minute ago you were a girl!"

"No, I wasn't."

"Well, I thought—I mean, I assumed—aarrghh!" He thrust forward again, this time hard enough to knock Trudy off him. "Have you even—have you had that . . . that surgery?"

"No, dear. I'm still intact."

"That's . . . disgustin'."

"You didn't think so a—"

Loving raised a finger. "Don't start that again."

"All right. All right." Trudy picked the wig up off the floor and plopped it lopsidedly back on his head. "How 'bout I put this back on and you just pretend you still think I'm a girl?"

"I haven't got that much imagination!"

"Oh, come on now. Do you really expect me to believe you had no idea what you were doing?"

"What's that s'posed to mean?"

"I mean, I'm good," Trudy said, batting both eyelashes, "but I'm not that good. Anyone who took a really close look—"

"I guess I didn't!"

"—and I could tell you were giving me some very close looks."

"What're you gettin' at? I had no idea, I'm tellin' you. No idea!"

"Uh-huh. Methinks the boy doth protest too much."

"Are you tryin' to say—" Loving inflated his massive chest. His T-shirt still hung around him in tatters. "Listen, buster, I had no idea. Got it? No idea. I'm all guy—like one hundred percent all guy. And I like girls."

"I can be your girl."

Loving was wild-eyed. "No, you can't!"

"Are you afraid I don't have the right parts to pop your cork? Because I can assure you, I do."

"Would you stop talkin' like that? There ain't gonna be any . . . cork-poppin'. Understand?"

"Maybe we're moving too fast. You're more of a traditionalist, aren't you? We should go out on a date first. Get some dinner. Maybe take in a movie."

"We are not goin' out on a date!"

"Why not? No one would know. About me, I mean. You didn't."

"Someone might!" He pounded the table. "No wonder all those

people laughed every time I said I was looking for you. They thought I—aaarghh!"

"So you're saying, as long as no one knows about me, it would be okay?"

Loving fairly shouted. "No! I am not saying it would be okay! It would never be okay!"

Trudy sniffed. "Suit yourself. But you're making a big mistake. You're missing out on the best time you ever had."

"Oh, right."

"And you haven't had any for a good long time."

"How would you know?"

"I know. Believe me, I know."

He pulled at his legs, trying to free himself. "I want you to let me loose, got it? Right now."

"Your wish is my command." Trudy produced a key and uncuffed his ankles.

"Thank you so very much. Mister."

Trudy looked into a nearby mirror and reattached the wig. "But even if we can't be together, we can still . . . work together, right?"

"No way in hell."

"Why not?"

Loving jumped off the bed. " 'Cause I don't work with . . . with . . ."

"Yes?"

" 'Cause I don't do that kinda stuff."

"What kinda stuff?"

"That . . . kinky stuff."

"Good heavens, man, I'm asking to work with you to get in to see Renny, not to nibble your pickle."

"You stop that kinda talk right now!"

"What kinda talk?"

"That—that—you know!"

"All right, all right. But you're still going to need me, so I'm coming with."

"Need you? At a redneck bar? Like I'm really gonna need a—"

"Yes?"

"A Trudy!"

Trudy made a few touch-ups with a mascara wand, then turned and smiled. Loving had to admit she—*he,* damn it—was gorgeous, even under the circumstances. "I think you'll find a Trudy is a very useful thing to have in this particular redneck bar. You're going to need some . . . distractions. I can provide that. Big-time. And face it, I know the territory. You don't."

Loving headed toward the door. His head was throbbing—for more reasons than he could count at the moment—but even if his head were missing, he was still getting out of this place. And he didn't want any part of . . . Trudy.

"Why would you help me? What's in it for you?"

"Maybe I just want to spend some more time with my new tall, dark, and handsome." Trudy leaned forward to peck him on the cheek. Loving recoiled.

"Don't even think about it!"

"All right, sweetie. Whatever you want."

"And don't call me sweetie!"

"Whatever you want, sugar."

"Would you stop that!"

"Of course I will, honey-pie. Now, are you going to drive, or shall I?"

35

Within thirty minutes of the close of the day's hearings, the news of the latest development in the Roush nomination was global. Every podium, every channel, every water cooler seemed obsessed with the same subject. In Ben's office and every other office in Washington, D.C., the phones were ringing nonstop and the fax machines were in perpetual motion. Ben's e-mail server was so clogged Jones eventually just deleted all messages and hoped he hadn't missed anything important. The Christian Congregation scheduled a rally outside the gates of the White House, and Richard Trevor was demanding that the President withdraw Roush's nomination based on his "decadent character." In response, numerous gay and lesbian organizations issued statements or scheduled press conferences to support Roush and demand that the President reaffirm the nomination, claiming that the references to character were a screen for homophobia. A pundit on MSNBC noted that Roush's partner Eastwick had never appeared in the hearing room, despite the fact that he was no longer in custody, and referred to him as the "gay divorcée."

"Well, that was about the worst thing that could possibly happen," Sexton said, *tsk*ing his lips as an indication of his disgust. The Roush support team had gathered in the conference room in Senator Hammond's office to concoct some plan for what to do next, while Roush himself was outside making phone calls on his cell.

"Agreed," Hammond said sadly, running his fingers through his long gray locks. "The man lost the support of his party before the hearing began. Now he's lost the support of our party as well."

"I don't get it," Ben said. He was pacing in circles around the conference table. "They're dumping him because he allegedly went to bars? Who in the Senate hasn't? Because he may have had consensual sexual relations? Who in the Senate hasn't?"

"The problem is that he's gay," Christina said, as she came through the door, a tall stack of styrofoam containers tucked under her chin. They had opted to bring dinner in. They didn't have time to visit any of the Senate cafeterias, and probably wouldn't have been left alone for ten seconds if they had.

Christina took a seat and began handing out the meals. "They may call it a character issue. But it's only an issue because he's gay."

"For once, I agree with the redhead," Beauregard said, speaking while simultaneously scanning the latest tracking polls. "This was a back-door way of making sexual preference an issue. Most Americans aren't all that comfortable with male homosexual sex anyway. Fox News has been going wild with it—sidebar stories on the 'gay lifestyle' and 'the dark world of sexual fetishes.' Larry King hosted a debate on whether gay bars should be allowed within a mile of public schools. *USA Today* has a feature story headlined 'Are Gays Really More Promiscuous?' Face it—they scored on us big-time the instant they got someone to say the phrase 'gay bar.' 'Orgies' worked well for them, also."

"And I must say, speaking as an image consultant," Carraway added, "the witness looked great on television. He obviously spent a lot of time considering his wardrobe. Gay or not, he made a positive impression."

"Even if he was a right-wing flunky?" Ben asked. "Even if he was paid?"

"I'm not sure it matters. Gay sex is not a vote-getter in Middle America. Toss in some threesomes and orgies—" Beauregard shivered. "Ugh."

"Any word on whether it's true?" Carraway asked.

Ben shook his head. "Roush keeps repeating his professional mantra: I will not discuss my private life. But honestly—orgies? I can't believe it."

"Ben always thinks the best of his clients," Christina said, by way of explanation. "Not necessarily a good thing."

"Come on. Roush is a federal judge. How long could he possibly keep something like that quiet?"

"How long did J. Edgar Hoover keep his homosexuality quiet? Like, his entire life? And he had a much higher profile than a federal judge."

Ben shrugged. "I still can't believe it."

"You don't want to believe it."

"I don't think there's anything wrong with it if it was all consensual. I just . . . don't believe it. Doesn't ring true."

"I've got people looking into this Gottlieb guy," Sexton explained. "See if we can find some motive for him to fabricate testimony."

"Maybe he's jealous of Roush's success," Carraway suggested.

"Maybe Roush dumped him," Christina added.

"Ah." Sexton smiled. "The Anita Hill counteroffense. After she testified against Thomas at his confirmation hearing, the Republicans did their best to cast doubt on her testimony. Problem was— she had no motive to lie. She hadn't even wanted to testify. So they started the rumor that Thomas had dated Hill, then dumped her. Suggested that she was insanely jealous because he married a white woman instead of her."

Christina pursed her lips. "That's just . . . revolting."

"Agreed." Sexton paused. "I wonder if it would work for us."

"We're not going to have an opportunity for any counteroffensive," Ben said. "Not for a while. They still have more witnesses to call, probably of the same ilk. We should start rounding up people who have worked with Roush but have not been propositioned and have not observed any inappropriate behavior."

"Not that it would disprove what we've already heard."

"Can't hurt."

"It could, actually," Sexton said, batting a finger against his lips, "if it sounds lame. Desperate."

"What we need is for the nominee to get angry again," Carraway said. "My polls show the public doesn't understand why he sits quietly while people say nasty things about him. That outburst at the end of the last session was good, but undermined by the fact that he didn't actually get to say anything. He needs to show some fire. Tell people off."

"I disagree," Ben said. "That would be playing into their hands."

"Americans respect fire."

"Not in a legal, or even a quasi-legal proceeding. Makes you look defensive. I've talked to hundreds of jurors."

"When are you going to get the message? It's not a courtroom."

"But the same principles apply."

"Not in the political arena. People will support a sex fiend sooner than they'll support a wimp. You need to tell your man to fight back, hard and fast."

"I will not. It's bad advice."

The deep breathing made Carraway's shoulder pads rise. "Kid, don't question me. I'm the expert here. Just do it."

"Are you intentionally trying to sabotage this hearing?"

Carraway glared at him.

"I won't do it," Ben said firmly. "No."

Sexton intervened. "Could you at least get him to deny the orgies part? I think that would go a long way."

"I'll talk to him. But I'm not optimistic."

Hammond laid his hand on Ben's shoulder. "Give it a go, Ben. I know how persuasive you can be. Talk sense to the man. He trusts you." The elderly statesman smiled. "I feel certain you can make him understand."

*　　*　　*

"Absolutely not!"

"Just hear me out."

"I won't do it."

"Just a tiny compromise."

"Not an inch. Not a goddamned inch!"

Ben had taken Roush downstairs into the subterranean chambers that underlined the main Capitol building, the home of unwanted office equipment, the world's most archaic (and noisiest) ventilation and air-conditioning system, and the private hideaways of the most senior and important senators. Ben didn't have one; at the moment, he was about ninety-ninth on the standby list. But it was still a good place to stretch your legs and get out of the office, however briefly, without being spotted by the media. Ben had hoped a little exercise might help Roush clear his head.

So far, wrong.

"If we give them an inch, even an inch, we could set a precedent that will haunt every Supreme Court nominee till the end of time," Roush argued. "People remember the Bork inquiry as the moment when standards began to erode. I won't have them remember the Roush inquiry as the moment when standards disappeared altogether."

"I don't think you need to go into any detail. Just deny the seedy nightlife stuff. Isn't that what you were trying to do?"

"I lost my temper. It was a mistake. Any response will constitute a tacit endorsement of these scurrilous tactics."

"You can think of an explanation."

"Explanation, or excuse?"

"Say you're doing it to protect Ray's reputation."

Roush arched an eyebrow. "Step forward to protect the little lady? I don't think so."

Ben paused outside the door to what had once been the hideaway of his predecessor, Senator Glancy. After the murder, even the most eager senators passed on the chance to claim it. The room had been converted into a storage facility for cleaning supplies. "Look, it comes down to one thing. Do you want to join the Supremes or not?"

"Of course I do! What kind of fool wouldn't? That's not the question. The question is: How low am I willing to sink to get on the Court?"

Ben grabbed him by the shoulders and looked him squarely in the eyes. "Please reconsider, Tad. Our only hope is that you will step forward and deny as many of these accusations as you can. Because if you don't—I can't help you in there." Ben released his shoulders and looked at him sadly. "You're on your own."

36

The next three witnesses all stated that they had seen Thaddeus Roush frequenting gay bars in and around the Annapolis area. Ben didn't feel that was the end of the world. The constant corroboration, however, would eliminate the possibility in many people's minds that the stories were entirely false—even though Ben knew from experience that if you could get one person to lie, it wasn't that much harder to get four people to lie.

The fourth witness at least demonstrated a certain variety. Alice Rodgers, co-owner of a local concert venue, testified that she had seen Roush shopping in a gay adult sex shop. She was there to pick up a gag gift for an office Christmas party when, to her surprise, she chanced across a member of the federal appeals court. She remembered the incident very clearly.

"At first, I couldn't believe it—I had seen Judge Roush's picture in the paper just the day before. And there he was. Browsing the dildos and the edible body paint."

"How long was he . . . shopping?" Senator Matera asked.

"Oh, I don't know. Ten, fifteen minutes."

"And you observed him the whole time?"

"Well, I tried not to stare. But you know. It was a bit distracting. Like seeing Cher in a strip club."

"And did he purchase anything?"

"He did. But I couldn't see what it was."

"Did you speak to him?"

"Oh, heavens, no," she said, covering her face. "I didn't feel it was my place."

Well, Ben thought, it could be worse. This testimony was not helpful, but it was hardly a criminal act. In a way, he was almost relieved—it could have been so much more damaging.

"But even though you didn't speak to him," Matera continued, "you're quite certain it was Judge Roush."

"Oh, yes," Rodgers said. "Absolutely. No doubt about it. Despite his best efforts, I recognized him."

"Despite . . . his best efforts?"

"Oh, yes." She blinked. "Did I not mention? He was wearing a disguise."

Matera's head tilted to one side. "A disguise?"

"Yes, ma'am." Dramatic pause. "He was dressed like a woman." Ben's eyes closed.

"He was dressed like a woman?"

"Yes. Wig, dress, padded bra. The whole nine yards." She paused, and her voice dropped. "Not very good with the lipstick, though."

"But—" Matera coughed into her hand, then wiped her glasses. "But you're still sure it was Judge Roush?"

"Oh, yes. I was suspicious from the moment I saw him. Walked like a man, you know? Some things you just can't disguise. Especially when you're not that accustomed to wearing five-inch fuck-me pumps."

The audio censor was able to bleep the offending word, but just barely. Those present in the gallery weren't sure whether to gasp or laugh. Except Ben. He was certain of his reaction. He wanted to cry.

The worst of it was: Ben knew the woman was lying. If he had no other indication, he could see how tightly Roush was clenching his fists under the table. Yes, this was a lie. A paid lie, financed by some lobbying outfit or under-the-table PAC fund distribution. But what could he do about it?

"It's now or never," he whispered into Roush's ear. "You no longer have a choice. No one will vote for a transvestite Supreme Court justice. You have to deny these charges. Emphatically."

Roush's face was stony, but he still managed to whisper his reply. "This is beneath my dignity—and the dignity of the Court."

Ben pinched the bridge of his nose. "Then you deserve what you get."

"Thank you," Chairman Keyes said, as he dismissed the final witness. "It seems we still have some time before our scheduled adjournment." All of which Ben knew to be planned. Keyes thought that if Roush tried to defend himself he would sound like a criminal defendant insisting that he was not guilty. Most people assume the accused are guilty, despite all protestations. He was counting on them doing the same with Roush. Although Ben had tried every trick he knew to get the nominee to speak out, a nagging doubt in the back of his head wondered if Keyes wasn't right.

"Judge Roush, would you like to make any sort of response?"

Ben didn't bother interposing an objection. It would only sound as if he were making excuses for the forthcoming refusal to speak.

"I just thought in fairness I should give you a chance to respond to the character issues raised by the previous witnesses."

No response.

"Earlier you indicated a desire to speak. To deny some of the accusations that have been made."

"No, sir," Roush said, his voice slow and quiet. "I wish to protest the progress of the inquiry from judicial matters of relevance to personal matters of no relevance. I will not sink to your level by discussing that which was not properly raised in the first place. I have said before that I will not respond to any testimony relating to my personal life. It is not relevant and it sets a bad precedent. For the sake of the Court, and the future of all men and women nominated to sit on the Court, I must remain silent."

Keyes tilted his head to one side, then shrugged. "Very well. If you have nothing to say, we'll proceed to the voting. Would the clerk please—"

"I have something to say."

A stir rose in the gallery. Keyes lowered his reading glasses. "Mr. Kincaid? My offer was not made to you."

"Nevertheless, I will be heard."

"You have not been recognized by the chair."

"Actually, I think you just did." Ben pulled the microphone closer to him and eyed each member of the committee in turn. "If you think I'm going to lecture you about what has taken place in this chamber recently, you're wrong." He paused, waiting for his words to sink in. "You all know what has happened. You don't need me to explain it to you. What you might want to explain is why you've allowed it to happen."

Senator Matera looked at him wearily. "Mr. Kincaid . . ."

"I currently have the floor, madam, and I will not yield. I know you and your colleague Senator Keyes are sticklers for proper parliamentary procedure. So be quiet."

Matera leaned back in her chair, eyebrows raised, and remained silent. Ben took a deep breath. He'd won many a trial in the closing argument. He had to give it his best shot here—however impossible it seemed.

"Some of you probably approve of what has been happening, approve of the result if not necessarily the tactics. The end always justifies the means, right? That's the mantra of partisan politics. That's why we have to debate whether it's proper to filibuster actions that are supported by the majority. That's why we spend millions of dollars digging up dirt on each new nominee. Sure, it's dirty. But it's a means to an end.

"And what about the rest of you?" Ben asked, changing the direction of his gaze. "Those who disagree with the tactics and the result, but remain quiet, because last time—and next time—it was and will be your party doing the dirt. And so it goes, goes, goes, goes, goes, goes—until someone finally has the courage to step up to the plate and stop it. To draw the line."

Ben turned slightly toward the nominee seated to his left. "Thaddeus Roush has drawn the line, ladies and gentlemen. And you should respect that, because in your hearts, you all know he's right. What you have been doing here is wrong. As someone recently reminded me, when Clarence Thomas was being confirmed, you dragged sex into the proceedings. The ostensible topic was sexual harassment, but everyone knew that was just an excuse to introduce titillating material. Justice Thomas accused the committee of playing to racial stereotypes about black studs and sexual immorality—and he was right. And guess what? The same thing has been happening in this chamber this week—only worse. Now you're introducing sex under the cover of a character issue, but it's really an excuse to play to the stereotype of gay men as decadent, promiscuous. Perverse. And it has been far, far worse here than it was in the Thomas hearing because that's what happens when you allow your standards to erode. Once you start down that path, it is very difficult to stop, perhaps impossible. Soon we'll be able to disregard judicial qualifications altogether and cut straight to the sex life. That's what Judge Roush has been telling you since the day this hearing was convened—but none of you would listen. You just went along the way you've gone along in the past, ignoring the reality of what you have become. What this proceeding has become."

Ben considered the expressions on the faces of the committee members. It was impossible to know how this was playing. The senators were pros at masking their feelings, and for that matter, they might not know what their feelings were until they got the preliminary poll results.

"I don't know why these witnesses have said the things they've said. Even if it were true, it would be an odd thing to talk about after years of silence, and I suspect I'm not the only one here who suspects that none of it is true. Some witnesses have probably been paid. Some would say anything to get on television. Maybe a little of it is true. I don't know. But I know this: I've been to heterosexual bars before, but no one would think of using that to impeach me. Heck, George W. Bush went to bars regularly for twenty years, but that didn't stop him from becoming President. I've dressed up for fun before and partied and so has every one of you. I've even had sex before." He paused. "Once. A long time ago." He waited for the mild laughter to subside. "But no one cares. These things have only become issues in this proceeding because, in the spirit of total honesty, Judge Roush acknowledged that he is a gay American. And just as the unscrupulous have used race and religion and gender as weapons to defame and destroy in the past, so sexual preference is being used today. If Senator McCarthy's ghost still haunts this room, he must be very pleased."

Ben paused. His lips were so dry they were splitting. He knew he needed to wrap this up; he was amazed Keyes had let him go on so long without trying to shut him down. But he had one last thing he needed to say. One last chance to remind them of something they already knew.

"Thaddeus Roush is a good man," he continued. "All of you know it. That's why he's here. That's why the President nominated him in the first place. He's smart, he's hardworking, and he's fair. He's a reasonable man. He is exactly what we need on the Supreme Court. That's what matters. So we're not going to make any more speeches. We're not going to call any more witnesses. There's no point. You know what you need to know. It's time to vote. Just remember this one fact—"

Ben made eye contact with every one of them in turn, then continued. "America is watching to see if you'll do the right thing. Please don't disappoint them."

37

"Aw hell," Loving grumbled. "You didn't tell me it was a strip club."

"What did you think it was going to be?" Trudy replied. "A sewing circle?"

"You said it was a redneck joint. You never said—aw hell." He stared up at the large neon sign flashing the name of the club: AC-TION. Presumably because if you got inside, you were either going to see some or get some.

"So what's the problem, big boy? Never been to a strip joint before?"

"All too often."

"Bet you've never been to one like this. Fifty of the best-looking women you'll ever meet in your life. And very discreet. They have to be: some of their clients are members of Congress."

"You're kiddin'."

"I'm not. And lobbyists. Lobbyists love this place."

"They come here to rub shoulders with politicians?"

"Well, they come here to get something rubbed." Trudy winked. "Let's go watch Your Government in Action."

Loving scanned the considerable line of patrons waiting to get inside. "Looks like there could be a wait."

"More than a wait, sugar. Dressed the way you are, you'll never get in."

"Hey, I put on this fruity shirt you gave me. What do you—"

"Don't get your butt in a swither. I can get us in." Trudy extended an elbow. "Escort me, baby."

"I am not going to . . . to . . . have you hangin' on my arm."

"Why not?"

"Because you're—you know!"

"Yeah, I know, and you know, but they don't know. At least not most of them. Do you want to get in or not?"

Loving sighed heavily. "Hell." He raised his arm as if it weighed a thousand pounds and reluctantly offered an elbow.

"Thanks. You've got big biceps, sugar."

"Don't call me 'sugar'!"

They walked toward the front of the line, ignoring the more than one hundred people waiting. "How much money you got on you, plum cake?"

"Don't—" He sucked in his breath. "About five hundred bucks. More than enough."

"More than enough? Here? We'll blow through that in an hour." She shook her head. "I just hope that's long enough."

Trudy approached the gatekeeper, a burly bodybuilder with a shaved head and muscles that made Mr. Clean look like a ninety-pound weakling. "Hey, Bones."

He tipped a finger in a small salute. "Good to see you, Trudy."

"Boss wants to see me."

"Then step right in," he said, but Loving noticed he didn't move.

"Any time now," Trudy whispered in his ear.

"Any time now what?"

"Pay the man."

"For what?"

"To get in."

"There's a cover charge?"

"No, there's a get-the-gigantic-traffic-control-bruiser-out-of-the-way charge."

Loving muttered again, then grabbed his wallet and offered a five.

"Don't be absurd." Trudy reached into his wallet and pulled out a fifty, then handed it to the gatekeeper. "Sorry for the delay."

He nodded graciously and let them pass.

"Fifty dollars to get a seat in a strip club?"

"Fifty dollars to get in. A seat would cost you another fifty."

Loving slapped his head in disgust and followed Trudy's lead. He was immediately immersed in more or less everything he hated most in life. Relentless pounding noise—he supposed they called it music—playing so loud he could barely hear himself think, all electronic synthetic technocrap. Colored lights swirled back and forth across the club so fast it made him dizzy. The crowd was worse than Disneyland on a Saturday afternoon; every step forward required aggressive action. The people were generally well dressed—well, the men, anyway. Most of the women were barely dressed at all. Unlike most strip joints he'd visited, there was no stage, no artificial dividing line separating the patrons from the professionals. The dancers were working on the floor, often surrounded by a cluster of men barely a foot away.

"Isn't that kinda dangerous?" Loving asked.

"How do you mean?"

"Lettin' those droolin' idiots get so close to the girls. Eventually one of 'em's gonna get drunk enough to try to reach out and touch."

Trudy smiled. "Not to worry. This place has more bouncers than the Senate. No one gets away with anything in here."

Loving shoved his way past a group of gagglers surrounding a tall blond woman writhing on the floor in a hot pink sequined bikini. "It's nice to know management cares about its key employees."

"They don't. It's all dollars and cents. They want to attract the best customers, and that requires them to have the best girls. You don't get the best girls if you can't take care of them. That's all a girl really wants, you know." Trudy snuggled closer and laid a soft head on Loving's shoulder. "A strong man to take care of her."

"Would you stop that!" Loving pushed forward into the crowd. "So where is this Renny, anyway?"

"I can't be sure. But he's usually in the back room."

"Of course. There's always a back room. And let me guess. Not just anyone can get in."

Trudy touched Loving's nose. "Ding, ding, ding."

"So what do I have to do to get in? Say the secret word? Beat up a squad of bodyguards? Solve the riddle of the Sphinx?"

"I'll show you."

Trudy blazed a trail through the jam-packed club. In many respects, the place was like a casino. There were no windows, no clocks, nothing to remind anyone of how late it was or how long they'd been there. He wondered if they pumped oxygen into the room to keep everyone a little high. Happy people bought more drinks. And whatever other luxury items the place had to offer.

Loving veered left to avoid a fight in progress, then almost tumbled over a dancer giving a guy a hand job. A guy Loving thought he'd spotted on the Senate floor, but he was too repulsed to look for long. He tripped and fell to the floor, and the minute he pulled himself up, he came nearly nose-to-butt with some dancer's naked buttocks. As he steadied himself and scanned the room, Loving wondered if there had been this many women taking off their clothes in a confined area since the court of Caligula.

"That dancer back there," Loving said. He was shouting, but given the general din, he could barely hear himself. "She was toasted."

"You could tell that from staring at her ass?"

"No, her eyes."

"Well, that's hardly unusual. Even in a high-class joint like this one, most of the girls do a few shots or maybe a line of coke before they plunge into action. It's a tough job. They need something to . . . distance themselves."

"Seems like management would put a stop to that."

"To the contrary. As long as they don't overdo it, management likes the girls to be a little looped. Loosens them up. Makes them much more likely to tolerate a little pinching or other inappropriate touching. Accidentally brushing your boobies against some drooling politico's face. That sort of thing."

"You sound like you're speakin' from experience."

"Are you kidding? How much could I take off before . . . you know. Some of my girlfriends are strippers, and they've told me about it. It's not an easy life."

"Then why do it? Go to typin' school."

"And spend the rest of your life fetching coffee for the man? No thanks." Trudy leaned in closer. "In an A-list place like this, a good dancer can make two thousand bucks a night."

"How?"

"By pleasing the big tippers."

"Pleasin' 'em how?"

"You probably don't want to know."

"You're probably right."

"For five hundred bucks, you can get a fabulously good-looking girl and pay a bouncer to look the other way while the two of you disappear into one of the many small side rooms."

"Disgustin'."

"Maybe. But very profitable."

Loving almost crashed into a waitress. He knew she was a waitress because she was wearing clothes. "Get you something?"

"Yeah. I'll take a beer. And another one for my . . ." He gestured toward Trudy. ". . . friend."

Once again he pulled a five out of his pocket, and once again it was refused. The waitress smiled. "Your money's no good here, big boy."

Loving blinked. "You mean it's on the house?"

Trudy whispered in his ear. "She means you need Action bucks."

"Huh?"

"This place issues its own scrip. It's all the waitresses—or the dancers—will take."

"Scrip? How do I get that?"

"Give the waitress a credit card. She'll sell you some. With a twenty percent markup."

"That's highway robbery!"

"Maybe so, but it's the only way you'll get a drink in here."

Loving shoved his wallet back in his jeans. "Then never mind."
The waitress shrugged and moved on. "Scrip? What kind of idiot
would agree to a rip-off deal like that?"

"Well, with most guys, when the most beautiful woman they've
ever seen in their life straddles them and starts doing a lap dance,
they don't want to make a trip to the ATM."

Loving plowed ahead, muttering to himself about how he was
gonna have to talk to the Skipper about a raise.

At long last, they reached an alcove where, unlike the rest of the
entire club, men were the center of attention. Most of them were
sweaty and had their sleeves rolled up. And at three different tables,
the men were arm wrestling.

"What's this about?" he asked Trudy. "Trying to impress the
chicks?"

"More like, trying to blow off some steam because you can't afford to do it with any of the chicks. Give me a minute."

Loving watched Trudy approach another gatekeeper. He spotted a windowless door at the rear of the alcove. The back room.

"I'm here to see the Boss," Trudy said.

The gatekeeper shook his head. "You're not on the list tonight."

"Doesn't matter. I need to talk to him. About a job I did."

"Sorry. You're not on the list."

Loving watched as Trudy snaked an arm around his neck
and leaned forward, pressing—what? rubber padding?—against his
chest. Fake as it all was, he didn't know how the gatekeeper could
resist. She—*he,* damn it—was a total hottie. "Surely you can make
an exception. Give a girl what she needs."

The gatekeeper grinned from ear to ear, but he didn't budge.
"Sweetheart, I'll be happy to give you what you need any time, any
place. But I can't let you in that room."

Trudy recoiled and stomped away in a snit. "I gave it my best
shot, Loving. I couldn't get in."

"So that's it? We give up?"

"Of course not. You're going to have to enter the tournament."

"The tournament? What, poker or somethin'?"

"Arm wrestling!"

"This is a contest? I thought they were just . . . you know. Showing off."

"No. The winner gets inside the back room. It's like, the grand prize."

"Why is that a prize? Does everyone want to see Renny?"

"I doubt if any of these rubes know who Renny is. But they've heard about the infamous back room. It contains some . . . rare delicacies."

"Just give it to me straight."

"Women. Real women. Willing to have sex with anyone. No questions asked."

"Prostitution."

"No money changes hands."

"Renny keeps them doped up."

"Point is, they're there, they're willing, and they're better-looking than anything most of these muscle-bound clods have seen in their dreams. So, done any arm wrestling?"

"Well, yeah."

"Good. Then we've got a shot."

"I haven't done it in a long time."

"Doesn't matter. You'll have me to help you."

"You? How the hell are you gonna help?"

She slithered up close to him. "By exercising my feminine wiles, sugar."

"Don't call me 'sugar'!"

38

"This just in," Beauregard said, flying into the conference room with a blue-rimmed piece of paper in his hands. "We've crossed the Rubicon."

Ben squinted. "I don't understand."

Senator Hammond smiled. "When Julius Caesar was fighting the Gallic Wars—"

"I understood the historical reference," Ben said, trying not to appear annoyed. After the day he'd had, he was a little tired of being cast as the political equivalent of the village idiot. "What I don't understand is what he's talking about."

"The latest instant polls indicate that more people favor the Roush nomination than oppose it. And this is the first time that's been true since he made his coming-out speech in the Rose Garden."

"Swell," Roush said. "Does that mean we're winning?"

"Hard to say. This was a poll of the public, not the eighteen members of the Judiciary Committee. Still, one tends to lead the other."

Carraway pushed her glasses up on her nose. "I'm getting the same intel from my media contacts. Apparently Ben's little speech touched a few of the right chords," she admitted grudgingly.

"What?" Ben said, pressing his hand against his chest. "Can this be? Are you suggesting that I did something right?"

Christina kicked him under the table. "Gina's trying to be nice," she muttered. "Don't push it."

"To be specific," Carraway said, avoiding Ben's question, "the reference to partisan politics played very well. People are sick and tired of partisan politics. At least that's what they always say to pollsters. In reality, of course, they love it. Scandal is great fun, and they'd much rather read about someone's sexcapades than their views on foreign policy. But at any rate, that bit played well. Also, the line about McCarthy's ghost. Pure genius. Who wrote that for you?"

"Actually," Ben said, "it just came to me as I was speaking."

She gave him a long look. "You're saying you . . . extemporized? Used a line that hadn't been tested? Instant-feedback polled?"

"I wasn't even planning to give a speech. But after Roush declined to respond, I knew I had to do something."

Beauregard stepped between them. "Your remarks were not vetted in advance? Not approved by the oversight committee? Not play-tested before a shadow audience?"

"Nope. Just made it up."

"And what the hell do you call that?"

"Ummm . . . speaking from the heart?"

Carraway pressed the heel of her hand against her forehead. "God help us. That's so . . . amateur. Hammond, I can't work with this."

Hammond smiled. "The kid did good, Gina. Leave it alone."

She closed her eyes, her disgust unmasked. "I'm a kingmaker," she muttered. "A kingmaker surrounded by peasants." She left the room, slamming the door behind her.

Hammond slapped Ben's shoulder. "I thought it was a hell of a good speech. Not the first time I've heard you do it, either. I hope you're giving serious thought to running for another term. I think you could pull it off."

Ben frowned. "I don't know. I can't decide. On the one hand, it seems wrong to pass on an opportunity to do some good in the world. On the other hand, the thought of undergoing a campaign is horrifying."

"Why?"

"Ben is afraid someone will dredge up his lurid sexual history," Christina said, covering her mouth with her hand.

"What? Don't tell me you go to gay bars, too."

"I most certainly do n—" He glanced at Roush. "I mean, not that there's anything wrong with that. But—"

"I thought you two were engaged," Hammond said.

"We are," Christina said firmly, when Ben didn't.

"Well, what are you waiting for? Get married. That'll make him more electable. It will stifle sexual speculations and put an end to any talk about Ben being gay."

"Since when has there been any talk about Ben being gay?" Ben said, sitting up straight—then noticing Roush glaring at him. "I mean, not that there's anything wrong with that."

Roush rolled his eyes, then turned to Hammond. "And this was the man you chose to be my chief advisor?"

Hammond chuckled. "Don't gripe, Tad. The man saved your bacon in there. Or at least kept you in the frying pan."

Bertram Sexton raced into the conference room, carrying his jacket. It was the first time Ben had ever seen him wearing only two of the three pieces of his suit. "Been trying to get a line on how the undecided members of the committee are going to vote. Without success. No one's talking."

A line creased Roush's forehead. "What does that mean?"

"Nothing," Hammond assured him. "Means they're waiting to see which way public opinion tilts."

"But we know Keyes and Matera are voting against me, no matter what happens."

"And Potter and at least five others who don't have the spine to buck the party line," Hammond conceded.

"But if everyone follows party lines, we were dead before we began."

"So we have to assume someone will show some courage."

"A rather tall order," Sexton commented icily.

"But not impossible. If we have public opinion on our side." Hammond thought for a moment. "And if we can make it seem like the right thing to do. Nothing a politician loves more than playing the hero for a just cause. Especially if there's no risk involved."

"Here's something else you might want to see," Sexton said, passing around photocopies of a brief report. "We've managed to trace funds from a right-wing lobbying group that somehow found their way into the bank accounts of two of the people who testified against Tad. Who accused him of . . . well, you know."

"So they *were* paid," Christina said, grabbing a copy.

"Of course, the organization is saying they were just expense reimbursements."

"Ten thousand dollars?"

"Yeah. Guess they stayed at a really nice hotel." Sexton grimaced. "I'd be willing to bet more money will follow. Once the heat is off."

"This doesn't help their credibility," Ben said, thinking aloud. "But it doesn't prove they were lying, either. Man, I'd love the chance to cross-examine them."

"I wouldn't mind taking a swing at them myself," Sexton agreed. "But it isn't going to happen. They're not even giving interviews. Their financiers are taking no chances."

Christina turned up the volume on the corner television set. CNN was running a recap of the day's hearing, a greatest-hits compilation, the shouting points, always culminating with a clip of Ben's closing—usually ending on the "McCarthy's ghost" remark.

"I for one am tired of hearing that," Ben commented. "Do you suppose if we called Ted Turner and asked him nicely, they'd stop running it?"

"We don't want them to stop running it," Sexton said. "The more people see it, the more chance we have of converting people to support our nominee."

"But the committee votes first thing tomorrow morning!"

"I know," Sexton replied, and for once, a trace of sadness tinged his eyes. "I never said it was a great chance. But it's the only one we've got."

39

Judge Haskins slammed the front door of his rented George-town home behind him, locked it, dead-bolted it, pressed his back against it, and breathed an enormous sigh of relief. "Vultures. Relentless vultures!"

"You should talk," Margaret said. Her hair was up in the usual beauty shop do, with a single strand dangling down the front out of place. "You haven't been here all day. I have."

"Vultures!" Haskins repeated, just to get the thought clear in his mind. "They have no right to harass us like this."

"Do you want me to call the police?"

Haskins frowned but said nothing.

"That's what I thought. Having the press hauled away might end your run of perfectly glowing stories."

"Do I detect a note of cynicism in your voice?" he asked. He wrapped his arms around his wife and gave her a firm hug.

"I suppose I'm just not accustomed to being married to a hero.

I mean, being married to a judge was good. Very good. Decent money, all the best parties. But being married to a hero—well, that's more intense."

"I'm not a hero," he said, shrugging uncomfortably. "I only did what any other man would do in that situation."

"That clearly isn't true." She kissed him lightly on the cheek. "You *are* a hero, darling. Live with it."

He shrugged. "What's for dinner?"

"Shrimp limone."

He gasped. "Dear Lord. Have I died and gone to heaven?"

"Not yet, Rupert. I rather think your next destination is a musty old courtroom in Washington, D.C."

"Now, Margaret, I've cautioned you—"

"I know, I know. No chickens before hatching. Not even sure you want it." She winked. "But I'm picking out my inauguration gown, just the same."

Haskins mounted the stairs, feeling as tired as he had ever felt in his entire life. What a day! He was a judge, for heaven's sake. He'd never expected to be caught in the middle of a media firestorm. The President's people calling him night and day, asking question after question, always something more they had to know—now. Why did you say this in that opinion? Passages he didn't even remember that were suddenly of critical importance. And they practically wanted documentary evidence of his heterosexuality. At least half a dozen friends had called to tell him they'd been pestered by investigators.

Bad enough that the Roush nomination had gone so sour so fast: people demanding his withdrawal, others accusing them of homophobia, others prying into Roush's personal life and finding the most unseemly details. Now they were saying there was just the slightest chance Roush might survive the committee, that there was a backlash created by Keyes and Matera's heavy-handed tactics, that his advisor had swayed public opinion with an honest and heartfelt expression of outrage. Didn't matter, of course—there was even more damaging information waiting in the wings.

Haskins still remembered the look on Richard Trevor's face as he passed him the all-important manila envelope. Like a little boy who had learned the secrets of the universe and couldn't wait to tell. Trevor was watching his reaction oh so carefully. Haskins made a point of giving him nothing. If he wanted to know how badly Haskins wanted a Supreme Court nomination, he was going to have to find out by offering him one. He wasn't going to get an advance peek by playing these stupid cloak-and-dagger games on Roosevelt Island.

It was so close now. So close he could taste it. If he could just survive all this attention. The hotline phone calls in the middle of the night and supposed power brokers wanting to meet in low-key yet public locales, secret files and the impossible need to be on top of everything without appearing to be aware of anything. He had to be above the fray and the master of it simultaneously. Like tiptoeing through a garden of eggshells. But here he was, bearing it all, keeping his head up, making sure that if his chance came—*when* his chance came—he would be ready. He owed that much to Margaret. And to himself.

To be a justice on the Supreme Court of the United States. To have the ability to quite literally change the world with a stroke of a pen. What wouldn't someone do for power like that?

40

In general, Loving knew all the fundamentals of successful arm wrestling. What boy who grew up in a small town in Oklahoma didn't? It was a survival skill. Only here at Action, it appeared that the arm wrestling would get him access, not information. With luck, it might at best get him into the mysterious and salacious back room, where he might be able to wheedle out some information.

Contrary to the popular opinion of arm wrestling, Loving knew that the most important factor was not brute strength, although strength could certainly come in handy. For the push—the offensive action—what mattered was your shoulders and upper back. For the pull—the defensive action—you needed brawny pecs and biceps. Loving worked out regularly and tried to keep his upper body in shape. At his size, the only choices were muscles or flab, and he preferred muscles. He hadn't been to the gym since he started this investigation, though, and he knew he wasn't in prime shape.

"Push ahead," Trudy said, standing behind him, giving him a little shove. "Take on the boy in black."

"Nah. He's the champ."

"You can take him, you imposing hunk of manhood."

Loving felt his teeth clench. "Don't talk to me like that," he sub-vocalized.

"I'm just saying what's true. What's wrong with that, sugar?"

Loving felt his neck stiffening. "Let me start with one of the newbies. I'll work up."

"No, take the top dog while you're fresh. Get us inside that room."

"I'm not sure I can take him."

"I am. I'll be helping."

"Right. With your"—his voice dripped with sarcasm—"feminine wiles."

"Don't underestimate what you don't understand."

"I understand that you're not—"

"Shhhh!" Trudy gave him a harsh look. "Don't blow our chances before we've started. This match is almost over. The boy in black is going to take that redheaded punk down any second."

"I'm tellin' you, I don't think this is smart."

"That's because you don't know your own strength." Trudy grabbed his biceps and squeezed. "But I do."

He shrugged Trudy off. "Will you stop that!"

Trudy pouted. "Don't you like me at all? Even a little?"

Loving's lips pressed tightly together. "It's not that I don't like you . . ."

Trudy brightened. "Then you do like me!"

"No! I mean—I just don't go in for . . . you know. Your kind."

Trudy's eyes widened like limpid pools. "I am what I am, Loving. I can't help it."

"I know. I just . . . you . . . oh, aarrghh! When do we start with the arm wrestling?"

"When you get in line, sugar."

"Don't call me—"

"Go." She pinched his butt. He jumped into line.

Standing next to the Boy in Black's table, it was easier for Loving to study his technique. He was obviously experienced. He knew that the key secret was to push with the weight of your shoulder, augmented by your back and chest—not your biceps. By leaning into your opponent, you could throw your entire body weight into the struggle. The biceps you held in reserve, using them only if you had to, probably in defense if the match started to get away from you. The Boy in Black knew all this, and it showed in his current battle against a homunculus with a bushy red mullet. The other guy was probably about twice his size, but the Boy in Black was creaming him.

Beating this dude would require Loving to be more than strong. He would have to be smart—not normally what folks considered his strong suit.

Well, if he couldn't be smart, he could certainly manage tricky.

After he triumphed over the red mullet, the Boy in Black—dressed in a tight short-sleeved black T-shirt and black pants, sort of a *Dukes of Hazzard* version of Johnny Cash—took a towel from a barely clad beauty and wiped his face and hands. He grabbed the woman around the waist and pulled her close for a smoocheroo.

"You are so hot," the woman said breathlessly. She wrapped her hands around his muscular abs.

"Cool it, sweetcakes," he said. "I'm still working." A thin smile—almost a sneer—emerged. "Can't let you get me distracted. Women sap a man's strength."

Loving tried not to barf. He decided he didn't like the Boy in Black, which was good. It would make this so much easier.

"Who's next?"

"He is!" Trudy said, pushing Loving forward.

The Boy in Black gave Trudy a long, hard, very unsubtle look. He was clearly interested. "Wanna sit by me during the match, baby?"

"Sorry," Trudy said, clutching Loving's arm. "I'm with him."

The Boy in Black frowned, then noticed Loving for the first time. "That right? The tramp's with you?"

"She's not a tramp. I mean, she's not—"

"Why settle for a cheap cut when there's quality meat inside, pal?"

Loving felt his lip curling of its own volition. "That's no way to talk about a . . . lady."

Trudy beamed.

"I think you owe her an apology, chump."

The Boy in Black was not intimidated. "Uh-huh. And who exactly is going to make me?"

"Boys, boys, boys," Trudy said, squeezing between them. "We don't want any violence. Let's settle this on the arm-wrestling table." She turned to Loving and winked. "My hero."

The Boy in Black sneered. "You think this big lug can take me?"

Trudy's chin rose. "I think he'll mop the floor with you."

"Well, then, let's get to it." He stepped up to Loving, sneering. "Haven't seen you here before."

"Haven't been here before," Loving replied.

"Sure you want to start with me? Be a lot easier to work your way up through the bottom-feeders."

Exactly the same opinion Loving had expressed a few moments earlier. But now that he had heard this obnoxious jerk say it, he was determined not to do it.

"I'm in a hurry to get inside," Loving said simply.

"But no one wants you inside."

"After that cover charge I paid at the door, I don't much care whether anyone wants me or not. I'm goin' in."

"But this room you have to earn, bozo. That's why they put me in as the gatekeeper." He grinned, revealing an unpleasant display of poorly cared-for teeth.

If his experience had taught Loving anything, it was that the best weapon against bravado was its polar opposite. He made a strategic about-face. "Well," he said, shuffling his feet slightly, "you'll probably humiliate me."

"He will not!" Trudy insisted.

"But I gotta try," Loving added sheepishly.

The Boy in Black commiserated. "I understand. Hell of a thing, being pussy-whipped in public."

Loving managed to keep a straight face.

The Boy in Black gave Trudy one more lascivious look. "Last chance to sit with the champ."

"No thanks," she replied, grabbing Loving's arm. "I told you already. I'm with him."

He turned to Loving. "That right?"

"Yeah," Loving said, steely-eyed. "*She's* with me."

Loving lowered himself into the chair.

"Wait a minute," the Boy in Black's bimbo said. "You gotta pay to play."

"I paid a bundle just to get in here."

"And you'll pay a bundle more if you want to rumble with my baby."

Muttering under his breath, Loving pulled out a wad of real money—not scrip Trudy had collected earlier. "That do?"

The Boy in Black swept it away. "That'll do." He put his elbow on the table and opened his fingers. "Ready to play?"

Loving was.

He could see almost immediately that they were evenly matched, at least in terms of strength. The Boy in Black could see it—and was surprised and irritated by it—as well. They both grunted and strained, but neither made any headway. At first, Loving had a slight edge: he could feel his opponent's fist tilting ever so slightly to the side. But the Boy in Black soon corrected the situation. This could potentially go on forever, but Loving knew he couldn't afford a protracted match. It had been too long since he'd been to the gym, and unless he missed his guess, his obnoxious opponent was a daily visitor. If it turned into a stamina match, he would lose. He needed a different approach. The Drag.

Every bar rat in western Oklahoma knew the Drag, but he was betting that this East Coast pseudo-redneck wouldn't. At a moment of equilibrium, Loving hooked his wrist around the Boy in Black's till his palm faced him. Then, pulling with all his strength, he tried to drag his opponent's wrist, not to the side in the traditional manner, but toward him.

The Boy in Black was not prepared for the Drag. He tried to compensate, but Loving could see it was a struggle. Loving pulled hard, bringing all the strength in his enormous chest, back, and shoulders to bear. In this position, the Boy in Black had to fight back with his biceps, putting him at a distinct disadvantage.

Pull! Loving told himself, trying to force all his might into the maneuver. He could feel sweat dripping down his brow. His arm began to tremble slightly, the first and surest sign that his strength was ebbing. He might have the power position, but maintaining it was tough. The longer this went, the harder it would be. The Boy in Black's arm descended lower, then lower still . . .

The kid made a loud grunting noise, heaved himself back, and restored his arm to the upright position. Square one. Loving had taken his best shot—and failed.

He looked up and saw the Boy in Black grinning, those sickening teeth glistening. Damn, he wanted to beat this twerp! But the kid had the edge, and Loving knew it.

"Hang in there, sugar," he heard a voice whisper in his ear. "We can take this steroid stiff."

We? Where was the "we"? Loving gritted his teeth and tried to hold on. His opponent had him on the defensive, forcing him to use his biceps to keep himself in play. He couldn't hold this position for long. He had one more trick in his bag, but he couldn't implement it while his fist was on the way downward. If he was going to have any chance, he had to get his fist back upright.

Slowly, surely, he righted his fist to the twelve o'clock position. The Boy in Black was sweating a little, which gave Loving no end of pleasure. He had a hunch it had been a good while since this overblown clod had done any real perspiring.

Loving took a deep breath. Time to implement the Roll. This move was designed to take advantage of the weakest part of the opponent's body—at least, the weakest part in play in an arm-wrestling match: his fingers. Instead of pushing against the other guy's palm, Loving abruptly switched to pushing the meaty part of his thumb against his opponent's fingers.

He saw the Boy in Black wince. Good. The Roll was having its desired effect. Ever so slightly, his hand was starting to bend.

Loving twisted his wrist around to roll the primary pressure point of his assault onto the tops of the kid's fingers. His limp wrist buckled. Loving pushed hard. The Boy's hand went downward.

Downward, but not down. Loving knew he was close, but not close enough. This arm-wrestling machine had recovered before. He couldn't allow it to happen again. But what could he do about it?

Once again he heard whispering in his ear. "I'll take it from here."

What the hell did that mean? Loving didn't know, and he certainly couldn't turn around to ask, but a moment later, he became aware that Trudy was not only standing behind him but . . . moving. Sashaying, perhaps. Swinging her—*his*—hips from side to side, no doubt in the most provocative manner possible. Loving could only imagine the facial expressions that accompanied the movement. Correct that: he did not want to imagine the facial expressions that accompanied the movement. He was pleased that he could not see what Trudy was doing.

But the Boy in Black could. He resisted at first, but as the match progressed and the pressure on his fingers became more intense, he glanced away more frequently, distracted by the show taking place behind Loving's back. It had to be good: several of the other men in the room were watching as well.

The primary tenet of arm wrestling, the single most important factor, is concentration. If your mind isn't on the game, you're going to lose. And sure enough, not thirty seconds after Trudy went into action, Loving managed to push the Boy's hand onto the plush red pillow.

He'd won the match.

The Boy in Black was furious. He leaped out of his chair, then turned on his attending bimbo. "How come you never make moves like that?"

Her face flattened. "I've never even . . . *seen* moves like that."

He whirled around to face Loving. "This wasn't a fair fight."

"I didn't break any rules."

"Yeah, but it still wasn't . . . wasn't . . ." This guy's vocabulary didn't have words for it. Loving wasn't particularly surprised. He knew the Boy in Black had lost more than a match; he'd probably lost his job as well.

"All right, damn it. You can go in. Both of you." He sneered as he opened the door. "After all, it was a team effort."

"Let's go then, partner." Trudy offered him an arm.

"I am not taking your arm," Loving hissed quietly.

"Show some gratitude."

"I didn't see you sweatin' in that chair!"

"I did my part. You know I did."

"Yeah, well . . ."

"It'll look better if we go in together."

Loving rolled his eyes, feeling as if he might explode at any moment. But the sad truth was—Trudy was right.

His linked his arm around hers. His. Whatever. And they stepped into the inner parlor.

41

Here he was again. Sitting at home. Alone. Because he had stopped taking calls days ago. It was too dangerous to make any. And his lover of seven years wouldn't speak to him.

At least the police had finally removed the crime-scene tape. That was a relief. He could pretend that his home was, once again, his home. Also home to a hostile roommate. But home.

Roush had never expected to be here. Never expected the nomination to advance this far. Maybe, truth be told, that was the real reason he had come out of the closet during his acceptance speech in the Rose Garden. Risky, ballsy, controversial—but if he derailed his own nomination, then it could never proceed far enough to uncover his real secret. The one for which he still bore the guilt. His failure would be attributed to homophobia, not any problem on his part, and the secret would remain secret.

Except that no matter how he might privately want this nomination to die, it didn't. Hammond was working too hard. Sexton was too influential. Even Kincaid was helpful, in a goofy sort of way. They kept pulling his fat out of the fire. And only he knew how disastrous that could be in the long run.

They all acted as if he had been physically raped when those paid whores started rattling on about gay bars. Not him. He knew that would come out. He hadn't anticipated all the lies about orgies and threesomes, but that was okay. Ironically, it had backfired, ended up reinforcing the claims of homophobia, especially when it was proven that the witnesses—at least some of them—were liars. Paid liars.

The truth always emerges, eventually.

That's what he was worried about. It was not possible to keep a secret in this town. At least not for long. Certainly not forever.

He tiptoed down the hallway to Ray's door, then knocked gently. No response.

Probably wasn't locked, but he wasn't going to test it. If Ray had shut the door to his room—the room in which he'd been sleeping for the past many weeks—he'd done it for a reason. Nothing good could come from entering a room where he wasn't wanted. It had been so long since the two of them slept in the same room that Roush couldn't even remember when it was. Before this endless media conflagration. Before his life was turned topsy-turvy. Which was mostly his own fault.

He just hoped Ray wasn't avoiding him for the wrong reasons. Not that there was a right reason. But if there were more to it than just his irritation, his humiliation at having his private life made public . . .

Well, Roush preferred not to even think about that.

Was withdrawing still an option? Could he decline the nomination, after so many had done so much to keep him in the game? How would he possibly explain it?

He couldn't. And so, tomorrow, he would dutifully walk into that Caucus Room, waiting to hear sixteen people decide his fate. With his friends, support staff, and co-workers. All the while knowing that, of all the hearts beating on the Roush confirmation team, his was the one that had the least faith in the nominee.

When Jessie Matera turned thirty—not yet a senator, but close—she had blown her first perfect smoke ring. Since then, she had mastered the art. She didn't smoke much; she didn't smoke cigarettes at all. But occasionally, in times of great stress or jubilation, she allowed herself a good old-fashioned stogie. Why should the boys have all the fun?

Except tonight, it wasn't working. This was her third attempt, and it still wasn't right. More oblate than circular. Like the shape of the earth as viewed from outer space.

"Care for a smoke, Richard?"

Trevor reacted as if he had been offered a sneak peek at a porn flick. "I don't smoke, Jessie."

"Sure? Might relax you a little."

"I'm fine. Smoking is a vice."

"You seem a bit uptight tonight. But then, you always do." She passed the humidor toward the young man in the blue suit. "Try one."

"No thank you." Trevor smiled a little. "Jesus never smoked."

Matera took a long drag on her cigar, then exhaled. "Jesus never lobbied Congress for favors, either."

"In a way, he did. When he turned over the tables in the temple and tossed out the moneylenders—"

Matera raised a hand. "Spare me. I'm too old for fairy tales."

"Are you suggesting that the Holy Bible is not the word of God?"

"Perish the thought." She took another long drag. "I know the party line. Every word contained in the Bible is literally true. Just like it says in the Gospels. Even though the Gospels contradict each other constantly, they're still all literally true. Somehow . . ."

Trevor pointed a finger. "Don't be sacrilegious with me. I won't tolerate it. I can withdraw my funding—"

"Don't threaten me," Matera said, cutting him off. She didn't have to point. She could get her message across with her eyes. "You need me."

"You need me, too."

"That, unfortunately, is correct. I mean, I don't, not really. I couldn't care less if Roush gets to wear a black robe. And I'm not planning to run for reelection, as you know. But I do care whether I get nominated for the vice presidency. I'd make a damn good Vice President. And our current Commander in Chief seems to share my opinion. All he requires in exchange is that I serve as his personal lickspittle and perform every nasty job he needs done between now and then. A small sacrifice for such a distinguished position, don't you agree?"

Trevor looked at her directly. "Hasn't been a Republican Vice President named in the last twenty years that didn't have the support of the Christian Congregation."

Matera covered her mouth and yawned. "You don't have to wave your dick at me, Richard. I already know how big it is."

"I don't appreciate that kind of talk."

"I know. Jesus probably never said 'dick,' either, did he?" She put the cigar to her lips and savored the slightly woody aroma. "What's your big interest in this thing, anyway? Is it just that you want what President Blake wants?"

"The President wants what I tell him to want."

"As I suspected. So why are you so dead set against Roush? He's a smart man, you know. A good judge. Fair. Rational. Has actually read the Constitution."

"The man is a sodomite. That's still illegal in some states, you know."

"So is spitting on the sidewalk. Seriously, though, is that all? You oppose him because he's gay? 'Cause that's a dying cause, you know. And I say that as a prominent Republican senator who raked the man over the coals about his gayness during the hearings. I can see the handwriting on the wall. This is another form of prejudice, and future generations aren't going to look on you any more favorably than current generations look on the KKK."

"The Bible expressly forbids—"

"You're talking about that bit in Leviticus, right? Which was written about . . . what, 1750 B.C.? That was the Bronze Age, for pity's sake."

"I had no idea you were a Biblical scholar. I myself just read the words and follow them, and the Bible says, 'A man shall not lie down with a man—' "

"Except, taken in context, it's talking about a married man, right? It's saying that it's still adultery, even if you aren't having intercourse with a woman."

"That's not how I read it."

"And God didn't say anything about homosexuality in the Ten Commandments, did he?"

"No, but—"

"So this Biblical imperative didn't even make the top ten. Did Jesus say anything about it?"

"Not that we have a record of, but—"

"So in the end, it's just that one Bronze Age passage from Leviticus. And scholars aren't even sure what it's saying."

Trevor lowered himself into the nearest available chair. It had been a mistake to meet Senator Matera in her office. Something about being on her home turf gave her too much confidence, just as the fact that she wasn't running for reelection gave vent to a singularly unpleasant rebellious streak. "Satan produces false evidence to tempt the weak. Sometimes even people of great power can be weak."

"Oh, don't be so touchy. I'm not trying to threaten your narrow little worldview. I can't oppose the Christian Congregation and we both know it. I'm just curious. Is that really all this is? Political gay bashing? Pandering to the public distrust of anyone different from themselves?"

Trevor hesitated. "I happen to believe the President made a mistake when he nominated Thaddeus Roush."

"But you must've approved it. Or he never would've done it."

"We didn't know then what we know now."

"Namely, that he's gay."

"That's just the tip of the iceberg. An indicator of so much more that's wrong with this man. It's a mental illness, you know."

"Being gay is a mental illness?"

"Many prominent psychiatrists have said so. On the record. Even in these PC times."

"Would these prominent psychiatrists be members of the Christian Congregation, by chance?"

"That's neither here nor there. The Mark Foley scandal did incalculable damage to our cause. This could be even worse."

Matera rolled the cigar between her fingers, still eyeing her companion closely. "You're a stubborn man, you know that, Trevor?"

"I believe the same could be said of you, Senator," he replied, with a tiny intimation of a grin.

"Did you by chance have a better candidate in mind?"

Trevor tilted his head to the side as if trying to decide how much was safe to say. "I prefer a national hero to a national disgrace."

"Right. Haskins." Matera was sad to see that her cigar was almost at its end. She really shouldn't have a second, not at her age. Even during times like these. "Is Haskins on board with this?"

"I think he has made it clear that he would be willing to step in, if called, assuming he felt there was sufficient support for his nomination. But he wants no part of the effort to defeat the Roush nomination."

"Understandable. So you're sure he's your man?"

Trevor stared at her through steepled fingers. "There is a . . . well, a test pending, if you will. A loyalty test. A measure of determination. Or character."

"Stop talking in riddles. What's he got to promise? To bury *Roe v. Wade?*"

"He needs to prove he's someone we can work with."

"Someone who will take orders when given?"

"I liked it better the way I said it."

Matera shook her head. "You're a devious man, Trevor."

"I prefer to think of myself as a clever strategist."

"As you wish." She ground her cigar butt into an ashtray. "Think this is going to get out of committee?"

"I'm not sure. But it doesn't much matter. If it doesn't get out of committee, that makes everything so much easier. But I have to be prepared for every contingency. That's what clever strategists do. When they play to win. And I always play to win. Yea, though I walk through the valley of the shadow of death, I will fear no evil."

"So that's it, then. Never mind the qualifications, the record, the man himself. He's gay, and you've decided that homosexuality is an unforgivable sin, so he's going down. The sad thing is, I can't even criticize you. I know you honestly believe what you say. For you, it's a matter of faith." She paused. "I just wish your personal faith had less to do with judgment and more to do with mercy."

Matera sighed, stood, and stretched. It wasn't the cigar smoke, but she nonetheless had a strong desire to take a bath. "I think this meeting is over, my friend. We both know where we're going." She shook his hand again, then clapped Trevor on the shoulder. "I really wish you'd have taken that cigar."

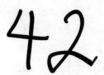

42

Loving and Trudy sashayed into the back room, arm in arm.

"Will you stop that already?" Loving muttered.

"What's that, sugar?"

"Don't—" Loving bit back his words. There were a lot of people in the room. Mostly naked men and totally naked women. Not many of either were paying attention to the new arrivals. "You're . . . swinging your hips."

"That's what girls like me call *walking*."

"Do you have to walk so . . . provocatively?"

"I am what I am."

"Well, actually, you're not."

"Details, details."

Loving swore silently. "Do you see Renny?" He'd been so concerned about winning the arm-wrestling match and getting in here, he'd almost forgotten the primary mission. They had to find the mysterious Renny, the man who had instructed Trudy to take Victoria to the Roush press conference. Which she didn't leave alive.

"Not yet. Why don't I work the room?"

"Okay. What'll I do?"

"What you do best. Stand there and look tall and manly." Trudy leaned over and gave him a peck on the cheek.

Loving's reaction suggested he was about to resort to fisticuffs.

Trudy held up a finger. "Temper, temper." She winked. "Sugar."

She sashayed off to the right. And Loving knew this because he was watching.

He closed his eyes and mentally chastised himself. Ogling a guy! A guy who looked like a really spicy chick, sure. But still a guy!

Loving mopped his brow. He had to keep his attention on the matter at hand. Renny.

The back room was far more glamorously appointed than the club outside. Loving was no expert on furniture, but he knew this was stuff of a higher order. Plush satiny chairs and sofas, lots of mahogany and oak. Most of the men in here looked foreign. Collarless shirts. Accents he couldn't distinguish. Eurotrash.

There was a lot of sex going down in the room, in all manner of positions and combinations, but that wasn't the half of it. A couple of the men in easy chairs were getting lap dances. One had his pants down; the other was jerking off while he watched the lap dance one chair over. These women were clearly of a higher order: well groomed, fit, statuesque, beautiful. Many of them had a foreign cast to their features. Mail-order Russian women? Loving wondered. Lured over with the false promise of marriage, only to end up strutting and grinding in this high-class dive? He hoped not.

Loving turned his eyes away from the various performances taking place throughout the room and directed his attention to the wall. There was a painting hanging just beside him, a beautiful oil depicting an Old World wooden ship at sea caught in a storm and many men on board trying to bring it to rights. Loving didn't know much about art, but he was certain he'd seen this picture before. But where?

Now that he noticed, there was a lot of art in the room, not only paintings, but sculpture and mobiles descending from the ceiling, and brightly colored Pop Art stuff that he hated. He had no idea if it was real or reproduced, valuable or Wal-Mart, but it certainly gave the room a different look from the usual illicit sex parlor. Why did Renny bother? Did he really expect anyone to notice an art show while he had a naked seventeen-year-old undulating in his lap?

He returned his attention to the painting, and a memory sparked. It was a Bible story, that was it. This was the *Storm on the Sea of Galilee,* and those men scrambling all over the boat—the fishing boat—were Jesus's disciples. This depicted the scene before Jesus walked across the water. He'd heard the story a million times when he was a kid in Sunday school. Maybe that was why the painting looked familiar. Maybe he'd seen it in church?

No, there was something else, something more. He just couldn't remember what it was.

Someone crept up from behind. "Found him, sugar."

Loving pivoted. "I told you not to call me 'sugar.' "

"I know. That's pretty much why I do it."

Stay calm, Loving told himself. You still need her. *Him!*

"So you found Renny?"

"Yeah. Wasn't easy. He had his face stuck in—well, you probably don't want to know."

"You're right."

"Anyway, he's done now. Let me introduce you."

Loving followed Trudy across the room, trying to ignore the various forms of immorality and debauchery taking place all around him. He wasn't normally that much of a prude, but this place was making him sick. All these people making out—if you could call it that—in front of a Bible-story picture! It just wasn't right.

He glanced at the painting one last time. Why did that picture bother him so much?

Loving found his quarry slumped in an easy chair upholstered in what appeared to be a corded green brocade—very fancy. Renny had that slightly dazed, vacant expression that Loving knew as the sure sign that the man had recently emptied his seminal vesicles. Loving supposed he should be grateful for the opportunity to question the man while he was in a dissipated, semi-comatose state.

Renny's eyelids fluttered. He looked up at Loving, who from his angle must have appeared to be about forty feet tall. "Trudy say you wish to speak to me?"

He had a thick accent—Russian, Loving thought, but he couldn't be sure—and a salt-and-pepper mustache and beard that was no doubt supposed to compensate for the thinning hair on the top of his head. Loving introduced himself, providing as little information as possible. "You know—or I should say, knew—a woman named Victoria."

His lips turned up in a sweet, trembly smile. "Ah, sweet Victoria. Such boobies on that woman! Not real, of course. But I have not been such a man as would care."

Loving pursed his lips and tried again. "I was wondering why you asked Trudy—"

"Trudy! Yes! Another fine example of the woman."

"She's—he's not a woman."

"Such a nitpicker you are. Trudy is charming and very pleasant for the eyes. What more does a man require?"

"Well . . ."

"Most importantly, she is so agreeable. She will do anything I ask her to do, you know what I say? Absolutely anything. All I do is pass a little money her way every now and then and she is mine to command. Every man should be so lucky as to have such a willing slave."

Beside him, Loving saw the topic of conversation doing a slow burn. Trudy was angry.

"But enough chatter about people such as these. Why do you ask me questions?"

"I'm trying to find out why you asked Trudy to escort Victoria to the Thaddeus Roush press conference."

Renny shrugged happily, still basking in the easygoing state of afterglow contentment. "That is easy to explain."

"It is?" Loving considered himself pretty good at this sort of thing, but even he hadn't expected the man to talk this quickly. "Why?"

"Because Victoria—such a lovely woman, but she did not drive."

"That's it? 'Cause she couldn't drive?"

"What can I say? A wonderful woman Victoria was. Extremely

talented. In so many unexpected ways. But she grew up in Manhattan. She never learned to operate a motor vehicle."

"But—" Loving tried to suppress his growing frustration. "There must be some reason you arranged for her to go to the press conference. I'm pretty sure she didn't have a press pass."

Renny's eyes lowered. For the first time, Loving had the sense that he was thinking before he spoke. "Ah. But there you touch on matters of business. I cannot discuss matters of business."

Loving squatted down till they were eye level. "That ain't good enough. A woman is dead. An innocent man has been accused. This could affect who does and doesn't end up on the Supreme Court. You're gonna have to talk."

"Ahh . . . I think not."

Loving leaned forward. "I think so." He reached for the man's collar.

"That would not be such a good idea."

"Oh yeah? You think you could take me?"

Loving felt a hand on his shoulder. Trudy. "That's not what he means, sugar." Trudy jerked her head backward.

Loving did a quick scan of the room. They were hard to see. The spotlights on the walls focused upon the art objects, creating blind spots in unusual places. But when Loving forced himself to focus, he was able to detect at least four men standing about the room, one against each wall. They were not paying the slightest attention to the women in the room. They were watching him and Renny—their boss, no doubt—very carefully.

Muscle. Hired muscle.

Renny shrugged. "So you see, Mr. Loving, we are at an impasse, are we not?"

Loving backed off. He could take those creeps one at a time, but they were unlikely to come at him one at a time. That's why there were four of them.

"This isn't over. I'll be back."

"I think not," Renny said, supremely confident. "It will take more than a strong arm to get you in here again. You will never get past the bouncers at the front door. So I fear that this is farewell, my friend."

Loving gritted his teeth. Much as he hated to admit it, the man was right. How would he ever get in here again? He wasn't a police officer, and even if he were, what would be the basis for a warrant? Even if he put on a Sherlock Holmes–type disguise, he'd probably never be able to get back in here again. He'd played his hand and lost. What a fool he'd been! He should have seen this coming. He should have—

"There's a back door behind the green sculpture," Trudy whispered in his ear, pointing.

"Huh?"

"Go." Trudy leaned forward over Renny's easy chair. "And just for the record, I never liked working for you, and you still owe me money, you Ukrainian creep!"

Renny looked almost as puzzled as Loving felt.

Trudy turned her attention back to Loving. "Count of ten, sugar."

"Huh? What are you gonna do?"

"What I do best. Create a diversion." Trudy winked. "Count of ten."

Loving began counting. Trudy disappeared. And ten seconds later, the lights went out.

A gun fired in the darkness.

43

Ben was closeted with his advisors—quite literally, since they were all standing in a janitorial storage closet down the hall from his office. The press had Ben's office, Senator Hammond's office, and the Caucus Room covered; this was about the only place left where they could meet without having to field the same question over and over again: Will Thaddeus Roush withdraw?

"Is there no hope at all?" Ben asked.

Sexton shook his head sadly. "I've talked to every senator on the committee who would talk, and the AA of every senator on the committee who wouldn't talk. This has become too much of a lightning rod—for all the worst reasons. It's going to go straight down party lines."

"And that means we lose," Beauregard added, as if Ben didn't know that already. "Ten to eight. The nomination dies in committee and President Blake picks someone else. Without ever being forced to take a controversial position on a controversial issue."

"Who can we call? Who could we work on? There must be someone who could be persuaded to vote his or her conscience," Ben said.

"What do you think I've been doing for the last forty-eight hours?" Sexton snapped. "It hasn't happened." He glanced at his watch. "And now it's too late. I hate to say it, but . . . it probably would be best if Roush threw in the towel."

The door cracked open. "That won't be happening." Roush stepped inside.

Sexton gritted his teeth. "I don't like it any more than you do, Tad. But I hate to see you rejected. You deserve better than that."

"I won't turn tail and run."

"If you go in that room, you force everyone to take a stand. It becomes a referendum on gay rights."

"Maybe it should be!"

"Let me correct myself. It becomes a referendum on gay rights—and the gay community loses."

"The first time. Perhaps we have to lose a few times before we can win. Better to start the process."

"I'm sorry," Ben said, "but I disagree. Better to wait for the right time. The first black Supreme Court nominee—Thurgood Marshall—passed because the time was right. The first female appointee—Sandra Day O'Connor—passed because the time was right. I had hoped that the time was right for you." He lowered his head. "But apparently I was wrong."

"So are you saying you want me to quit?" Roush looked at him, his face twisted in a knot. "Is that what you're saying? After all we've been through? I should quit?"

Ben thought for a long time before finally speaking. "I think you should . . ." He tried again. "I think you should do what's best for you, Tad."

Roush laid his hand firmly on Ben's shoulder. "Then let's get our butts into that Caucus Room."

"Before we begin," Chairman Keyes said after the hearing had come to order, "I have a few words I'd like to say to the people in this room. An opening statement, if you will."

"Point of order," Ben said, pulling the microphone to his lips.

"This is not a courtroom." Smart-alecky, yes, but he wasn't likely to get another chance.

To his surprise, Keyes grinned. "Yes, Mr. Kincaid. Thank you for that clarification." He looked to the side of the gallery, which Ben knew equated to looking directly into the camera. This speech wasn't for the people in the Caucus Room. It was for the folks out in television land.

"There's been a lot of discussion about this proceeding in the press of late. Too much, if you ask me. And too little of it has focused on things that actually matter."

Like what, threesomes in gay bars? What was the purpose of this? The man already had the votes he needed to give the President what he wanted—Tad's head on a platter. Didn't he?

"Let me make one thing perfectly clear. Throughout these proceedings, I—and I think I speak for my colleagues as well—have been concerned with one thing and one thing only: the professional and personal qualifications of the nominee. So when we cast our votes today, ladies and gentlemen of the press, you may be assured that we are voting on that basis. And that basis alone."

Very sweet, Ben realized. He's basically arguing that he and his companions could conceivably kill Tad's nomination without being considered anti-gay.

"Every man and woman on this dais has a conscience, and those consciences place integrity and loyalty at the epicenter of—"

"Point of clarification," Ben said, interrupting. What the hell— this thing was over, anyway. "Do Robert's Rules of Order permit the chairman to attempt to influence the committee members with a so-called opening statement right before the vote is taken?"

"Mr. Kincaid!"

"I mean, I know you've been doing it for weeks, but in the hearing room, on national television? I don't know. It just seems sort of tacky."

Keyes's nostrils flared. "Mr. Kincaid, I am grossly offended by your suggestion that—"

"Well, I was grossly offended by your self-serving opening statement."

Keyes pointed a gavel. "Consider yourself fortunate that I don't find you in contempt of Congress."

"I could hardly be more contemptuous of certain members of Congress than I am at this moment."

"Mr. Kincaid!"

"Why don't you call this what it is? A pathetic attempt to save face even though you and the other members of your party are about to kill the nomination of a worthy man because your partisan masters wish it. Because it turned out the nominee had a different sexual preference than you do and wasn't afraid to tell everyone."

For the first time since the start of the proceedings, Keyes appeared barely able to contain his rage. "You are out of order."

Ben started to reply, but Keyes cut him off. "I sat patiently and listened to your speech yesterday, appallingly self-serving though it was. Now you will afford me the same courtesy. And if, as I think may be the case, you don't know the meaning of the word 'courtesy,' I can direct you to the nearest dictionary."

Ben settled back into his chair. There was no reason to continue—he'd made his point. Anything more would just seem obnoxious. Not that he particularly minded being obnoxious to Senator Keyes, but it wouldn't do Roush any good.

"As I was saying," Keyes said, rediscovering his oratorical voice, "this assemblage has always acted with pride and dignity as befits these chambers, so let no one dare to cast aspersions, let no one congregate with the wicked, but let us only cast our votes as our hearts, our minds, and our Creator directs us."

Ben tried not to roll his eyes. It was the first time he'd heard anyone violate the Constitution three times in a single sentence.

"All those who favor sending the nomination of Thaddeus Roush to the full Senate with a favorable recommendation for confirmation should so signify by saying 'aye.' All those opposed should signify by saying 'nay.' The clerk will call the roll."

As had undoubtedly been arranged in advance, the clerk started with those sitting to the left of the chairman—the Republicans. One after another, they fell in with the party line. Eight votes in a row, all against.

Roush sank progressively lower into his seat. "It's over," he said quietly.

"Senator Matera of Wyoming," the clerk called out. "How do you vote?"

There was a pause, long enough to cause every head in the room to turn her way.

Keyes leaned into his microphone. "Senator Matera? It's your time to vote."

"Yes, I know that." She batted her finger against her lips, then sighed. "I've been thinking a long time."

"Senator, we need your vote."

"And you mean that in more ways than one, don't you?" She smiled a little. "I've got to tell you—despite outward appearances, I've been troubled about this business for a long time now."

"Senator . . . ," Keyes said, a deep furrow crossing his forehead. "This is not a time for making speeches. You do not have the floor. You just need to cast your vote."

"Well, now, Mister Chairman, you got to make your little speech, even though it was not proper procedure, so you can just hold your breath a moment while I make mine."

A mild titter of laughter spread through the gallery. Ben realized he was clenching his pencil so tightly his knuckles were white. What was going on here?

"I came into the Caucus Room today expecting to do . . . well, just what everyone expects me to do. I've been the good chairman's attack dog, and now I'm supposed to deliver the final bite to the throat. But I've been troubled. Since the start, I suppose. I mean, I don't mind asking questions. Anyone who wants to sit on the Supreme Court ought to be prepared to answer some tough questions. But what's going on now . . ."

She seemed lost in thought for a moment. "It disturbs me. Right down to my core. I had a conversation last night that disturbed me even more. Reminded me where the real power in this town is now, and how far that is from where the real power is supposed to be. In the long run, I suppose one little vote isn't going to make that much difference. But you never know, right?"

Ben gasped. Was it . . . possible?

Chairman Keyes cleared his throat. "Senator Matera, do you feel quite well?"

"Fit as a fiddle."

"And . . . you understand what you're doing?"

"Yup. Kissing the vice presidency good-bye." She shrugged, tugged on the flared lapels of her jacket. "Stupid job, anyway. Who wants to carry the President's luggage for four years? I'd rather go back to Wyoming and spend some time with my grandchildren." She sat up straight and turned slightly so she could face her fellow Republican committee members. "So on behalf of all of you—whether you like it or not—I'm going to do what you should've done. What you perhaps wanted to do but couldn't find the courage to do. Because every one of you knows that Thaddeus Roush is a fine man and a distinguished jurist. Smart as a tack. Your reasons for voting 'no' have nothing to do with his qualifications. And that's a shameful disgrace that I find myself unable to countenance." She stopped, then started again. "And one more thing, just for the record: if the founding fathers had any inkling what these confirmation hearings would turn into, they would've never given us the damned advise-and-consent power in the first place."

Matera stared directly at Keyes, who looked almost as flabbergasted as Ben felt. "I vote yes, Mister Chairman."

Ben was stunned, but not so stunned he couldn't add. Matera's vote was unexpected, but even if every Democrat on the committee voted yea, it would only produce a tie. Chairman Keyes would break the vote, and he knew all too well how that would end.

As it turned out, Senator Matera wasn't finished. "And what gives me particular pride—and hope for the future—is that I've managed to convince Senator Potter, the youngest member of this committee and thus the one most able to change the old-guard politics, that confirmations should be based upon qualifications, not party politics. Isn't that right?"

Senator Potter nodded. "I second that, Senator. And I also vote yes, Mister Chairman."

The room was thunderstruck. One after the other, every Democrat on the committee voted to confirm Judge Roush.

With the vote at ten to eight, Keyes would never have a chance to cast a tie-breaking vote.

While everyone else was still gaping, not sure whether to applaud or hiss, Thaddeus Roush rose slowly to his feet.

"Thank you, senators," he said quietly. "You honor me. And may I perhaps express my special thanks to you, Senator Matera, for reminding me what government is supposed to be."

"My pleasure, sir," the senator from Wyoming said, her eyes twinkling. "Now get over to the full Senate hearings and give 'em hell."

44

"What's going on?"

Loving had no idea why the lights had gone out, except that he was certain Trudy had made it happen. He would have to remember to thank Renny for being stupid enough to piss her off. Later.

Piss *him* off.

Someone had fired a gun. Loving didn't know who, but it stood to reason it was one of the four bodyguards he had made earlier. Even though he couldn't see anything, he could hear movement from all corners of the room, above the loud cries and protests from various quarters. Total darkness probably took a lot of the fun out of a good lap dance.

He knew the bodyguards would be heading his way. He didn't have much time.

He leaned into the place he last recalled seeing Renny's ear. "You're gonna come with me now."

"No."

"Yes. And it would be better for you if you came peaceably."

"I do not think so. Over here, Dmitri!"

Have it your way. Loving grabbed the green sculpture behind him. He hoped it wasn't a priceless antiquity, because it shattered into about a million pieces when he clubbed Renny over the head with it.

One of the bodyguards managed to stumble into Loving. Loving grabbed his shoulder so he could get a bearing on where the rest of his body was, then punched the guy hard in the kidneys. He went down fast.

Loving didn't wait for another thug to find him. He lifted Renny's limp body, threw it over his shoulder in a fireman's rescue position, and hightailed it for the back door Trudy had indicated to him earlier.

It was tough to find the door because he kept tripping into naked women and priceless objets d'art, but as he got closer to the back wall, he was able to discern a thin trace of light down below. It was the light from outside seeping through the crack in the door, enough to indicate where he wanted to go.

The noise behind him was increasing, and increasingly close. It would be only a matter of seconds before the bodyguards caught up. He hoped Trudy had her escape plan worked out in advance, because he had no opportunity to look for her. He reached for the doorknob and—

The lights came back on.

"There he is!"

Loving didn't wait to see which of the thugs was doing the shouting. He threw open the door and plunged into a back alley. A trash Dumpster was just beside the door. Loving dropped his bulky Russian package, grabbed the Dumpster with both hands, and pulled it in front of the door. A second later, someone tried to push it open—without luck. The Dumpster didn't budge.

Loving didn't kid himself that the obstruction would hold, or that it would take the hired muscle long to run through the front door and circle back to the alley. He hoisted Renny back up on his shoulders and headed for the street. Luck was on his side for once. The alley let out just a few hundred feet from where he had parked the car.

Trudy was not waiting for him.

He wished he had a chance to search, but he knew that waiting around would only get him captured, probably killed. He threw Renny into the backseat and peeled out. As he left, he saw several men he recognized from the inner parlor racing toward him. Too late, suckers!

He thought he had at best a few minutes before Renny woke up. He decided to drive back to the motel room where Trudy had held him. He knew where it was, knew it was private, and knew it was unlikely that any of the thug patrol would show up there. And if Trudy returned, he would know she had gotten out safely.

Not that that mattered. Obviously, it didn't matter at all where some damn transvestite went. But . . . he'd just feel better if he knew she was all right.

He. If he knew *he* was all right!

Loving didn't have to wait long before Renny regained his senses.

"What happened?"

Loving sat in a chair facing the captive, his arms folded across his chest. "You declined to come quietly."

"Ernst!" He tried to stand, only to find he'd been tied to a chair. He could barely twitch.

"None of your bullyboys are gonna help you. They're far, far away and they don't have a clue where you are."

Renny arched an eyebrow, seemingly unafraid. "You are certain of this?"

"I'm absolutely positive. I left them in the dust. I wasn't followed. And they had no way of knowin' where I was takin' you."

"Well then." Renny stopped his useless struggling. "It would seem that I am at your mercy."

He said it, but he didn't seem nearly worried enough for Loving's satisfaction. "So now maybe you'd like to answer some of my questions."

"I suspect that I would not."

"You will," Loving said, staring him in the eye, "when you know the alternative."

"You do not strike me as such a man as would kill simply to obtain information."

Loving shrugged. "You're right. I usually gravitate more toward slow and painful torture."

"I think that you are bluffing, my friend."

Loving punched him in the solar plexus.

Renny doubled forward as much as the rope would allow, which wasn't much. A few moments later, after he had recovered, his sneer returned. "Still bluffing."

Loving hit him in the jaw.

"You know," Loving said, "I'm really not enjoyin' this. Are you?"

A trickle of blood ran down the side of Renny's mouth. Loving wiped it away.

"Do you really think that I would betray my business for so little cause, my friend?" Renny asked. "My enterprise is worth millions. *Millions.* It will not be brought down by one stupid brute. You are a fool if you think otherwise."

"The only thing I'm thinkin' is that we're both reasonable men and we could save a lot of time if you told me what I wanted to know without me havin' to get rough."

"What is it you wish to know?"

"Told you already. Why did you have Victoria taken to the Roush press conference?"

Renny stared at him for a long time before finally responding. "You proceed from an incorrect assumption."

"And what would that be?"

Renny hesitated even longer. Loving rose to his feet, pounding one fist against the other.

Renny spoke. "I did not wish for Victoria to attend the conference. I cared nothing about the conference."

"Trudy told me you arranged the whole transportation setup."

"That much is true. But it was not because I wished it. It was because Victoria wished it. All I did was make the arrangements. Victoria and I have done . . . much business together. Both professional and personal. Naturally, I hoped for this relationship to continue. So it was a simple matter to arrange the ride for her."

"Why did she wanna go?"

"I believe that she and someone at the conference . . . had unfinished business. She owed me money. And she believed that this visit might assist her fund-raising efforts."

"How?"

Renny's eyes narrowed. "Now you are asking me questions such as I cannot possibly answer. As I said, it was her business, not mine. And now she is dead."

"You must have some idea. Especially since you two had this close relationship."

Renny did not respond.

"I'm waitin'," Loving said impatiently.

"I have told you what I know. Anything more would be speculation. Or might endanger other professional relationships. With the living."

"What relationships? What the hell are we talkin' about? What were you and Victoria into?"

Renny paused for a long time, then sighed wearily. "It is so difficult to know how to begin. Do you know anything about art?"

"Art? You mean, like that picture in your back room of the bearded guys on the boat?"

Renny's eyes traveled skyward. "Yes, like that priceless Rembrandt—*Storm on the Sea of Galilee*. Which has been missing for many years."

"Missin'? I just saw it."

Renny only smiled.

"Look," Loving said, "I'm tired of these games. I want to know what this Victoria person was doin' at the press conference. I want her real name."

Renny seemed to be staring beyond him, not making eye contact. "That I cannot do."

"That you will do, you Europimp, or I'll take you apart piece by piece."

"If I give you her name, then you will be able to learn everything."

"That's the general idea."

"That, I cannot allow."

Loving rose to his full height, inflated his chest, and pounded his fists together. "I don't see that you've got a hell of a lot of choice. You'll tell me what I want to know and you'll do it now, or I'll separate your neck from your head!"

The door behind them slammed open.

Loving whirled around. To face Max and Pretty Boy.

They were both armed.

Renny smiled. "I guess I would say that I see the situation differently than you, Mr. Loving. It is, after all, simply a matter of perspective."

45

"We're not out of the woods yet," Ben kept saying, but no one was listening. Everyone in Washington he knew, and several people he didn't, were packed into his office. Champagne glasses were clinking. Everyone was congratulating Roush, shaking his hand, slapping him on the back. He appeared pleased—a little stunned, perhaps, but pleased. It was a brief but heartfelt celebration. Another fifteen minutes, and then they had agreed they would put the booze away and let the press in. Then things would really become chaotic.

"Appreciate it," Roush said as Ben approached the center circle where Roush was speaking to Sexton, Carraway, Senator Hammond, and others. "But I can't take credit. I owe this one to Senator Kincaid."

Ben waved the compliment away. "I had lots of help."

"I know. And I'll thank everyone. But you turned the tide. You made the people of America sit up and listen, voice their opinion, give it a second thought. You made it possible for Senator Matera to do what she did."

"Maybe," Ben said quietly, "but remember, we're—"

Everyone present recited the rest of the sentence in unison: "—not out of the woods yet!" And then burst out in riotous laughter.

Christina approached with a trayful of champagne refills. "Ben, don't be a wet blanket. We're celebrating here."

"But we don't have anything to celebrate yet."

"Tad got out of committee, fooling every pundit in the city. I'd say that's worth celebrating."

"But he still has to go before the full Senate. And the Republicans hold a majority there, too."

"Then you'll turn them around just like you did the committee."

"I'll be lucky if I'm allowed to speak. There won't be a hearing. The senators will debate, then vote. Period."

"Polls show an increasing groundswell of support for our nominee," Beauregard said, clutching his clipboard and somehow holding a champagne glass at the same time. "More and more people are setting aside their problems with homosexuals and focusing on his qualifications. Much as it pains me to admit it—you made that happen, Ben."

"I think Senator Matera had a little something to do with it, too."

"She fanned the flames. You started the fire."

"Got to agree with that," Senator Hammond said. "And speaking as the Senate Minority Leader, let me tell you that this is a service that will not soon be forgotten. You need to get your hat in the ring for reelection, Ben. I think you'll be surprised by how much support you get."

"Speaking as a lowly lawyer," Sexton said, "I think anyone with your natural skills is wasted in the courtroom, Kincaid. You've found your niche here in Washington, and you've been given a lucky break most people would covet. Make the best of it. The voters will remember what you've done here today."

Ben shrugged. "All I did—"

Christina hung on his shoulder. "Ben, stop resisting and accept the compliments." She bounced up on her tiptoes and kissed him on the cheek.

Ben's face instantly turned bright red. "Christina," he said under his breath, "I've told you before—"

Once again, the crowd finished his sentence in unison: "—not in the office!"

This time the laughter was so loud, so infectious, Ben couldn't help but give in and smile.

"Hey, you wild and crazy party animals!" Jones was standing on his desk, trying to be heard above the fray. "Are you taking media calls yet? I've got a reporter from the *Post* just dying to talk to our Supreme Court nominee."

Roush started toward the phone, but Ben stopped him. "This is your party," Ben said. "Enjoy it while it lasts. I'll take the call."

"Are you sure?"

Ben nodded. "We told them to wait till six. I think I'm capable of saying 'No comment at this time' as well as you are."

Ben wove his way through the crowd and took the phone receiver from Jones. "Look, we don't have anything—"

The female voice on the other end of the line cut him off. "This is Brandi Barnett with the *Washington Post*. Do you have a comment on the Fox News report?"

Ben found himself swallowing air. "The what?" He started over. "We have no comment at this—"

"I understand from a highly placed anonymous source that the Republicans are planning to filibuster if they can't muster the votes to stop the confirmation process. Can you confirm or deny?"

"Can—the Republicans? What—?"

"I also have a White House source saying the President is going to publicly ask Roush to step down and that he has already done so privately. Can you confirm or deny that?"

Ben didn't know what to say. Information was speeding by much faster than he could process it. "What are you talking about?"

"Should I take that as a denial?"

"You should take that as an I-don't-know-what-the-hell-you're-talking-about."

And then she told him.

Ben returned to the celebratory circle, a somber expression on his face. "Tad," he said quietly. "I need to talk to you."

Roush took one look at Ben's face and the smile on his own disappeared. "What is it, Ben?"

"There's an unconfirmed report on Fox News . . ."

Hammond waved a hand in the air. "Then I think we can dismiss it without even hearing it."

"There's . . . There's apparently some evidence . . ." Ben stammered. "Tad, we should talk in private."

"No," he said firmly. "We'll do it here. I have no secrets from my friends." The strange thing was, Ben didn't sense that Roush was dismissing the importance of the report. He just wasn't going to hide from it. "They'll all hear soon enough, I'm sure. What is it?"

"They're saying . . ." Ben swallowed. "They're saying that you had a child. A long time ago. But I know that's not possible."

"Because?" Roush tilted his head to one side.

Again, Ben noticed that he wasn't denying anything. "Because, you know . . ."

"I have had heterosexual relationships, Ben. Before I came to grips with who I really am. Almost got married once."

Ben noticed that Christina's hand was trembling. As always, her instincts were excellent. "Then," she said quietly, "this story . . ."

Roush threw his shoulders back and assumed his best military posture. "Yes, it's true. I fathered a child."

"Out of . . . of . . ." Ben found himself stammering again. "Out of wedlock."

"Yes. I know, I should've told you. But I didn't want to bring any unnecessary embarrassment. On me or the mother, okay? So I didn't, and I apologize for that. Satisfied?"

Ben wished he could answer in the affirmative, but he was still troubled. "But that reporter . . ." He took a breath and started again. "I mean, that reporter was saying that the Republicans were all up in arms. Planning to filibuster, if necessary. And the President was going to make some kind of public statement."

"And you don't think an illegitimate child is enough to merit that kind of backlash?" Roush set his glass down on a tabletop, then walked to a window, his back to the crowd. The sun was setting just behind the Washington Monument. A beautiful spectacle, but one that, at the moment, did not comfort Ben in the least. "You would be right."

"We can still go someplace private," Ben said, stepping behind him. "But I need to know. I need to know everything."

"Like what?"

Ben threw up his hands. He hardly knew where to begin. "Like who has the child now?"

"No one."

"You mean, you put the baby up for adoption?"

"No. There is no baby."

Ben struggled to understand. "You're saying the baby died."

Roush turned slowly, looking a hundred years older than he had only moments before. "I'm saying the fetus was aborted." His once erect posture sagged, as if tons of weight had been yoked across his shoulders. "You see the problem. From a political perspective."

Abortion. The only major political bugaboo Roush hadn't already transgressed against. Ben clenched his eyes shut. "And you knew about the abortion?"

"Knew about it?" Roush picked up his drink and downed it in a single swallow. "I paid for it."

46

L oving darted behind Renny, positioning his rope-bound body between himself and the assassins.

Renny only chuckled, laughter distorting his thick European accent. "So, in a mere matter of seconds, I am transformed from your punching bag to your human shield. Do you perhaps see some intrinsic worth in me now?"

"Just shut up," Loving growled, putting an arm lock around the man's neck. He looked up at the two assassins, both with their sizeable guns poised and ready. "What's it gonna be, you clowns? You gonna take out the boss, or you gonna leave quietly the way you came?"

The two men in the long coats exchanged an expressionless glance.

"What's that supposed to mean?" asked Loving.

"It means they are men of few words," Renny said. His chuckle had escalated into a full-out laugh. "They are obedient, but not chatty. I like this in my trained killers."

"Trained by whom?"

"By the best in the entire world."

Loving scoffed. "I've spent some quality time with the Pretty Boy, and I'm here to tell you—he could use a few more days in the swamp with Yoda. Maybe a couple of years."

Pretty Boy's grip tightened, but he managed to restrain from pulling the trigger.

"Enough with this childishness," Renny said, suddenly ominously serious. "Feodor. Take this fool out."

Like a robot responding to command, the older of the two assassins raised his weapon.

Feodor trained the gun on Loving's face. He squinted his right eye closed and focused . . .

Loving pulled Renny up higher, till his head totally covered his own. Then he began rocking the man's head back and forth, just to make sure there was no clear side shot. A flesh wound to the ear probably wouldn't kill him, but it might sting enough to make him release the hundred-and-eighty-pound burden that was currently the only thing keeping him alive. Feodor readjusted his aim; Loving moved the human shield in response. Back and forth, back and forth . . .

"Please," Renny said, exasperated. "You are making me dizzy."

"My heart bleeds for you," Loving replied.

"And how long do you think you can keep this up? Already I feel that your arm is weakening."

"I got two."

"So that will give you twice the—what?—three minutes you have held me already? And then these gentlemen will perforate you like a fishing net. And the alley dogs will eat your corpse."

"Very colorful. You Europimps really got a way with the language." He tightened the lock on Renny's throat.

"Very well. Shoot his arm."

"It'll go through my wrist to your throat," Loving warned. "If I think I'm goin' down, I'll choke the life out of you first."

"Empty threats."

Loving clenched the man's windpipe. "Maybe I'll just start the process now. Call your men off or you're dead."

"If I am dead, then you have no shield." Despite the lack of air in his lungs, Renny managed a perverse smile. "Either way, you will die."

Loving continued choking, but his mind was working the entire time. What the creep said was unfortunately all too true. He needed an end-game strategy, one that didn't result in him being dead. He could delay all he wanted, could threaten Renny, perhaps even kill him, but he'd still end up dead. Dead, and without the satisfaction of having obtained the information he wanted. That Ben needed.

"If I'm goin' down," Loving grunted, still choking the life out of Renny, "then chokin' isn't good enough. I want you to experience pain." He grabbed the man in the crotch and squeezed. Renny screamed. The two assassins leaned forward, adjusting their aim, but Loving warned them back, pushing Renny forward and squeezing all the tighter.

What looked like desperate cruelty had, of course, been done for a reason. With two hands posed at either end of the man, Loving was ready to make his move. It wasn't a very good move, but it was all he had.

Mustering his considerable strength, Loving hoisted Renny into the air, chair and all, and threw him at the two assassins.

Feodor and Pretty Boy toppled several steps backward. Renny crashed to the cold hard floor. Both guns fired, but Loving didn't know where the bullets struck because he was already out the door and thirty feet down the parking lot. All he knew for sure was that they hadn't hit him. And that was good enough.

Loving knew he didn't have time to get to his car and get it started. Instead, he wove his way through the parking lot. If he could make it to the highway, it was just possible he could attract some attention, enough that the two hit men would back off. He knew the darkness would help protect him. On the other hand, a pro like Feodor probably didn't need to see his target to hit it. All he had to do was keep flinging bullets until he got lucky.

Sure enough, Loving heard shots ringing out behind him. He ducked but continued moving, low to the ground. Those two men had major-league firepower. Pretty Boy was still firing his automatic weapon, not that he really knew how to use it. Most of his shots were flying a foot over Loving's head. He obviously thought that if he just fired often enough, the law of averages would eventually give him a hit. A killer who trained on Nintendo rather than the firing range. Pathetic.

But still potentially lethal.

Loving kept running at top speed. What else could he do? And for that matter, how many times now had he been reduced to turning tail and running? How many times had he allowed himself to become the hunted, racing away from people who were trying to kill him? He couldn't stay lucky forever. As soon as he got out of here, he was going to turn the tables. Go after the hunters. It was the only way he could come out of this case alive. As soon as he was safe, he would start planning his attack. The best defense is a good offense. So that's what he would do. As soon as this parking lot emptied out into the street. Just as soon as the parking lot—

Loving put on the brakes, stopping his forward momentum as best he could. But he still had to hold up his hands to prevent himself from crashing headfirst into the brick wall.

The brick wall.

This parking lot didn't empty into the street. It was a dead end.

Loving whirled around, ready for action. But there was nothing he could do, nowhere he could go. He was trapped.

Feodor stepped quietly forward, gun poised. Like the pro he was, he showed no trace of emotion. He didn't have to. Loving could feel the pleasure emanating from him.

"It would seem," he said, with a thick German accent, "that this merry chase has come to an end. You have been a worthy opponent. But now our revels are ended. Go with peace."

Loving backed against the wall. He had nowhere to maneuver. "If it's all the same to you, I'd just as soon not go at all."

"Alas, regrettably, that is not a choice." Feodor raised a gun. It was smaller than the one he had brandished before, but all the more terrifying as a result. He held the gun so close to Loving's chest he couldn't possibly miss. And then he fired.

Book Three

All the Rest Is Perjury

47

In the dim light of the conference room, the television flickered with a blue glow. All at once, the screen flooded with a white light so intense it was momentarily blinding, then faded and resolved into a sienna-tinted head shot of Thaddeus Roush. The voice-over narration was delivered by the warm, crisp voice of a well-known wrestler–turned-actor–turned politician.

"He said he'd be there for the poor, the oppressed, the underprivileged." The camera began a steady zoom toward Roush's eyes. "He said he'd be there for those in need, for those who seek justice. Equal justice." By this time, Roush's huge eyes were all that remained visible. "But when it mattered, he wasn't even there for his own child." A hideous, dissonant, cringe-inducing organ chord sounded, followed by the growing black-and-white image of two fetuses expanding out of Roush's enormous eyeballs and merging into a single horrific image.

All at once, the screen went white again, and the musical sound track was replaced by the sound of a baby crying. Then two babies crying, then three. Soon the speakers were rattling with the titanic sound of so many unhappy babies.

"Every year," the somber voice continued, "almost two million parents choose to have their own babies killed before they are even born. Thaddeus Roush was one of them. Do you really want him on the Supreme Court?"

Ben turned off the set.

"That's just disgusting."

Christina was slumped in a chair munching on a tuna fish sandwich. "Better than the last one. It managed to squeeze in gay bars, orgies, and abortions, all in thirty seconds."

"Where are these coming from? Who's paying for them?"

"Someone with a lot of money. A new PAC formed just to oppose the Roush nomination. Gina Carraway is calling her media contacts, trying to track its funding. But what does it matter what the names are? It's some right-wing group with loads of cash."

"I wish I understood better how people can raise so much money so quickly."

"I wish you did, too. Especially if you're going to run for reelection." She looked up. "And you *are* going to run for reelection, aren't you?"

"What makes you ask that?"

"Knowing you. For a long time."

"So you know I'm hungry for power?"

"I know you can't resist a professional challenge. The chance to be in a position to help people." She paused. "Even if you'd be better off if you didn't."

"You're saying you don't want me to run?"

"Not at all. You should do what you feel called to do. All I'm saying is . . ." She finished the sandwich and wiped her mouth with a napkin. "I think you're an incredible attorney, and getting more incredible all the time. You belong in the courtroom. It's your highest and best working environment, the place where you can make the greatest contribution. The political arena is fine, I guess. And I certainly don't blame you for accepting the governor's appointment—who wouldn't? But it isn't really you." She sat up and brushed the crumbs off her dress. "At least I don't think it is. Am I wrong?"

"I don't know. I haven't made up my mind whether to run or not."

"And I don't mean to pressure you." She placed a hand on his shoulder. "As long as I'm not pressuring you, wanna set a date for our wedding?"

"Christina—"

She held up her hands. "That was a joke, Ben. A joke."

Gina Carraway entered the room, her cell phone glued to her ear. "No, sir. What I'm asking is that you exert your considerable influence to help finance a counteroffensive." She stood by the table and paused. "We're looking for three million dollars." Pause. "I know it's a lot of money, sir. That's why we called you." More pause. Carraway flipped her clipboard and scanned her address list while simultaneously carrying on a conversation. "If we don't, sir, the Christian Congregation is going to choose the next Supreme Court justice. Is that better?"

She looked up at Christina, shrugged. Christina made a slashing gesture with a thumb across her throat. Carraway shook her head and pointed a finger toward her open mouth, making a gagging face. Christina pulled an imaginary wallet out of her back pocket and started counting out the dough. Carraway gave her a big nod and two thumbs up.

Ben marveled at how an entire detailed conversation could take place without a word being uttered.

"Yes, sir, I know the party will appreciate your contribution and sacrifice." Pause. "Well, no, the party can't officially endorse the nominee. He's a Republican." More pausing. "No, the Republicans aren't endorsing him now, either. But despite rumors to that effect, the President hasn't asked him to withdraw." Pause. Pause. Mild drumming of fingernails. "Well, not yet, anyway."

She switched the phone to her other ear. "Yes, sir. We need three million dollars just to get this off the ground." The voice on the other end of the line was so loud Ben could hear it clear across the room. "Yes, that's still a lot of money. But it's less than the Republicans spent the first day after Roush got out of committee." Pause

pause pause. "Yes sir, I know nobody knew this latest revelation until after the committee vote, and doesn't that seem a little suspicious to you? Like maybe someone was holding the silver bullet and saving it until they were sure it was necessary? Don't you think—" Carraway winced, then pulled the phone away from her ear and shut it off.

"I gather that's a no?" Christina said. "Possibly a 'hell, no'?"

Carraway pursed her lips. "The exact words were: 'I'm not going to put my money on the line for a horny homo baby-killer.'"

Ben pinched the bridge of his nose. "And you thought this person would be a likely contributor?"

"Sadly, yes. I thought he was our best shot. It will all be uphill from here."

"Swell."

"Problem is, Roush has no support base anymore, not in either party. Everyone sees him as being totally on his own, abandoned. And if there's any truism to which everyone subscribes in this town, it's that you can't do anything without money." She tossed down her clipboard and stretched. "I haven't been able to locate the source of the funds for the anti-Roush 527s. Originally, it was a consortium of pro-life groups, but they've gotten some extra seed money from other organizations, all of them new. The Republican National Committee can't get formally involved, but a lot of its biggest contributors can and have. Which is not to say there have been no contributors from the left side of the fence. There have been. Lots of them."

"This is so wrong," Christina said. "Tad is a man without a country." She turned toward Ben. "How is he?"

"I don't know. He called and asked if it was necessary for him to come in today. I told him it wasn't."

"When will the full Senate debate the nomination?"

"It could be as early as Monday. Certainly the President wants it over and done with as soon as possible. He wants to take advantage of this latest firestorm. Besides, all these TV spots are expensive."

"That's too soon," Christina said. "How can we possibly turn around public opinion by Monday?"

Carraway cracked her knuckles. "What could we do to turn

around public opinion if we had a year? Hope the world develops a case of collective amnesia? This nomination is over. Finished. Dead in the water. Gay, I could work with. Gay bars, even, I could work with. But abortion? It's hopeless. If Roush has any brains, he'll withdraw."

"But he won't," Ben said quietly.

"Then he'll wish he did."

Ben sighed. "At least it couldn't possibly get any worse."

Annabeth hated it when the boss failed. It didn't happen very often. Maybe twice in the ten years she'd worked as his AA. Keyes had one of the most successful track records in the history of the Senate—that's how he ended up chairing the Judiciary Committee in the first place.

"Massage your neck?" she asked. It had always worked in the past.

"If you insist," Keyes grumped.

Annabeth walked behind his desk, removed her glasses, and began slowly and gently kneading the elderly man's shoulders. "You didn't fail, you know. How could you possibly know Matera would do a Benedict Arnold on you?"

"I should've known. It was my job to know."

"She's just a sad old woman who wanted to do something memorable before she goes gently into that good night. I don't think she had a prayer of getting the VP nod; I don't care what anyone says."

"And I'm just a sad old man who would happily accept the vice presidency if it were offered, but my chances went down like the stock market on Black Friday when Roush got out of committee. Especially when those scheming bastards on the other side made it a matter of conscience." He swore silently. "I hate matters of conscience."

Annabeth kept stroking, sinking her long fingernails into Keyes's almost gelatinous flesh. She could see the short hairs rising on the back of his neck. "So what's the problem? Surely you don't think the Senate will confirm his nomination. Not after the abortion revelation."

"Not a chance."

"Then what's to worry about? He's going down."

"Yes, he's going down. But he's not going down because of me!" Keyes shrugged off her hands. "I'm supposed to be the power broker in this chamber. Nobody should be able to get to first base without my help. Instead, in this mess, I come off looking like a doddering old has-been who couldn't even keep a goddamn baby-killer from getting out of committee!"

"I think you're taking this much too seriously," Annabeth said. She was trying to sound soothing, but he was making it increasingly difficult. "A few months from now, no one will remember that you didn't ground him in committee. They'll just remember that he didn't get on the Supreme Court. You'll be blameless."

"Have you learned nothing in the time you've been working for me, woman? In this town, there's no such thing as blameless."

"Come on," she said, wrapping her arms around him and hugging tightly. "Where's that Texas optimism? There must be a silver lining in this somewhere. When Thaddeus Roush steps into the Senate chamber, you'll destroy him."

"Wish me luck with that," Keyes burbled. "Probably the only comfort that man has at this point is, no matter how bad everything is, it couldn't possibly get any worse."

Judge Haskins's cell phone popped open. "I told you never to call me on an open line."

"You told me never to call you at home, too."

"So take a hint. Don't call."

Richard Trevor sighed heavily into the receiver. "I'm sensing some hostility here, Judge. What's the matter? Haven't you read the papers? Or watched television?"

"Of course I have. How could I miss that influence-peddling barrage? It's the most embarrassing display since LBJ's little girl with the daisy."

"But it's working. Polls show—"

"I don't care about your polls. I don't want any part of your seedy operation!"

"That's not what you said last week."

"Last week you promised me the Roush nomination wouldn't

get out of committee." Haskins made sure the doors to the bedroom were closed and his wife wasn't listening. He must remember to keep his voice down, no matter how excited he got. "You were wrong."

"Details, details. Roush will be rejected. Monday. Probably before the lunch break."

"I don't care! Don't you see what you've done!"

"No," Trevor said wearily. "Why don't you explain it to me?"

"You've made it dirty! Before it was supposed to be a clean, aboveboard affair. The nominee turns out not to be the person the President thought he was, so the committee rejects him and the President picks someone else. I could live with that. But now it's something entirely different. Now it's more like the committee found nothing wrong with him, so some big-money power players dug up some dirt because they have a vendetta against homosexuals!"

"I can assure you, that's not the way it's playing in the public eye. I've seen the tracking polls."

"I want you to stop calling me, stop trying to meet with me. I want you to leave me alone."

He heard Trevor's long exhalation on the opposite end of the phone. "So does that mean you are no longer interested in being a member of the Supreme Court?"

Haskins didn't answer.

"That's what I thought. You want it so bad you can taste it. You just want to get through the confirmation process and emerge squeaky-clean. Like a hero." He chuckled in a way that set Haskins's teeth on edge. "Don't worry, hero-boy. You'll be okay. You can stay as far away from me as you like. But stay close to the President, okay? And when the time comes, I expect you to remember who got you the job you've wanted your entire professional life."

Haskins's lips pressed together; his eyes were livid. "I don't know what you're talking about."

"I think you do. Have a nice weekend, and fear not. Roush will not be confirmed."

"How can you know? He's risen from the dead before."

"I know. This time, I know."

"What, like you have even more dirt you haven't used yet?

Don't make me laugh." Haskins stared at the cell phone, tempted to throw it across the room. "If I know nothing else, I know this: no matter how bad it is for Roush now, it couldn't possibly get any worse."

Roush was getting used to sitting alone at night. The price of fame, he liked to tell himself, as if he hadn't paid that price enough times already. But he knew that this wasn't what it was really about. This was his own fault. All of this mess was his own fault.

He'd known this could happen. He'd known it all along. He took the risk, he decided to keep the truth to himself, and now he was paying for it.

Of course, if he'd told anyone about the abortion, he wouldn't be here at all. Wouldn't have been considered at all. Had he made the right choice? It seemed so pathetically unfair to be automatically disqualified just because of a foolish mistake he made all those years ago. He was just a kid. She was just a kid. He didn't even know who he was—obviously—or he wouldn't have been with a woman in the first place. Why couldn't the past remain in the past?

Asking himself rhetorical questions wasn't getting him anywhere. He was rationalizing, trying to come up with excuses for—well, if not lying, withholding the truth. Funny. This whole thing began to go sour when he chose not to hide the truth, chose to be honest about who and what he was.

Without telling Ray first.

And now he was being hanged by one tiny thing he had kept to himself.

Ben had called three times today, trying to put together a strategy session. What was the point? He was smart, sort of, but naïve in so many ways. Ben still believed in him. Worse, Ben still believed he had a chance, when everyone else knew better.

Self included.

But then—he knew something Ben didn't. He knew what everyone was thinking: it may look bad for Roush now, but at least it couldn't get any worse.

But Roush knew that it could.

48

Pretty Boy slammed a fist into Loving's face. Given the force of the blow, Loving should have fallen backward about ten feet, but the rope—Trudy's rope, from the motel room—held him tightly to his chair. So Pretty Boy hit him again.

Blood gushed out of Loving's nostrils. It looked as if the light in the storage closet at Action was blinking on and off, but Loving knew the only thing blinking was his tenuous grasp on consciousness.

This had been going on for almost an hour. His face was so cut, bruised, and bloodied that Loving suspected it barely resembled his usual handsome self. But at some point, even he had to worry about how much he could take. Or how long before Renny would get sick of the game and just kill him.

Renny stepped into the light cast by the low-hanging lamp descending from the ceiling. "Would this be a time when you would be feeling comfortable talking to me, my friend?"

Loving licked the traces of blood from his lips. He wanted to wipe away the blood dripping into his eyes, but his hands were tied behind him. "Never been much of a talker," Loving managed. "But the ladies tell me I'm a great listener. Why don't you do the talkin', and I'll just keep my ears open."

"Fool." Renny's irritation was almost as pronounced as his cruelty. "You were tough and merciless when you had me strapped to your chair. Do you find torture for information so amusing now as you did then?" He snapped his fingers at Pretty Boy. "Hurt him some more."

The next five minutes were not among the most memorable that Loving had experienced. Okay, they were memorable, he supposed, but nothing he'd remember by choice.

Could be worse, he tried to tell himself. Not too long ago, he'd been certain he was a dead man. He saw Max—no, Feodor—press the gun against his chest. He'd seen him pull the trigger, heard the action fire. When he'd lost consciousness, he felt quite certain it was for the last time. Except a funny thing happened. Turned out that gun wasn't one of your garden-variety firing mechanisms flinging molded pieces of lead. It was a taser gun. About a trillion volts of electricity rocketed through his body. Renny was wearing a dog collar—an electronic homing device—on his ankle, like a criminal on parole, which explained how his paid assassins were able to find him so quickly. Loving woke up later in this tiny storage closet in the back of the club, with barely enough room for him and Renny and Pretty Boy.

"Perhaps I have not made myself clear enough to you," Renny said, clipping off each word with a bitter emphasis. "These men here—they do not like you. My young son Wilhelm, he in particular does not care for you. It would seem that you have embarrassed my boy Wilhelm. Badly. At a public place. A shopping mall. In the ladies' department, no less. It is all much too horrible to contemplate." He leaned forward. "Confidentially, my friend, I am not surprised. I have tried to protect Wilhelm with experienced partners and big guns, but at the end of the day, some problems cannot be remedied."

"Hey!" Wilhelm protested.

Renny waved a hand. "Do not bother. It is true and we both know it."

"He's not so great. All he did was sneak up behind me. Like a coward. He hit me with Alexander's gun. It hurt!"

Renny shook his head, eyes closed. "Do not make it worse than it already is, my son. This man Loving—he has no need for surprise. Take away your gun and he could use you for a sledgehammer even now."

"Not sure I could now," Loving grunted. "But I like the sound of it."

The corner of Renny's lip turned up. "Let me cut to the chase, my friend, or we will be forced to continue cutting your face. Wilhelm would very much enjoy the chance to kill you, and I cannot say that this would cause me much pain, except for my own security and that of my associates. I would like to know how much you know and how you came to know it and who you have told about it. That is all. It could not be more simple. So there you have it. You tell me what I wish to know and you will live. You fail to cooperate and you will die."

Loving spat out the blood dribbled between his lips. "Liar."

"You do not believe me?" Renny said, a hand pressed against his chest. He feigned offense for a moment or two, then gave it up. "All right then. You are correct. There is in fact no chance that you will walk out of here alive. You have embarrassed me too greatly. Even if I was not concerned about the information you have learned—and I am—I could never let you leave. But I can very much rearrange the manner in which you die. One bullet to the cranium and it will all be over in an instant. Quick. Painless. Or we can make it a much slower, more protracted, more . . . memorable affair." He leaned in close. "We will make you feel such pain that this simple torture you have undergone so far will be as nothing. It will seem like your mother's sweet kisses compared to what will follow. So what will it be? The quick death, or the excruciating one?"

Loving grimaced. "Geez, I don't know. I've always been a choosy shopper. Can I have some more time to think about it?"

"I think not." Renny lunged forward and pinched Loving's nostrils closed with one hand, covering his mouth with the other, squeezing so hard it hurt. Loving's senses were immediately over-whelmed by the loss of air. He wanted to gasp for breath, but the fingers on his nose remained firmly in place. He soon depleted the remaining air in his lungs and worse, had no way to release the car-bon dioxide building in his system. His head felt as if it might ex-plode; his eyes were bulging out of their sockets. Blood trickled down his throat.

Just at the instant he was certain he would pass out, Renny re-moved his hands.

Loving lurched forward—or at least his head did, the only part of his body that wasn't tied to the chair. He coughed and wheezed and gasped for air, desperate to get something circulating through his lungs.

"A nasty way to die, isn't it?" Renny said. "But even at that, much too quick. Much too painless. I want something that you will experience with more . . . extended pleasure. Unless you are perhaps ready to tell me what I wish to know."

Loving wanted to be defiant, but found he was unable to form the words necessary to do it. How much longer could he hold out? He knew every man, no matter how tough, had a breaking point. And he feared he was very much approaching his.

"This is your last chance, Mr. Loving. Talk to me!"

Somehow, some way, he managed to find words. "No, thanks. I'll go with Option Two."

"Idiot!" Renny threw up his hands, enraged. He grabbed the lamp behind him, jerked the electrical cord out of the base of the lamp—without unplugging it—and peeled back the rubber coating. Once he was able to reach the wiring beneath, he pulled the two threads apart, careful not to let them touch.

"Americans," Renny swore under his breath. "You have such stupid notions, these preposterous ideas of what it is to be a man. Where did you learn your lessons, from the James Bond movies? Let us see if your little secrets seem so important after this."

Loving felt a surge of raw electricity delivered to his chest. His entire body lurched up and down; his heart beat wildly. Renny had only begun his work. He touched the exposed wires to Loving's forehead, his cheeks, his damaged nose. He ripped apart Loving's T-shirt and touched the wires to his nipples, and when that wasn't enough, he touched the wires to his crotch. Loving fought to stay awake, fought to avoid cardiac arrest, fought to keep his lips closed a little longer.

What would it hurt to talk? he heard the evil voice in his head saying. Ben and Christina could take care of themselves. He didn't even like Thaddeus Roush. Who was he trying to protect? His investigation had come to a dead stop. What was it he was trying to save this time? What exactly was it he was going to die for?

And then the answers crystallized in his head. He wasn't going to die. He wasn't going to take Option One or Two. He was going to live—live for the chance to turn the tables on Pretty Boy and Renny. He had to pull through. If nothing else, for that.

And perhaps for that beautiful painting of the disciples on the Sea of Galilee.

"Damn you!" Renny shouted. He continued electrocuting Loving, but Loving had removed his mind to another place, had focused on thinking, not feeling. Nursery rhymes, country music lyrics, the Pledge of Allegiance, anything to distract him. He couldn't even be sure which parts of his body had been electrified. All he knew was that he had survived it.

Renny was furious. "We need something better. Something that hurts even more! Something this monster can't ignore!"

"I'll get to work on it, Father," Pretty Boy said.

"Don't bother. I have had all of this one that I can stand. If he has told what he knows to someone else, they will soon show their hand. And then we will kill those people. We will kill that senator for whom he works and everyone in his office. We will kill everyone he knows, if necessary. But we will start with him."

He clasped his hand tightly around Loving's throat. "Play time is over, my oversized friend." He squeezed even tighter. "Your death is now upon you."

49

The radio spot began with a voice-over in the usual clipped stentorian tones over a driving electronic beat that had been sampled from an action-picture sound track.

"Do you believe liars should be trusted?"

DUH-duh, duh, ta-da, the electronic heartbeat boomed in the background. DUH-duh, duh, ta-da.

"Do you believe sex offenders should be running the justice system?"

DUH-duh, duh, ta-da. DUH-duh, duh, ta-da.

"Do you believe a murderer should be on the highest court in the land?"

The music swelled, adding a pizzicato electric guitar riff that elevated the tension level of the music to the magnitude of a slasher flick. Then, all at once, the music disappeared. And after a moment of silence, the chorus of baby cries began, a mass cacophony of infant pain.

The stentorian voice returned: "Then tell your senator you don't want Thaddeus Roush on the Supreme Court."

"Paid for by the—"

Christina switched the car radio off. "You know, I was hoping for some Sarah McLaughlin or Alicia Keyes. Maybe John Mayer. Radiohead."

"I've got a Susan Herndon CD in my briefcase," Ben said, keeping his eyes on the road as he navigated the winding avenues of Montgomery County.

"Thanks, but no. Upon reflection, I realize that great music shouldn't be wasted on a sour disposition."

Ben briefly took one hand off the wheel and gave her knee a squeeze. "It was inevitable that the extreme pro-life lobbyists would emerge as soon as the news about Roush's past broke. But that's not going to sway everyone. Polls show a plurality of Americans still think abortion should not be criminalized."

"Now you're starting to sound like Beauregard."

"Well, if you hold a bad penny long enough, you're bound to turn a little green." Christina giggled. "I spoke to him earlier. He's not ruling out the possibility of more backlash. People are tired of judicial appointments turning into political footballs. This has only made it worse."

"Ben." She looked across the car at him, her big blue eyes glistening. "I know you like Tad, but—honestly. Alan Ginsberg's nomination was derailed because he admitted he once experimented with a marijuana cigarette. Remember the big fuss when it was discovered that Justice Roberts advised a gay rights group? He came very close to losing the support of his President over that one. Here we've got not only gay rights but the only other political football that could possibly be more controversial—abortion. People are still split all over the map on abortion and gay rights. Put the two of them together, and I don't see your man getting onto the Supreme Court. Certainly not when the Republicans control the Senate."

"He's a good man, Christina."

"I know that, Ben. But Senator Matera's speech notwithstanding, that's not really the primary qualifier for the Supreme Court, is it?"

"It should be."

"But it isn't."

"But it should be."

"But it isn't!" She grabbed his shoulders and shook him as hard as she possibly could without causing an accident. "Ben, you have to live in the real world."

"That's what people say when they're giving up."

"Well—"

"Don't." He kept his eyes on the road, but his expression was fixed. "We've been through tough cases before. We never gave up."

"But this isn't a case, Ben. That's just it. There's no courtroom. We can't control public opinion." Her face turned downward. "Better to let it go and forge ahead. Concentrate on your reelection campaign, if that's what you're going to do." She lightly touched the ring on her finger. "Maybe even give some thought to your personal life."

Ben paused at a stop sign and turned to face her, his expression stern. "Christina, we are doing the right thing. I will not give up."

The wheels screeched as he pulled away from the stop. "I know," she said wearily. "That's what I love about you. Sort of."

Ben admired the sunroom overlooking the expansive garden in the rear of Roush and Eastwick's home, but he had liked it better the first time he'd seen it, when it was filled with people and excitement, fraught with anticipation and intrigue. Today, with only Eastwick present, and he barely speaking, the excitement was subdued to the point of extinction.

Eastwick was seated in a footed chair with red upholstery and arms that extended into an eagle's beak. He hadn't moved from the chair since Ben and Christina arrived.

"I really don't see how I can help you," Eastwick said, speaking slowly and almost as if his voice were detached from his body. Ben noticed that there was a half-full brandy decanter on a table not far from his chair, and a small glass beside it bearing a trace of the dark, smoky liquid. "Tad never tells me anything."

Christina tried to seem sympathetic. "I'm sure he's trying to shield you from the worst of the media blows. He's been taking some serious hits."

"What am I, a child? I don't need to be protected. I need to—"
His voice caught. "I need to be able to pretend that I'm his partner.
A true partner. Not just a political football."

"I can imagine how you feel," Christina replied, moving to the
chair nearest his. "But let me say that I admire the courage you've
displayed throughout all this. Not only during the police interrogation but even before, having the courage to come out during the acceptance speech and be forthright about—"

"I had nothing to do with that," Eastwick snapped.

Christina hesitated. "Well, I know you weren't the one making
the speech, but still, you understood—"

"I most certainly did not. Thaddeus never told me he was planning to mention his sexual preference. We didn't even discuss it."
His eyes shrank until they were almost the same color as the liquid
in his glass. "I was outed."

Ben's lips parted. No wonder Eastwick had remained so distant
from the confirmation campaign.

"He—He didn't consult you?"

"Not even a hint."

"To be fair," Ben said, doing his best to defend the clearly
indefensible, "Tad did tell us he didn't plan to reveal his sexual preference. But when he stood before all those people and all those
cameras—"

"Yes, I know. His sense of propriety overwhelmed him. Doesn't
that make him a wonderful person? And doesn't that make me—
what? A prop? A tool?"

Christina touched his hand sympathetically, but he acted as if he
did not even feel it. "I'm sure he didn't mean it that way. How did
he explain it to you?"

"We haven't talked. Not really. Not since the disastrous press
conference when the body was found and the police hauled me
away. Nothing. Not even a 'Hi Ray, glad you're not sharing a cell
with Big Bruno.' "

Ben pressed his fingers against his forehead. The resentment
threshold in the room was so high it was palpable. This was going
to be more difficult than he had imagined. "I understand that you
may be having some negative feelings right now. Still, can you give
us any information about the baby he lost?"

"Shouldn't you be asking Tad that question?"

"Believe me, I have. He's not answering. It's like some kind of wall. Someplace he won't go."

Eastwick laughed, a short, bitter cackle. "And for good reason." He rose from his chair, moving as though he weighed a thousand pounds. He poured himself another brandy, downed it in a shot, then walked unsteadily toward the bay window that overlooked the green expanse behind the house. "What you may not know is that for the first thirty years of his life, Tad was perfectly straight."

No, Ben thought, I didn't know, but what else is new?

"That's probably partly why the President's investigators didn't trip onto the truth. There was plenty of evidence of heterosexual affairs in his past. He claims he always was gay, deep down, but he was trying to sublimate it, trying to overcome it. Never quite worked, which might explain why he never married. Might also explain why he tended to favor women from the . . . seedier side of the tracks. No one who would ever make a suitable wife."

"When did he, ummm . . ." Ben could feel his face coloring. How do you put these things?

"When did he realize he was gayer than *La Cage aux Folles*? Later. When he started going to those gay hangouts, more in an effort of self-discovery than because he was stalking action. He claims he was never really sure—until he met me." Eastwick stared through the sunroom window, as if wishing he could bury himself in the loveliness of the peonies and the stately hedges. "At least that was when he first openly acknowledged it. I had had male lovers before, but not Tad." He pressed his palm against the glass. "Despite what you heard at the hearing, I was his first."

"How did you meet?"

"At an art gallery. A showing for one of the Maryland Court of Criminal Appeals judges who painted on the side. Talented woman, actually. I was there because I was clerking for Senator Hammond and I love art, and Tad was there because, well, it came with his job. He brought a date, a homely little thing from the poor part of Annapolis, but I could tell there was nothing between them. Between Tad and me, however, that was different. Instant chemistry, just like in the movies. Instant."

"That's nice."

"It was more than nice. It was fantastic. It was a miracle. It was quite literally what I had dreamed of my entire life. Our first few months together—" He shook his head. "That's when my life began."

"And you've been together seven years?"

"Until now."

"You're not thinking about—about—"

"Can't quite think of a word for it, right? Can't call it divorce, because we're not allowed to marry. But after seven years, there should be something."

"I'm sure you're exaggerating the problems," Christina said reassuringly. "It must seem overwhelming right now. I've often said that these times of stress—trials, hearings, what have you—they're tough on the subject, but they're even tougher on the—the—"

"Still can't think of a word for it? Partner, Tad usually says, but that makes us seem more like lawyers sharing an office than lovers sharing a bed. The law, that sacred cow to which Tad has devoted his life, won't give us a word for what we are. You want to say, 'It's even tougher on the spouse.' But you can't. Because I'm not a spouse."

"Maybe some counseling . . ."

"When? Tad's too busy with this interminable and increasingly impossible quest to get on the Supreme Court, so he can sit on a bench with a bunch of no-life losers and decide the fate of people they've never met. That's all he cares about. Not me."

Ben drew in his breath. If this went on much longer, he was going to be pouring a brandy for himself. "But getting back to the subject of the abortion . . ."

"That happened before we met. Well before."

"I understand, but I still thought he might've mentioned it to you."

Eastwick turned suddenly, and his face was streaked with tears. "He did. And how do you think that made me feel? To know that he'd had a child with someone, someone he didn't even . . ." He covered his face with his hand.

"But why won't he talk about it? We need details to prepare a response."

"Doesn't matter," Eastwick said with a wave of the hand. "It will all come out. Soon."

"No doubt, but we have to prepare, think ahead, and we can't unless—" Ben stopped mid-sentence. A cold chill enveloped his heart. "What do you mean, it will all come out soon?"

"It's inevitable. So many people have been looking into it. For so long."

Ben was confused, but his brain was beginning to work its way out of the muddle, and the only explanation was one he didn't like at all.

"What are you talking about?" Christina asked. "The FBI investigation of Tad's background?"

"No. Well, yes. But—no."

"If you could perhaps be just a bit clearer."

"I'm talking about the police."

"The police?" Christina shrugged.

"The *local* police," he snapped. "I'm sorry. You didn't deserve that. But that's what I'm talking about. Not the feds. The locals. Lieutenants Fink and Albertson."

"But they're looking into the murder of the woman at the press conference. The one no one can identify."

Eastwick collapsed forward, his head practically in his lap. "Don't you see? *She's* the woman."

"Who is?"

"The woman who was killed. It's her! I knew it the moment I saw her. Even though I've only seen photographs. Even though she's done everything imaginable to alter her appearance."

Christina threw up her hands, then turned to Ben. "Do you understand what he's saying? Because I sure don't."

"I fear I do." Ben edged closer. "I think what he's saying is that the murdered woman . . . is the mother."

"The mother of who?"

Eastwick looked up at her with red-streaked eyes. "The mother of the child Thaddeus chose not to have."

50

Renny squeezed Loving's throat all the tighter. Loving could feel the life quite literally oozing out of him. He knew he didn't have much time, knew that Renny wouldn't break it off at the last possible moment. This was for keeps. If he was going to do something to save himself, it had to be now.

"I—I—erg—" Loving tried to speak, but the hand clamped around his windpipe made it difficult.

"Do you think I am such a fool?" Renny said. "You think once again that you will bait me into sparing you so I can hear whatever nonsense you have to say. You are wrong."

Loving gritted his teeth and tried to force the words out, despite the odds. "Y—y—you better."

Renny laughed. "Still you have the temerity to threaten me? It is to laugh. I could crush the life out of you with a flick of my wrist."

"I—know—art—stolen—"

Renny pulled his hand away as if he'd been bitten by a scorpion. "You know what?"

"I know you're an art thief," Loving managed to spit out. He desperately wanted to massage his neck, but his hands were still strapped to his side. His throat was so sore it ached with every syllable. "That's what this is all about, ain't it? Art. All that stolen stuff in your sex den."

Renny laughed, but the merriment was not nearly so hearty as before. "And am I to believe that a homunculus such as you knows anything about fine art?"

"I know it's a good way to make money," Loving rasped. "I know art theft causes more losses than any other form of crime other than drug smuggling. A two-billion-dollar-a-year business, last I heard. I figured you were into drugs, until I saw your private room at the club."

"Drug smuggling is for criminals. I am a patron. This is not crime. It is more like a gentleman's high-stakes poker game."

"Don't kid yourself. You just figured out an easier way to make a living. Drugs are policed and prosecuted with vigor. But art theft is practically ignored, at least by comparison. Security at most museums is pretty light. Even morons like you and your henchmen who couldn't possibly run drugs might be able to run paintings."

Renny slapped the back of his hand across Loving's cheek. "You will not talk to me in such a manner. I am a connoisseur of art. I do what I do out of love, out of respect. I take art from those who do not deserve it, from those who cannot protect and preserve it. I give it a good home. I ensure that it will last for the ages. Safe."

"Safe someplace no one can see it but you," Loving snarled.

"Once again, you are the fool," Renny said. "What do I care if the great unwashed are able to see a priceless Vermeer? Can they protect it? Would they know how to preserve it? Are they even able to appreciate it? I think not."

"So that makes it okay for you to steal it from the rightful owners?"

"Don't be infantile. I do not steal. I leave that to penny-ante players such as Victoria. I buy from those who do. I implicate myself in nothing. What do I know of the provenance of a particular piece of art? I assume the seller has come by it honestly, and if I am wrong . . ." He smiled and shrugged. "Well. Then I am wrong."

"You're a crook."

"Can you prove it? Can you trace any of the art that you saw? I think not. The statute of limitations on art theft is usually less than ten years, a pitifully small period of time to store a great work of art. While I wait to sell it freely, it only increases in value. In Switzerland, the statute runs a pathetic five years. Imagine that! Barely any time at all. In Liechtenstein and the Cayman Islands, a painting can come out of a bonded free-port warehouse in seven days. Seven days! Do you know that the recovery rate for stolen art is less than ten percent? Hardly a high-risk enterprise. Even for famous works, such as that Rembrandt with which you are so enamored, the recovery rate is less than fifty percent. The international art community is disjointed and pathetic. The Art Loss Register in New York and Geneva has improved the situation somewhat, but not nearly enough to slow me down. The worldwide market remains largely unregulated. Interpol is useless. Most countries have rejected the latest UNESCO treaty on art and antiquities. If I wish to sell, I need only go to the right country to do so. If I wish to keep the art, to admire it and treasure it, I need only remove it from its place of origin. No law requires a buyer to research the provenance of a work of art or to try to determine whether it has been lawfully obtained or stolen. And as a result, almost no one does. My work is preposterously simple—barely even a challenge. It would be more difficult to rob your local savings-and-loan than to heist a world-famous van Gogh."

"So that makes it okay?"

"I take care of my possessions!" Renny shouted. "I save them from perilous hands! Even in museums, standards for preservation and restoration techniques are dangerously uncertain. I am much better able to maintain and protect these priceless gems for the common good of humanity."

"Pretty funny," Loving grunted. His strength was beginning to return, but he knew he was nowhere near ready to make a move. "Hearing you babble on about the common good of humanity while you're torturin' a guy tied to a chair."

"Many sacrifices have been made to bring art into the world," Renny opined. "You will barely be a blip on the cultural horizon."

Totally delusional, Loving realized. But he wouldn't get anywhere by pointing that out. It was just possible this was his opportunity to extract some information. "So Victoria—was she an art freak, too?"

"Victoria?" He made a snorting noise. "She knew nothing of art. All she knew was how to steal. And she wasn't all that good at that."

"So why was she at the Roush press conference?"

Renny ignored the question. "If that woman had any real talent or intelligence, she'd have been working the stock exchange. Or robbing payroll shifts. Box-office proceeds. Instead, she made do with podunk palaces like that five-and-dime museum in Boston. And she practically screwed that up. To her eternal detriment. Failed to notice what rich fathers she might offend." He shook his head. "After that, the doors to the art world were closed to her. She was limited to penny-ante crime. Convenience stores. Liquor stores. Running petty errands for politicians and their cronies."

"But what was she doing at the Roush press conference?" Loving asked again, even more insistently.

"You have too many questions. Now I do not believe you know anything. And even if you do, I do not believe you have told anyone."

"You're wrong."

"Am I? We have cut your face—tortured you with electricity. Where is your cavalry, eh? Where are your saviors? I think they are not coming. I think they do not exist."

The door to the storage closet opened and Wilhelm entered the room. He was carrying a space heater and a long iron rod with a sharpened tip. He plugged in the space heater. And waited.

"Do you know what it feels like to have a red-hot iron shoved into your body?" Renny asked.

"Happy to say that I don't," Loving grunted.

"That is about to change. I do not suppose this would be the time when you would like to talk?"

Loving shook his head.

"I thought not. Pity. I have almost grown to—well, if not like, then at least respect you."

"I'm ready, Father," Wilhelm said. The red tip of the iron rod illuminated the barely lit storage closet.

"Very well. Proceed."

Wilhelm did not hesitate. He jabbed the red-hot iron into Loving's exposed gut. Flesh sizzled. Loving cried out, unable to stop himself. And then Wilhelm jabbed him again. And again.

Loving slumped, all his strength oozing out of him. If he hadn't been tied to the chair, he'd be a puddle on the floor. Renny said something, but Loving's brain was no longer able to process the language.

Loving fought as hard as he could to hold it together, but it was useless. His body needed a release from pain more than his brain needed to register understanding. In a matter of seconds, blackness enveloped him.

51

Ben was huffing and puffing by the time he reached the top of the three-tiered marble steps outside the D.C. Circuit Court of Appeals building. After convincing the weekend security staff to let him in, he found the elevators inoperative—budget cuts required shutting off some of the interior systems during the weekend. After mounting three more flights of stairs to get to the top floor, he was near exhaustion. By the time he located Judge Roush's office, he was limping and clutching a stitch in his side.

Perhaps Christina was right. Maybe he did need to get more exercise.

He found Judge Roush in his chambers, a wonderfully ornate room reflecting the Federal architecture of the era in which it was built. Rococo crown molding linked all four painted wood walls to the ceiling. Roush's desk looked as if it was at least two hundred years old; it had a sliding removable lap panel for writing upon and a secretary's rack for sorting correspondence. Judge Roush looked as if he belonged in this Old World environment—far more than he ever did in the brighter, more modern Senate building or the Rose Garden of the White House.

"So," Roush said, barely looking up, "you found me."

"Yeah," Ben said, leaning against a high-backed chair and wheezing. "And it took me all day. Next time leave a note."

"I didn't want to be found."

"That much seems clear." Still gasping a little, Ben slid into the chair. "So what gives?"

Roush leaned back in his desk chair. There was a tranquillity on his face that belied the fact that he was in hiding. "Wonderful office, don't you think? I still remember the first day I came here. Thought I'd reached the pinnacle of my career, the summit. Beautiful office, nice home in the suburbs, good salary—what else was there? I'd made it to the federal court of appeals. The only position higher would be the Supreme Court—and that was so unlikely it didn't even bear consideration. I mean, what were the odds? Not even worth thinking about." He sighed. "I would've been better off if it had stayed that way."

"Don't say that," Ben replied. "You were chosen for a reason. I sincerely believe that. And I don't mean a political reason."

Roush smiled, but Ben knew it was a smile that meant his words had been mentally brushed aside and ignored. "I've been happy here. Always. Love my work. Love my colleagues. Would've been perfectly content to spend the rest of my days working in this office."

"You could," Ben said, even though he didn't want to. "It's not as if you've resigned. Withdraw from the Supreme Court confirmation process and just stay."

He shook his head slowly. "No. Much too late for that. Thomas Wolfe was right—you can't go home again." He stared at the green ink blotter on his desk. "Especially not after all the scandal. Wouldn't be fair to the other judges. I'd be an object of suspicion and mistrust, a blight on the court." He inhaled deeply. "No. Like it or not, this part of my life is over."

"Then let's work together to start a new life. On the Supreme Court."

Roush pursed his lips. "I know you've been to see Ray. I assume he told you."

Ben chose his words carefully. "He confirmed my suspicion that the woman who was murdered at your home was also the mother who conceived the child that was aborted."

"Do the police know?"

"I haven't heard anything. But it's only a matter of time. Both the press and the Republicans are pouring millions into investigating this new aspect of your past. Frankly, I'm surprised they haven't already made the connection. But for that matter, I'm surprised they haven't been able to identify the victim."

"There's a reason for that," Roush said, but he left it hanging, without explanation.

"I did warn you," Ben said, trying to fill the silence. "I advised you to tell me everything. Better to give me the bad stuff up front and let me prepare for it than to allow me to be blindsided."

"You feel as if you've been blindsided?"

"I feel as if I've been sucker-punched by a Mack truck."

Roush nodded. "I really thought that maybe, just maybe, I could slip by. Especially since the Republicans were in such a hurry. I thought it was possible it wouldn't come out."

"I must say," Ben replied, "that there's something odd about the way it was never revealed during the committee hearings, but was revealed the instant you got out of committee. It's as if someone was holding it back, waiting to use it only if it became necessary to derail your confirmation." Ben waited for some explanation. He got none. "But you were naïve to think there was any chance it wouldn't come out. And you're talking to someone who more or less majored in Naïve."

Roush smiled but said nothing.

"Tell me what happened, Tad. Please."

He looked up abruptly. "You mean about the murder? I have no idea. You don't think—"

"No. I mean about your past."

"It's all dead and gone. Over with. A long time ago."

"Evidently not. There must be some reason she came to see you on the day of your press conference." Another interminable silence. "Tad, please."

"No. I . . . can't. I'll just withdraw, that's all. And then it will be over and I can retreat into obscurity and—"

"Listen up, buster," Ben said, his voice acquiring a new and unaccustomed strength. "Do you have any idea how many people have poured hours and hours of their time, not to mention thousands and thousands of their dollars, into your nomination?"

"I know you've worked very hard."

"Forget about me. There are literally hundreds of us. Hundreds of people who put their necks on the chopping block for you. Do you know how many phone hours Christina has logged, working for you instead of that Wilderness Bill that means so much to her? Or the Poverty bill? What about Senator Hammond, the Democratic leader backing a Republican appointee—how often does that happen? You can't just crawl away in a fit of self-imposed martyrdom." Ben's lips tightened. "You haven't got the right. You owe them better."

"Ben," Roush said, spreading his hands wide, "there's nothing more I can do."

"Of course there is. You can tell me what happened. Everything, this time. Every single bit. Then we'll see where we can go from there."

Roush sighed, weariness etched in his brow and the creases circling his face. "All right," he said, finally. "But you aren't going to like it."

52

Was he still bleeding? Loving wondered, as his eyes lolled around in their sockets. Was he awake? He was fairly certain he was awake, because not in his worst nightmare had he ever felt like this, as if a huge gushing hole had been opened in his stomach, a hole punctured by a very hot, very sharp stick. Because it was true.

But still bleeding? He wasn't sure. He liked to think that the heat had cauterized the wound. But he was still tied to the chair. How long had it been now? Hours? Days? It seemed like days, but he knew time moved slowly when you were being tortured. One of those great truths of life, he supposed. One he had never hoped to experience.

He knew he had blacked out at some point, and that made establishing a timeline all the more difficult. He had no way of knowing how long he'd been unconscious. For all that Renny talked about wanting to kill him, he sure as hell wasn't in any hurry about it. Even after he came back around, Loving kept his eyes closed.

After a while, Wilhelm threw down the hot iron in disgust. Renny had tried to comfort him, saying that Loving would wake up soon and Wilhelm could start his fun up all over again. Such a loving father! You could see why the bond between them was so strong. The family that plays together, stays together . . .

The iron rod was lying on the floor, just a few feet to Loving's left. It was still glowing hot. That meant he couldn't have been out too long. Presumably, any moment the Torture Twins would return and resume their activities. And there was nothing Loving could do about it, not as long as he was tied to this chair. He was helpless, pinned down like a butterfly in a collection, barely able to move.

His attention returned to the glowing iron. Still hot. Not far away from him . . .

Could he do it? His brain was so addled that making any kind of coherent plan was difficult. He certainly couldn't be assured he would fall where he needed to fall, and if he missed, it would be over. Renny would find him lying on the floor and he would be enraged. Loving wouldn't get a second chance.

On the other hand, this storage closet was very narrow. It wouldn't be possible to go too far wrong. Even if he hit the wall, he could ricochet back into place. In fact, it might be best if he hit the wall . . .

There were times in a man's life when careful planning was advisable, Loving mused. And there were other times when the best damn thing a person could do was just go for it. Too much thinking would make it all the less likely it would ever happen.

Loving turned to the left, which predictably twisted his insides into a knot and made his perforated stomach burn as if it were on fire. He'd have to overcome that if he was going to get anywhere. He clenched his teeth, took his mind to a better, kinder place where he wouldn't feel the incredible pain he was about to experience, and threw himself down, chair and all.

He flew off to the left of the storage closet, clattering against some rickety metal shelving. Something sharp punctured his arm, but it was nothing compared to the agony he was already experiencing. He slammed down on the hard concrete floor, hoping the noise hadn't been heard by anyone outside.

The fall knocked the breath out of him. He inhaled deeply, quickly, trying to regulate his breathing and gather some strength.

Loving fell facing away from the wall, so he couldn't see the hot iron. But he could feel heat emanating against his bound hands. Thrusting with all his might, he moved himself and the chair ever so subtly backward until the iron was within reach. Then he placed the rope that tied his wrists together directly on the iron.

The problem with having a red-hot iron between your bound wrists was that, no matter how effective it might be at burning the rope, there was no way to prevent it from also searing the flesh on those same wrists. He could feel his skin melting, peeling away. Flesh burned so much easier than rope. By the time his wrists were free, there might be nothing left of them.

Loving squeezed his eyelids tight. Tears crept out of them. The pain was excruciating, but that had been the case for a long time. And that would be the case again, if he didn't get free.

In the end, he couldn't wait until the iron had severed the ropes completely, but he got them weakened sufficiently that he could pull them apart. Good enough. Once he had his hands back, the rest was duck soup. He still hurt like hell. But he was free.

Of course, that was just the start. Now he had to get out of there, which would be a challenge, since he had only the vaguest notion of where "there" was. If he could get to a phone, he could call Lieutenant Albertson. Boy, did he have some information to share with the man now! Or he could call Ben. Or both. Get some help and get the word out. He already had a pretty good idea of what had happened, why Victoria had gone to the press conference, what Ben needed to know to clear Thaddeus Roush and his partner once and for all.

Slowly, carefully, Loving pushed the closet door open. The hallway outside was dark, but he could hear the thumping sound of dance music not far away. He was somewhere in Renny's club. Someplace even more private than the room he'd had to arm wrestle his way into. If he wandered around long enough, he was sure to find one of the public areas. And from there, it would be just a short walk to the—

He froze. There was noise in the corridor. The sound of swishing. The swishing of corduroy slacks. And the only person he knew who had been wearing cords . . .

"It seems I have arrived just in time."

Pretty Boy. Wilhelm. Whatever you wanted to call him, he wasn't a welcome sight.

Loving knew that the space of a second could be critical. He raced forward, hoping to clock the creep before he had a chance to respond.

Wilhelm pulled a gun. And it wasn't a taser.

"This is a shame. I had hoped to prolong the amusement for ever so much longer."

Loving felt his throat clutch. Pretty Boy's father might be a delusional sadist, but at least he was sane. Wilhelm, he was not so sure about.

"Your daddy doesn't want me dead."

"You are mistaken. He sent me back here for that very purpose. As much as we have enjoyed our little fun with you, he has determined that you are too dangerous to remain breathing."

"You'll regret this."

"The only thing I regret is that I won't have any more fun with the iron. But all good things must come to an end. I doubt that I could get you tied up again without the taser." He sighed heavily. "So I will just have to kill you and be done with it. Pleasant dreams, Mr. Loving."

He raised the gun and pointed it directly at Loving's face.

53

"Ray was absolutely right," Roush explained to Ben. "I was bottom-feeding. Trawling the seamy side of the street. Looking for Ms. Goodbar in all the wrong places. I hadn't come to grips with my sexuality yet—wouldn't let myself admit it. So I dated women, or tried. Even slept with them. But I always made sure it was someone utterly inappropriate. Someone I would never be tempted to marry. Someone who would never be tempted to marry me." He laughed bitterly. "I'm not sure some of them even liked me."

Ben cleared his throat uncomfortably. "Are we talking about . . . prostitutes here?"

"Oh no, no, no. I never paid for it. Nothing like that. We're just talking, um, what's a polite term?"

"Women of low repute?"

"Very good, Ben. What a way you have with words! English major?"

"Music."

"Close enough. Anyway, yes, in my spare time, which was never that extensive, I was cavorting with trailer trash and barflies, and on at least one notable occasion, a thief."

Ben frowned. "You mean, like, a shoplifter?"

"Please. Give me some credit. I had better taste than that. I'm talking about an art thief."

"Oh," Ben said, arching an eyebrow. "Well, that *is* better."

"Nothing but the best for young Thaddeus Roush. Okay, maybe she actually stole art only once, but I like to think the job improved her entire résumé." He closed his eyes and continued his story. "I met Vickie, short for Victoria, at a bar in Georgetown. On the outside she seemed eminently trashy—exactly the sort of woman I was drawn to at the time. Ripped-up jeans, tight T-shirt. Fourteen different tattoos, some of them in places that are . . . unmentionable. She was a piece of work, no doubt about it. But the more time I spent with her, the more I realized that she was, well, not as dumb as you might've guessed. The outward appearance was more show than tell."

"Like maybe she was slumming, too."

"Exactly. Of course, that made her all the more intriguing. A little frightening, too. And she was tough, very tough. Exactly how I didn't feel, at the time."

"So I assume this led to a relationship between the two of you. And that eventually this relationship led to the two of you becoming sexually involved."

"I think we became sexually involved the first night I escorted her out of that bar. In time we developed something that you might be able to call a relationship."

"And this tryst eventually produced a pregnancy?"

"Not at first. We were on again, off again. I had my world, she had hers. And the more I knew about hers, the more I realized it could have nothing to do with my judicial work. We hooked up when we could, when we wanted. Sex, that is. When we wanted sex."

"And that was . . . ?"

"At first, ridiculously often, particularly given my confused sexuality. I wonder if she didn't get that, at least a hint of it. Some of the things she did, some of the ways she . . . humored me." He took a deep breath. "In retrospect, it's almost as if she knew before I did."

"How long did this relationship last?"

"In the first phase, about three months. Till Jerry showed up."

"Ah. A rival?"

"Oh, no. A business partner. Partner-in-crime, I guess you'd say."

"Had they worked together in the past?"

"No. Jerry was new. And very different from Vickie."

"How so?"

Roush held up his hands. "In about every way you could imagine. He was much less adept at disguising his patrician roots. He had a pronounced Southern accent and it was clear he was used to money, if not at present then certainly at some point in his past. It didn't matter how ragged his T-shirt looked; you always sensed he'd be more comfortable in a Polo. Drove a Maserati, for Pete's sake— said he'd won it in a lottery. He wasn't fooling anyone. Could've been a Vanderbilt for all he belonged in those dive bars."

"Then what was he doing there?"

"Said he had a big score, a chance to make some easy bread—he actually used that word, *bread*. He just needed someone with a little experience in the conning and cat burglary department to bring it off."

"And that was where Vickie came in."

"You got it."

"So what was it he wanted to rip off—his daddy's summer cottage on Cape Cod?"

"It was actually more ambitious than that. He'd scoped out a small but affluent museum in Boston. Somehow acquired a lot of information about it: interior schematics, the strength and schedule of the security force, that sort of thing. And he wanted Vickie to partner up with him."

"Did she do it?"

"Oh, yeah. The robbery was in all the papers at the time. For a place with such a valuable collection, it was pathetically under-protected. But somehow or other, it all went bad."

"They got caught?"

"No. No one ever got caught. But Vickie showed up on my doorstep the next day bleeding from about a hundred places. She was practically dead."

"Why didn't she go to the emergency room?"

Roush gave Ben a long look.

"Oh. Right. Thief."

"Yeah. Thief very much being sought by the police. Fortunately, I know a little first aid, at least enough to get by. Most of the wounds were superficial, all but a bad stab wound near the clavicle. Her left arm was in horrible shape—she had quite literally wrenched it out of its socket. Fixing that was no pleasure, I can assure you. I poured bourbon down her throat, but I know it still hurt like hell."

"Where was Jerry?"

"That was the million-dollar question. I kept asking. She wouldn't answer. Finally, one night, when I think she was too weak and too drunk to resist, she told me what happened to her partner."

"Did he go on the job with her?"

"Oh, yeah. She couldn't do it alone."

"So, he was hurt even worse than she was?"

Roush let his eyelids flutter closed. "She killed him."

Ben's lips parted. He hoped his jaw wasn't drooping, but it was impossible to be sure.

"Said she had no choice, of course, but that didn't make it any better. Falling-out amongst thieves, something like that."

Ben leaned forward. "So what did you do?"

"What else could I do? I'm a judge! I told her she had to turn herself in."

"I'm guessing that idea didn't appeal to her much."

"You guess correctly. She screamed and shouted, threatened. Told me that if the cops knew about her I'd be implicated, too. And she was right, of course. But it didn't matter. I mean, cavorting with a thief was one thing. But this was murder!"

"I have a feeling this story isn't headed for a happy ending."

"Your instincts are impeccable. I waited until she was stronger. The police still hadn't made the slightest break in the case. With my connections, I was able to monitor their progress, or lack thereof, pretty closely. They didn't have a clue. Finally, I told Vickie she had to turn herself in. And I told her that if she didn't, I would."

"How did she respond?"

"Two simple words: 'I'm pregnant.' "

Ben fell back into his chair. Now, at last, it was all beginning to make sense.

Roush rose, glancing toward the imposing bookshelf behind his chair, as if selecting something to read to help pass the time. "What was I going to do? Turning in your lover and implicating yourself was one thing. Turning in the mother of your child—that was quite another. We argued for days, back and forth. Mind you, she didn't want that child; it was just a blackmail device for her. I've always hated the idea of abortion—still do. But what business did I have raising a child? Me, an unmarried man preoccupied with sleazy women, a man increasingly realizing he was not entirely heterosexual. Was I going to raise a child with this woman? Was I going to raise a child without this woman?" He leaned his head against the leather-bound books. "It was an insoluble problem."

"So you reached a compromise."

Ben could only see the back of the man's head nod. "She got an abortion. I paid for it. And then she got the hell out of my life and never bothered me again." His eyes turned toward the ceiling, catching a glint from the fluorescent lighting. "I was appointed to the D.C. Circuit. I bought a beautiful house. I met Ray." A smile briefly flickered across his face, then faded. "Life was good. For a while."

"She didn't stay gone, did she? She came back. The day of the press conference."

"She, like everyone else in America, had seen all the publicity the day before announcing my nomination and my voluntary outing."

"Did you talk to her?"

Another nod. "My housekeeper let her in, though she fibbed about it later to protect me. I didn't recognize Vickie at first. She'd totally changed her look—and I don't just mean a new hairdo. I'm talking plastic surgery. Major changes."

"Nose job? Breast augmentation?"

"More like total reconstruction of the facial features. Seems the heat was on her pretty hard after the robbery. Jerry's body was discovered, and some rich relatives called out the dogs. There was a concerted effort to find his killer, financed by not only law enforcement but some major-league big bucks. Somehow they figured out she was involved. She had to disappear, totally disappear. So she changed her name, got some fake ID, redid her face. Even altered her fingerprints, apparently. That's why she's been so difficult for the police to identify. She's not only no longer Vickie—she's a person who doesn't really exist. Victoria. No past. No records of any kind. A phantom figure. Not even the IRS had anything on her. And that's saying quite a bit."

"What did she want?"

"Three guesses."

"Money."

"Got it in one." Roush sighed. "Once a thief, always a thief. Tried to shake me down. Figured a potential Supreme Court nominee with a dark secret was good for something. Figured it wouldn't help my chances if the world knew I'd paid for an abortion. Threatened to expose me unless I came across with a million bucks. Said she'd already given all the proof to a third party. It was pay up or kiss the Supreme Court good-bye."

Ben swallowed. "So you—"

"I didn't kill her, if that's what you're thinking. I wouldn't have opened that door during the press conference if I'd had any idea she was there. But I knew better than to blow her off. She wasn't bluffing when she said she'd expose me. So I told her I couldn't deal with this at the moment, with reporters and a zillion other people running around the estate. It wasn't like I kept a million bucks lying around the house. Told her to hide out behind the arbor gate till everyone was gone and we'd talk about it. I went back to my business and, well, you know the rest. Next time I saw her, she was dead."

Ben batted a finger against his lips. "Dead, and positioned in a place where her body was bound to be found during the press conference." He looked up suddenly. "And Ray—"

"I'm certain he had nothing to do with it. I'm certain."

"He was near the body."

"I don't care."

"Disguised or not, he knew who she was. And what she could do to you."

"I'm telling you, Ben—it wasn't him."

"He had a motive."

"Hell, *I* had a motive!" Roush's voice shattered the stillness of the room. "But I didn't kill the woman. And I don't know who did. But it wasn't Ray!"

Ben rose slowly out of his chair, one hand pressed against his aching forehead. "*That's it.* That's what this is all about!"

"I don't follow you."

"The murder. The way it was done. It was about giving you a motive."

"What are you saying?"

"I'm saying you've been framed, Tad. You and Ray. Intentionally. By someone who knew who that woman was. And that proof Vickie gave to a third party—when her confederate heard she was dead, he or she must've forwarded it to a right-wing political interest group that leaked it as soon as you got out of committee."

"But who would kill that woman just to get at me?"

"I don't know—yet. That's what we have to figure out. As soon as possible. It's the only thing that can save you now."

"How are we going to do that? The police don't have a clue."

"I don't know. But if we can tell your story, if we can show that you've been framed, that this is part of some conspiracy to keep you off the Court—" A light shined in his eyes. "Dear God, I wish you'd told me all this before. This changes everything."

"I don't see what you're so excited about."

"Finally, this game is being played on my home turf." He batted a finger against his lips. "We expose the true murderer, show that you're the victim of a frame-up, and the rest of these objections to your nomination will seem trivial by comparison. Political puffery. Part of the scam."

"I'm still not following you."

Ben leaned across Roush's desk. "Since this whole thing began, people have been dragging me along, trying to get me to do things I don't know anything about. Representing you at the hearing, which I was pathetically unsuited to do. Dealing with politics, which I don't even begin to understand. My performance has been pitiful. But clearing an innocent man who has been intentionally framed . . ." Ben's eyes met Roush's, a determined expression on his face. "That's what I *do*."

54

Loving stared at the gun Pretty Boy held at point-blank range. Had he made it so far, suffered so much, only to come to this? He had put up with Renny's torture, had seared his own flesh to get free, only to be drilled by this ignoramus?

"Now, wait, Pretty—er, Wilhelm. I don't think you wanna do this."

"Really? Because I am pretty sure that I do. Paying this debt will give me enormous pleasure."

"Well, yeah, you, sure. But I'm not so sure *I'm* gonna enjoy it."

"I am rather certain you will not." He readjusted his aim, pointing the gun at a somewhat lower part of Loving's anatomy. "I will make the first six or seven shots nonlethal, yet highly painful. I will cripple you. I will eliminate your manhood. I will let you bleed. Then at long last, I will kill you."

"Gosh, Wilhelm, I can see you still bear a grudge, but this seems like a bad way to work it out. Perhaps we could just arm wrestle?"

"I do not think so." Pretty Boy extended his gun arm.

Loving swallowed hard. So this was it, this was really, truly it. There was nothing he could do, no place he could run. His bag of tricks was empty. Nothing left but getting drilled by this Eurotrash moron.

Pretty Boy's trigger finger tightened. "Sweet dreams, Mr. Loving."

"Sweet dreams to you, sucker," said a voice in the darkness. And a second later, Pretty Boy tumbled downward in a heap on the floor.

Loving's eyes fairly bulged. "What in the—"

Trudy stepped into the light. Holding a baseball bat. "How do you like my swing, slugger?"

Loving was so astonished—and relieved—he could barely speak. "I think you're so incredible I could—"

Trudy's eyelashes fluttered. "Yes?"

Loving pulled Trudy close and delivered a kiss right on the lips.

"My, my," Trudy said when it was over. "Has my big handsome gotten over his teeny-weeny difficulty?"

"Not likely. But a debt is a debt." He grinned. "Thanks for showin' up and savin' my bacon."

"I just wish I'd gotten here sooner, sugar. You're a mess."

"Don't worry. I clean up pretty good. What are you doin' here?"

"Did you really think I was going to leave my boyfriend all by himself?"

"Trudy—"

"After we split, I kept a low profile but hung around the club to see what, or who, emerged. When Renny returned to his private lounge without you, but with traces of blood on his hands, I knew something was up. I saw him whisper something to this lug down on the carpet, who got a great big grin on his face I didn't like at all. So I followed him."

"And the baseball bat?"

"I keep it in my car. A girl has to protect herself."

Loving wiped blood from his brow. "Remind me not to tangle with you."

More eyelash batting. "You're welcome to tangle with me anytime, lover boy."

"Later. Any idea where Renny is?"

"Uh-huh. He just took his bedtime downer and headed for his upstairs apartment. There are guards."

"There always are. Lead the way, Trudy."

"Sure you're up to it?"

"No choice, really."

She smiled at him, then puckered up. "Another kiss? For luck?"

Loving returned the smile. "Sorry. Not on the first date."

Renny had just snuggled into the satin sheets of his huge bed, prepared to sleep the sleep of the content, a good day's work complete. He liked to keep his sleeping quarters private. There were plenty of places downstairs for indulging in the pleasures of the women who drifted in and out of the club. This was his sanctuary, his fortress of solitude, a place where he could be alone with his thoughts. No women were allowed, nor anyone else for that matter. The boys on the landing made sure he wasn't disturbed.

At least, that was how it was supposed to work.

His eyes had barely closed when he felt a hand wrap around his throat.

Renny tried to sit up, but the strong hand pinned him to his pillow.

"Don't bother strugglin'," Loving whispered. "You couldn't outmuscle me even if you weren't doped to the gills. And you are."

Renny tried to speak, but the hand crushing his windpipe made it difficult. "What—where—"

"Your guards? Lying in a heap on the plush shag carpet, which by the way may be hot stuff in Europe, but here in the United States is totally passé. Very 1970." He tightened his grip. "Don't bother callin' for them. They're likely to be immobile for some time. Apparently they don't play baseball back in whatever country you recruited them from."

Renny's legs and arms thrashed back and forth. Loving barely twitched.

"Here's the deal," Loving said. "I know you understand how quickly a person with a collapsed trachea can die, since you were briefing me on exactly that subject earlier. So I'll give you one chance to tell me what I want to know. One chance. You will tell me why Victoria went to the Roush press conference. You will tell me about this political favor Victoria did earlier in the year. You will tell me about the Boston museum job. You will tell me everything else I want to know—anything that might be of interest to me. And in exchange, I will let you live to see the authorities clean up this den of sex and stolen art. You will serve a long prison sentence. But you will be alive. If you tell me what I want to hear. Are we clear on this?"

Loving continued choking Renny for a few more seconds, just to make sure he got his point across. When he finally released the man, he sat upright, coughing and sputtering, massaging his sore neck. His eyes watered with pain. He coughed up blood. He hyperventilated. Then he fell back against the bed, utterly exhausted.

"All right," he said, his voice feeble and cracked, "where shall I begin?"

55

"Judge Haskins!"

Several stray members of the White House press corps caught sight of him as he crossed from the West Wing to the driveway where his ride was waiting. He was nattily attired in a navy blue suit, both buttons buttoned, and a dynamic red tie. His hair was freshly cut and appeared to be sprayed into place. When the bright lights of the minicams switched on, a faint trace of base makeup was discernible at the ridge of his jaw.

He paused, as if thinking about whether he really wanted to deal with the press, then let out a small sigh and turned to face them.

"Have you been talking with the President?"

Haskins dipped his head slightly. "I have had that pleasure, yes."

"Then it's confirmed. After the Senate rejects Thaddeus Roush, President Blake is going to nominate you."

He held up his hands. "I don't want to presume to know the mind of the Senate."

"You must be aware that Roush lacks the votes to be confirmed," the brunette representing CBS said. "After he's out of the running, the President will want to put someone up fast. While he still can."

"If Judge Roush's nomination fails, it is my understanding that the President wishes to move forward with all deliberate speed."

The AP stringer tried to cut past the polite gobbledygook. "He's going to nominate you, isn't he?"

Haskins gave them a gosh, shucks shrug worthy of Ronald Reagan.

"I have three unnamed sources who say you're going to be the pick," the CBS woman added, egging him on. "The President would be crazy not to choose you. How could the Senate reject a national hero?"

Haskins held up his hands. "Look, I want to make one thing perfectly clear. I bear no animosity whatsoever toward Judge Roush. He is a fine man, a fine jurist, and he would undoubtedly be a fine member of the Supreme Court. I have no desire to take that away from him."

"But if the Senate does reject him?" the AP stringer asked.

"As it will," the CBS representative added.

Haskins tilted his head to one side. "In that unfortunate instance, I would of course consider accepting any nomination, were I so honored as to be selected."

"And the President has in fact already selected you, hasn't he? It's a done deal."

"Again, I don't want to presume to know the minds of others. Especially not the leader of the free world."

A new reporter pushed to the front, a short, wiry man whose age was demonstrated not so much by his balding head as the fact that he was actually using a pad and paper. "Judge Haskins, this is a matter of great national importance. You've met with the President for three consecutive days. We know he's had his people running background checks on you. We know his staff has pored over every opinion you've written in your time on the Tenth Circuit. And today, you've been closeted with him for more than two hours, which is the functional equivalent of spending a week with anyone else on earth. The people have a right to know—are you going to be the next nominee for the Supreme Court?"

Haskins sighed, as if overwhelmed by the force of the questioning. "It is my understanding that . . . in the event that Judge Roush's nomination should fail . . . the President has indicated that I have his support."

A dozen cell phones flipped open. The press corps' fingers raced to be the first to phone the story home.

"In fact," Haskins continued, "the President has asked me to be present in the gallery of the Senate when the vote on the Roush nomination is taken so that, if the nomination is rejected, he can immediately present his replacement."

The reporters chatted all at once into their cells, making it pointless for Haskins to continue. He turned toward the limo that had pulled up behind him while he was speaking.

"Congratulations," the limo driver said, as he opened the rear door.

"Let's not be premature. Even if Judge Roush is rejected, there's no guarantee they won't reject me, too."

"Reject the man who saved a baby from a burning building? I don't think so." He stood erect and saluted. "I think I have the very great privilege of chauffeuring the next member of the Supreme Court of the United States."

"Well," Haskins said, smiling shyly, with a tiny twinkle in his eye, "I just hope you're right."

56

"You're sure about this?" Ben barked into the phone.

"Positive, Skipper."

"And you can prove it?"

Loving hedged. "Well, I'm workin' on that. But this creep had no reason to lie."

"Loving, you were threatening to kill him!"

"Aw, all I did was squeeze his scrotum a little. That pansy-ass leaked like a sieve."

Ben took a deep breath. "You'd better be right."

"I am. Anythin' else I can do?"

"No. When you're finished with the police, get to the hospital."

"Ah, I don't need—"

"I want you checked out, tough guy. There could still be internal bleeding. I don't want my personal information highway to kick off. After the docs clear you, get back to the office as soon as possible." Ben wiped his brow, unsure whether to be elated or horrified.

"I've got a lot of thinking to do. And a lot of work to complete before morning."

Ben wasn't surprised that he couldn't get an appointment to see Senator Keyes, but he wasn't going to let that stop him, either. He called Senator Hammond and got him to make an appointment—even Keyes couldn't turn down the Senate Minority Leader on the eve of the confirmation debate. Once Ben knew Keyes was in his office, he marched past the poor receptionist, who appeared to be even older than Senator Keyes and accustomed to senators behaving with proper decorum—not crashing through the gates during someone else's appointment. When Keyes looked up from his desk and saw Ben, he appeared more bemused than annoyed, although a little of both. He told the receptionist to retake her position, before some new barbarian crashed the gates, and offered Ben a chair.

Thirty minutes later, Ben was still begging.

"C'mon, Senator. Work with me."

"And why would I want to do that?" Keyes said, his Texas drawl in full force. "Working against you has been so pleasurable."

"Was it that pleasurable when you got out-voted in committee?" Ben knew it was imprudent to cross swords with the leader of the Judiciary Committee, but desperate men took desperate actions. "We smoked your butt."

"You got lucky."

"We smoked your butt."

"And you wouldn't have even gotten lucky if it hadn't been for those turncoats Matera and Potter. Woman must be going through menopause or something. She's got one foot in the grave so she decided to cultivate a conscience. You can't take credit for that."

Ben raised an eyebrow. "Are you sure?"

Keyes peered at him through bushy eyebrows. "Perhaps I have underestimated you, Senator Kincaid."

"No 'perhaps' about it."

"But what you're asking now is out of the question. Help you? Good God, boy—I'm getting telegrams from home telling me I should organize a filibuster. Even though the man has no chance of rustling up the necessary votes for confirmation. They just want to be sure."

"A filibuster would mean the Senate doesn't get to exercise its constitutional right to approve and confirm."

"That's about the size of it."

"There hasn't been a filibuster against a Supreme Court nominee since Abe Fortas went up for Chief Justice back in the sixties."

"Doesn't mean it can't happen now."

"Surely you don't want that. How can we go on pretending you're honoring the Constitution if you won't even let it come up for a vote?"

Keyes shrugged. "Did you think you were working in a candy factory, son?"

"No, I thought I was working in a democracy. Are you going to filibuster?"

He shrugged diffidently. "Haven't decided yet."

"Please don't. Let this case be decided on its merits."

"Kincaid, it isn't a courtroom."

"Yes, I believe you've mentioned that once or twice. What I'm saying is—instead of screwing around with all this political BS, why don't we see if we can actually uncover the truth?"

"You're so naïve."

"C'mon, at the end of the day, don't we both want the same thing? The truth?"

"Speak for yourself. All I want is to get the damn leader of the free world off my back."

"You're too smart and too—forgive me—too old to be nothing but a political pawn."

"You're right." He smiled. "I'm going to be a political pawn and the next Vice President of the United States."

"So anything goes? As long as you get what you want?"

"Well, perhaps not anything. But a great deal."

Ben looked at him squarely. "I never thought I'd say this, but— you're better than this."

"Better than the vice presidency?"

"Better than letting an innocent man be hung out to dry."

Keyes turned his head to one side and drummed his fingers. Ben knew from the hearing that this was not so much a sign of irritation as a sign that he was doing some deep thinking. "How can you be so sure about his innocence?"

"I've shown you what I've got."

"It's not enough."

"I'll make it work. You'll see."

"You'll make it work, huh?"

"If you give me a chance. If you kill the filibuster. And if you recognize me during the debate."

Keyes's eyes went skyward. "Recognize the junior senator from Oklahoma? A known supporter of Roush? His counsel at the hearing? My party would hang me out to dry."

"I don't believe anyone can hang you out to dry."

"Well." Keyes sniffed, shrugged his shoulders. "That is as it may be, but . . ."

"Will you do it?"

"And what would I get in return?"

Ben pursed his lips. He should have anticipated this response, this being Washington. But he wasn't sure what to say. "What do you want?"

"How about you use your influence with Senator Hammond to get that pansy-ass Wilderness Bill killed?"

"I can't do that. My fiancée has been working for months on that bill. It's very important to her."

"Like the vice presidency isn't important to me?"

"The Arctic National Wildlife Refuge is our last untouched wilderness area. We can't let it be devastated by drilling, no matter how badly Americans want to drive their cars."

"Nothing you're saying is persuading me to give up the vice presidency."

"You don't have to." Ben leaned forward. "I think I can swing it so you can do the right thing and still be the President's top choice."

Keyes arched a bushy eyebrow. "Is that so? And that's because you're so tight with the Commander in Chief?"

"No. But I still think I can make it work. Please. Give me a chance."

Keyes stared at him for a long time, not making a sound other than the drumming of his fingers. A minute passed, then another. After a while, the silence seemed deafening. Ben imagined he could hear the carpet rustling in the air-conditioned breeze.

"All right then. I'll make sure there's no filibuster." He made a harrumphing sound. "Didn't care much for the idea, anyway. Little too partisan, even for me."

"And you'll make sure I have a chance to speak during the deliberations?"

"You'll have the same chance to be recognized as every other senator."

"I need a promise."

"And what if it all goes bad? Where will I be then? What happens if you put on your dog and pony show and it doesn't work?"

"It will work," Ben said, a soft but firm voice. "It has to work."

"There are no guarantees in politics, son."

Ben nodded. "This isn't about politics. This is about justice."

57

"Comfortable, Angel?"

"How could I be comfortable with all these television cameras around? My stomach is churning enough to make butter."

"It shouldn't take too long." Judge Haskins had a front-row seat in the gallery above the Senate chamber. In only a few minutes, the confirmation debate would begin. In compliance with the President's request, he and his wife were attending, reminding the senators that they had a ready alternative. "There's no point in a protracted debate. He doesn't have the support. Keyes will probably push for an immediate vote."

"I only hope you're right," Margaret said. "I don't like being in the public spotlight."

"It won't be for long. How many spouses of Supreme Court judges can you identify?"

"Umm, none."

"Exactly." He took his wife's hand and squeezed it. "Once the confirmation process is over, no one will be interested in you any-more."

"Well, I think you could've phrased that a bit more gallantly." She grinned. "But I understand what you're saying."

He scooted closer to her. "I know you're uncomfortable with all this. I apologize for dragging you through it."

"Don't be daft. What were you going to say? 'No, Mr. President, I don't want to be on the Supreme Court. It might upset my wife's tummy.'"

"You've put up with quite a lot from me, over the years. Don't think I don't know that. I don't deserve—"

She placed a finger over his lips. "Shhh." She leaned forward and kissed him on the cheek. "You're my hero. My knight in shining armor. You saved my life."

He shrugged. "That fire was no big deal."

"I was talking about the day you married me."

They settled back into their chairs, hands clasped tightly together.

Ben sat at his assigned desk in the Senate, staring at the mass of people surrounding him, wondering how he had ever gotten into this mess, wishing he were at home watching this on C-SPAN. Or not.

The Senate floor was packed. Every desk was filled. All one hundred senators were in attendance, and each seemed to have at least three clerks or assorted other flunkies at their bidding. The gallery was packed with spectators and interested parties. Ben, like everyone else, had noticed that Judge Haskins and his wife were sitting in the first row, front and center. Richard Trevor, the head of the Christian Congregation, was sitting directly behind him, a sure sign that his organization intended to throw its support to Haskins as soon as the opportunity presented itself. Even the lame-duck Vice President was present, making one of his rare appearances in his constitutional role of President of the Senate, just in case he should be needed to cast a tie-breaking vote. Unlikely—all the polls indicated that Roush's nomination would fail by at least ten votes. The Republicans clearly had the forty-one votes necessary to sustain a filibuster. Ben had to count on Keyes's promise that the threat would not be exercised, or Roush's nomination would never come to a vote at all.

Christina was huddled in the back of the room, sitting with Bertram Sexton and Kevin Beauregard and Gina Carraway and her clipboard. Right up to the last minute, she had been analyzing data and trying to root out any potential weakness in the opposition, possible undecideds. She hadn't found any.

Jones and Loving were also in attendance. If Ben was going to pull this off, it would be because of them.

Thaddeus Roush stepped through the back doors of the gallery. A sudden silence blanketed the room, followed almost immediately by an intense volley of whispers. Roush ignored it. It was ironic, really: this debate was all about him, but he had to sit up in the gallery.

Roush walked to the front row, looked both ways—then took a seat beside Judge Haskins, directly in front of Richard Trevor.

Ben shook his head. He didn't care what Roush had done in his confused youth. He had guts. This country needed him on the Supreme Court.

Ben watched as Christina folded a note and passed it to a Senate page. More polling data, no doubt. Probably some new survey Gina had transmitted via Instant Messenger.

He took the note from the page and unfolded it.

I LOVE YOU, it said. GO GET 'EM, TIGER.

He had to smile.

The Vice President gaveled the Senate into session. Game on.

58

Ben was hardly surprised when the Vice President and President Pro Tem recognized Senator Keyes, chairman of the Judiciary Committee, to orchestrate the debate, and Keyes promptly recognized a series of die-hard Republicans to speak first.

"... and what are we to tell our children, good Christian American children who have been taught to exercise restraint, to practice abstinence, that abortion is a crime against God and nature? Are we to tell them that the murder of an innocent fetus qualifies them for appointment to the highest court in the land? Is that the message we want to send to the children of America? Or perhaps, do we want to send a different message? A message that says that there is still such a thing as morality in government. That strength and character still matter to the people of the United States. That the Supreme Court is no place for those who would desecrate and offend the fundamental values of this great land."

Ben saw the senator subtly adjust his speaking position. At first, he thought the man must be positioning himself for the C-SPAN camera, but then he realized that what he was really doing was turning his back to Judge Roush, seated above and behind him in the gallery. Apparently the coward wanted to confront him without confronting him. He needn't have bothered. Roush maintained a perfect stone face, neither smiling nor scowling, just letting it all roll off him.

". . . but if not now, when do we draw the line?" the senator continued. "Do we want to live in a world where homosexuals control the law of the land? This man has been engaged in an ongoing relationship with another man, a relationship that is still illegal in many states and will always be an abnegation of God's word. Now we learn that before he embarked on one sinful relationship, he had yet another, that he actually paid for a murder. A legalized murder, to be sure, but no less horrendous for it, no less shocking to the conscience, no less offensive to our collective consciousness." His voice boomed. "What will happen to us as a nation if we allow this abomination to be enshrined in the Supreme Court?"

Ben pondered. A plague of locusts? Death of the first-born? Armageddon?

"Judicial activism! That's what will happen!"

Ah. Well, that was my next guess.

"We cannot open the door to judges who seek not to interpret the law, but to make the law. Lawmaking is the sovereign right of this body, this Congress, and no judge has the right to force his own decadent beliefs on the laws we create. Look where these people have put us today. No prayer in school. Immigration run rampant. A Swedish minister arrested for condemning homosexuality. The world is in chaos! This is no time to allow—"

"Pardon me," Senator Keyes said, gently interrupting. "I believe that your five minutes on the floor are over."

That was the first time today Keyes had enforced his own time limit. Was it possible he was just as tired of this tirade as Ben was? One could only hope.

"Mister Chairman," said Senator Bening from Colorado. "Could I be permitted to say a few words about a man from the great state of Colorado who does tremendous justice to the bench on which he sits, Judge Rupert Haskins?"

"Point of order," Ben interrupted, before Keyes had a chance to respond. "Aren't we supposed to be debating the nomination currently before the Senate?" His voice dropped a notch. "Rather than speculating about the possibility of any future ones?"

Keyes made a clucking sound. "Well, I'm sure Senator Bening intends his remarks to relate to the matter at hand. The Chair recognizes Senator Bening of Colorado."

Ben didn't need to listen to the oration to know where it was headed. He'd seen the crowd of Haskins supporters, many of them bused in from Colorado, outside the Capitol building carrying signs with slogans like: HERO OR HOMO?

". . . and I concur with Senator Scolieri about the need for judges who know the meaning of the phrase 'judicial restraint.' Judge Haskins has been on the bench for almost twenty years and his record is utterly unblemished. He decides the cases before him without overreaching to reshape society in his own image. He knows what it means to be a judge of men and a defender of the law."

Ben rose to his feet. Bening saw him from the corner of his eye.

". . . and so as we consider the nomination of Judge Roush—"

Ben sat back down. Very smooth transition.

". . . this is not an all-or-nothing proposition. It is not as if the rejection of this candidate will create a permanent vacuum on the Supreme Court. It only means that we can return to the drawing board and reconsider, perhaps make a more measured analysis of what this Court needs, what this country needs. I think you all share my conviction that—" He glanced toward Haskins, sitting in the gallery, and smiled, "—that it will not be difficult to find an alternative candidate."

He paused, then looked squarely into the television camera. "Ladies and gentlemen. When you have the chance to go with a hero, why settle for anything less?"

Despite their previous conversation, Ben was still surprised when Keyes's fickle finger of fate turned next toward him. "The Chair recognizes the junior senator from the State of Oklahoma." He smiled thinly. "You have five minutes, sir."

There was an audible stir in the chamber, including the gallery. Ben wasn't the only one who was surprised.

"Then I'd best get started." Ben stood beside his desk and turned so he could see the entire assemblage. He'd never spoken to such a large group in his entire life, certainly not if you considered the countless people who must be watching on television. He felt his knees wobble a bit just thinking about it. So, he reasoned, it was best not to think about it. Concentrate on what he was doing. Even if this wasn't a courtroom, the primary rule of closing argument for the defense was the same: bring it back to the person.

"This has been a very long process," Ben began, trying to slow the pace of the rhetoric a bit. "At least, it seems like a long time to me. It seems like an eternity to me." Mild chuckles from the gallery. "But imagine how it must feel for Thaddeus Roush. Imagine how it must feel to have your name dragged through the public dirt, to have your secrets revealed, your previously unblemished reputation tarnished, and for what? Because the President chose you for the Supreme Court."

He turned, wondered briefly if his better profile was to the camera, then got on with his speech. "Thaddeus Roush never asked to be on the Supreme Court, never expected to be asked. Sure, he didn't turn it down when it arrived—what sane jurist would?—but he never asked for it. The President came to him. And where is that President now? Well, as we all know, the President has silently withdrawn his support from his own candidate. What can you say about a President who commits his people but then does not support them? And what is the basis for the President's withdrawal of support, and the vast majority of the abuse that has been heaped upon Judge Roush since his nomination? The fact that he refused to hide in somebody else's closet. He resolved that if he was going to present himself to the American public, he was going to present himself as the person he truly was. He wouldn't try to fly under the radar. He wouldn't try to be bland and innocuous so he could slippery-slide through confirmation, even if what he did was controversial, even if it might destroy his chances of confirmation. Why would anyone do such a thing? Because, for some people, honesty is more important than popularity. Integrity is more important than success."

Ben paused, hoping some of this would soak in. "Isn't that the kind of man we want on the Supreme Court?"

He turned again, facing a different part of the floor. He didn't have as much room to maneuver here as he might in a courtroom, but he would have to make do.

"I know some of you are disturbed because, when Judge Roush was a very young man, he assisted a woman in obtaining an abortion, a fact which, I would remind you for the record, he has never attempted to deny or excuse. The fact is, Thaddeus Roush regrets it more than anyone. He considers it the greatest mistake of his life. But which of us did not make some mistake when we were young, hmm? I'd like to see that person cast the first stone. We all make mistakes when we're young because, frankly, we're so stupid. And I'm not sure I'm that much smarter now. But I know this: a good man should not be rejected because of a mistake he made twenty-some years ago and has regretted ever since. If youthful transgressions, even serious ones, were a prohibition to public service . . ." He smiled a little. ". . . this chamber might well be empty."

He paused. Was this getting through to anyone? Was he persuading the undecideds? Were there any undecideds to persuade? There was no way of knowing.

Less than two minutes on the clock. He had to plow ahead.

"I listened with great interest to the remarks made by Senator Bening, but I must respectfully disagree with his conclusion. It is not appropriate to reject one candidate because we think we have inside information about the President's mind and prefer another choice to this one. You don't reject your meat and potatoes because you think there might be dessert. And it seems particularly inappropriate when the dessert has been stage-managing events from behind the scenes, promulgating negative information about the current nominee, actively campaigning for the job in contravention of the history of judicial practice in the United States."

The stir in the chamber wasn't loud enough to drown out the clattering of the gavel or the outrage of the senator from Colorado. "Will the speaker yield?"

"I will not," Ben replied.

"Mister Chairman, I move that the speaker's remaining time be revoked!"

"Senator . . ."

"I will not stand here and allow this partisan advocate to tarnish the reputation of a great Coloradan, a bona fide hero. I ask him again to yield."

"And I say again that I will not." Ben glanced up at Chairman Keyes. "And I'd like the time consumed by the senator from Colorado's interruptions added back to my remaining time."

"It will be," Keyes answered. "You have a minute and a half remaining, Senator. Speaking for us all—this had better be good. Congressional immunity won't save you if you're making accusations without proof."

"In my world, Mister Chairman, we don't say boo without proof. Wish that were the case here in Washington." He turned back toward the chamber. "Many people have remarked upon the coincidence that the dirty secrets of Thaddeus Roush's past were only revealed after he was approved by the committee. Almost as if someone was holding them in reserve, only using them if it became necessary. There was a great deal of inquiry directed toward determining whether the information was correct. But I've heard very little inquiry about where that information came from. There's a reason, of course. Ultimately, the information was revealed by a reporter for the *Post,* and there is a tradition of journalists not revealing their sources even when ordered to do so by the courts. There was a widespread feeling that even if the reporter in question were brought before the courts or the Congress, she would remain silent. She had committed no crime and did not appear to have abetted one. There was no reason for her to talk."

Ben took a deep breath. "So I didn't bother asking. I sent her a Congressional subpoena for the original documents that were leaked by her anonymous source. And then I had them fingerprinted."

Creased brows crisscrossed the gallery. Everyone seemed to be practically leaning out of their desks. He had their attention now.

"Good thing all law students preparing to take the bar exam are required to be fingerprinted. Guess who touched the documents?" He paused a beat. "Judge Haskins."

The murmuring in the chamber rose to a full buzz. Ben raised his voice; he couldn't afford to let the tumult consume his remaining time.

"I don't imagine for a minute that Judge Haskins did the investigating. The documents were provided to him . . ." He glanced up at the gallery, where Richard Trevor sat behind Judge Haskins. ". . . by some other interested source, who in turn received them from an agent of the woman who obtained the abortion in question. But Judge Haskins leaked them when he saw his chance. It was all part of his campaign for the job, perhaps the most clever campaign imaginable—a campaign based upon appearing to refuse to campaign. It worked. He became the heir apparent. Even before the previous nominee had been rejected."

"Point of order!" Senator Bening practically screamed. "I will not continue to listen to this defamation of Judge Haskins. The man is a national hero!"

"I think it mitigates against your status as a hero," Ben said quietly, "when you're the one who set the fire."

This time, the chamber exploded. Both the Vice President and Senator Keyes were pounding their gavels, to no avail. Everyone talked at once, some fascinated, some outraged. Judge Haskins had a stricken expression on his face; he shook his head vigorously from side to side. His wife clutched his arm apprehensively. Judge Roush looked at both of them, his expression still blank, but his eyes scrutinizing them carefully.

"Point of order!" Senator Bening continued shouting. "I demand an apology. I demand an explanation!"

Chairman Keyes pounded his gavel a few more times. "I'm afraid Senator Kincaid's time has expired."

"I respectfully request a five-minute extension," Ben replied.

"Absolutely not!" Senator Bening exclaimed. "I oppose!"

"Well," Ben said, "he did demand an explanation. How can I do that if I can't talk?"

Maybe it was Ben's wishful thinking, but Chairman Keyes appeared to be suppressing a grin. "I'll give you another three," he said, "with an option for two more if you're saying anything of interest."

"Thanks," Ben replied. "I will be." He turned back toward the gallery. "I don't have time to go into the details, but all the supporting documents will be made available to the press by my Chief of Staff—" He nodded toward Christina. "—as soon as we recess. My investigator has been working the past month to uncover much of this information. He was trying to learn the identity of the woman who was killed at the Roush press conference, an investigation that led him into the world of art theft because, as it turns out, the murdered woman was a longtime thief. A thief available to anyone who needed a dirty job done."

Ben lifted an envelope from his desk and removed several documents encased in plastic. "But to make a long story short, since I'm already talking on borrowed time, the investigation of that woman's past led to the discovery of another crime. An arson-for-hire job at the downtown Denver Hilton. She was paid ten thousand dollars, which might not seem like much to you, but was the score of a lifetime for her, especially since she owed money to an extremely dangerous trafficker in stolen art."

He took a breath and continued. "My office manager is very clever with computers. Always has been. Even before I could afford one." In the back of the room, he saw Jones beaming. "He was able to go online and find all of Judge Haskins's bank accounts. Even the secret one in the Cayman Islands." The buzz began to build again. "To be perfectly honest, I'm not entirely sure that this squared with the federal privacy laws, but I figured we had a good reason. Because, as this printout shows, there's a ten-thousand-dollar cash withdrawal just before the date of the fire. Of course, there could possibly be some other explanation . . ." He tilted his head to one side. "But I doubt it."

Ben glanced up into the gallery. "No wonder you reacted so much more quickly and heroically than anyone else, Judge Haskins. You knew the explosions were coming. You knew exactly where they were and how dangerous they would be. Because you planned the whole thing."

Up in the gallery, Haskins rose to his feet, his knees trembling. "It's . . . it's not true! It's . . ."

Ben tossed a stack of paper down on his desk. "The documents speak for themselves. You probably arranged for the doors to be stuck, too, didn't you? To create a crisis situation that only you would be prepared to resolve."

Senators and spectators rose from their seats, whispering and shouting, waving their arms in the air. Ben clasped his hand over the microphone, causing a skull-shattering feedback. In the aftermath, the room fell quiet.

"Well, that worked nicely," Ben said. "You might consider that as an alternative to the gavel, Mister Chairman."

Keyes gave him a small salute.

"One last thing," Ben added. "I can't prove Judge Haskins killed that woman at Thaddeus Roush's home during the press conference. But I can prove he was there. And I know he was willing to put hundreds of lives in danger as part of his quest to get himself a higher profile, and we know he was willing to deal with the devil to smear Tad Roush. Is it really so difficult to imagine that he would kill one woman to insure there was a vacancy he could fill? I've contacted Lieutenant Albertson of the Washington PD and suggested that they get a subpoena for the Haskins local residence. I think they might just find something that will eliminate all doubt about what really happened."

The room was almost completely out of control, but Ben insisted on finishing. "Just one last thing," he said, shouting above the fray. "Now that the dessert is out of the way, why don't we confirm the meat and potatoes? Thaddeus Roush is a good man and you all know it, a good man who's been subjected to a frame and a smear campaign and a lot of other trouble he never asked for. He is enormously qualified and he deserves to sit with the other Supremes. So for once, let's do the right thing."

Ben turned toward the front of the room. "Mister Chairman, this is a democracy. So I move that we put this thing to an immediate vote."

Keyes was about to speak, when at the front of the room, he saw Senator Matera rise slowly to her feet.

The chamber became quiet once more and everyone strained to hear her voice. "I'd like to say one thing. This is the last time I will be present in the Senate chamber, and the last vote I'm going to cast. I'm going to vote for Thaddeus Roush to be confirmed in his appointment to the Supreme Court. I'd be obliged if the rest of you would do the same."

All at once, Ben heard someone clapping, then another, and another, and then it grew until it became a groundswell of thunderous applause. The senator to Ben's right rose, still clapping, then the other Democrats did the same, and before long, more than half the Senate was on its feet.

Ben raised his hand upward toward Judge Roush. Roush stood and returned the salute. Their eyes met. And that was enough.

59

Chairman Keyes let a few more people speak after Ben so every-one could have a clip for their local news, but less than an hour later, he called for the vote.

"The matter presently before the chamber is the nomination of Judge Thaddeus Roush to the Supreme Court of the United States. The question before us is this: Does the Senate advise and consent to this nomination by right of exercising its powers granted by Article 2 of the United States Constitution? I will direct the clerk to call the roll."

"Senator Armstrong."

"No."

"Senator Bernard."

"No."

"Senator Byers."

"Yes."

And so it began. Ben sat at his desk, elbow to elbow with his fellow senators, and watched the votes trickle down. Most of the senators were voting along what passed for party lines in this convoluted mess—Republicans voting against the nominee of their President, Democrats voting for a die-hard Republican. Ben was pleased to see that at least his party was falling into line; there was considerable doubt about whether Roush could even muster that vote after the abortion revelation. So far, though, they hadn't gotten anything from the Republican contingent. And they couldn't win without it.

Five minutes later, the clerk was approaching the middle of the alphabet.

"Senator Matera."

The prior rhythm was altered as the clerk paused to allow Matera to rise to her feet again. It wasn't required, but Matera wanted to do it, and no one was going to stop her.

"I vote yes." Her voice crackled a bit, and as she said it, she peered down at a number of her colleagues. Ben knew who she had singled out. She wasn't glaring at random. She was staring down the handful of Republicans who were considered moderates. The precious few who might conceivably change their vote given the proper motivation.

The first moderate to vote was Senator McHenry. He voted no. Ben saw Matera give him the evil eye, but no words were spoken.

The second moderate to vote was Senator Norwood. She also voted no.

But Senator Palmetto voted yes. The second Republican to do so.

"Senator Quince."

Ben could feel the man's eyes burning down on him as he spoke. "I know this isn't the time for speeches," Quince said quietly, "but I just wanted to explain that, although I still have some reservations about this nominee, I am moved by the words of the senator from Oklahoma. This chamber should be focusing on the qualifications of the nominee for the job to which he has been nominated. When we focus on anything else, we encourage people to create scandal, which appears to me to be exactly what has happened in this unfortunate case. We must stop this before it robs the process—and the Constitution—of its dignity." He took a deep breath. "Accordingly, I vote yes."

Ben's heart almost leaped out of his chest. For the first time, he allowed himself to believe confirmation was just marginally possible.

The murmur in the chamber was audible, but the clerk continued calling names as if he did not hear it. In the course of the next five minutes, five Republican senators voted yes. No one had abstained. The vote was almost even, the nays only slightly ahead.

"Senator Wellington."

"Yes."

"Senator Wyatt."

"Yes."

The chamber and gallery alike held their breath. The vote was fifty yeses, forty-nine nos.

"Senator Yarmouth."

There was an understandable pause. He appeared to be staring at the tote board as he spoke.

"Well, under the circumstances . . . I vote yes."

Ben's eyes widened with stunned surprise. A loud hue and cry ballooned up from the gallery, but the Vice President banged his gavel, cutting it off.

"Accordingly," the Vice President announced, "the yeses number fifty-one, while the nos are forty-nine. The Senate therefore does advise and consent to the nomination of Judge Thaddeus Roush to the Supreme Court. We are out of session."

He banged the gavel again, and this time there was no stopping the whooping and laughing and crying, the ecstatic outcries and disgruntled grumbling. One hundred senators and six hundred spectators spoke at once, all of them amazed at the historic event they had just witnessed.

Senator Hammond pushed his way down the aisle to Ben. He grabbed his hand and began shaking it with great force. Tears were in his eyes. "Damn it," he said, smiling, "I knew you were the right man for this job. I knew it!"

Ben shrugged. "We got lucky."

"In politics, there's no such thing." He pulled closer so he could be heard above the growing tumult. "Listen to me, Ben. You have to run for reelection. You have to. We need a man like you in the Senate."

"Well, thank you."

"Will you run?"

"I have to admit, it hasn't been quite as horrible as I thought it might be."

Christina came running down the aisle, pushed several senators out of her way, and threw her arms around Ben's neck. "I never doubted you for a minute," she said, hugging him tightly.

"Then you were the only one," he whispered in her ear.

"No, I wasn't." She looked toward the gallery where, amid the noise and the tumult, Thaddeus Roush stood in the front row looking down at them. A throng of people were trying to get to him and offer their congratulations, but for the moment he was holding them at bay.

Even though Ben couldn't hear, he didn't need to be a lip-reader to know what Roush was saying: "Thank you."

Ben nodded back at him. "It was my pleasure."

"I talked to Lieutenant Albertson on my cell," Christina told Ben. "He's working on a subpoena to search Haskins's home, office, and the place he's been renting since he came to D.C. And he's sending a security detail to pick him up from—"

Her eyes turned upward again. Ben followed her gaze. In the front row, just to the left of Judge—soon to be Justice—Roush, Margaret Haskins still sat, her hands covering her face.

But Judge Haskins was gone.

60

Loving practically had to promise his firstborn child before Trudy would let him leave the hospital. All that talk about his delicate condition—it was almost as if they were married. Which wasn't likely to happen, at least not in this universe. Still, Loving had to admit, his association with her—*him*—had loosened him up a little bit. Made him perhaps a little more accepting. Helped him see the value in people very different from himself. Trudy had saved his life. After that, minor details such as gender and wardrobe choice seemed pretty minor.

Loving was waiting covertly in Haskins's front yard when his Cadillac came careening around the corner and down the circular cul-de-sac. Haskins's eyes were wild; his movements were frenetic. Sweat dripped from his face.

As soon as he left his car, Loving stepped out of the bushes.

"Evenin', Judge."

Haskins froze as if he had hit an invisible wall. "Who—who are you?"

"Name's Loving. I'm here to make sure you don't do nothin' you shouldn't."

"Like what?" Haskins snapped.

"Like destroyin' evidence."

"What makes you think there's any evidence here?"

"Well, you were drivin' in an awful big hurry."

"You have no proof. You just came because that damned Kincaid said all those horrible lies about me."

"The Skipper has been wrong, once or twice. And if he's wrong today, fine. But I think I'll keep an eye on you, just the same."

"You can't do that. You're not with the police."

"No, I'm not. But the police have obtained a search warrant and they're on their way. I'm just babysittin'. Till they get here."

Haskins tried to push past him. Loving blocked his way.

"You have no right to be here."

"You know, I 'spect you know a heck of a lot more about rights and stuff than I do, bein' a judge and all." He looked at the man levelly. "But I'm still not gonna let you destroy evidence."

Haskins rushed forward, tackling Loving. Loving's feet hit the porch steps and he tripped, falling backward. Haskins caught him with a punch to the jaw on his way down, then rushed past him.

Ow! Loving wasn't sure which hurt more—the slug to his face or his head thudding against the concrete sidewalk. As if he hadn't taken enough pounding lately. For an old geezer, Haskins had a darn good right arm.

He pulled himself up and rushed to the front door. Haskins had locked it, but hadn't had the time to secure the dead bolt. Two good body slams with Loving's strong right shoulder and the door began to crack. Two more and he was inside.

He found Haskins in the living room, crouched by the sofa, clutching a gun in both hands.

"Don't make me shoot," the judge said, his voice trembling.

Loving held his place, barely five feet in front of Haskins. The man shook from head to toe. Judging from his wild-eyed expression, he had taken complete leave of his senses. Loving had no confidence that he was in control of his trigger finger.

"You don't wanna do that," Loving said, holding out one arm.

"Stay back!" Haskins cried, shaking the gun back and forth. "I *will* shoot! Why shouldn't I? I've got nothing left to lose."

"Lemme tell you somethin', friend—everyone's got something left to lose."

"Not anymore. I'm ruined. I've lost my job, my reputation. My freedom."

"You still got a wife who loves you, right?"

Haskins hesitated, his gun wavering.

"How's she gonna feel when she comes home and finds out you plugged someone in the living room? What's she gonna think about you then?"

Haskins's face contorted with pain and desperation. His hands quivered even more wildly than before.

"Margaret . . . always believed in me," he said, his voice choking. "Even when I didn't deserve it." He stared at the gun in his hands. "Like now."

Loving took a step forward. "Look, just gimme the gun. We can work out all the details later. I'm sure—"

Outside, they both heard the sound of sirens approaching.

"Oh, no. Oh, no." Haskins's voice was barely a whisper. "They really are coming. They're going to lock me up and humiliate me and—and—"

"Whoa," Loving said, taking another step closer. "Let's stay calm here. The police are just comin' to help."

"No one can help me now. My life is over."

Loving watched as Haskins slowly turned the gun barrel away, toward his own face.

"Hang on there," Loving said. "You don't wanna do that. Think about your wife. Think about—"

"Prison," he muttered, staring at the gun. "Instead of the Supreme Court. Prison. Public disgrace. Margaret." His eyes grew even wider. "I'm sorry, Margaret. I'm so sorry!"

"Don't!" Loving shot forward, but he wasn't fast enough. Haskins put the gun inside his mouth and pulled the trigger.

"*No!*" Loving turned away just before he fired. The scattered remains of Haskins's head rained down, blood and brain tissue showering the room like a filthy rain.

The front door opened and two police officers rushed inside, their weapons drawn. "What the hell happened?" one of them asked.

"A tragedy," Loving muttered. "A damned tragedy. Or maybe the end of one."

Loving sat on the front porch of Haskins's rented home, hands on his chin, disgusted with himself.

"Don't take it so hard."

Loving turned and saw Lieutenant Albertson standing behind him.

"There was nothing more you could have done. The man thought his life was over, ruined. So he took the easy way out." Albertson frowned. "Hard thing for a good Catholic boy to say, but I'm not so sure he did the wrong thing."

Loving didn't attempt a response. "What's in the Baggie?"

Albertson held up the plastic evidence bag he was carrying. "A pair of garden gloves. Found them hidden in the bedroom closet. They've been washed, but a luminol bath has already revealed microscopic traces of blood, and my expert says it's the victim's type. We'll do DNA typing on the blood, if there's enough, but there's no real doubt in my mind. He must've found the gloves in Roush's garden and put them on to avoid leaving prints when he killed the woman. When you wouldn't let him get to them, he knew the game was up. He was going down for murder."

"So he shot himself in the face." Loving felt a mixture of disgust at the thought of what Haskins had done, and disgust at himself for not preventing it.

At the far end of the driveway, Loving saw another patrol car silently pull up, lights swirling. A moment later, a plainclothes police officer helped Margaret Haskins out of the car.

"Man, I do not want to be here for this," Loving said, pushing himself to his feet. "Do you need me for anythin' more?"

Albertson shook his head. "I know where we can find you. Thanks for your help."

Loving took a deep breath, then marched down the driveway, his head hung low. "Yeah. Anytime."

61

*B*en knew he had better things to do—most of his senatorial duties had waited on the back burner while he was obsessed with the Roush confirmation—but he couldn't help himself. He was addicted to the CNN coverage of the whole affair. The Roush confirmation vote had been dramatic enough, but coupled with the discoveries about Judge Haskins and his subsequent suicide, it became an even more major news event. Pundits bickered about every aspect of the case, whether it held hope for a more bipartisan approach to judicial confirmation or evidenced a gross eroding of standards. Everyone weighed in on the subject—everyone except the President, who had remained silent. Ben's final speech in the Senate had been replayed and sound bit almost nonstop, and after the twentieth viewing or so, Ben finally stopped wincing every time he saw himself on the screen.

"Ready to go?"

Christina stood in the office doorway wearing a bright blue tea-length dress with a brilliant opal brooch.

"You look stunning," Ben said.

She curtsied slightly and fluttered her eyelashes. "Well, I try."

"Where have you been?"

"In Senator Hammond's office. We're still working double shifts, trying to get that Wilderness Bill out of committee. We think there's a chance. If anyone can do it in the current political climate, it's him."

Ben placed his hands on her hips and smiled. "How is it we work together every day but still don't see enough of each other?"

She returned the smile. "Well, part of the problem is that we live in separate apartments."

Ben coughed into his hand. "Yes, well, umm . . . one thing at a time. May I escort you to the Capitol steps?"

"I'd be honored," she replied, offering him her arm.

The President was present on the East Wing balcony, feigning pleasure that his nominee had been confirmed, but what pleased Ben most was to see Ray Eastwick in attendance. He was seated in the front row behind the podium, just beside Roush, the seating sending an unequivocal message to every spectator or viewer. He wondered if they'd made up—or had even had time, given all that had happened so quickly. He felt certain the wounds would heal, eventually. They were two intelligent, successful men; they knew better than to waste their lives sulking when they could be celebrating life to the fullest.

And today was a great day to celebrate.

On cue, Roush took his position, put his hand on a very large Bible, and gazed across at the Chief Justice of the United States.

"Please repeat after me."

Roush closed his eyes, said a silent prayer, and began. "I, Thaddeus Ronald Roush, do solemnly swear to protect and defend the Constitution of the United States . . ."

The newly appointed Justice Roush's remarks were brief, so in less than half an hour the entire ceremony was over. Ben was anxious to congratulate Roush, but so were about a thousand other people, so he patiently waited his turn. Now that the excitement was over, he was back to being a less-than-one-term junior senator from Oklahoma, and as such did not get cuts to the front of the receiving line.

"He'll make a fabulous Supreme Court justice," Christina said. "I can tell already."

"And what makes you so sure?" Ben asked. "His probity? Honesty? Integrity?"

"I was more focused on that pin-striped suit he's wearing. What a snappy dresser! I'm always impressed by a snappy dresser."

"I assume that's what attracted you to me."

"Mmm. No comment."

Ben heard a buzzing sound from her purse. She took her cell phone out and reviewed the screen.

"Gina's Instant Messaging me. Seems the police have learned even more about Haskins's victim. She's been linked to at least five different heists. And they've uncovered the name of her partner on that museum job, the one she killed. Jerome Charles."

A synapse fired inside Ben's brain. "Where was he from?"

Christina continued to scroll through the message. "Doesn't say where he's from. But they've disinterred the body from a Beaumont cemetery and—"

Ben's head jerked around. "Where?"

"Beaumont. South Texas."

Ben pressed the heels of his hands against his head. "No," he gasped.

Christina's eyebrows scrunched together. "What is it?"

"How could I have been so stupid?"

"Ben, you're creeping me out. What is it?"

"I've got to get out of here."

"You've—Ben! What's going on?"

"I'll tell you as soon as I know. As soon as I know for sure."

"But where are you going?"

Ben kissed her on the cheek. "To have a very serious talk with Ray Eastwick."

en had to wait almost two hours. It wasn't enough for him to
talk with Eastwick; he needed to talk with the man in private.
Eventually, after all the well-wishers had finished well-wishing, while
Roush was still chatting with the press, Ben managed to pull Eastwick away. They reentered the Capitol building, found the nearest
empty conference room, and locked the door.

"Ben—what's this all about?"

"I need to talk to you, Ray. And I thought you'd want to do this
in private."

"Why? I have no secrets from Tad."

Ben just hoped that was true. "You two getting along better?"

One corner of his mouth tugged upward. "Yes, thank you. It
seems there's nothing quite like being appointed to the Supreme
Court to buoy a man's spirit. Even when you only slip past the Senate by the hairs of your chinny-chin-chin. We finally sat down and
had a heart-to-heart."

"And?"

"Well, I'm not going to suggest that everything's all perfect now. But I think I understand a little better what was going on in his head. It really was a spontaneous act—revealing his sexual orientation at the press conference. Outing me. Outing us. I'm not saying I think it was smart, or even acceptable. But I'm beginning to understand."

"I'm glad." Ben wished he didn't have to go any further, but he knew he did. "Ray, I have to ask you about something."

"Then get to it. What is it you want to know?"

"The day of the press conference. In your garden."

"Yes?"

"You . . . saw the woman. The woman who was killed?"

"Yes. I've never made any secret of that. I told the police I saw her. What's the problem?"

"The problem is, I think you more than just saw her. I think you knew who she was."

"I've already told you I knew she was the woman Tad had the affair with. The woman who had the abortion. I just . . . sensed it. The moment I saw her."

"No. I think you knew she was the murderer of Jerome Charles. That's the real reason you became so agitated when you spotted her on the premises, isn't it?"

Eastwick peered deeply into Ben's eyes. "What makes you so sure?"

"Something you told me the first time we met." Ben pulled out a chair. "Sit down, Ray. We're going to be here awhile."

Senator Hammond pushed open the door and leaned into Ben's office. "Coming to the victory celebration?"

Ben barely looked up. "I'd like to."

"Then what's stopping you, son?"

"I'm not sure what to do."

Hammond stepped inside. "What's the problem?"

"The problem is, I know something. About someone I admire. And I'm not sure what to do about it."

"I take it this something you know is something bad."

"Very bad."

Hammond pulled up a chair. "Well, son, I've been around a long while, and in my experience, no matter how bad it is, the best approach is to confront the person straight on. Just come out with it. Put it on the table."

"Yes, but—" Ben sighed. "It's very hard to do." He looked up at Hammond. "Because I'm talking about murder. The murder of Victoria Danvers."

"What?" Hammond's forehead creased. "I thought that was all over and done with. Judge Haskins committed the crime."

"I thought it was over, too. I was wrong."

"But the police found the bloodstained gloves at his home. And the man killed himself."

"The man had a lot to feel guilty about. Paying someone to set that fire, for instance. But he wasn't feeling remorse about the murder of Victoria Danvers. Because he didn't do it."

"But he put the gun in his mouth—"

"The shame of having people think he was a murderer—wrongfully—may well have contributed to his suicide. The gloves were planted in his home."

"How could anyone know the police would be coming to search?"

"Because the murderer—the real one—knew I was going to expose Haskins as an arsonist on the floor of the Senate. And he figured that once people swallowed that, it would be a short hop in the public eye from arsonist to murderer. Which it was."

Hammond's back stiffened for a moment, then he slowly settled back into his chair. "How did you figure it out?"

Ben shrugged. "It wasn't hard. Not once I heard the name of the man Victoria killed all those years ago after the Boston museum robbery. Not once I heard he was buried in your hometown. You told me about the loss of your son, how it devastated you, all those years ago. You even told me you named him Hieronymous Carroll—and that you loved Latin. I guess your son did, too. Because Hieronymous is the Latinate form of Jerome. And Carroll is Latin for Charles. Hieronymous Carroll became Jerome Charles. He never took your last name because he was born out of wedlock. That's why most people didn't know about him. That's why even now, his disappearance hasn't been linked to you. But I figured it out. And then I confirmed it by talking with Ray Eastwick. Your former clerk."

Hammond's eyes slowly drifted downward. "He was raised by his mother, a sweet little thing from a good family in Beaumont, Texas. Rich as the devil. But married. And she had no use for me, other than as an occasional plaything." He sighed heavily. "I thought she'd be a good mother to him. But apparently I was wrong, given the way he turned out. They had some disagreement, she cut him off, and he turned to crime to keep himself in the style to which he had become accustomed."

Hammond turned his face upward to keep his eyes from spilling. "I loved that boy, in my own way. Only child I ever had. I kept an eye on him from a distance—she wanted it that way. Too distant, as it turned out. Next thing I knew, he'd vanished into the European underworld without a trace. Got messed up with some art thieves. And then he disappeared—until he turned up dead. No one knew what had happened to him. So I hired a detective to find out. Took the man years to piece it all together. That woman—Victoria Danvers—had not left many clues behind. Smart. She was a philosophy major, did you know that, Ben?"

"No," he said quietly.

"How does someone go from being a philosophy major to being a coldhearted killer? It was incomprehensible. But true. The detective finally found some snitch who put him on the right track. He identified Danvers."

"But Senator—why murder?"

"She killed him, Ben." His voice reacquired some of its usual fire. "Killed him in cold blood. Killed him mean. Some kind of falling-out after the Boston job. He got greedy, probably, and she challenged him. I don't doubt that he did something to provoke her irritation. But she murdered him. Murdered the only son I ever had. Ever would have. More than that—she punished him. She was deliberately cruel, hurting him long after he had any ability to defend himself. Dragging his face in the gravel. She mutilated him, Ben. So I started looking for her, without success. Hired even more detectives to find her, but they couldn't. I understand why, now. She'd changed her name, changed her whole appearance. Even changed her damn fingerprints. After a while, I almost started to forget—or at least to not obsess over it every day and night."

"What changed?"

Hammond wiped away the tears that streaked his face. "Where I come from, we were taught that murder is wrong, no matter what the circumstances. We were also taught, an eye for an eye."

"You recognized her at the press conference."

Hammond nodded. "The detective had shown me photos of the woman. No amount of plastic surgery was going to fool me. Her face was burned into my brain. Knew her the second I saw her. Felt it in my gut. And she didn't deny it, either. She laughed at me, wanted to know what I was going to do about it. And—and—I don't know what happened to me. Something just broke. Something inside me. I saw the gloves and the garden shears and I grabbed them and—well, you know the rest. I didn't have time to hide the body, so I did just the opposite. Put the body where it was certain to be found."

"And certain to divert suspicion to Thaddeus and Ray."

Hammond looked down, his face somber. "I like to think that if the police had ever gotten serious about charging either one of them, I would've come forward." He paused. "But I guess we'll never know, will we?"

"You didn't seem to have any problem framing Judge Haskins."

Hammond laughed bitterly. "The man caused a fire that could've killed hundreds of people. If he wasn't a murderer, it was only by happenstance. I didn't have any moral qualms about pinning the murder on his sorry little ass."

Ben rubbed his eyes. It had been a long day. And it wasn't over yet. "Thank you for telling the truth."

Hammond looked away. "Sounds as if you knew most of it already anyway."

Ben nodded sadly. "You don't know how much this pains me, Senator. You've been my mentor—at times, my only friend in Washington. I wish there was some alternative. But there isn't. I'm going to have to tell the authorities."

Hammond drew in a deep breath, wiped his face again. "No, Ben. I don't think you will."

"What—is that a threat?"

"Of course not. I just know that you're a reasonable man."

"You can't imagine that I'm going to keep silent just because we're friends."

"No, son. I think you're going to remain silent because I'm the Minority Leader of the Senate. And in a year, I just might be the Majority Leader. And you don't want to screw that up."

Ben stared at him uncomprehendingly. "You must have mistaken me for someone who cares about politics a good deal more than I do."

"Really. And does that pretty little fiancée of yours feel the same way?"

Ben stopped short.

"You know, if I'm not in the Senate, that Wilderness Bill your little filly cares so much about will go down in flames. Will never get out of committee, in fact."

"What are you saying?"

"Just a simple fact. If I go down, so does the Alaskan wilderness. How will Christina feel about that? And how will she feel when she finds out it was your fault?"

"Christina will understand."

"Maybe. Maybe not. How will you feel about it? Do you want to see oil rigs in our last unblemished wilderness?"

"You know I don't."

"For that matter, what about the antipoverty bill? That'll go down in flames if I leave the Senate. The education bill? History. Fifty million dollars to fund education in the state of Oklahoma alone—gone. All thanks to you."

"I won't listen to this."

"I know you care about the death penalty. This is the time to strike. I could get an anti–death penalty bill passed if you like, and with Thaddeus on the Supreme Court, it'll be upheld. Don't you see, Ben? You need me to keep my job."

"That doesn't matter," Ben said, pacing agitatedly behind his desk. "This is a question of justice."

"Is it? Is it just that all those people living below the poverty line should go on suffering so you can fulfill some quixotic quest to punish a man for executing the career criminal who murdered his only son? Does that really make sense to you?"

Ben ran his fingers through his hair. "This—this is all confusing and—and irrelevant. What it comes down to, is—"

"I'll tell you what it comes down to, son." Hammond rose to his feet. "What it comes down to is what do you care about most? Your sense of justice? Or Christina? Because if you care one whit for that girl, you won't let the projects she cares so much about and has worked so hard on go down in flames."

Ben felt an ache in the pit of his stomach. His head throbbed. He felt hot, stifled. He desperately wanted to be gone, anywhere but here.

"It's a simple decision, Ben," Hammond continued, in the same even, measured tones. "Lock up an old man. Or save the world. What's it going to be?"

Ben closed his eyes, inhaled deeply, then opened them. He walked to Hammond and stood barely an inch away from him. "Listen to me, Senator. And listen very closely. You will not always be the Senate Minority Leader. You will not always be a senator at all. And the second that you're not—I'll be waiting for you." He paused a moment, then added, "There's no statute of limitations on murder."

The corner of Hammond's mouth turned up slightly. He stepped toward the door. "I guess we understand each other."

"I guess we do."

"I'm sorry it had to be this way, Ben."

"Not as sorry as I am."

"Don't take it personally, son. It isn't personal. It's politics."

And he closed the door behind him.

63

Christina arrived at the office at the usual time, and was more than startled to see that Ben was already there.

"Now this is a surprise," she said. "What on earth brings you to the office at the appropriate time of the morning?"

Ben rose from his desk and smiled. "I had a lot of plans to make."

"I'm glad to hear it. Because I've got a list a foot long of things you need to do. Your mother called—you forgot her birthday again. And Loving wants to take an extended vacation. Evidently he's got a new flame, someone named Trudy. I told him he could go, but I also said I'd be pretty irritated if he got married before I did. He just laughed; don't ask me why." She took a deep breath. "And there is that minor matter of whether you're going to run for reelection."

Ben walked around his desk and clasped both her hands. "You got a free hour or so?"

"Are you joking? I don't have a free minute. I'm supposed to meet Senator Hammond before I—" She paused. "Which reminds me. Someone told me he came to your office last night. What did he want?"

Ben barely hesitated a moment. "Nothing important. Just tying up some loose ends."

"Nothing bad about the Wilderness Bill?"

"Of course not."

"That's a relief." She glanced down at her book. "But I still have a packed morning. I've got to meet with the administrative assistant for the—"

Ben pulled her close to him. "How would you feel about going on a little trip?"

"Huh?"

"I thought we might go visit Tad."

"Tad? Tad Roush? Are you crazy? The Court is in session."

"I called ahead. He'll be waiting for us."

"Why?"

Ben pulled her even closer, till they were practically nose-to-nose. "Christina—how would you feel about being married by a justice of the Supreme Court?"

Christina's lips parted. For a brief moment, she didn't even speak. "By—what—?" She tried again. "You mean, get married to you?"

"That was what I had in mind, yes."

"You mean—now?"

"Can you think of a better time?"

"But this is awfully sudden."

"Is it? Seems like this relationship has been dragging on for several novel-length years."

"I meant sudden as measured in Ben Kincaid time." She smiled softly, then touched the side of his cheek. "Are you going to run for reelection?"

"Does it matter? No matter what we decide to do, we'll be . . . partners."

Her crystal blue eyes sparkled. "Partners?" she said breathlessly. "Really? Partners?"

He pressed his nose against hers. "Till death do us part."

ABOUT THE AUTHOR

WILLIAM BERNHARDT is the author of many novels, including *Primary Justice*, *Murder One*, *Criminal Intent*, *Death Row*, *Hate Crime*, *Dark Eye*, and *Capitol Murder*. He has twice won the Oklahoma Book Award for Best Fiction, and in 2000 he was presented the H. Louise Cobb Distinguished Author Award "in recognition of an outstanding body of work in which we understand ourselves and American society at large." A former trial attorney, Bernhardt has received several awards for his public service. He lives in Tulsa, and readers can e-mail him at wb@williambernhardt.com or visit his website at www.williambernhardt.com.

ABOUT THE TYPE

This book was set in Sabon, a typeface designed by the well-known German typographer Jan Tschichold (1902–74). Sabon's design is based upon the original letter forms of Claude Garamond and was created specifically to be used for three sources: foundry type for hand composition, Linotype, and Monotype. Tschichold named his typeface for the famous Frankfurt typefounder Jacques Sabon, who died in 1580.